1

Manifesto From a Woman

We all have the key, to our own happiness, let's open the door.

Lady Kondo

ISBN 978-1-3999-2927-1

I dedicate that story:
To my mother, to my father for giving birth to me,
To my sisters, without you, I wouldn't be who I am.
To Jimmy, in my next life, I promise you, I will marry you.
To all Sarcoïdosis sufferers, and other forms of chronic maladies.
And to you, you know who you are.

'There are all sorts of revolutions: political, economic, scientific, artistic. Each has its own significance and, often, necessity. But no matter what one changes, the world will never get any better as long as people themselves, the guiding force and impetus behind all endeavours remain selfish and lacking in compassion. In that respect, human revolution is the most fundamental of all revolutions, and at the same time, the most necessary revolution for humankind.'

Daisaku Ikeda

My name is Kondo. Kondo means Chief or Leader. It is a male name given to the first child. Then I became Lady Kondo.

When the moment comes, I will tell you why I inherited that name. For the time being, I want to concentrate on a subject that dominates our everyday lives: "Desire!" I hear the sound of pleasure ringing to my ears, just thinking about the word. It spurs me to dream.

The art of desire, that topic has been observed and explained by all our great philosophers. Even though, desiring is seen as necessary, because it propels us towards a reality, one would want to perceive as a source of possible satisfaction, that need, that irrational wish can also draw out so much sufferings.

There is nothing more eloquent than to bring to life our desires, to offer a decor to those desires, and to shape them accordingly. That is why, I am going to tell you a fairy tale, a tale about Desire, with Buddhism at the heart of the story.

Once upon a time, in the twenty-first century, in a city where rainy days rhymed with romance and carrying an umbrella, regardless of the size, the shape, its colour, was regarded as a fetish accessory, perfect to protect oneself, against its showery mood swing, where the Thames River flows confidently through its historical buildings; —yes, you have guessed it well, —London, there was a Guinean woman called Issata Sherif. —The name Issata comes from African origin and means: *kind willing person*. It is also said that it derives from the Arabian name, Aicha. and implies: —*She who struggles*! In conclusion, any woman called Issata could be identified, straight away as: —*She who struggles to become a kind willing person!* And how to honour such heroic definitions? Issata was looking for Mr. Right to dance through life with. Yes, times have changed! Prince Charming sounds so outdated these days! —No man wears the crown anymore, except for Prince William and Prince Harry! Plus, as far as I am concerned, it must be painfully heavy to carry the royal blood over one head for lifetime after lifetime. A fortiori, it is not fair for men in general to be regarded as a prince only based on the simple and lucrative fact that they possessed a title.

So, let's be honest, what are the real qualities of a Prince except for being Charming? That is why he had to be Mr. Right!? —Physically? Tall and handsome of course, with a smooth and naturally tanned complexion.

She needed to be able to smell the famous acacia honey, crawling on his golden skin, so that the option to lick it or not, the honey, wouldn't appear as a choice.

His body had to come in the perfect shape. With a mind as creative as hers, she had already designed in her imagination, some discreet but well-maintained muscles, till the opportunity to taste the goods presents itself.

After all, business is business.

He will need to possess a cultivated spirit because she loves to debate and always makes sure she wins. Mr. Right must offer her, flowers and invite her to romantic places. Coming from her, that appeared as common sense.

But most importantly, he must have acquired the art of kissing as described in *The Kiss*, the famous painting from Klimt. Issata's theory on finding the perfect man lies in the kiss. The kiss was holding the key to reaching paradise.

A man lacking experience in that department, couldn't be a good lover. Nothing to do with sex! Making love and having sex are two completely different exercises! You don't need a man nor a woman, to release any orgasmic pleasure. You can do it yourself, by making use of your natural resources or with the help of little devices.

—Morality, a man who doesn't know how to kiss, get out!

—So, for Mademoiselle Sherif, it had to be Mr. Right, and he had to make her dance through life. —Just dance! She was raised in France but moved to London as an au-pair at the age of twenty to study English. Years later, she was still living in London; perhaps still learning English. As much as she enjoys her lifestyle, big cities can be a lonely place for a woman. —Where are the men, she used to ask herself?

—No, wrong question, as men were everywhere. Except in her bed and her pants. How to meet them was the dilemma? Times have changed indeed, and yet, the quest for finding *The One* was still a difficult task for some.

Issata is a Buddhist and a member of the Soka Gakkai International, mainly known as SGI. She chants Nam-myoho-rengekyo, the expression of the mystic law, based on Nichiren Daishonin's teaching. Who is he? Some guy, that you will encounter throughout the novel.

No, Issata doesn't walk around dressed in a long orange robe! Maybe sometimes, depending on the fashion trend but not for religious reasons, and she eats meat. That's right, let's remember that first, she is of African and French nationality. And the French love their steak very bloody! In fact, bleu! Even though the flesh is red. Don't ask why bleu? You know how the French are, such romantic species! Have you ever tried a *Chateaubriand*, a *Bavette d'Aloyau* or simply a *faux-filet?* Just try, no gastronomy can compete with the taste of France! Right, I think I might attract some enemies! Who cares, us French love revolutions! And yes, I am Franco-Guinean, in case you wondered. Anyway, all this to explain that she eats meat and sausages… The only common ground she might have had with a Buddhist monk was the hairstyle. She kept her hair very short. That is to say that she was normal.

She had encountered Buddhism at the University at the age of nineteen and philosophy had always been her favourite subject. She discovered similarities between the work of *Rabuch Spinozza* Dutch philosopher from the 17th century and the one of Nichiren. Spinozza would say:

'The desire is the essence of man'. That is why *'Earthly desires leads to Enlightenment'* and *'Transforming karma into mission'* fascinated her. Desire, that strong feeling of wanting, wishing, yearning, for something to happen, could lead her to elevate her spiritual insight? That is so cool, but I don't want to become an old lady! I just want a boyfriend! —And karma? —That is your karma, she loved saying, because she sounded intelligent!

She works as a *Chef de Cabin* at Voyage Europe, a new train service, known as VoyE, located in Waterloo station.

At the launch of their latest project *Service à la carte* for their business lounges, she was recommended for the London site. Her mission consisted of establishing the profile of the very important clients, the Business First. Issata added her personal touch and renamed the group: 'BFirst.' VoyE covered destinations, in Paris, Brussels, and Germany. —80% of travellers, inspired the wild testosterone. But no one caught her attention.

Until one day, he came along.

Part 1

MR SMITH

-Earthly Desires Lead to Enlightenment-

1

It all began in October 2011, '*The Year of Capable People and Dynamic Development.*' Every big organisation strives to live up to their vision statement. SGI's mission is to promote peace, culture, and education. Every year, Daisaku Ikeda suggests a theme, as a spiritual directive, in line with the time. Who's that man? I will introduce him later. —Capable People? —In what sense, Issata questioned, when she heard the theme!
—And on top of it, I have to grow dynamically?
—As if I had nothing else to do! She was joking of course!

The year was coming to an end, and she was not near seeing her dream of sharing her life with a great man coming true, but she kept hope that Mr Right would manifest one day soon. —What if he turned up in the shape of Shrek, she panicked one day? —Princess Fiona loved him; she would answer. —But I am not Fiona!' Then she realised: In the fairy tale, most princesses had to turn a frog into a prince!

Her afro black hair, neatly trimmed to her scalp, a mixture of the hairstyles of Dee-Dee Bridgewater and Angelique Kidjo, two different women, but real symbols and inspirations in the music world, Issata arrived in front of Voyage Europe security gate, at half-past five, her starting time. *Air in G String was* ringing in her ears through her iPod. That melody belonged to her favourite classical music pieces. The kind of music we want to hear when happy, in love, lost or even confused. The type of music which speaks to our feelings, listen to them and most importantly understand them. When listening to this melody, she felt free to explore all her fantasies, allowing the vibrations to transport her soul. Each key contained the expression of her sensibility, her Romanesque spirit, her femininity. *Air in G String* to her described that call forcing her to believe. She removed her uniform trench coat, unveiling a silhouette so elegantly designed in a ruby colour dress-suit, the same colour as her coat, which silky texture, blended perfectly with the shade of her flawless black skin and flattered her slim mermaid legs. —Bach doesn't follow me in the lounge! She took off her headphones, acknowledging the security guard faithful to his morning position with a: 'Hello Kwame,' 'Issata sis, how are you?' 'I am fine, thank you.' He scanned her badge and she headed towards the lounge reception.

'Hello Issata, how are you?' It was Michael her colleague. He came from Jamaica and his hair was always neatly presented in cornrow style, the famous African hairstyle where the hair is tightly plaited on the scalp.

'Michael, hello I'm alright, thank you.' She welcomed him with her sweet and bountiful gap-toothed smile, which she inherited from her father. That kind of dentition is a synonym to happiness or tooth luck. —She has *Les dents du bonheur*, would say the French expression. To understand its origin, let's go back to Napoleon's Era. Soldiers who were equipped with a bridge between the first two front teeth were exempt from participating in the war. Therefore, they were lucky and had the good fortune to escape the bloody fight. And what have the teeth got to do with the war? Well, on the battlefields, soldiers were obliged to use their teeth to load their shotgun as it was mandatory that they kept their rifles in their hands. That is why they had to use their incisors to cut the wrapping paper containing the loading powder. No easy task to perform with a big gap between the teeth. Some soldiers even decided to remove one tooth to escape the war. Luckily, Issata didn't have to go to war. But she had another battlefield to win. —Mr. Right! And she had the smile for it. 'And you?'

'All good, we have the list of our Business First travellers and one of them is actually travelling this morning. He should arrive any minute.' 'Who is he?' she asked, intrigued.

'Mr Smith.'

'Finally, I get to meet him, thank you!' She walked away. She had heard a lot about this man from her colleagues but had never managed to meet him. He was a lawyer, that was all she knew. While getting ready, which meant swapping her silver ballerina shoes for her black high heel leather pump and swallowing an espresso coffee, her phone rang.

'Tell me,'

'Mr. Smith is just passing through security.'

'Ok, thank you.'

The lounge was built on two floors. —Ground floor and a first level which could be accessed by an impressive helical staircase, made of marble light pink. People could also use the lift. Issata worked on the first floor, regarded as *Le Salon.* It comprised a capacity of two hundred seats for optimum comfort, a central bar and a series of theatrical boxes where passengers could enjoy their time prior to their train. Every box was featured with a large sofa, upholstered in red cherry velvet, a small pedestal pine table and the latest connectivity services. But what differentiated Voyage Europe, to other Business train services, was observed through its unique creation: — Business First, or as Issata would call it *BFirst,* tailor-made, to Elites only. The company had set up a private area for the important clients to relax alone or meet other travellers, in an intimate atmosphere, within reason.

She was checking the VIP section on the far-right corner of the lounge, separated by a translucent divider and her phone rang again.

'Yes,' she picked up.

'He is going up now, you can't miss him!' And he was right!

A strong presence pervaded the atmosphere. From the top of the stairs, she perceived a red head positioned on a perfectly elongated body, covered by a very light grey suit, which material could only cost a lot of money. The redness from his hair, neatly shaped on his skull, illuminated the skin of his face, extremely white. Puzzled, she borrowed her eyes to observe the contrast in those colours, approaching her. Puzzled, she borrowed her ears to listen to the sound of his steps. It sounded like exquisite caresses, on the marbled stairs, caresses leading to a gracious dance, the kind of dance, she wished to dance with her Mr Right. She fixed him, curious to discover his face. —Who is hiding behind that stature? Her heart trembling, she checked all his gestures. He followed his way methodically; the path of a man in control. Then he stopped, as if he had waited for the perfect moment. He lifted his head and she crossed his blue and striking gaze. It pierced her with violence. She received an electric shock, travelling down to her stomach. Never had she encountered, some eyes filled with so much force! They shone like a magnetic power. Issata felt naked. He smiled, and within ten steps, met her at the top of the staircase. Unable to pronounce a word, she observed him in all his splendour and studied his oval's face, splashed by soft freckles. The colour of his small lips, underlined by a thin moustache, shed light on his pink shirt, revealed under the three greyish pieces of suit, he was wearing. Effectively, his wardrobe cost a lot of money. He was holding a cream trench coat, a brown briefcase in one hand, and a brown chocolate hat, matching the colour of his calf leather shoes, in the other hand. The soft lustra enhanced the smart toe cap finishing. From the red soles, she recognised Christian Louboutin's signature. She couldn't tell his age. He was neither old and neither young, but he inspired beauty, power, wealth. Mr Smith inspired her to believe in her fairy tale. And hop, she landed in the twenties, the crazy years and transformed herself into Josephine Baker, dressed with a large feather crown embellishing her African heritage, attached to her infamous mini banana skirt. —*Chiquita Madame de la Martinique"* rang in her ears. And she sang to herself, *Issata Madame from the Business Lounge, today is the day where your fairy tale begins...*Ready to perform the Charleston in the middle of the lounge, she heard coming from far: 'Good morning,' a deep and melodious voice, similar to those officers of yesteryear, trained to announce the king's arrival. She was melting in awe, when the sound of the lift opening, slapped her ears. —Get real girl! You are not at *Les Folies Bergères,* —Plus Voyage Europe wouldn't be impressed by your performance, she warned herself.

'Good morning, Mr. Smith,' exclaimed her heart-shaped face nervously.

'How do you know my name?' That same deep tone wished to know.

'Michael at the reception informed me, and I am Issata,' she threw, trying to play cool.

'In that case, can I call you Issata?'

'Sure!' Uneasiness printed on her face, she checked: 'Can I get you something to drink?'

'No, thank you, I have a very important call to make. I will see you when I leave.' He walked away, heading towards the VIP area. She watched him pick the FT from the newspaper rack and settled in the private area.

—That is Mr Smith, she praised herself. Fascinated and destabilised by that masculine presence, permeating the room like a scorching force, she was not taking note of her regulars, but strolled on her first floor, insisting on the reserved zone. She caught him, looking in her direction. He detained an impeccable visual contact. Blue occupied her mind and she saw blue everywhere, the same colour we admire on postcards. Naturally, the soundtrack of the French movie *Le Grand Bleu,* resonated around her and she found herself diving into an imaginary ocean. This music was the first electronic sound, she had fallen in love with. The emotional power narrated through the music of the movie was contained in that sound. —A mood, rich in complexity, sometimes serene, sometimes capricious;

—A magical mood, a romantic story between two men in love with deep waters.

—*Ladies and Gentlemen, the boarding for the train 7:37 has started.* She had to emerge from her swim. She hadn't plunged that far but felt drenched with emotions.

'I hope you enjoyed your stay with us?' she commenced softly when she approached him.

'I have indeed Issata, thank you,' a continuous spur, escaped from his mouth, while putting his coat on.

'You have an accent,' she stammered.

'I am German, but I studied Law at Harvard University in the United States.'

'Very impressive,'

'Walk with me' he suggested, leading the way.

She obeyed. 'Do you travel every Monday morning?' she asked.

'Yes, normally on the 10:17, I have an early conference in Paris today.'

'Oh, that is why I have never seen you before, perhaps you arrive when I am on my break,' she gasped.

'Perhaps,' he repeated, and paused briefly, looking at her. She realised they had reached the exit. —Shall I escort him further, she wondered? His sex appeal convinced her when he began to go down. He walked down the same way he climbed onto the stairs, in control, without failing to glance at her sexy legs. Visual exchanges were created between them, animating a sexual tension. She felt weak on her knees and was afraid that she might fall. Fortunately, they arrived at the end of the stairs. Mr Smith stopped again. He smiled at her, forcing her to confront his gaze. She felt his blue magnetic power opening her dress and visualised it falling down along her Amazonian legs. Specific drops only harvested in those kinds of situations, began to drip down her cotton panties. She took a deep breath, preparing herself to say goodbye but he beat her to it:

'See you next Monday Issata.' He offered his hand.

'See you next Monday.' She accepted it.

He held it for a while and she couldn't help noticing, the very expensive looking watch dressing his right wrist.

—A Rolex, precisely!

'Mr Smith, what a character!' she got to Michael, out of breath.

'I knew you would like him,' he teased her.

'He is so damn hot! His eyes are haunting me already… And he called me by my name.'

'You never know!'

The following Monday, her show was back on. The morning went very fast and smooth. She welcomed all her regulars like she would greet her own guests at home.

At nine o'clock, it was time for her forty-five minutes break. She sat quietly in the reserved area to update her travellers' file. She had created a portfolio, illustrating the profile of every regular, and had developed a method she had named '*Getting to know you.*' —Mr. Smith will arrive any minute, she got to remember. She put her folder away and went to the ladies to freshen up. On her way towards the lift, Michael called.

'Yes?'

'He is coming.'

'I am in the lift.' As she came out, she saw him climbing the stairs, dressed in black. His Borsalino hat, covering his head. 'Mr. Smith,' she called, and headed quickly towards him. He looked in her direction. His jacket opened, over a black shirt nicely fitted, revealed his muscled torso. He didn't wear a tie. She admired him in all his elegance, skimmed his black leather shoes, meticulously polished which seemed to have been made exclusively for him. The darkness in his look aroused her senses.

'Issata, I was afraid I might not see you today.'

She giggled nervously. She had missed his deep and sensual voice, that rich and luxurious smooth sound.

'I was coming down to welcome you.'

I am happy to see you!' he let out, when she stood in front of him. He plunged into her brown eyes with amusement and savoured every instant of their proximity.

'Me too!' she exclaimed; a rush of excitement glittered in her eyes.

'That is a declaration!'

—Damn, what a fool I am! She spoke inside.

'In that case why don't you sit with me and tell me all about your weekend?' He began to walk without waiting for her response. —He is definitely a lawyer. How to resist such an invitation, a small voice answered inside? 'Sure, I will get some water.' She moved away from him.

'Today you are my VIP! Tell me about you?' he ordered when she joined him.

'What?' She felt sweat dripping under her armpits.

'Is there any problem? Please have a seat.'

She laughed and sat straight facing him. Her right leg draped over her left one, she maintained both arms crossed and tight against her body.

'What would you like to know?' came out of her mouth.

'Now we are talking. What is your role in the lounge?' His eyes surveyed her from head to toes. They lingered on her glossy juicy lips, as if he was imagining their use and effectiveness in action. They could sip, siphon, imbibe, gasp, gulp, stroke, kiss, suck… She gasped and let out hurriedly:

'My role is to look after our Business First travellers, like you.'

'What does that mean concretely?'

—He is damn right, how to explain my mission here? 'Let's say that you are part of Voyage Europe elite and I am here to make your experience with us memorable.'

'Do I get special treatment?' the rascal checked.

She went red with embarrassment, but her black radiant skin helped her mask her masquerade. At least, she had her blackness as a shield and it was a natural one. 'You can always put forward your suggestions,' she defended.

'It is high time they found someone like you! I have been travelling with VoyE for the last seven years, and none of the staff have spent time with me as you are today. I feel very special, thanks to you, Issata.'

—Thanks to me, he feels special? 'I will pass that on,' she uttered.

'Good weekend?'

'Nothing exciting!'

'A man in your life? Surely you must have a boyfriend with legs like yours.' He paced his gaze on her shiny tights, caressing her with a naughty smile. She froze and spoke abruptly: 'No, I don't have a boyfriend... Even with legs like mine.'

'Have I crossed the line?' he asked, but didn't apologise. Men like him are unapologetic.

'I just don't know what to say!' she chuckled.

'Issata, you are a very attractive woman, and you should enjoy receiving compliments. I must confess, I was looking forwards to seeing you this morning.'

'Mr. Smith,' she tried to speak.

'And, I bet you have hidden talents which many men would die for, to discover.' He spoke very slowly, almost singing a serenade. —Had she heard right? His eyes didn't leave her the least. She understood that he was looking to hear her arguments, like those provided, when filing a court claim.

'Why don't you tell me what made you become a lawyer?'

'Touché, my father was a lawyer, and I grew up with the belief that everyone deserves to be protected. Does this answer your question?'

'In which field do you specialise?'

'Criminal law!'

'Are you serious?'

'Very serious, and I can't say no more!'

'I understand, because you might find some evidence against me.' Instantly, she felt guilty. Guilty of what? Being a woman? Or guilty for desiring him?

'Now you are revealing yourself! I like you Issata, and I would like to take you for a drink soon.'

The boarding for his train was announced.

'Time to go now.' Mr. Smith organised his things and stood up.

'Let me walk you down,' she proposed, standing up too.

'No thank you, I can find my way! But think about my invitation. I really want to get to know you.' Issata couldn't believe what she was hearing. 'I will think about it.'

'What is your favourite drink?'

'Champagne.'

'To our champagne rendezvous soon, then.' He put his hat on and walked off.

—I must tell Jimmy!

Monday had become the best day of the week, where a woman named Issata, incarnated the happiest woman in the world. One could wonder why?

December made its entrance, with its long greyish dress, highlighted by black and white patches. —If December was a woman, she used to contemplate, she will be sincere, trustworthy, and generous, and would transform the whole winter season, into a time of care and compassion. She would remind all of us that *Winter always turns into Spring,* would say Nichiren. And that women born in December are special!

Issata was already sitting in *Eat Tokyo* restaurant, a Japanese cuisine renowned for its authentic taste, when she saw Jimmy conversing with a waiter, pointing in her direction. They made eye contact and she greeted him with her precious smile. Dressed in a blue-purple straight cut robe, fold-out collar, sleeves stopping at the elbows, a long pearl necklace, with matching pending earrings, decorated her petite chest. The smoky black shadow, dramatically painted on her eyelids and the glossy blackberry lipstick, sensually brushed on her African lips, were depicting the image of a cabaret actress, ready to climb on stage to welcome her audience.

So, who is Jimmy? —His real name was James, but Jimmy for the intimate. That's right, you guessed it well, he was Issata best friend, who also worked for VoyE Company as a Strategy customers service manager. He was French and German, tall and handsome, elegantly fit, caring and sexy! But there was one *little hic*, he was Gay! Nothing wrong with being happy even though in some countries it is still a crime. He represented, everything Issata was looking for in a man. But he loved men. They met through a colleague's birthday party and since then, these two had become inseparable. She watched him, fraying his way through this compact restaurant. A Herringbone cap, covering his head, he was draped in a grey tweed, three quarter length coat and resembled some of Jean-Paul Gaulthier, models parading on a podium. When he reached the table, she recognised the pair of Burgundy Jimmy Choo trainers, she had bought him for his birthday a year ago.

'Jimmy!' she exclaimed, rising to her feet and throwing herself into his arms.

'Darling, you looked amazing!' They hugged.

'Thank you, you looked stunning too.' she observed, detaching from his embrace.

'Thanks, that is for you!' He gave her a small pack from Chanel, expensively wrapped.

'Jimmy, you shouldn't have!' But took the bag from his hands, guessing what it contained.

'Give it back to me then,' he expressed and took off his coat. He revealed, black skinny trousers and a cashmere pink turtleneck jumper, nicely fitting his svelte silhouette.

'I think, I will make an effort to keep this one!' Giggling, she tore up the wrapping paper, within seconds.

'*Allure Sensuelle,* thank you so much!'

'Pleasure darling! Let's celebrate now!' He made a sign to the waiter who greeted him.

'And your new role, are you enjoying?'

'Well…'

'What?'

'There is this man…' Mr. Smith blue eyes penetrated her senses as if he was standing in front of her and she chuckled mischievously.

'Who?'

'Mr. Smith.'

'Tell me.'

'Champagne,' interrupted the waiter, placing a bucket on their table. He presented a bottle of *Laurent Perrier*.

'Jimmy only you can treat me like a queen!' Issata was moved to tears.

'Because you are worth it!'

The waiter opened the bottle and served their glasses.

'Happy Birthday Miss!' he said and disappeared.

'Santé!' Jimmy rose his glass.

'Santé!' She copied him and they slurped their golden liquid, ecstasy printed on their face. 'Mr. Smith,' he wanted to know. She giggled innocently and explained the facts about her Monday morning rendezvous, since the appearance of this man in her life, even though he had only stepped into the business lounge, but for Issata, the lounge representing her life, it seemed logical that Mr. Smith belonged to her life. —That he was making her hormone go so wild. And she was having multiple orgasms, just by his presence. Without forgetting all the signs, proving that he must be so into her. Jimmy listened to his friend's story patiently, shook his head sometimes, imagining her, so worked up to appear natural. He knew her so well, and cared for her so much. She was the Issata, he loved. She was so unique and made him laugh.

'New role and a new adventure!'

'But what do you think?'

'He is definitely flirting with you. Find out what his intentions are.'

'You should see the way he looks at me. Sometimes I think he is just looking for attention. He is handsome, he is a lawyer and has power.'

28

'You have your answer! Is he on Facebook?' Jimmy pulled out his phone from his pocket.

'I have never thought about it! I guess you are used to this, with your *Tinder* and *Happn* dating applications' she teased.

'What is his first name?'

'Daniel.' And Jimmy began an advanced search on this man who was part of the life of his friend. Each time he would click a profile, her heart would bang inside her chest, at the same vibration of her disappointment, when a picture was revealed. 'Not him!' she would sigh disheartened. 'And this one?' 'Neither!'

Jimmy pursued his mission, as determined as the hope marked on his friend's face. When suddenly she exclaimed: 'But Jimmy, do you know how many Smiths they are in the UK? It would be almost like looking for Mr. Martin in France!'

'I guessed you will have to continue your homework alone at home!'

'I guess you are right!'

'Let's drink up!' Jimmy led the way. She followed his footsteps and he refilled their glasses.

'Are you ready to order?' The waiter checked on them.

'Shall we go for bento?' said Issata who always chose the same menu.

'Good idea! Let's go for salmon and chicken teriyaki.'

'More drink?' checked the waiter.

'A large bottle of warm *sake*!' answered Jimmy.

'You want to make me drunk!'

'It is not very complicated sweetheart! So, what are your plans with Daniel Smith?' Jimmy pursued when the waiter left.

'If only I know! I don't know what to say when I am close to him. My heart beats so fast that I am scared he hears it.'

'Just enjoy his compliments.'

'His presence is hypnotic Jimmy!'

'I understand, he hypnotises you, that is why you become wet in your pants, without realising!'

'How on earth?'

'You said it darling!'

'I just want someone to dance through life with,' she whispered, contemplating a dream which seemed impossible to realise.

'You want a fairy tale, don't you?'

'Yes, exactly!'

'To your dance with Mr. Smith then!'

She giggled.

'And which princess would you want to be?'

'Cinderella!'

'Why her?'

'Did you actually know that the name Cinderella has the connotation; *One who unexpectedly achieves recognition or success after a period of neglect and obscurity?*'

'Interesting.'

'I just don't want to have to return home before midnight.'

'I see, you want to wake up the next morning in a hotel.'

'You are perfectly right, us women have fought hard for our rights, for our emancipation, we might as well stay till morning, with champagne for breakfast.'

'Honey you are hilarious!' They both cracked up. 'You never know; you might be the next Cinderella of the twenty-first century.'

'There is no black princess in Walt Disney!'

'Yes, there is!'

'Which one?'

'Princess Tiana in *The Princess and the Frog.*'

'I forgot about her, you surely know your Walt Disney Classic too, but this is the only story with a black princess.'

'Write your own fairy tale then,' smiled Jimmy.

'I wish so, but how?'

'Change the tide.'—Changing the tide, she spoke in her head. 'I feel so stupid now, I am thirty-seven, and I am dreaming of a fairy tale.'

'Darling Issata, me too I want a Prince, there is no fairy tale for gay men.' They burst into laughter again, tears shining in their eyes, describing the colour of their complicity. But behind their laughter, there was also a profound truth.

'But enough of me, what about you?' she said, taking a slurp from her drink. At that moment, their meal arrived.

'Good appetite!' the waiter said leaving swiftly.

'So?' Her eyes questioned, before attacking her bento. Jimmy took a deep breath.

'Do you remember Andrew?'

'The personal fitness instructor?'

'Yes,' he exploded laughing. A naughty look spiced up his face.

'And?'

He plunged his chopstick into his salmon and shoved the marinated raw flesh in his mouth. Chewing quickly, he explained: 'He contacted me again, and we had a date.' Jimmy had noticed Andrew at his local gym a while back. Then Andrew stopped attending. Then he reappeared a month ago. He was a cute Brazilian guy, and kept his dark curly hair, always tied on top of his head, secured with a red bandana. His big round chocolate eyes, highlighted his Latin blood and could burn any fragile flesh, if not

31

vigilant. —So recommended, with moderation. His Egyptian lips as juicy as a ripened peach seemed to be blowing kisses to anyone rapid enough to catch them. According to Jimmy, he looked like a god. They only met once for a drink, and Jimmy liked him. Issata knew what was coming.

'Did you paint Van Gogh?' she asked.

'Yes, we painted Van Gogh, and Gauguin, and Co…'

And they exploded in waves of laughter again. Now let me explain to you the Van Gogh theory. According to Issata and Jimmy, the art of painting rhymed with sex and vice versa. Why? They viewed art as a means to explore one's unique creativity and the description of one's own freedom. And why Van Gogh, a very tormented man? In fact, Issata had suggested the annotation: *'Did you paint Van Gogh?'* One day, they had spent an afternoon at the Tate Gallery, where the works of the artist were exposed, and they pondered on the famous painting *The Starry Night,* which as the title suggests, portrays an intense night, and most probably the state of mind of Van Gogh himself. She received the violent flashes printed on the canvas like a cosmic energy. Rather than dooming this painter as someone who couldn't find peace, she began to feel a sexual release through all his paintings, by the boldness of the colours he chose, his dramatic impulsiveness at expressing landscapes and still life in his work. Voilà! That is the story! And Gauguin? They were just friends.

'Was it good?'

'I think I am in love!' Typical of Jimmy who loses his heart easily, as he believed in connection.

'So, what is next?'

'Now, it is my turn to invite him.'

'What do you have in mind?'

'To go for dinner, and to spend more time talking with him.'

'I understand, last time you were too busy painting Van Gogh.'

'Yes, we are meeting next week, on Tuesday.'

'We have to celebrate this; we both have a story to report.'

'Absolutely darling, to our fairy tale!' He poured the last drop of sake in Issata's cup and placed another order. In the middle of their meal, he asked: 'But tell me how does Mr. Smith fit in your Buddhism?

I think, I owe to shed the light on that person called Nichiren Daishonin. In the history of Buddhism, early Buddhist doctrines expounded that those earthly desires caused sufferings, and those sufferings were manifesting through various cravings, such as attachment, delusion, and destructive impulses. It was explained that greed, anger, and foolishness represented the main poisons at the root of earthly desires. According to these theories, to reach a state of happiness, all desires had to be extinguished. Because Desires and Enlightenment were regarded as facts of life, which could not coexist. And came Nichiren Daishonin, a priest from the thirteenth century. What for? He wanted to understand why Buddhist teachings had failed to guide people to happiness. —If mankind were to continue to follow earlier Buddhist reasonings, people would then have to wait, a very long time, to reach illumination, making it impossible to ever consider leading a happy and fulfilling life. Such insane blindness was doomed to fail, he deducted and went searching. Through his quest, he acquainted himself with the Lotus Sutra, which overturned these previous teachings by proclaiming that all people have the potential to reveal their Buddha nature in their present circumstances. Because, as so long as there was life, desires would continue to exist. And a desire remained a desire, a sincere wish, which emerged from the heart. If not, what about eating? People would die from hunger if they could not satisfy their vital needs. What about sexual desire, humanity would also perish if we didn't procreate if we didn't fulfil our basic needs. 'And Lady Kondo to add, sex is part of life! I cannot see myself giving up on it! It represents a very important factor to maintain relationship alive. Healthy relationship thrives on passion, excitation and sexiness. I tell you a secret, for me, I see sex like an Arpaggio, you know that Italian word which signifies, playing on a harp. After all, we all have our own rhythm, haven't we...? After vigorous studies, Nichiren came to realise that the greatest teaching of Shakyamuni, the first historical recorded Buddha, was the Lotus Sutra and concluded that Nam-myoho-renge-kyo, the title itself of the Lotus Sutra, hidden in the teaching, could liberate humanity. He discovered that the source of desire was innate to life itself. To be alive was a primal instinct and the greatest desire in itself. From that realisation, the idea that human being associated their desire to happiness was an act so commonly human that he owed to defend. On 28th April 1253, he proclaimed Nam-myoho-renge-kyo.

Issata smiled, recalling when she took part in this teaching. If she was to be honnest with herself, it was mainly the idea to achieve her desires that seduced her in chanting.
'To be honest, I don't know. I am going to trust what is revealed within my heart and let the universe play its job.'
'That's it?'
'That is a start!' she smiled.

'But what do you think about when you chant?'

'What do I think?' she repeated, 'Thoughts are what make us alive, aren't they? And '*I think, therefore I am,*'

'Descartes!'

'Touché!' she sighed. 'I guess I would like to go on a romantic date with him!'

'And if you don't go on a date, does it mean he is not the one?'

'He had better be! Because I am fed up to wait!'

Jimmy giggled. 'Do you chant every day?'

'Yes.'

'For how long?'

'It depends on what I need to realise, but I normally chant one hour every day.'

'In a go?'

'Yes, when it is possible! At the moment due to my early start, I chant for thirty minutes before going to work and then finish my hour in the evening.'

'I am very impressed!'

'I see my Buddhist practice as my spiritual exercise, just as you would go to the gym, to watch sexy bodies.'

'What a metaphor!' he giggled

She smiled. 'Let just say that in the world we are living, it has become necessary to offer healthy food to our mind. And my Buddhist represents my fertilizer to cultivate my wisdom.'

'Darling, I just want enough wisdom to fuck!'

'You can always chant about it then!' she guffawed.

'Right now, I am dying for a fag!'

'Me too! Let's finish up quickly then, and decide after!'

'Deal!'

They plunged back into their box, scrapping till the last grain of rice. Jimmy paid.

'What's next?' she asked, once out. She pulled on her Marlboro Gold super king, the only cigarette, she had ever smoked since she had begun her dangerous liaison with that drug.

'You know where!'

Layers of dried saliva coated on each corner of her mouth, the feeling that an axe had been planted in her brain, waves of nausea hitting her throat, Issata opened her eyes to her dimly lit room. They were forced to confront the light of ray piercing through her blinds. She moaned. Lying flat on her large metal bed, baroque style, which invaded most of the space in her flat, her head buried into her memory pillow; she couldn't think straight. She fixed the cheap two doors white wardrobe, full of clothes located near the entrance of her studio. She kept her uniform hung on it. Next to it, she organised her Buddhist sanctuary. She managed to find space for a huge plasma television, which she kept on top of a wicker basket, congested with items, she probably wouldn't remember that she possessed. And of course, a panoply of DVD and CD, stacked together, covered the four corners of her flat.

How did her night go? Flashback of herself dancing with Jimmy, stimulated her memory. They ended up at the Georges and Dragon pub, the well-known gay venue in Shoreditch, notorious for total fun and mindless hedonism.

Then they jumped into a taxi, with another guy.

He kept saying: —Te Quiero. He was kissing Jimmy. Jimmy was looking for something in his trousers.

36

—I wonder if he had found what he was looking for, she analysed in the most natural observation. Because that was what the most normal person, suffering from a hangover, would contemplate the day after, in order to alleviate the sentiment of guilt behind their self-sabotage. Or maybe, the day after, a lot of those wild animals like Issata, would wake up in the universe of Edward Munch, that Norwegian painter, the great expressionist in the history of art. Why in his world? Simply because, it is the name of one of his paintings: *The Day After.* The canvas represented a *Madonna* in a bedroom, laying on a bed in an inviting posture. Her arms opened alongside her voluptuous body, her long black curly hair sweeping the floor, she is wearing a white corset which reveals the heaviness of her breasts possibly in need to be emptied. Not far from the bed a small table was located, where a bottle of liquor and two glasses were placed, suggesting, that the woman was not alone, contrary to Issata. Not only she was alone, and her body was hurting. —*The Day after* was clearly reflecting her state of being after a wild night. No response about Jimmy's finding emerged. —Maybe, I should sleep it off, crossed her mind, wishing she was twenty again, free from any responsibilities. But she was thirty-seven and her bladder's plea was more convincing than the suppressed desire of a teenager. She shoved her duvet away. To her surprise, she was wearing her sexy pink cami nighty dress, long enough to cover her private part.

—How did I get in? Who cares, I didn't get laid! Still feeling fragile, she placed her feet carefully on her lino floor, attempting to stand. She succeeded. Her eyes fixed the bathroom's door.

'Alleluia!' she exclaimed, when she dropped her derrière on the toilet seat. She sprayed the sink with her warm and golden water and listened to the violence of the jet flow. —It's great to pee, she moaned with pleasure.

A naive smile printed on her face, her head resting against the wall, she remained in her vulnerable position for seconds. Her legs spread opened, she felt the elastic of her black lacy panty, that no one had the privilege to touch, to smell and to pull off, tied to her ankles. She wiped her fanny, and drew the little strength she had left, to lift up her buttocks. —I am getting old, her brain denounced, facing her reflection in her mirror. She couldn't miss the marks of what was left of her make up and washed her hands. —It is because of you Jimmy, never again! She covered herself with her old dressing gown that has lost its creamy colour and returned to her main room. The kettle on, she lit up a Marlboro Gold and sat at her bistro table. A *ding* sound came from her iPhone. She knew it was Jimmy. She hurried to grab her phone; another *ding* melody followed. —Ok, he has found what he was looking for, she deducted reading his texts and laughed. The kettle whistled; she went to remove it from the stove. Her coffee ready, she returned to her seat. She was holding in her hands, a huge white cup on which a massive red heart was printed, offered by Jimmy. Her lips welcomed the flavour and the smell of the hot drink with deep gratitude. But she was constrained to swallow her liquid slowly, feeling a bit fragile. This was not helping her mind clouded by the millions of Vodkas and Tequila shot she had engulfed. Guilty of her crime, she watched the smoke of her fag, disappear around her. Then she remembered their search on the person of Daniel Smith. —No way! Yes way! And she logged into her Facebook account, to pursue her investigation. The list of names under Mr. Smith appeared endless. She gave up and her eyes met her Buddhist altar.

—I know, it is time to chant! In no time, she killed another fag and carried her mug with her. On her knees, in front of her shrine, she grabbed her prayers beads, also called *juzu* in Japanese. She opened her butsudan and looked at the Gohonzon her object of worship. She rubbed her hands, and expressed *sansho,* which is to chant Nam-myoho-renge-kyo, three times. No, she didn't wash, nor change her clothes to pray. After all, as the expression would say in French:

— *L'habit ne fait pas le moine,* translated as '*Clothes do not make the man'* in English. Issata looking for Mr. Right, didn't mean that she had to wear a wedding dress to pray and wait for him to knock on her door. This explained why most of the time, she was naked beneath her bathroom robe.

—*You are probably asking yourself, as to what her Buddhist practice actually entails? As far as what you have read, she repeated these strange words, sometimes for hours, that she calls the mystic law. What if she was practicing the voodoo? Being an African woman, that unusual behaviour could validate a very plausible theory? Impossible, this ritual was born in Haiti! Africa, is best known the grand marabous. So let me try to explain to you, what is that Buddhism.'*

First, the butsudan, literally meaning Buddhist altar, is a wooden cabinet. Well, that precious furniture encloses and protects a Gohonzon or religious icon. Issata's one was made of cherry red oak wood, decorated with two brass-coloured knobs for handles, a model she had designed. The word Gohonzon is a term for venerated religious objects and takes the shape of a scroll or statue, in Japanese Buddhism.

'Honzon' signifies object of fundamental devotion, and 'Go' an honorific prefix, is translated as, with honour. Simply put, Gohonzon means to worship with honour, and in Nichiren Daishonin Buddhism, it refers to a mandala, a hanging calligraphy paper, containing Chinese and Sanskrit characters, appearing like little drawings. In the middle, of it, we can see written in big, Nam-myoho-renge-kyo, Nichiren. His own signature, as proof that has revealed enlightenment, the essential purpose of his teaching.

This object of veneration is the physical representation of the Mystic Law inscribed by Nichiren in 1279. That religious tool represents the graphic reflection of enlightenment, often compared to a mirror, helping us to bringing out the life condition of the Buddha, called Buddhahood. It is expressed through wisdom, courage, compassion and life force.

when Issata discovered that, that piece of paper, nicely decorated could be identified as a clear mirror, to perceive her true self and her relationship with her environment, she recalled the story of Mami Wata.

—Did Nichiren get inspired by her legend?

Mami Wata was an African goddess and a legend deriving from African history who lived in the sea. This explains the English pidgin, Mami Wata, translated as 'Mother of the water' in modern languages. She was believed to be a woman, with half-human and half-fish appearance, like a mermaid. But the story tells, she had also the ability to turn wholly into any shape of her choice, such as snake, while keeping her upper body as a woman, and appearing topless.

And what does she had to do with the Gohonzon?

40

I will get to that point, let me just tell you more about this mysterious creature. Obviously, she carried an enviable beauty with her long black hair and her dark enthralling mysteriousness. Such splendour always carries supernatural advantages. That said, she possessed immense powers, such as healing and fertility and provided spiritual and material benefits to her worshippers. As well as her magnificent life style, she guarded the water bodies as their protector. And in order to sustain peace in her kingdom, some traditional groups in Africa refused to attend beaches or exerting fishing activities. Nonetheless as much as she had great intention for her people, she also possessed like all human being, an imminent weakness, a perversive taste for lustfulness. Guessed what she did? She captured men to satisfy her insatiable appetite for carnal pleasure. After she had abused them, she made them swear faithfulness to her! And if they refused, she punished them by plugging them through extreme poverty, by destroying their relationship if they were married or she sentenced them to the capital penalty: Death! —What would be like to capture men, the way Mami Wata went about? Issata did wonder. Then she realised: —I can't even catch one, that is not for me!

—Back to the Gohonzon being compared to a mirror.

Mami Wata drew all her power from a looking glass that she carried with her at all time. Through her fetish tool, she was able to conduct rituals, where her devotees by staring in the mirror, could access her sacred power and entered her world. That was what the allegory, the Gohonzon being regarded as a mirror, brought home to her mind. So, I cannot say whether Nichiren had encountered this myth in his lifetime.

By the knowledge of her appetite to fundamental darkness. I can only deduct, that he simply avoided her.

But he explained in his writings, On Attaining Buddhahood in this lifetime,' — *'It is the same with a Buddha and an ordinary being. When deluded, one is called an ordinary being, but when enlightened, one is called a Buddha. This is similar to a tarnished mirror that will shine like a jewel when polished. A mind now clouded by the illusions of the innate darkness of life is like a tarnished mirror, but when polished, it is sure to become like a clear mirror, reflecting the essential nature of phenomena and the true aspect of reality. Arouse deep faith, and diligently polish your mirror day and night. How should you polish it? Only by chanting Nam-myoho-renge-kyo'.*

Although the title implies reaching a state of being, for what I have understood, attaining Buddhahood lays in engaging in a spiritual transformation. In order to draw forth our infinite potential, our life is being tested by plunging into the abyss of our own existence, so that we can reveal the best version of our humanity, a self that nothing can *destroy.*

—Time to observe the daily routine of her practice.

She then dusted the base of her butsudan, a cream cabinet, where she kept most of her Buddhist guidance and books; checked that her fruit offering was still shining with freshness, replaced her tea candles; added cool water in her greenery vases, two of them she possessed, which she kept on each side of her Buddhist altar, offered some fresh water in a small sake cup and burnt one stick of incense. No rules existed in regard to the gifts offered to the Gohonzon.

However, the altar being the focal point in Nichiren Daishonin's teaching, any efforts dedicated in showing respect towards the Gohonzon, is an expression of great sincerity. And in accordance with the strict law of causality, those endeavours will be manifested in one's life. The offering of water belongs to old Indian tradition where water is considered to be of very high value. That is why members offer that precious liquid to the object of worship. The evergreen, symbolises the eternity of life.

The candles express the light and this light is the manifestation of the buddha wisdom which illuminates our lives. Incense illustrates the function of fragrance. At the same time, if one suffers from allergy after using it, it is best not to burn it. It is common sense.

When it comes to food, only the heart matters. Members of SGI mainly offer fruits, sometimes sweets, cakes, chocolates, even wine. Issata loved placing a bottle of champagne on her Buddhist altar, because at the end of the day, she would be the one, enjoying the golden liquid. Her altar being cleaned, not that it was ever dirty, but I had to explain the ceremony, she began Gongyo. That is right, it takes efforts to become happy.

Gongyo represents her daily prayer which she performs morning and evening, as a supplementary practise, to her chanting. The word gongyo means assiduous practice and this practice entails the recitation of the 'Hoben' and 'Juryo' chapter from the Lotus Sutra, which conveys the heart of the Buddha. For Issata, she understood this ritual as an expression of gratitude for life. And she made her own commitment, to realise the wish of the Buddha via her own actions. The prayer ends with a vow: *'At all times I think to myself: How can I cause living beings to gain entry into the unsurpassed way and quickly acquire the body of the Buddha?'* Very clear! A Buddha is someone who constantly strives to find a way to encourage others.

Three prayers are offered during Gongyo. And one in particular is dedicated to personal wishes: *'I pray to reveal my Buddhahood, carry out my human revolution, change my karma and fulfil all my wishes.'* Once she expressed Gongyo, she began her meditative prayers. —Nam-myoho-renge-kyo…

And what does it actually mean? Let's travel back to France to *Paris 8 University Vincennes-Saint-Denis* where she studied English and Literature. No, she spent her time partying and falling in love. Obviously, she failed her first year! That time also marked the year, when her papa passed away. He died of a heart attack. A very handsome man, tall and generous, anti-tobacco and alcohol, however his fate decided that his time was up at the age of seventy years old.

The following year, she encountered Jeanne, who was studying the same diploma as her. She introduced her to chanting Nam-myoho-renge-kyo, equally called Daimoku.

In a more detailed explanation, here is what it means:

Nam is the act of devotion or dedication and derives from Sanskrit, an ancient language in India, now mainly used for religious purposes. *Nam* also takes the meaning of returning to one's source.

Literally speaking *Myo* means Mystic or Wonderful and expresses the essence of life, visible and invisible. *Ho* is the manifestation of life or actual occurrences that can be observed and the manifestation of the law itself.

Looking at it, together *Myoho* is the Mystic Law. It is called the Mystic Law because it is difficult to comprehend the working of this Law intellectually.

Renge signifies the Lotus flower. In Asian culture, it is seen as a symbol of purity and nobleness. The characteristic of the Lotus flower is that it produces the flower and the fruit at the same time. Therefore, it symbolises the simultaneity of cause and effect. The Law of Causality explains that we are directly responsible for our fate and since we can create our destiny, we can also transform it.

So, reciting Nam-myoho-renge-kyo, brings out simultaneously the effect of Buddhahood, which will manifest at the right time. Just like the Lotus flower can only grow thick and healthy roots and bloom in a muddy pond where its flower remains immaculate, the same principle can be observed in our own lives. The pond illustrates our worry-filled world, the lotus is Issata, you, who are reading, me. And the mud represents our problems —the indispensable nourishment for our spiritual growth. No matter how muddy or dirty the pond is, the lotus flower always blossoms beautifully, so can human being.

Kyo means sutra, the voice, or teaching of a Buddha.

It represents vibration and interconnectedness of the universal energy that permeates all life. The character originally meant warp of clothes and later came to have an additional meaning as to the thread of logic, reason, and law. It was used in a sense to preserve a teaching.

We could say that the *Kyo,* of Myoho-renge-kyo, indicates that Nam-myoho-renge-kyo, is the law of eternal and unchanging truth. Simply said, each time we articulate Nam-myoho-renge-kyo, we are actually saying:

I dedicate my life, I devote my life, I return my life to the Mystic Law, the law of cause and effect, the law of the eternal and unchanging truth. Issata insisted on the fact that chanting Nam-myoho-renge-kyo was not magical.

Nonetheless, by basing our lives on this law, we can transform all sufferings and hardships, into a source of joy.

Straight away, she connected with Jeanne's warm attitude. The life of this new friend was overflowing with boundless compassion, something which Issata hadn't found anywhere, not even with Mum. Mum will be the name I will use, to refer to Issata's mother. Secretly, she was holding immense anger toward her, an aggressive feeling which she protected through a filial love for her younger sister Sophia.

At first, articulating Nam-myoho-renge-kyo appeared difficult. She encountered a lot of struggles in finding the rhythm of these six syllables, and before anything else, she didn't like hearing her voice. She found her tonality too deep and was often compared to a man when she spoke. As time went by, she managed to get her rhythm. Jeanne also encouraged her to chant, to see tangible proof that chanting worked. Why proof? Because the purpose of chanting lies in guiding anyone to achieve their goals in life. Every beginner is encouraged to chant five minutes morning and evening, to test the truth of Buddhism. Issata wanted a boyfriend and chanted to make it happen. She attended Buddhist meetings, where she met other French members. Their approach to life moved her. They all looked confident and free, but they were also older than her. Her mother didn't see any objection to her new spiritual path.
'What matters is your happiness!' she told her. Sometimes, Sophia would chant with her.

After chanting for one year, not only she didn't have a boyfriend but failed her studies again. —Finito with chanting, and went to London as an au pair.

Her debut in London was not easy. She felt lonely and that loneliness was manifested even more in her inability to express herself in English. This is when she decided to give another try to Buddhism. But the family she was living with, didn't accept the idea of her, articulating these strange words loudly in their home.

She was desperate and prayed a lot. Another au-pair, she had during the school trips, encouraged her to seek legal advice at the Citizens Advice Bureau. She met a lovely Nigerian woman, looking for someone to take care of her two children. She didn't mind her choice of faith. This is when Issata ended up in North London.

Was this proof of chanting or just a coincidence? She found a local group that she considered as her SGI family. Her daily practice became stronger and she felt like a powerful force was pushing her forward; a sense of connectedness with her environment; the sentiment that she belonged somewhere. She concentrated more on listening to her voice, until one day, she realised: —My voice is my identity! —My voice reveals the truth about who I am. At the age of nineteen, she discovered something new, a way to life which gave her hope, and she was ready to explore more. In her limited English, she studied as much as she could Nichiren Daishonin's philosophy. A year after, practicing steadily, she realised that she didn't have a clear goal in life. And now? —What did I know about life when I was nineteen, let alone about relationship, she smiled?

Her love story with the mystic law, was born in October 1994 and she married the philosophy by receiving the Gohonzon in 1997.

In 2005 she commenced her job at Voyage Europe as a stewardess. Working for VoyE was her pride and her good fortune. She had the freedom to visit her family easily.

She confessed to me that she used to hide at waterloo station behind the crowd, admiring the parade of the stewardess, walking elegantly, their make-up immaculately applied, their eyes shining, probably from tiredness, which Issata couldn't envisage, driving their carryon confidently with one common message: 'Red, for Voyage Europe'. One day, she approached one of them and asked for advice on how to get on board. —I have started as a stewardess, and now a few years later, there I am, PR Lounge coordinator.

Mr. Smith enigmatic energy, penetrated her being. His bright blue eyes undressed her with violence and insolence and she felt the caress of his provocative smile, kissing her senses. —Jimmy is right, how do I chant about it? That was not the real question! Her dilemma was that she was afraid to chant about it. Because her wishes had never come true! While listening to her voice, she could feel a heavyweight, resting on her heart, a tight pressure. That weight inspired an odour, a pounding smell, reminding her of those dark years tainted by the word solitude and her inability to attract Mr. Right. Tears flowed in her eyes.

—But Mr. Smith, surely must be a sign of the universe? Desperately wanting to believe, she broke down in tears. Because, the idea of believing rhymed with deep faith. Jesus, Mohamed, Nichiren himself had demonstrated faith throughout their life. —How could I implement such faith, when I have never experienced it? Just thinking of it, stirred up a profound pain. No place existed anymore in her heart, for her to dream. Her wet eyes fixed the

Gohonzon, with the hope that a little light would illuminate her way, like a fairy Godmother operating her magic trick.

Well, her iPhone made a sound. Jimmy, shared more photos of his time with the guy he slept with, which she never got the name of.

'I look forward to seeing yours with Mr. Smith, Darling! XX'

—Oh Jimmy, only you can believe such a thing could happen, she giggled. And in her amusement, came out from her mouth: —To believe is like my friendship with Jimmy. It is about trust! The light began to brighten inside her. On reading, her friend's message, a spontaneous determination, prompted her to decide: —By 16th March, Mr. Smith will invite me on a romantic date. *'My darling Jimmy, I love you so much, XXX.'* She answered excited.

Why that date? Simply, because, it was a symbolic day for the members of SGI. It commemorates an occasion that took place on March 16th 1958.

Josei Toda, the second President of the organisation made an impassioned speech to 6000 youth, entrusting them with the future of the Soka Gakkai and the widespread of the humanistic philosophy of Nichiren Buddhism. How did he come to Buddhism then? At the age of nineteen, he met Mr Makiguchi, an educator, author, and philosopher. Josei Toda being a teacher himself was touched by his warmth and his vision in introducing a more humanistic way to life, based on the creation of values. A theory which he had presented into three distinctive categories: the value of beauty, the value of gain, and the value of the good. —*Beauty* for its sensory impact on aesthetic awareness, *Gain*, a measure not just limited to material goods sustaining our lives, but towards the holistic advancement of life and *Good,* a measure of contribution to social or public well-being, therefore mankind as a whole.

For Makiguchi, creating value is determined when any action undertaken, adds to the advancement of the human condition. And it was mainly through education that he chose to implement his value theory. To his eyes, education existed to serve the students and he explained his educational ideas and theory in a work called 'Soka Kyoikugaku Taikei (The System of Value-Creating Pedagogy).' Of course, he encountered opposition as his views contradicted the military government's politics in place at the time.

They both began practicing Nichiren's Buddhism in 1928 and founded Soka Gakkai, in line with their thinking. Makiguchi took the lead as the first president before it became the SGI in 1975.

Originally it started as Soka Kyoiku Gakkai which means, Society for value-creating Education. *'I could find no contradiction between science, philosophy, which is the base of our modern society, and the teaching of the Lotus Sutra,'* he declared when explaining why he took faith in Nichiren Buddhism. Rapidly, Toda and Makiguchi grew confident, that his teaching was the only vehicle able to help people reach absolute happiness. *'With indescribable joy, I transformed the way I had lived my life for almost sixty years,'* stated Mr. Makiguchi. That's how grateful, he felt, for having encountered, that extraordinary philosophy of life. He could clearly grasp that transforming society begins through individual transformation. And that was why education was important. Education to become happy and not for the sake of passing exams.

For someone like Makiguchi, education had to derive from real life experiences, so that new ideas and new ways to learn could emerge. Unfortunately, his beliefs didn't sit well with the authority who imposed the Shinto as the state religion for their war campaign. They were both arrested on 6th July in 1943 because they refused to follow the religious policy of the Japanese military. Mr Makiguchi died of extreme malnutrition in 1944 at the age of 73 in Tokyo's Sugamo prison. Whereas Mr. Toda was released on the 3rd July 1945. When he came out, the whole country was in despair, and the Soka Gakkai had collapsed. From that day he started to rebuild the organisation on his own and took the presidency. Today, thanks to his great determination millions of people have taken faith in Nichiren Daishonin's teaching. Going back to 16th March, fostering the younger generation had always been at the heart of Josei Toda's vision. So, he invited the Prime Minister to one of their general meetings in order for him to meet the youth of the Soka Gakkai.

Everyone strove their hardest to make the day a historical event. Indeed, the day turned out to become a historic moment, but not for what those youngsters had hoped for. The head of their country declined the invitation at the last minute and sent his family on his behalf instead. Witnessing the response of the Prime Minister, anger and disappointment ravaged the heart of President Josei Toda. However, seeing the spirit and the passion of the young people to actualise this big event, he dedicated that day as 'Youth Day' in honour to them, also called Kosen Rufu day. Kosen Rufu is the main goal of SGI, and I will come back to it later. The significance of this day is to honour a new era led by the youth division, a spiritual fight which embodies the mentor and disciple relationship, another

51

important aspect within Buddhism that we will discover together throughout Issata's journey. From that day, 16th March shed the light on a new departure. Just as our date of birth would mark our history in this world, those anniversaries' dates narrate the history of SGI and the actual proof of the expansion of its movement. That's the reason, she chose that date! Will 16th March be her lucky number?

She travelled to Paris for Christmas, taking place at Sophia, her sister; mother of three children, married to Bertrand, Senegalese, and an IT consultant. Her first son, called Malcom was a product of her youth. His father, a white man, didn't want to recognise the child. Years later, she met her husband with whom she has Nelson and Rose.

—One week with Mum, she contemplated anxious, on her journey there. Let's remember, that she carried a lot of anger towards Mum, which, she didn't understand. That emotion was taking a perverse pleasure by casting a shadow in her heart while spying on her thoughts. From the start of her chanting, that resentment had been sitting in her heart silently. But visible enough, for it not to pass unnoticed. It was waiting there in the centre of her entity, like a boat parked in a port. It anticipated the arrival of the owner to sail away. She had shared with Jeanne, that burden associated with her mother. She encouraged her to chant for her mother's happiness and to repay her depth of gratitude for giving life to her.

Nichiren Daishonin wrote an important letter called: 'The Four Debts of Gratitude' where he discussed his views, from the perspective of Buddhism. In Hinduism, the

52

word 'Krita-jna' is a Sanskrit expression which meant gratitude. Literally, 'jna,' means 'Acknowledging' and 'Krita,' 'What has been done on one's behalf.' Therefore, when one 'acknowledges' and 'appreciates' what has been done for one, their next phase is to lead a life dedicated to the welfare of others to establish the transmission of 'Krita-jna.' In other words, it is the knowledge and the spirit of gratitude for the support and care received from others that contribute to one's personal growth, which must be cultivated, and the most obvious people are our parents.

As predicted, Mum's company reiterated the anguish she had dreaded. A heavy malaise was digging a hole in the relationship; a malaise activated by a terrifying sentiment, her mother seemed to evoke in her. In reality, that was all she knew, nothing except for that primitive engulfment, to scream, to cry, to yell, just by staring at her. But she never dared cross the line. A lack of fulfilment was tainting her mother's life, even though, she had Antoine, her companion. They had met two years after her husband's death. He was a nice friendly man in his mid-sixties whose roots derive from Portugal, director of a marketing company, patiently preparing his retirement. What was the problem then? Her mother too was working part-time as a receptionist, in the school, her daughters had attended. She was the only black woman, to whom Madame Leroix, the headmistress of the school had entrusted the front desk responsibility. And when Sophia was born, being a good employee, she was able to come back part-time. Her retirement pension was assured too. Unless Antoine's friendliness didn't fit her mother's personality? What was actually the real problem? Her mother's unhappiness or Issata's anger? Whatever the reason, something was weighing heavily on her chest. It was rock solid and she worried that a day would come when she won't possess the strength to carry that burden. And that day will end her sorrows. Fortunately, the cheerful presence of her nephews helped her maintain, a healthy state of mind. She adored them. Especially Malcolm, born on 18th November 2004. I 'll get to 18th November, later. Ok, let me give you a little insight. That year, marked her thirty fourth birthday and she made the determination to meet her Mr. Right by 18th November. On that day, Mr. Right didn't manifest but Malcolm made his appearance in the world. From the moment she held him in her arms, she felt connected to the essence of his life. He is very intelligent; however, school describes the place where he meets most of his difficulties. Sophia even explained that he didn't express himself. What to think, considering, she has trained as a psychologist, but didn't understand one of her children? No one can judge! That is the little summary about the existence of her nephew that she loves dearly.

'Issata, I am so happy to see you!'

It was December 31ˢᵗ, she celebrated New Year's Eve with her very old friend Agnes, ten years, her oldest. Agnes came from Sweden and embodied the perfect personification of Scandinavian women whose features rhymed with tallness and slimness, pale milky skin, light eyes, square jawlines, and a small nose as pointed as a kitten muzzle, except for her hair. Wavy and long, reaching above her waist, her ebony hair was floating graciously on her shoulders.

There was a glimpse of Sophia Lauren in the expression of her ravishing blue eyes and her generous sensuous smile. Normal, her genes contained Greek blood. In a nutshell, she was a bombshell. She lived in North London with her husband Abdul, half Indian and Somalian. Abdul was a strong and muscled creature. A gentle and fierce gaze emanated from his oval shape face. Always perfectly dressed, his name was well-known in the fashion industry. He designed lingerie's for women and men. It was during the year of his fortieth birthday, that this eighteen-year-old phenomenon, that all international designers were fighting to have on their podium, entered his life.

They met in Milan, where he had just signed a contract with Versace house. Straight away, he fell in love with her wild innocent eyes, the shape of her juicy lips, the heaviness of her pear shape bosom, which revealed the woman child, residing inside her, the type of woman any man would want to protect. And the slenderness of her legs, which inspired the smell of tropical palm trees, those trees one cannot resist to caress, until its fruits fall down the ground.

No man could resist her sex appeal. And she chose him. They span the perfect love for five years, then Agnes got pregnant and was forced to give up her world. Mother of twins, Joseph and Louis, she decided to dedicate her time to raising them and coordinating charity events, while Peter travelled the world.

Issata and Agnes had known each other for twenty years. They met at a Buddhist meeting. They had nothing in common, except for a connection they couldn't explain. In spite of her glamorous appearance, Agnes had a big downfall: —She never listened and could be very careless, bouncing with extreme negligence. Without qualifying her as stupid, she lacked common sense. If Issata ever tried to make her reflect, she would be welcome with her favourite catch phrase: *This is who I am!* What to say to this?

She even wondered what Abdul could perceive in her except for her beauty. Abdul inspired gentleness and compassion, and his mind resembled a huge dictionary of knowledge. On the contrary, Agnes was an attention seeker. Anyway, Issata never addressed it either. —Maybe, she is right, that is just the way she is, she deducted! The evening unfolded joyfully, with plenty of food, drinks, and laughter. All guests were couples with children, mainly friends of Agnes and Peter.

In the morning, she went home to Valley Park, at number 66. Those golden figures were nailed to a varnished black door. The windows borders were also painted in black. Issata named the propriety the black and white villa. The entrance more than inviting, gave a view from the outside to an immense residence built on three stories, converted into ten studio flats. The whole building had been completely refurbished. A large palmer tree planted in a black ceramic pot, occupied the little patio beside her flat's window. That was the reason she took the place. No one could ever miss the black Jaguar, always parked at the front of the house, so brilliantly polished, that anyone passing by, could admire themselves as if looking through a mirror.

But it was impossible to peek inside, as all windows were armoured. Rajeev her landlord owned that car, the famous XJ6 model.

She walked alongside the slab white and black mosaic looking, meticulously placed on the ground. When she opened the main door, her eyes travelled alongside the long and luminous corridor, leading to the communal kitchen. The walls were covered by angels' paintings and a massive photo of the Taj Mahal. She spotted some lights coming through other flats' doors, but the house was quiet. Issata didn't really know the tenants. There were men and women all working, all keeping themselves to themselves. Regularly, she would discover new faces.

'2012 is the year to move out from this place,' she sighed, slipping into her nest. —Why? The house is clean and refurbished. Little angels were watching over her.

Buying a flat was a desire as equally important as finding Mr. Right. Kicking her shoes off, she stared at all the stuff she had accumulated.

Let me give you a little portrait of her landlord Rajeev Harijan. In the history of India, a *Harijan* person represented a member of the lowest caste, often referred as *Untouchable* or *Dalit*, literally translated as 'broken' or 'scattered' in Sanskrit. They were regarded as *Untouchable* due to their social and ritual status and labelled as primitive. As a result, they had segregated Hamlet outside towns and villages boundaries. It was forbidden for them to enter many temples and schools as their touch was seen as seriously polluting to people of the higher caste; and even reported that the sight of some of them was held to be polluting. That was why the tribe was forced to live in a nocturnal existence. Thankfully, the modern Indian constitution formally recognised their plight by legally establishing their *Scheduled tribe*. Rajeev's family, from his father's side, was then able to access education. But the story explains that in the Indian caste system, caste cannot be changed as it would upset the cosmic balance. In other words, they inherit the caste from their parents. Rajeev was sent to a military camp at a very young age. His only ambition was to get the recognition that his caste never received. And he was aiming for the Field Marshall Rank, the highest rank attainable in India's Army.

This rank was above General Officer. Rajeev served the army for fifty years and retired to look after his family properties. He was an only colonel when he left, while all his comrades grew to higher positions.

Issata had met Rajeev, a year before, she began her new role at VoyE. He presented himself in his green bottle, military uniform, a red Indian turban, placed on his head.

A thick moustache designed in the shape of a plaster, hardened his facial expression. Nonetheless, he looked like a very respectable person.

She noticed the amounts of medals pinned on his uniform, five to be precise. He explained the significance of each one of them. — It is my honour to serve others, he kept saying. He even confessed that his wife had abandoned him with his daughter. —She has never understood my mission, in helping others, he would cry out! —My daughter is everything to me, she must find a nice husband who can love her and her son, he used to say. His daughter got pregnant in her teens. But he never shared what had happened. Issata didn't know what to make of him. Why was he sharing something so personal with her? But she knew what to make of his nasal voice, which was the sound of his life. She had never heard such a high nasal pitched frequency. His timber resonated like a complaint, an escape, somebody hiding something. That thing was hidden in his voice. And his eyes? He possessed deep penetrating dark eyes which answered her theory of a dark secret buried inside him.

—And me how did I end up here in the first place, she contemplated that morning?

2

2012 '*Year of Developing a Youthful SGI*' began.
—Another year of development, she commented when the theme was announced. —And I have to make it joyful! —Clean up your mess, yourself!

Work is great! *Le travail c'est la Santé* would say the French song from Henri Salvador. —Waking up at four o'clock in the morning to sell dreams to travelers was the ideal job of every woman. Even more so, when there is a man called Mr. Smith as an incentive.

'Good morning, Michael,' she greeted and hugged her colleague.
'Hey, welcome back Issata, and Happy New Year!'
'Happy New Year to you too!' 'Good celebration in France?'
'The usual, eating and drinking!'
'Tell, me about it! Are you ready to see him?' he laughed.
'Someone is reading in mind,' she walked off.

The first hours disappeared like a weaving thread. They coloured her morning with smiles and kindness, a weaving cloth dear to her heart, because she had produced it with her own hands. She brought to it, her stitch of patience and gratitude.

Break time came, she left the lounge for some fresh air. When she returned, *Le Salon* was still very busy. Even the VIP area was crammed with *BFirst* travellers. One of them began complimenting her on her beauty and explained that he was working in Dakar. Issata not the least interested, couldn't help thinking: —Mr. Smith should arrive any minute! 'Very nice meeting you,' she tried to escape. Her gaze darted frantically towards the big roman clock, decorating the wall of the reserved area. But the client continued his conversation. Her heart was pounding like a bomb on a timer, ready to explode at that crucial moment. She had been waiting for their precious reunion for three weeks, where she would stand by her imaginary balcony, her senses dancing with joy, looking out for his arrival.

—Someone has got to help me please, her brain wailed. Her tears began to shine in her eyes. Then her phone rang.

'Michael,' she picked up.

'He is on his way!' he let out.

'Ok!'

She smelt his tasty presence. Yes, she could taste his unique aroma, which even the best food critic would find difficult to detect. Issata had the gusto for it. Then she heard his famous footsteps, the tap dance. Mr. Smith's steps, produced a very distinct sound, like a musical phrase guiding his feet. For Issata, his steps guided her heart. His presence grew heavily.

'Nice meeting you Sir, I must go now.'

'I am travelling again next month.'

Moving away from him, she scanned through the crowd. Her pupils searched for a tall and handsome man, freckles splattered on his white skin, red hair, and eyes as blue as the Indian Ocean. That shouldn't be complicated to catch. Well, no one was matching the description in this very

61

busy and noisy lounge. —Damn, where is he? —Why didn't he join the reserved area? —Surely, he would know by now, that he would find me there! Her eyes scrutinised every corner of the lounge without forgetting those areas, cleaners often leave untouched. Most of the travellers displayed concentrated conversations with others voyagers. Some approached her and she feigned a smile. —Thanks Buddha, they can't read my mind, she commented behind her professional composure. Losing her patience, she was about to call Michael, when the soft lustra from a brown leather shoe with a red sole caught her attention. She recognised the signature.

Mr. Smith was sitting, hiding in a corner, reading his newspaper. He noticed her. Easy, she represented the woman in red. No, she was not the only employee wearing red, nor was she the only black woman in the lounge. But she was the only person who gave justice to that sacred colour. He devoured her secretly, glimpsing above his FT, a triumphant signal, lightening his eyes. At that moment, those five minutes of tension, which had seemed interminable, gradually left her body and she walked slowly towards him. *Air in G String,* resonated in her and guided her movement. He observed her advancing towards him and listened to the melodic sound of her steps, his blue eyes caressing her long legs. She moved in a slow motion. Clapping on the floor, her heels expressed the only majestic sound deriving from the expensive Vienna marble flooring. The large tiles, looking like a checkerboard, dominated by three complementary colours, milky white, beige caramel, and a warm nuance describing a mixture of copper and chocolate, took a sublime dimension. How many times during the weeks, months, did she venture on that ground? Those tiles invited millions of people trampling on each other toes as if they were practicing the tango. On several occasions, she watched them swirling with their suitcases, performing the last dance, before catching their train. But that particular Monday denounced a unique reality, an authentic truth. That particular Monday would remain her red-carpet moment for eternity. Nervous, she reached his seat and her eyes lingered on his pink silky shirt, put in evidence by a dark costume, with thin white lines.

'Good morning Issata, I was waiting for you.'
As soon as his voice rose, her heartbeats accelerated, a confirmation that she was still alive. —You were waiting for me? her mind repeated bewitched, by the persuasive power guiding his voice. Mr. Smith's words melted through her being. They sounded like a delicious French butter, softening slowly in a frying pan. She could add a pinch of salt, black paper, some garlic, white wine…And? Issata parted her lips, to accommodate a rapid respiration.

'Good morning,' she stammered. 'Why didn't you come to meet me?'

'I just told you! I didn't want to have to share you with other travellers.'

'I see,' she sighed, embarrassed.

'Happy New Year!' he pursued.

'Of course, happy New Year!' That was all, she could say. Mr. Smith didn't lose sight of the show. He stared at her, very hard, excited, and confident because victory belonged to him. His opponent was an easy target. The kind of woman dreaming of romance and seduction, even if it meant plunging into a dangerous game.

Moreover, men like him only strove to win. The word defeat didn't exist in their dictionary.

63

She remained stuck in the Lagoon of his eyes, sweat dripping under her armpits. She shivered. —Happy New Year, that is all you say? And pleaded guilty. Mr. Smith was divinely handsome. She was discovering a new beauty emerging from his being. The red dominance from his ginger hair turned into a more marron chestnut shade. Could this explain the contrast between his white skin and his persistent controlling blue stare? What was she trying to confirm? That beauty was only revealed through an obsessive behaviour? Either, or, that an obsessive character strives on desire to define beauty? Or was she simply observing the famous quote from Oscar Wilde: 'Beauty is in the eyes of the beholder.'

That observation didn't help her to relax. Quite the contrary, she felt stupid and defenceless. She worried that if she was to move, malodorous evidence from her wetness would be spotted on the luxurious floor. Losing her breath, she feared to faint. Strangely enough, images of those women from the past, trapped in their corset, caressed her mind. How did they manage to respire those poor things, with men's noses, always stuck in the middle of their boobies?

As if he had heard her question, Mr. Smith let out, in the most natural manner. 'Issata, I want to see more of you this year, outside the lounge!'

She widened her eyes. Her heart leaped from her chest but she managed to prevent it from breaking her ribs. She opened her mouth. Her lips trembled. Her mind froze.

—Someone is not Josephine Baker anymore, a little voice murmured. Amused, he surveyed her

'Me too!' detonated from her mouth.

Not the least surprised, 'At least we both want the same thing!' was his reply.

—What an idiot I am!

'Good celebration?' he continued.

'My celebrations? I went to France!' she mumbled.

'Alone?'

'Yes, and you?'

'I was in New York…'

'New York?'

'I spent Christmas with friends.'

'Oh?'

'Only friends!'

They heard the boarding announcement. He rose to his feet and adjusted the knot of his tie. A destabilised Issata watched him put his long black coat on.

'Are you allowed to take me to the platform?' From the tone of his voice, she understood clearly that she had no choice.

'Of course, let me get my coat!' She walked off anxious, her teeth chattering. —Just calm down, you are only doing your work, she warned herself. When she met him, he was standing by the lift with two other travellers. She didn't know them. She smiled at them. The lift appeared shortly after. She encouraged everyone to get in. The heat from his body rubbing against her, she respired his wild odour flirting with her hormones. Her nostrils continuously simmering, she wondered if the two men could detect the chemical energy bounding them. There was no time to find out as the door opened and they all came out.

'Everything ok Issata?'

'Yes, thank you, it was a bit suffocating inside,' she answered, feeling exposed.

'*Moi aussi J'avais un peu chaud mais pour des raisons très différentes,*' he rambled in French, nurturing an insatiable hunger.

' You speak French ?'

'*Je parle plusieurs langues Issata, dont une en particulier.*'
He insisted on the last word, a naughty smile, printed in the corner of his lips, probably revealing that linguistic expertise, that made him so proud. She could have investigated more about his unique talent, but chose to throw her head back, and laughed stupidly.

'I think we should get moving now.' She began to walk. He followed her, not commenting.

They passed the reception, in front of a Michael amused and impatient to cook up his colleague. They found themselves again, shoulders to shoulders on the escalator, crowded with passengers. She watched straight ahead, afraid of crossing his view. When they stepped onto the platform, she looked in his direction and caught him fixing her.

'Coach 14,' he smiled.

They marched silently. Regulars waved at her. She answered with a polite nod in order to block off the millions of thoughts buzzing in her brain.

'Here we are!' he said when they reached his coach.

'Bon voyage Mr. Smith!'

'Issata, from now on I want you to call me Dan!' he ordered.

'Pardon me?'

'Dan is my nickname,' he murmured and kept his attention, solely on her.

'If you want.'

'I just told you so!'

'I will need to get used to it,' she stammered.

'Just try!' he insisted.

She opened her eyes, widely.

'Say my name, you will see, everything will be fine.'

'Dan!' she uttered, laughing.

'Didn't I tell you? It was not so difficult, wasn't it?'

'You'd better climb on the train,' she cut short.

'I wish I could take you with me,' he spoke softly and moved close to her. Without shame, he rubbed her hand, looking into her eyes.

'Mr Smith!' she removed it abruptly.

'Dan,' he rectified.

'Ok, Dan, but I am at work!'

'Am I not attractive to you?'

'Yes, I am!' she laughed, then felt all eyes on her.

'So, see you next week!' He winked at her and climbed on the train.

'So?' Michael asked, when he saw her, rushing towards him.

'He wants me to call him Dan!'

'He is flirting with you big time, darling!'

'He is also a client!'

'But you like him!'

'I admit, and I feel bewitched by his presence.'

'Are you not the African woman? Shouldn't you concoct an African elixir?'

'Michael,' she chortled.

'See what he is after Issata! By the way, have you lost weight?' He stared at her, analysing her silhouette.

'I don't know!'

'I think so darling, be careful.'

'I will.'

'How are you my dear?'

She heard a nasal voice, when she introduced her key in her door. —On no, she chewed her words. She swallowed her pride and turned around. 'I am fine, thank you, and you?'

'I cannot complain! I am here to serve you! My tenants are everything. Without you, my business cannot survive, and I will be a nobody!'

—And here he goes again, with the same sweet phrases.

'How is work?'

'I am just back from my shift.'

'I see, you must be very tired.'

'Effectively, did you need anything from me?'

'No, not at all, I like to maintain friendly relationship between myself and my tenants.'

'Thank you for informing me!' She pushed her door.

'Of course, my dear, look after yourself and God bless you. You are like my sister, if you need anything, don't hesitate to contact me.'

She entered her flat, and locked herself in. —Don't you have anything to do with yourself? she analysed, kicking off her shoes. —Always in the house as if something had happened. —And that hideous green colour of that uniform of yours, it looked like an omen! Methodically, she removed her clothes, beginning with her stockings, her panties, ok the tong, then worked her way up to the dress. During that religious activity, the image of those black birds, from Alfred Hitchcock famous movie, *The Birds,* crossed her mind. The story begins with two beautiful green lovebirds, but behind their charm, their purity, laid a deep family secret. —Rajeev too, looks very clean, in fact a bit too clean!

She followed her habitual routine: —To swallow a glass of Prosecco or two, nibble, usually the leftover from the local Japanese food store, inhale two fags, before her nap. Two hours later, she would emerge from her siesta, make use of her pink toy. —Take a shower and will start again the next day. On that Monday, she added a *Girls evening* in her agenda.

'Sweetheart,' Agnes exclaimed, welcoming her friend, in her home. She was standing on silver high heel shoes, revealing her painted red toes, which highlighted a long evening red dress, with a plunging décolleté. Issata wore a woollen grey jacket, sailor 'style, which one could guess was covering a black slim jeans and black jumper, turtle neck. Her prune beret, matched the colour of her high heel's boots.

'Hi Agnes,' she embraced her friend. 'Are you going to gala?' she added, not the least surprise, because money and comfort were the only souvenirs, she had kept from the times she honoured the Vogue and Gala covers' magazine.

'Tonight, we celebrate! You should have made an effort, especially if you are looking for a man.'

—And who tells you, that I haven't met him, she wished to say? 'Some of us have to work!' her lips defended.

'Darling, I know that, let's go to the kitchen.'

They traversed a long and spacious corridor, separating the main lounge reception to the kitchen. Agnes had prepared everything. A bottle of Dom Pérignon selected for the tray of *fruits de mer,* waiting for them.

'That is the reason, I love being your guest!' Issata announced, devouring the feast with her eyes. Oysters, langoustines and smoked salmon, were deliciously dressed with lemon and parsley, ready to confront their destiny.

'Make yourself comfortable.' Agnes said, and busied herself with opening the bottle. The pop sound was heard. She poured the golden liquid in two flutes. The sparkling sound resonated in the kitchen. Issata settled on one of the wooden high chairs.

'Cheers,' Agnes offered the drink to her friend.

'Cheers,' Issata echoed. They brought drink to their lips.

'Champagne is the only real drink,' she savoured.

'There is plenty,' answered Agnes.

'And how are the boys?'

'Good, in Milan with their father.'

'Lucky them!'

'Yes, I am lucky!'

—I was talking about your children and Abdul, Issata observed in her mind.

'We had a good time on New Year's Eve!' Agnes pursued. I had not drunk that much for a long time! I love having everyone around me. It reminds me of my times on the podium,' she threw and lit up a fag. Pulling a long drag, her eyes shone, shedding light on the souvenirs of her youth.

'I am guessing that your role as a mum must have affected the rhythm of your life? I do admire couples who have children today, even though I don't want any. It is a huge responsibility!' Issata recognised, lighting a Marlboro too.

'That's right, and I can't complain! Abdul and my sons represent everything to me!' her diva's voice declared. 'Actually, it is high time that you meet somebody, too. Surely, there must be a cute Business man in the lounge, for you!' —That is so you Agnes, she thought! And the worse thing to throw at a woman! It is already difficult

70

enough to admit to oneself, but on top of this, having to hear a friend reminding me that I am still single? Tears rose to her eyes. —How can you be so insensible to others, she wished to scream? Me too, I wish to meet somebody! Me too I would love to have a big house and feel the presence of a man, who encourages me, reassures me, and inspires me. In that moment, Dan's smile came to rescue her. Flashing in her mind, his perfect smile was giving her the hope that it was possible for a masculine soul to find interest in her.

—Because you think that you are irreplaceable? Perhaps Abdul is fucking around! After all, he is surrounded by pussies all the time! She took a deep inspiration and it came out: 'Maybe there is someone!' She swallowed in one go the remaining of her champagne, presenting her flute for a second refill.

Her heart pounded hard because for once, it was her story, her romance.

'Little dark horse, spit it out!'

'Drink first!'

Agnes executed the order, without forgetting hers.

'Champagne madame.' They gulped their Dom Pérignon.

'What is his name?'

'Daniel Smith and he is a lawyer'

'Lawyer, that is good, and?'

'He is handsome and sexy and he speaks French. This morning, he asked me to escort him on the platform and told me to call him Dan!' She ended her résumé, panting. She hadn't shared much, but just talking about him, made her happy.

'Smashing! He must take you out!'

'He suggested it, we'll see!'

'Honey, we have to celebrate this! Oh, and let's eat those little creatures before they all melt! They have been looking elegantly chic for us!' laughed Agnes, admiring her seafood tray.

'Agnes only you can come up with such metaphors!'

'I know, I am so funny!' They both giggled.

'Thank you so much, I needed to talk about it.' Issata commented. 'If only you knew, how much I want to believe!' She grabbed a langoustine and broke it with her hands to access the flesh.

'And what does your mate Jimmy think? He is a man and gay men know these things!' Agnes has only met Jimmy once, at Issata's birthday. He was so not impressed by her mundane's attitude and questioned his friend how she had befriended someone like her. 'I don't know,' she had replied.

'Of course, he is excited for me!' she attempted to make herself heard. The flesh from the fish was still swimming in her mouth. 'It is delicious!' she managed to say clearly.

'I ordered them at Scott's Fisherman!'

'They are good I get mine there too!' she swallowed more champagne and demanded: 'But tell me honestly what do you think about Dan?' Issata was dying to share the slightest details about her moments with that man.

'Darling, don't worry, you will find the right man! Look at me, I met my prince!' she threw and snatched an oyster. She slurped it like a cat would drink his milk. 'When I met him, it was love at first sight and we travelled the world together...' —Please, for once let's talk about me, she bled inside. She knew the in and out of Agnes stories, to the part where she felt obliged to listen about the first time, she had sex with Abdul. Too late, Agnes enumerated the same stories, that her friend had listened for millions of times in their many years of friendship. She had no other choices, except for listening to this woman. She read contempt in her eyes, which reminded her, she was alone. And that her Agnes, lived with her husband and their sons, in their luxurious castle. Fortunately, the champagne lifted her spirit. Getting up the next day was hard and so followed the rest of the week. Her only motivation was named *Monday*.

'I have a surprise for you,' said Michael, excitement in his eyes, when he saw her approaching the reception.
'Tell me!' she hugged him.
'It is his birthday on 16th February.'
'Who?'
'Your Mr. Smith!'
'Are you serious? That is in a few weeks?'
'I had a look at his profile in the database, he is born 16th February 1962'
'You are a star!'
'You could offer him a card on behalf of the lounge team?'
'Great idea!'
'But do be careful, you lost a lot of weight' he surveyed her, worried.
'Really? I can't see it!'
'You brought so much to the team. It will be sad if something was to happen to you.'
'Thank you, Michael.' She slid away, her heart beaming with joy.
'Good morning' 'How was your weekend and all forms of politeness were expressed here and there, like every week, as soon as she reached her floor.

At 9:45, she took her position and waited patiently for her colleague's call.

'Hello,' she picked up at the first ring.

'He won't be travelling today, his secretary just called.'

'What? Tears filled her eyes.

'She said to tell you that Mr. Smith had an urgency and that he was impatient to see you.'

'No way!'

'I guess it gives you time to find the perfect card.

'What about next week?'

'No mention of his next visit!'

'Michael, I don't know what to think. Surely the fact that he advised his secretary to contact the lounge, that is a sign, isn't it?

'You will need to discover this for yourself.'

How did she manage to finish her shift? She had only enough strength to take off her smelly shoes when she got to her flat and collapsed on her bed. When she opened her eyes, she could not define how long she had slept. However, the grey light coming through her windows, denounced that she must have been gone for a long time. Effectively she read six o'clock on her iPhone's screen and discovered that she was still wearing her uniform. Shaken by panic, she managed to rise but the fatigue was taking over. —What's wrong with me? She lit up the lamp on her bedside table, and undressed. She stood naked like an earthworm, in front of her mirror. While confronting her silhouette, her mind acknowledged: —It's true, I have lost weight! Her legs so nicely designed since her adolescence, evoked those dried branches on the verge of breaking. Her arms looked like flowers stalks, ready to fade away. And her breasts, only her tits comparable to bud roses, maintained them visible. She sighed and headed to the bathroom to pass her water. Her eyes watched the shower cubicle. —It will have to wait tomorrow, she murmured and that same state of mind sent her back to bed. She only wanted to sleep.

The same scenario was performed throughout the week. She would wake up in tears, eaten away by pain. Curled up in her bed, she didn't dare move. Alone, in the middle of her mattress, she resembled a foetus. No one by her side to protect her. One movement was sending flames of distress to her nervous system. Never did she experience such physical agony. It burnt! It stung as if she was bombarded by enflamed needles. Her suffering began from her pelvis and moved alongside her legs. The fire went back and forth in the flesh. She began to cough nastily and suffered a heavy headache. She felt that her skull was going to split. But she had to go to work. Every day she would step into the lounge, charged with a cocktail of painkillers swimming in her blood. Pills that didn't work. Everyone was worried, her colleagues as well as travellers. —I am tired, she defended.

Arrived Saturday. Knocked down by burning pain, she opened her eyes. Weakened by fatigue, those same eyes wandered around her room, looking like two feeble lights, abandoned in this troubled world where she was losing herself. —I am so shattered, resonated in her mind! And she was still in bed. Plus, she was meeting Jimmy later.

—I could cancel, he would understand? She moaned shaken by agony. Her woman's body demanded a miraculous potion to relieve her from the dolour. 'Are we still meeting today?' A text which helped her decide.

—I need to see him. It will do me good.

'Darling are you ok?' He caged her shoulders with his hands, staring at her. As soon as he saw her, entering *l'Auberge* a French restaurant, located at Waterloo station, he noticed straight away that something was not right. After their brief exchange, she deserted her bed, found refuge in the bathroom, and took root under the shower, for some time that she can't recall. She just knew she had to rush. She had a pair of blue jeans on, her prune mini boots, a black woollen jacket from Zara, and a black bonnet with a pompon covering her head. She purposely didn't apply some makeup on her face. She was just not inspired.
'My Jimmy, I am very exhausted lately.' She fell in his arms.
He held her against his chest and placed two kisses on her cheeks.
'But you have lost an enormous amount of weight.' he insisted, moving away from her.
'A lot of people have mentioned. I will seek medical advice.'
'Right, do it quickly, and let's spend a good time!'
They sat and Jimmy waved at a waiter, a young man with curled dark hair and tanned skin.
'So, he didn't travel?'
'No, and it feels so strange! Almost as if I had received a shock emotional for not seeing him.'

'Well, considering that he is a businessman, he must be very busy.'

'I know, but he transmitted a message for me.'

'Issata, your priority is to take care of yourself. Because with those crazy shifts you are on, I wouldn't be surprised that you have caught some kind of nasty virus!'

The boy returned with a bottle of champagne, a tray covered with charcuteries, cornichons, and peanuts.

'My Jimmy,' she let out.

'That should cheer you up!'

Jimmy not being indifferent to that young waiter, observed him opening the bottle and filling their glasses.

'I will come back later to take your order.'

'Perfect!' he smiled. 'Santé darling,' he raised his flute.

'I saw how you looked at him.'

'I wouldn't mind, but we are here for you.' They gulped their drink.

'Now tell me, do you see Pascal?' Pascal was her manager and the coordinator for all VoyE lounges.

'To be honest, I must have seen him three times since I began that new role. VoyE proposed that idea and I made it happen.

'That means, there is no job description for that role?'

'It looks like it! I was so excited to do something new. Anyway, next week, I am on holiday. A good week off will recharge my batteries.

'Me too, Monday I leave for Brussels for ten days. But promise me you will use the time to rest, and contact Pascal. It is not normal for you to have lost so much weight. Look at your eyes! That is not you!'

'For the eyes, I couldn't be bothered to make up today!' she threw, a rictus in the corner of her lips.

'Issata, I feel there is something going on with you.' His compassionate gaze surveyed her.

'I am going to follow your advice. Now tell me about Andrew?' The tenderness on his face turned into guilt.

'Oh my, that is finished since last year! We went to the *Rodizio Rico,* the Brazilian restaurant in Angel... He was just boring!

'You didn't paint Van Gogh?'

'Yes, we painted a bit. A bit, a lot and that's all we share in common. Painting is the story of my life!'

'I wish to paint too!' she sighed.

'Soon darling.'

'If you say. So, finished, finished?'

'He is a good fuck but far too young for me.'

'Too young or you are too old?'

'Did you decide?' the waiter intervened.

'Steak Frites?' Jimmy suggested.

'Sounds good.'

'And a bottle of Côtes du Rhône' he added.

Throughout their meal, Jimmy didn't feel his friend. Even after swallowing two bottles of wine.

She didn't see Sunday passing. She remained in bed all day. She dragged herself to work on Monday. He didn't travel and no message was sent. Within days, her health deteriorated, with the same intensity she wished to see this man. Her figure shank at a rapid speed, consuming her breathing and forcing her lungs to work harder.

At night, she began to swim in her sweat and would wake up completely drenched in the middle of the night as if someone had poured water all over her.

During the daytime, she resembled a wilted flower doomed to die. She experienced white lights, flashing in front of her very eyes. It aggravated her ability to see. She lost her appetite. Irritability became her second name. In the lounge, everyone noticed her radical change. She would confine into deep silence and be found sleeping in the private area, an indigo colour, emanating from her face. When walking in the street, strange anxiety would arise inside her. It was translated as her conviction that someone was following her. She perceived an entity. That thing was fraying its way through her brain and haunted her like a demonic ombre. It flickered continuously watching out for the moment to strike. Even, her Buddhist practice where she drew her strength and hope, had turned into a heavy and painful austerity.

—What is wrong with me, she dared ask? But only tears and confusion answered her alarming cry. They formed her new reality. She was losing it.

It was as if being alive was killing her.

—I am finally on holiday, she sighed, Friday at half-past two, when she entered her home. She kicked her shoes off and guided her ass on her bed. She unzipped her coat nonchalantly. She stretched her thighs and turned her ankles to relax her contracted burning muscles. Her eyes caught the mirror. They met the sadness of a black woman, whose brown eyes had lost their spark, its exoticism, that scintilla which illuminated the life of many people. She approached the reflection and pressed her fingers on her eyes. She massaged her eyelids quickly. She opened them slowly, and the woman still appeared deeply lost. Her image revealed a profound suffering.

—Who are you? Tears escaped from her eyes, like those tiny bubbles of water, on a summery morning, which greets the flowers from their profound sleep. They crawled on her cheeks and ended their journey in the collar of her uniform. The woman cried too but didn't reply. —Speak to me, she insisted, shaken by waves of anxiety. Her sobs flooded her tired eyes. The woman still didn't respond but mimicked her gestures. Her heart pounded. She trembled and her anger was spurred to wake up. A deep desire to scream seized her brain. Her neurons only searched to respond to the murderous call, emerging from her heart. So, she held her index in a threatening manner: —I am warning you! I am not afraid of you! Tell me what do you want? She compressed her fingers into a fist and maintained them so tightly closed so that the articulations of her phalanges looked like tiny daggers. She foresaw the strength of her hand hitting the mirror, and anticipated blood splashing on her face. Petrified, she blinked. There was no blood and her hand remained safe. In her stupor, she realised, she was addressing herself. —No, that is not me! she wailed. A desperate sound escaped from her dried throat. She rushed to her bed and hid her face in her pillow. —Why, she cried, churning with dolour. She was lying flat, banging her legs on the mattress, desperate to choke her agony. Her tears circulated on her face, like a glacial torrent, responding to the cadence of her physical and emotional sufferings.

—I want the pain to end, she begged through her tears.

It didn't stop. It followed its own path, which is to hurt. The pain turned into an army of leeches. Glued on the bank of the victim's skin, the army furrowed its way through Issata's flesh, stabbing her with the same intensity of heated blades. Behind each attack, it left a clear sign of the invasion. Issata felt like balls of fire were exploding beneath her pores. The flames spread rapidly and proliferated at the speed looking-like larvae, preparing its hatchings. An invisible force was determined to seize her body. A murderer who had decided, to keep her body under its power. She felt defenceless. Exhausted, she smelt her own odour, mixed with the scent of the lounge and the effluvia of a tired young woman. Sick to vomit she recognised that she was still wearing her uniform.

She found herself, her arse flattened against the ground of the shower. The water fell down on her violently. It slapped her face, punched her, tortured her. Confuse and weak, she held her knees with both arms. She resembled a young girl, seeking a hug.

How long did she remain in the shower? She only remembered drying her skin and sliding into her bathroom robe. When she returned to her main room, her eyes encountered the fruits and the greenery on her butsudan. They were dying in their mouldiness. She couldn't care less. Her back against her headboard's bed, she lit up a fag and contemplated the smoke evaporating silently in the room. She was attending the mise en scene of a vertiginous malaise. A melodramatic storm was visiting her brain. The villain sequestrated her thoughts, her words, her willingness to act and to live. She was under the threat of emotional blackmail, weakening her body and reducing all mental coordination. Any hostage, in the truest sense of the term, would entertain an indisputable panic. They would hope that someone would rescue them. Issata didn't want to fight. She found herself obliged to verse a ransom. She chose to settle the price with her emotions. A crime was about to be committed. She was casting for two roles at the same time, the hostage and the witness. She pulled on her fag, and analysed the circles of nicotine, stumping around her. Captured by the scenery, she starred in the emptiness and watched the movie of her life, being reduced to smoke. She was gnawed with sudden fatigue. Was it real or was she plunging into a dream which would stop existing when her eyes would open? Then nothing. From what she had reported to me, she was sleeping and dreamt of fume, deeply encrusted in her everyday life. It followed her. The smoke had a smell, a traumatic scent calling her subconscious. The smell began to irritate her senses. The touch on her skin prompted her to sneeze. She coughed heavily, losing her breath. Then, she opened her eyes. The smell persisted. Confused, she trembled and turned her head around. She noticed the smoke dancing next to her. Her Marlboro was burning her duvet. —Oh my, she yelled! The dream? —No, it was not a dream!

Her eyes looking like a peeled tomato, she visited her surgery the next day. The whole in her duvet blanket in which, she could have disappeared, was the wake-up call! She explained all her symptoms to the doctor available. Suspecting an infection, he prescribed her a course of antibiotics for a week as well as codeine to ease her dolour. —You should also have your eyes checked, he advised her. —An infection, she whispered, once outside. —It could make sense because I am so exhausted. She rushed to her chemist to collect her medicine and went home. —Can twenty-one pills, three times a day, during seven days could turn everything around, she wondered? She swallowed her pills and lay in bed. The codeine revealed its soothing power within minutes. Her muscles were more relaxed. Her thoughts deserted her mind. Issata plunged into a serene grogginess and fell asleep like a baby. It took a succession of vibrations for her to decide to open her eyes. She checked her iPhone. —Three o'clock, she managed to read and to see the missed calls, coming from her mother. —I don't have time for you mother! she expressed irritated. —When I think that I was sleeping so peacefully! Mum had left a message. She didn't listen to it. She straightened herself on her bed, and felt weak. She realised; she hadn't eaten since she had left work. —Come on then! she left her bed, to inspect her cupboards. They were empty or rather congest with crackers, those new rusks which most women crave: —The *Ryvitas*. —Right, she whistled and opened the fridge. Nothing exciting either, yes, some bubbles as always. —On an empty stomach? —I did swallow a cocktail of medicines earlier! — After all, why not was her conclusion? —And surely, there must be something to eat with those crackers? She moved about, a few Tupperware half full from leftovers, and spotted some brie cheese and mushrooms pâté still in their packaging but out of date. —Expired, since last week, that will do. And organised a tray that she carried with her to the bed. A burning sensation manifesting again inside her legs, she bit into her toast, and swallowed two pills of codeine with a glass of sparkling wine. —it is so good, she smiled. —And those little sandwiches, not bad at all, after all! —What is all the fuss about those expirations' dates? The sparkling tonality of her voice surprised her. Laughter, a word which inspires cheerfulness, rhymes with good health, the memorandum of freedom, this sound which had deserted her weeks ago, was finally paying her back a visit. She exploded into laughter, trembling from wonderment, under the euphoric effect, her happy voice was producing to her being. She gulped another glass of bubble; her senses being guided by the contentment she was experiencing.

—The doctor must be right; it is only an infection! She devoured her biscottis and indulged herself with her alcoholic beverage. A determined force surged within her. One could question how? And Issata just wanted to believe. That desire spurred in her, the need to listen to music. She lit up a fag, grabbed the remote control of her stereo system Sony, pressed the 'play' touch, and there, 'Air in G string,' escaped from her speakers. The moment, she heard the first notes, tears rolled in her eyes. Her body turned into a cord instrument. She represented the violin, changing into a viola, then a cello, contrabass, without forgetting the Kora. It didn't matter which instrument she chose. The chord sonority fascinated her. They allied into lianas and lifted her through their musical strength, guiding her to believe in her dream. Nicotine invaded her lungs.

The sound resonated around her. All her organs vibrated, under the repetitive and romantic caresses of the strings. Issata encouraged her tears to dance freely on her cheeks. There were no words to convey what was brewing inside her heart. Bach owned the indescribable magic, in implanting that ounce of hope, in people's heart. It was beautiful, soft, rich, special. It was Bach.

Now, it is time I tell you how she has fallen in love with Bach. She was thirteen. She discovered him at college thanks to Mr. Lawrence, her music teacher, a fervent admirer of Bach. He commenced all his lessons with that masterpiece and explained to those teenagers, dressed in hoodie jumpers and wearing Doc Martens, what elevated him to the stature of a genius.

—Bach's motto was: —To practice! That was how Mr. Lawrence started his classes. —His talent today derived from the fastidious labor, he operated throughout the progression of his life. —Bach incarnated the explorer of musicology. He had found the musical code and brought a new dimension to the sonorous world. —The Master of compositions, this is Bach, the eternal Master. —You are young, and I am asking you to compose the harmony of your own life. Find the rhythm of your own melody! Add as many counterpoints needed and write your story! We all have our own talent! Find yours, he used to say, with the hope that one day, one of them would become the next virtuoso. It was also thanks to his passionate spirit in instilling in their heart, that thirst to learn, that she was able to acquaint herself with the reason behind the choice of the title 'Air in G string'.

Originally, it was called Orchestra Suite n°3. So why this change? Most of Bach suites, consisted mainly of dances: 'La courante' the French Suite, the tempo rhymes with liveliness, 'La suite Allemande' denounces a moderate tempo, 'La sarabande' a Spanish Suite, is more of a slow tempo. Those styles belonged to the baroque era. Having said that, in the heart of suite n° 3, emerged an air, a ballad which grabs and penetrates us, as I have tried to describe, through Issata's moods.

Back to the suite, round about one hundred and fifty years following the death of Bach, someone named August Wilhelmj, German violinist, infamous for his rendering intellectual and artistic elegance, had fallen under the spell of that air. He invented a new way to play this piece by transposing the melody on a lower octave, which inspired him the idea to transfer the violins solo on the 'G' string as the main key note. That was for the little historia!

Issata is a bit of a naughty girl, isn't she? As years passed, away from M. Lawrence's class, still captivated by this soft and majestic ballad, having experienced it on numerous occasions, one day her mind placed the light on the greatest mystery of mankind.

—Eureka, she exclaimed, everything is linked to the 'G' point! —Newton with his magnificent discovery on the gravity point, then Bach and Wilhelmj on Air on the G string! Obviously, she made sure to notice the difference between cultures. Newton being English, could only demonstrate that reservedness, which suits so well an Englishman. He observed the genius idea to put the accent on the gravity. That might explain why Great Britain is floating in the middle of the Channel River. The country's duty was to protect its G point. Whereas the German, they literally danced on the string. But in French the word gives

nature to that piece of garment separating the derrière,
from left to right. How gracious! Came her conclusion:

—Guys it would have been much easier to ask a
woman! I have deducted that Issata's musical skills were
limited to the G point.
—Oh, where was I in the story? That's right, I remember
now…. The romantic melody wandered around our dear
lady, leading her to contemplate her own heart. —Bach
gave birth to this reverential air, the air of the baroque age,
*the air of the French overture. —*Mr. Lawrence was right; I
must find my key! I must get myself together, it is only a
bit of fatigue, she tried to convince herself.
—Tomorrow, I will have my eyes checked.

And her conscious mind met the decomposed offerings,
dying on her butsudan. —Not very catholic, she sighed!
Her fag out, she presented herself in front of her butsudan.
—Only the Buddha would know how long I had left you to
rot. She removed all debris and engaged her heart and soul
in polishing her sanctuary. She dusted the doors of her
sacred box, cleaned the wax residues from her vintage
candle holders, and restored order in her Buddhist library.

In her endeavour, she felt a reassuring lightness,
infiltrating her being. —*Everything's Gonna Be All Right,*
she decided. It was her sincere devotion to preserve the
purity of her faith, which motivated her, to consciously
take responsibility in polishing her own life. She cleaned
her studio as well. Reconnecting with the brightness of her
familiar surroundings, she knelt to perform her prayers,
something she hadn't observed for a while and sincerely
prayed to appreciate what she possessed. —I have a roof
over my head, a job that I loved, I think, my Jimmy,
money. I doing not bad! As she pronounced the last Nam-
myoho-renge-kyo, her iPhone vibrated. At the sight of the

interlocutor, she hesitated to pick up. —I can't hope to polish one aspect of my life while keeping another part tarnished.

'Hello' she answered, faking her enthusiasm.

'Issata, it's mum,'

'I know, it's you. How are you?'

'I left you three messages.'

'I have heard them!' No, she was lying.

'You could have called me,' Mum complained.

—Here, she starts again! 'I was going to call you, I have just finished my prayers, she cut in.

'Send me some texts messages sometimes,' she pursued, without taking notice of her daughter's comments.

'Yes, you are right, and how are you really?' Issata added, knowing too well that engaging in an argument with her mother, wouldn't serve any purpose.

'I only wanted to hear your voice.' The sound, coming from Mum's words warbled like the voice of an abandoned child, in a foreign country. A world, where she had to learn the language and the culture. Her daughter listened to that long and heavy moan, that Mum seemed to constantly entertain in her silent mood, as well as when she spoke. It was as if she was looking to be heard, to be seen under this role, which the word mother had upholstered her existence, as a woman. —Mum, I only asked you a simple question, *'How are you?'* her brain was ready to let out. She heard herself panting in her handset and felt rising in her heart a familiar irritation, similar to what she had experienced, when she saw the sad the woman in the mirror. That sensation, she had just heard it, the noise of a truth not being said. Perturbed by her analysis, she forced herself to explain:

'You know I have a new role, and my early starts are not easy.'

'Me too, the doctor said that I have to avoid certain food because my blood pressure keeps going up.'

'Did you hear what I have said?'

'Yes, yes, well be careful,' threw her mother then paused, looking for something to say. 'I am tired too; I am waiting for my retirement.'

'And Antoine, how is he doing?'

'He is fine, he will never find someone like me!' Issata had listen to Mum's comments many times, her heart swelling with exasperation. When her parents lived together, her mother's deepest desire rested on buying a property.

It didn't happen. With Antoine, she was actually sharing a five-bedroom house, equipped with two bathrooms and an immense garden. Despite this comfort, the grandeur of the house had put light on a pit, dug long ago in the driveways of her life. And as time was going by, she could witness her mother sinking in her own gulf.

'Ok, as long as everything is fine, that is the most important,' she hurried to say. She just wanted to end that insane conversation with her mother.

'One day, you will understand, when you live with someone, you have to adapt.'

'Of course, mum now I have to go.'

'Send me some texts sometimes, ok?' Mum continued to beg for pity.

'Yes Mum, I said, I will!'

'Oh, goodbye then, my darling.'

'Bye mum.' She grabbed her notebook kept by her altar and went to sit on her bed. —I MUST SPEAK TO MUM, she wrote, in capital letters, reading loud what she had just scribbled. How? I don't know. Writing represented her true passion in life. During her childhood, the word reserved defined the only adjective, she could associate herself with. And the sole mean she detained, in observing that reservation was to confront it on paper where she would express how she felt. In her garden secret, she planted all her worries, all her fears and all her dreams freely. A lot of those seeds had ripened, and had turned into beautiful plants, which gave birth to the fruits of the tree of her life. So far Issata had harvested thirty and seven years. But some, like *Love* still remained in the dormancy phase, awaiting patiently for the right condition to unfold so that the germination may begin. It became an adventure, where she had to break down all barriers in her heart. Through her own vocabulary, she portrayed, how she viewed the world. She saw that activity as a trip in finding herself. Writing was her rendezvous with her true self. Flicking through the pages, she whispered: —One day, my prince will come…

The optician noticed some serious inflammatory lesions in the corner of her pupils and confirmed an infection. He sent her to Moorfields's hospital. She was submerged with deep worry on the way to the clinic.
—Maybe, I will become blind, tears pearled in her eyes. When she got there, she was assisted by Dr Kyle. He effectuated test after test, and observed the damage on some nerves due to the inflammation. The verdict resulted in Issata suffering from Sarcoidosis.
'But what is it?' she questioned panicked.
Sarcoidosis is an illness specific to the immune system. It takes place during a change in the lymphatic system. The cause is unknown, but Dr Kyle tried to explain.
—That change is observed when an antigen, a foreign substance, invades the human body. That imposter

provoked a reaction. The immune system will anticipate an immune reaction, orchestrated by the lymphocytes B and T, special agents, whose mission is to detect viruses. That immune reaction is specifically directed at those intruders. In our scenario, the cells recognised an abnormality. Even though they proceed accordingly, the process leads to granulomas identified as reddish parches on the skin, which played a dominant role in the inflammation of the body. The others symptoms tailored made by the illness can be examined through a large amount of weight loss, nocturnal sweats, joint pain, without forgetting the deep fatigue, exactly what Issata had experimented.

—No wonder, I was constantly tired, she thought.

'Can I be cured?' she cried.

'There is so much mystery behind this condition. And as doctors, we don't have all answers.'

'What can I do then?' she cried.

'I am going to prescribe you some prednisolone.'

'No, I don't want to take steroids, it makes your face puff!'

'It can help you fight the inflammation. And I will send your medical tests to your surgery, for them to look at your lungs.' 'I don't know what to say' she sobbed.

'You will be fine; I will see you every week at least for a month to control your ACE level (Angiotensin-converting enzyme). He handed over her prescription. She went to collect her medicine from the hospital pharmacy.

—Sarcoidosis is an unknown malady without cure and of course, I had to catch it up, she told herself back home, in front of her Gohonzon. —Why? Her tears rained on her face, pumping out like a storm. She heard them splashing on her lino. They sounded like drops of rain falling down a roof, violently She spent the rest of the week in her place and started her 100 g of prednisolone with omeprazole as advised by Dr. Kyle. She informed Jimmy. He was worried and relieved that they had found something.

'Hello Michael,' Issata greeted him when she reached the reception.
'Hello my darling, he hugged her. 'Nice holidays?' he asked.
'I must admit, I needed it.' She wondered if she should tell him about her illness.
'Glad to hear this, but your eyes are very strange.'
'To you, I can say,' she sighed.
'What?'
She explained the symptoms and the diagnosis.
'I am not surprised! Look at your work conditions!'
'Do you think work could have contributed to this?'
'Of course! Five days a week at half-past five, is completely inhuman! I truly hope your treatment works, and remember, I am here for you!'
'Thank you and please keep it to yourself!'
'Not a word!'
'Do you think, he will travel today?'
'Who knows, in any case, I call you' he empathised.
'Michael, do I really look strange?'
'You are beautiful just as you are, but look after yourself!'
He hugged her one more time and let her go.

As soon as she stepped onto her floor, she was welcomed by: 'Nice seeing you Issata,' 'Did you have a good rest?' 'You looked refreshed' 'Take it easy.' 'Thank you,' she could only answer. And in her mind, she proclaimed to herself: —I have sarcoidosis, an incurable illness.
That confirmation changed the light on the surrounding.

The Issata, they knew was disappearing in this imaginary palace, she had painted through her dreams. While it continued to shine in its splendour, the mistress of the house was fading away slowly.

At quarter to ten, instinctively she walked to the stairs and took the position. She listened to her heartbeat softly, like a woman in love. She was anticipating his sublime and enthralling odour. His perfume was already tickling her nostrils and stimulating her senses. She just wanted to believe. She could hear the innate sound of his steps; she had composed in her head before receiving Michael's call. Then her iPhone would ring once. She would answer: 'Yes' and he would say: 'He is here!' She would sense, his naughty smile, in his voice. Issata waited alone for some time. His perfume was fading away. Then the magic behind his steps disappeared too, crushing her heart. Michael didn't call her but observed her from the bottom of the stairs. He moved his lips and she read: 'Don't worry! You will be fine!' 'No!' her eyes replied. —Dan is a player!' she concluded moving away from her stage.

High on steroids, Issata reached the end of her week, less tired. She observed milder pain throughout her body. To her surprise, she was feeling better, and put on a bit of weight. However, her eyesight worried Dr Kyle. He increased her dose of cortisone and sent her for a lung MRI. What are her eyes got to do with her lungs? He wanted to establish how severely attacked her body was by the illness.

So, sarcoidosis? What is the story? Here is what she discovered! Dr. Jonathan Hutchison, an English surgeon, dermatologist, ophthalmologist, pathologist, venereologist shared the news in 1876. It was presented as a dermatologic reaction, turning the skin into a purple bloody shade. This reaction activates a cutaneous eruption over the face and the body. —98 years later, then I was born, she reflected. In 1888, the term itself was invented by Dr Lupus pernio Ernest Besnier, a dermatologist whose structural histology was recognised in 1902. Then this rare illness manifested in the eyes, bones, lungs and was identified as a systemic illness by Dr Schaumann. To understand its etymology, the word sarcoidosis, as most words of our encyclopaedia, comes from Greek. *Sarco* signifies: 'flesh', -*(e) ido,* means, « resemble or similar to » and *sis* « condition ». Simply said, sarcoidosis would imply 'A *condition which resembles to raw flesh or alive'*. It is also known as the (BBS) disease named after three hard-working doctors, Besnier - Boeck - Schaumann.

—Fascinating, she declared overwhelmed. —I am suffering from a condition resembling to raw flesh. There is an antigen attacking my cells and my immune system is fighting hard to defend my body. —Even specified as an orphan disease, rare, non-contagious, and whose genetic configuration represented a great risk to the human organism. —Fine, you burn everything! I am taking note! —Present yourself to me and I will challenge you! She was amazed at her discovery.

—Maybe I should observe my diet carefully, one day her consciousness, summoned her. Because it is denounced that '*You are what you eat.'* She searched and read: —To avoid red meat! Impossible as she liked her steak! It was preferable to eat whole wheat food such as pasta and bread. —I won't mind, she claimed. When she got to the part most doctors recommend, she was not happy. —To avoid caffeine, tobacco, and alcohol, —No way, she riposted loudly! —I am French, I need my caffeine! Nicotine has been part of my life for the last fifteen years and it can't live without coffee and sex. Well, tell me about it, I don't know when this will happen, she giggled!

One Monday morning, after her so well-performed show, she rested in the private corner. Engrossed in her task, she didn't give much attention to the time. But her nostrils absorbed a familiar odour. Her heart beat fast. She lifted her head and saw the lift opening. There he was, coming out, looking in her direction. 'Dan,' she murmured and stood up. He honoured a navy-blue royal suit, as electrifying as his piercing look. A red tie neatly attached around his white shirt was blending perfectly with the colour of his hair. His cream coat dropping over his left arm, he walked slowly towards her, the dangerous smile, he never parted from, dressing his face. She remained stoic; her hand glued to her chest. She squeezed her throat out of fear of falling down.

'Issata, good morning,' his suave voice expressed.

She fixed him, panting, not believing he was standing in front of her. But the liquor sliding from her vagina's lips reminded her, it was real.

'Good morning,' she muttered.

'I missed you and Happy Saint Valentin.' He pulled out a red rose from his bag and presented it to her.

'Dan!' she exclaimed.

'You remember?'

'Thank you.' Admiring her gift, she looked as mesmerised, as a little girl, in touch with joy for the first time, in her existence.

'Please forgive me, for my long absence.' He smiled and grabbed her left hand on which he placed a soft kiss. Paralysed, she didn't move. Her hairs rose all over her body, especially those in contact with her panties. Still holding her hand, he declared confidently:

'I would have invited you for a glass of champagne, on that day dedicated to love, but I have a lot of things to deal with. Can I join you?'

'Of course,' she sat and kept her arms crossed in front of her belly. To her surprise, he settled by her side. He turned towards her and wrapped his right leg over the left one. His right elbow was against the back of the chair, he used one of his fists, to hold his head.

'That is better!' she heard him say.

'Well, seen like that,' she chortled and said: 'So where were you then?'

'I was in Berlin and New York, to deal with my family inheritance. Did you get my message?'

'Yes, thank you. All sorted?'

'No, that is why I will be absent for three weeks. A few days in Paris and will travel back to New York for my fiftieth birthday.'

'Oh yes, 16th February!' she let out, feeling guilty.

—I should have bought the card!

'You knew it?'

'Let's just say that we have access to your profile!'

'I see,' he smiled. 'Do you know Paris?' he checked.

'Like a tourist.'

'I have never visited Notre Dame, you know.'

'Is that so?'

96

'Because like you, she is very impressive!'

'Dan,' she giggled.

'And I envy all those men who penetrated her territory.' He leaned towards her, animated by that savage desire, she had always known of him. He stared at her. His gaze smiled at her, talked to her, caressed her. She was under his spell and felt his erotic charm conversed with the secret parcels of her womanhood. She shivered. They were alone in the perfect scenery, *le salon*. Her heart trembled. Intense sensations travelled through her body.

M. Smith maintained his eyes contact. She could feel his hands, his mouth, stimulating her pleasure. Her lips slightly opened; her pussy enflamed, she controlled her breathing and tightened her thighs. She watched his hand moving towards her knees. —He is not going to? her eyes questioned. The boarding was announced. Staring at him, her heart jumped. 'Shall I come with you? came out of her mouth.

'No, Issata, it won't be necessary.'

He stood up and gathered his stuff. 'I will take you out when I return.' He pierced her with his gaze and walked off.

Thank you for the rose,' she mumbled.

—How interesting that a few weeks ago, I have been diagnosed with a mysterious malady and now that I feel better, he reappears! —I must be ready for his return, motivated her determination to bounce back, every day!

She looked deeply into ways to heal and included food supplements in her diet, starting with Lactobacillus acidophilus. What is it? Acidophilus is a friendly bacterium deriving from *lactobacillaceae* family, often found isolated in the mouth, the human and animal digestive tract as well as the woman's vaginal flora. It is equally observed in the milk, during the mixture of wholemeal flour and water used to make bread...And, and, and, listen to this: —The red wine! No need to tell you that our friend Issata, as we are learning about her, didn't fail to implement that healthy bacterium in her daily diet! She added a cocktail of multivitamins, containing antioxidants A, C, E, as well as Omega 3 Fatty acid, hence the importance of fish. What did she learn? The Fish contains the highest level of vitamin D in comparison to other types of food. The Fish makes people happy. Because according to tests, Fatty acid omega 3, found in fish, enables to limit the effects of depression. The Fish is good for the heart! It helps reduce heart attacks. It is beneficial to our eyesight, thanks to the vitamin A, found in this aquatic animal. All this to say, eating fish is good! —But I eat Japanese food every week! Maybe not enough, she observed! Blueberries, figs, prunes followed her every day in a Tupperware box. And essentially, she reintroduced sport, or to say long walks.

Dressed in jeans, a red sweater, her brown perfecto and white converses, she marched to Regent's Park. A soft air was floating around her, announcing the arrival of spring. She could guess the impatience of welcoming sunny days, inscribed on the face of the few people, she had encountered, all honouring light clothing. She penetrated the park and strolled alongside *Primrose Hill,* the famous pathway where a panoramic view of London could be admired. Watching couples, walking hands in hands, she remarked to herself: —They look happy! The more she engulfed in the park, the more she watched the crowd ambled from everywhere. Children were running and playing in the grass, away from the concrete road. Some moved on bikes, rollers skate, and even skateboards. But Issata followed her lane. She borrowed a walkway only she knew existed. It guided her to the *Queen Mary's Rose Gardens*. She smelt her odour. When she reached the Triton Fountain, an assemblage of sculpture, the mis en scene of a god of the sea, blowing into a shell, surrounded by two mermaids resting at his feet, her heart beat fast. From where she stood, she could see her crane, her foliage red and bushy, resplendent like a wild crown which nature had neatly studied and prepared. Moved to tears, she ran to her, contemplating the immensity of her thirty meters height, firmly rooted in her modest palace.

That's right! Sayon was a tree, an oak tree deriving from *Quercus coccinea* family and called scarlet oak, due to its flamboyant colour during the bloom period. By pure chance, ten years ago, their path met. Issata was a nature lover. She enjoyed losing herself in this mystical world. She was inspired by the force of nature in traversing all seasons. As a good student, she was keen to learn the rhythm of life. And one day, in her melancholic mood, she found her.

She was standing there as if she had been longing for her. That's right, Issata had decided that she would incarnate a woman. The moment she placed her eyes on that vegetal being, her life was enveloped by a majestic grandeur.

It was love at first sight. During that inexplicable coincidence, she recalled the first book she had read when she was seven years old, *My Sweet Orange Tree*. The author José Mauro de Vasconcelos, relates the story of Zézé, aged six, a young Brazilian boy. His family was poor and to escape the weight of his miserable life, he plunges himself into an imaginary world, where he befriends a tree with whom he communicates his secret dreams…And the tree talks to him too. That story remained with Issata ever since and her passion for books came to life thanks to Zézé. Secretly, she wished to possess her own tree too, which would comfort and protect her. That tree she had so long waited for, was finally offering her branches to her, via various nuances of red. In that instant, Issata visualised the image of a mother opening her arms to her child. She still remembered, her hypnotic energy, vibrating through her barks. In the most natural way, she asked: 'Can I touch you?' A soft wind blew through the tree's leaves, enabling the branches to shake. A bond had been created, biding a daughter to her mother. A fusion, nothing could destroy. Moved to tears, she embraced the tree with all her strength. The trunk fitted perfectly her arms' diameter so that she could touch her own fingers. 'I have found you,' she exclaimed proudly! 'And I am going to call you Sayon.' Why this name? It came from Guinea, a name she had discovered in *L'Enfant Noir'* an autobiographical story told by Camara Laye, where he talks about his childhood in Kouroussa, his education in Conakry, and eventually his departure for France. Sayon signifies wisdom. Issata saw the bark of her new friend turning into golden skin, and she took that sign as an expression that her tree had accepted her new name. This is how their story commenced. 'Sayon,' she exclaimed! She hugged her and kept her head against her dried skin, respiring her woody perfume. 'I missed you so much and I am very sorry, not to have come to visit you. How are you?' A ray of light pierced the sky, lighting Issata's face, confirming she was fine. 'I must tell you about Dan!' There and then, she opened her heart. Words leaked from her mouth, following her thought happily, in line with her own desire. Her words echoed to the intensity of her own sentiments. The more excited she felt in sharing every detail, the more foods for her soul emerged from the romantic abyss, she had dug in her heart. Only her, could swim into it. Free she felt, to share her heart with nature! Someone was listening without judging her. Then, she heard a rumbling coming from the tree. She recognised a call, denouncing, she might have forgotten to say something. 'Sarcoidosis? I was going to tell you!' she murmured. And her feeling of excitement turned into anxiety. 'I know, great health is the basis of everything! I did some research. I made some changes in my diet and we will see.'

Three Mondays went by. Dan invited her.

On the morning of that auspicious day, she opened her eyes overworked and tormented by dolour. Those terrible next days since her diagnostic filled the chapters of her health battle. The inflammation possessed all power on her limbs, even more so, her legs. The fire deriving from the malady, infiltrated her muscles, her flesh, and took root through her cartilages. Issata cried and swallowed two codeines. She laid in bed, conserving the white pastilles on her tongue. She anticipated the effect of opium. That's right, codeine had become her elixir of youth. Through opium, she was only searching to ease her physical and emotional pain. The medicine melted in her mouth, but she didn't obtain the desired effect. Irritated, she took two more and slid into a peaceful motion. Her muscles managed to relax. She was able to empty her head and palpate the joy submerging through her. Then, the energy to straighten up rose at last. Checking her phone, she read, half-past eleven, but the date changed it all for her!

—16th March, she let out! —How come I didn't realise?

—It must be a sign! Excited, she jumped out of bed. Pipi, coffee, fag, vitamins, meditation, and... *Laissez-moi danser...* song from Dalida, supported her preparations. She knew what dress to wear. A black dress, she had purchased at Massimo Mutti, but which shoes will take her to the ball? She pulled out from under her bed, a plastic with her shoes collection. Most of them had never left their prison cell which explained the price still tagged on them. She contemplated a series of pairs from different styles and colours, all measuring maximum ten centimetres high, while dancing with Dalida. She opted for L.K. Bennet pumps, in pink and black suede and wooden high heel.

—And what to hide, beneath the little black dress, she analysed, admiring her sexy legs? She headed towards her wardrobe and tugged a rectangular red rattan basket. Taking place on her bed, the box by her side, she untied the cream cotton string, bidding the precious container to its lids. Revealing what it contained, the smell of lavender hit her nostrils. She loved keeping soaps with her underwear. Proud of her collection, she enjoyed the erotic exhibition flattering her senses. They all came from luxurious boutiques. She caressed the display with her eyes and imagined each material covering her tits and her behind. In awe, she noticed a lacy suspenders corset in pink and black silk and took it out. Her feet still sequestered in her L.K. Bennett, she removed her nighty and let her screaming parts feel the sexy fabric. Facing her image in the mirror, she placed her hands on her breasts to weigh the fullness. They didn't contain a lot of meat, but filled her cup perfectly and married her torso admirably. A glorious smile confronted her to which she answered, adjusting her string.

— You'd better be a good fuck Dan, for the price I got the dress! She burst into laughter. A sound caught her attention. 'Ready?' A text from Jimmy. She panicked when she noticed the time.

—Shit, four o'clock already! 'No! Still have the jungle to mow! And paint my nails!'

19h45, Issata entered the Connaught, covered with a cashmere black coat reaching her knees, a pink pashmina protecting her neck. Under her right arm, she carried a black leather clutch. She looked like an African goddess.

'Good evening, Miss,' a tall and skinny man, fifty years old looking, short greyish hair, whose light brown eyes inspired a touching fragility, welcomed her.

'I am meeting Daniel Smith,' she pronounced nervously.

'Issata Sherif?' he checked.

'Yes,' she murmured, surprised.

'I am Jason, Mr. Smith has asked us to look after you. Would you care to follow me?'

They walked through a small corridor and he pulled a red curtain where a lounge bigger than her studio flat was ready for her. In the middle of this boudoir, two flutes made in crystal, and a bouquet of red roses was placed on a table, covered with a white silk cloth. She couldn't miss noticing in the corner of the room, a Louis XIV sofa, covered with red velvet material, above which, a gigantesque mirror in gold was adorning the wall. —He thought about everything, she could only think, hypnotised by so much beauty.

'Can I help you with your coat?'

She handed over her woollen trench. A velvety black dress, rounded neck, falling down her shoulders, was covering her body. The long sleeves fabricated in lace were falling loose on her arms. The cut of the garment, rendered her legs thinner than usual, but she still looked beautiful. Jason placed her coat on the divan.

'Won't take a minute,' he smiled and walked out.

—In five minutes, he will be here! *'Still waiting for Dan but the place is amazing!'* She texted Jimmy. The minutes which followed, encouraged a malaise that she didn't want to envisage. Jason returned pushing a silver trolley. It transported a bottle of champagne, cooling in an iced bucket, a tray with smoked salmon nicely presented in thin rolls, cheese, and mushrooms pastries, tomatoes bruschetta, and olives. Although everything looked deliciously presented, confectioned with high quality products, her appetite had deserted her, like a fugitive in conflict with her anguish.

'Champagne?' Jason presented a bottle of Louis Roederer and opened it.

'Cristal? Of course!' she smiled. —He went the extra mile for me, surely, he won't let me down. Tears rose to her eyes. The pop sound exploded in the room.

'Madame,' he gave her the flute.

A sad thank you slid from her lips. She gulped her drink and watched him place the delicatessen on the table.

'It is very good,' she had to admit.

'Enjoy and I will see later.' As he left, her iPhone vibrated.

'Jimmy,' she picked up.

'So?'

'He hasn't arrived yet!'

'He won't be long!'

'It is already twenty past eight.'

'You are right for a first rendezvous it is not very courteous! Why don't you call?'

'To tell him what?'

'At least you will know.'

'He has organized everything, a special room, Cristal champagne, and some canapés,' she moaned.

'Call him and let me know. There must be an explanation!'

'Ok,' she hung up. She finished her glass and searched for Dan's number. She saw it inscribed like those gambling games where all symbols had to be similar, in order to win the price. Her eyes remained glued to the screen for seconds, while she listened to her heart pumping out her blood with vigour and fear animating her fingers. Any sound drew her regard in the direction of the curtain. She hoped to see him rushing towards her. He would apologise and even carry a big present. —That is probably the reason why he is late, he must be busy looking for the perfect gift for me, she wished naively, so she wouldn't have to press the button. Eventually, her finger gave in. It was ringing but there was no possibility to leave a message. She repeated the operation several times until the famous recorded message by many providers erupted: *'We are unable to connect your call, please try again.'* She stood in the middle of this magical scenery, heaviness in her chest, her tears burning in her eyes. —No, her heart screamed, fighting to prevent them to flow.

—Why, she addressed the three letters on her phone? It didn't answer. —Dan why? Not wanting to believe that he had abandoned her. That was how she felt. She paced the room. That painful insight activated her tears, to slide on her cheeks like an avalanche. She trembled incapable of thinking straight and observed her head rolling in the room. Her head resembled a huge snowball, collecting flakes of sadness, stuffed by embarrassment, looking to expose her anger. Within that horrendous moment, she met her regard in the mirror. Her eyes blinked and she walked closer towards it. —You, she spoke aloud defying the reflection. The reflection wrapped her body with her bruised and accusing eyes. Issata's heart pounded consequently. It hammered in the middle of her chest, confronting this imposter, whom she suspected was her dream stealer, the sorceress determined to take away her right to believe.

—This is all your fault! She pointed her finger at herself! Her heart drummed violently. Her breathing slowed down. She felt a pressure, grabbing her neck as if some hands were looking to choke her. She was unable to move, nor to speak. Her mobile still hidden in her hand, rang. She jumped, but couldn't hide her deception when she saw the name of the caller. 'Jimmy,' she stammered.

'He hasn't arrived, has he?'

'No, I have tried several times. I heard the ringing, then the connection got lost!'

'Try again, he is probably stuck somewhere!'

'How can he do that to me?'

'There must be an explanation!'

'He stood me up! That is the only explanation! I feel so stupid!' She broke down in tears.

'Ok, I am coming to get you!'

'Yes, please come and get me!'

Jason entered the room when she hung up and found her in tears. 'Something wrong Madame?'

She redoubled her tears for answers.

'He is not coming, is that so?' he approached her.

'I just can't believe this!'

Jason sighed and took a serviette from the table.

'Here is it.' She grabbed the cloth.

'Madame,' he began and placed a friendly hand on her shoulder. 'I don't want to interfere but that is not the first time.'

She stared at him through a glance which sought some explanations.

'Mr. Smith.' He paused as if looking for his words. 'I have observed a lot of women just like you, waiting. And all of them left the Connaught in tears.'

'No, no, no,' she shook her head.

'This is the truth!'

'Surely, we are not talking about the same person!' she raised her voice.

'A tall handsome man, ginger hair, German-speaking, Italian looking, and notorious lawyer.'

Issata shook her head, not believing what she was hearing.

'I shouldn't tell you this as I could lose my job. Mr. Daniel Smith is a predator. You have so much class Madame. As soon as I saw you, my heart began to cry for you.'

She moved away from him and landed on the red sofa, sobbing. —I should have guessed it! What a fool! Jason followed her and sat by her side, listening to her sobs.

'I feel ashamed with myself!'

'That is not your fault! Men with power think that they can buy everything. Money can't buy love.'

'Why are you telling me all this?'

'Mr. Smith has been our client for ten years and he is a married man!'

'Married? I had never seen any ring on his finger.'

'It is easy to remove it, Madame.'

Her hazelnut eyes were flooded again. Debris of her make up, scattered on her face, her visage was resumed to an unfinished painting.

'I feel so stupid!'

'Issata?' she heard.

'Jimmy!' She stood up and ran to him. 'What am I going to do?' she hid in his arms. Jason observed them, envious of their complicity.

'I'll take it from there!'

'Very good! The bill is already sorted so make the most of it. And I will add the taxi on it.'

'Thank you, champagne darling?' Jimmy looked at his friend.

'That would kill me! Take me away from here.'

'Shall I call a taxi then? Which address?'

Jimmy sorted everything.

'What am I going to do?' she asked when Jason left.

'He doesn't deserve you! It must be a protection from the Buddha because you are a precious woman.'

'And tomorrow I will have to see him.'

'I don't think you should go.'

'I have to confront him.' She pulled away from him to collect her stuff.

'We could at least drink the champagne before leaving. Plus, it is Cristal!' He filled the two flutes.

'To Daniel Smith!'

'He is a bastard Jimmy!'

'To the bastard then!'

'Jimmy please!'

He smiled and swallowed his drink.

'Nothing exceptional!' He gulped the bubble of his friend.

She giggled timidly.

'At least, I have made you smile.'

'Your taxi is here,' Jason announced.

'Thank you.'

'Madame, you will be fine.' He bowed to her.

She pouted and Jimmy escorted his friend to the taxi. The journey remained silent. She kept her head on his shoulder all throughout the drive.

'Do you want me to come in?' he checked when they reached her home.

Her visage covered with tears, mixed with the little resemblance as to what beauty represented, she muttered:

'No,'

'Ok, try to sleep and we meet tomorrow after your shift.'
She nodded as a response.

Once inside, she removed her dress, tugged her pull-ups, her underwear, and threw everything on the floor. She cleaned the left over from her make up, avoiding the eyes in the mirror, and laid naked in her bed. In the dark, she attended her own concert, the cascade of tears, orchestrating the propagation of those existential malaises, those ailments which profound roots derived from gloomy and infectious emotions. A recurrent sound dominated the fanfare, recalling in her an odour, a perfume following her, like an undesirable stench. That was how she felt, undesirable. She stayed awake waiting for the alarm clock to buzz, with her internal pain for sole blanket. Quarter past four, she dragged herself to the bathroom where she put on her uniform without washing. She didn't pray either. What for? Five o'clock, she carried her huge bag on her shoulder and walked to the bus stop under the heavy rain. Fortunately, it was not far. She arrived at VoyE terminal completely absent, looking like a ghost floating in this touristic decor.

'Issata,' called Michael. As soon as he saw her, approaching the reception, he noticed something was not right. He rushed to her. She lifted her head and gazed around. The voice activated an explosion in her cells. It was like a metaphysical energy, splitting her skull. Becoming aware of her brain flexibility, she could hear the poundings of her heart from two parallel worlds. A reality surrounding her and a tainted sentiment perceived through her own mind. An intense battle emerged between her mind and her soul. A vast variety of sounds captured her attention when suddenly, her eyes caught her own reflection amplified via several versions of her face.

Shaken by uncontrollable spasms, she trembled frenetically.

'Issata, it's me!' Michael got to her. Her pupils rolling under her eyelids, she recognised his image and stammered, through a stream of saliva, running from the corner of her lips: 'He...dididin't coocome...' and collapsed in his arms.

Agnes and Jimmy observed their friend annihilated on this hospital bed, shocked to see this woman that they loved in their own unique way, buried in her dolorous sleep. Her black skin had turned into a faded blue. An oxygen mask covered her face. They listened to her breathe. As their next of kin, they were the first to be alerted. Jimmy burst into tears at the news. —I should have prevented her to go to work, he blamed himself.

Michael, who called the ambulance, explained the situation to the paramedics. He told them the change in her behaviour, her weight loss, and that she had begun a steroid treatment. But in his heart, he questioned her role at VoyE. How could the company implement such a position without assessing the risks? In the evening, she opened her eyes but was unable to communicate. Confined in her mutism, she looked straight ahead, like a dead body waiting for someone to shut her eyelids.

They met Dr. Reynolds, a sexagenary tall black man, kinky hair which defined African men of his generation. He took note of her condition and suspected that she was experiencing an emotional shock. —Daniel Smith is definitely the key to this equation, Jimmy believed. He could still watch the desperation, the betrayal printed on her face. The same hurt dressing her eyes in that hospital bed. Agnes was sad to discover that her friend hid the illness from her.

'I will prescribe her some antibiotics and place her under perfusion and order some blood tests. I will also ask the nurse to keep her jacket uniform on her, because if that is what I am suspecting, she needs a catalyst.'

'Hello Sophia,' Jimmy welcomed the younger version of Issata. Long thin plaits were falling on her shoulders. It was the first time, they were meeting. As soon as he found out, he contacted her via Facebook. Mum was desperate to come and protect her daughter, the flesh of her blood, but the universal wisdom opted for a reason. Sophia had to honour that role. He organised her train ticket and offered his flat for her stay.

'Jimmy, thank you so much,' she moaned, in tears.

'She is a fighter' he empathised. They went to the hospital. Agnes was already there. Sophia broke down at the sight of her eldest sister. She had always been her rock. Watching her lying in a hospital bed was devastating.

She looked like a patient suffering from deep psychological troubles. To one exception, she was not strapped to the bed. Her tears crawled on her cheeks; she escalated souvenirs from the time they lived together. Issata chose the clothes to dress her baby sister and exhibited her talent in doing her hair. —She took great pleasure in cradling me with fairy tales so that I could plunge into agreeable dreams. —My second mummy, she whispered, sneaking towards the bed.

'She is strong,' assured Agnes. She stood up to embrace her. They were meeting for the first time too.

'Issata,' Sophia whispered her sister's name softly.

She lifted her eyes but didn't answer.

'It is me Sophia, your baby sister,' she continued shocked.

Issata could only stare at her. Her eyes as larges, and elongated as almond nuts, weakened by the perdition to shine, to charm, described an inexplicable naught on an emaciated visage. And how to read them?

'What is wrong with her? She can't speak?'

'They think, she had a shock!'

'What can we do?' Sophia held the hand of her sister and called her name again. Silence remained the same answer.

'Please, tell me the truth. Did something happen?' She stared at both of them, despair in the eyes.

'She began a new treatment,' murmured Jimmy.

'Which treatment?' she cried.

'To build back her immunity system. It has happened suddenly!' He held her in his arms.

'Do you think work could have contributed to it?'

'Absolutely!' Agnes's anger rose in the room. 'It is definitely not normal to collapse in a workplace, like what has happened to your sister.'

'And why does she have her jacket on?'

'Dr. Reynolds suggested it. He said that the red colour is very powerful.'

'My mother and I are truly grateful for what you are doing.'

Four days went by, still no improvement. Dr. Reynolds commenced to lose hope but refused to envisage her transfer to a psychiatric hospital.

It was a very dark time. The surrounding seemed busy. Tones of images appeared like mirages. She could see, but her brain could not register, what she believed to have recorded. Human shapes sharing the same similarities walked in and out, around her. Food was inserted in her mouth. She couldn't' taste a thing. People washed her. she slept, but didn't dream. She was alive, but didn't exist.

There was heard a loud sound, she recalled, like the barking of thunder and she woke up with a start. Her eyes headed towards the large windows. She observed the greyness in the sky, tainted by torrential rain. Her heart banged rapidly at the same speed of the storm. Her gaze caught the cold blue colour covering the wall of the room. She trembled. That colour evoked a troubling sensation. She shut her eyes, searching. When? Where? To her greatest surprise, she became aware of her own faculty to think, as if she was discovering that privilege. Everything happened fast. She witnessed herself running about with no destination. There was no shape, no sign, no message, only Issata in the middle of her own darkness. She was deflated but refused to resume her race. —Red, she uttered suddenly, as she spotted a light, lanterning her way from far. The sound of her voice resonated in her soul. She pushed her blanket away and noticed the red jacket. — Blue, red, her mind repeated. Emotions emerged without words, nor thoughts to explain them. Her eyes moved frantically from one colour to the other. —I have seen these colours before, she overheard herself. Those colours looked like a drop of blood in the ocean. Trembling, she touched the material of her jacket and that thunder exploded again. Her ears followed the provenance of the noise. She admired the force coming from the water dropping. They fell from the sky, like fire bullets, being shot from different directions. —I know that sound! She straightened herself and closed her eyes. She was assisting to an orchestra, with the rain, the thunder, and the wind, as principal instruments. —There was water and it was dark, her mind reacted. The tempo grew intensively.

—Where have I heard that melodrama symphony? Images flicked through her head. She sees a restaurant. A bottle of champagne. She notices a woman looking familiar. The woman wears a black dress. Then she is in tears. A man takes the woman in his arms. The woman is in red. The woman falls down. Her heart pounded violently.

—What does it mean? The rain stopped.

—No, she exclaimed, her voice echoing in the room.

—I can speak, she spoke aloud. So moved, her tears began to crawl on her cheeks. She fixed the windows, through her wet eyes and begged the sky to give her back the music.

—Please! Instinctively, she entwined her ten fingers together and her mouth formulated: —Nam-myoho-renge-kyo, Nam-myoho-renge-kyo, Nam-myoho-renge-kyo. The characters vibrated inside her being on the tonality of their true meaning: *I dedicate my life to the mystic law, the law*

115

of cause and effect, and eternal truth. A sentiment, she was turning into a hot balloon, ready to take off, rose inside her. Simultaneously, the sky brightened up, offering her a rainbow. In Chinese culture, the rainbow symbolises the bridge of happiness and good fortune. Issata watched the sky, captivated by the explosions of lights. The colours floated in front of her very eyes. She envisaged herself dancing between each drop. She resembled a little girl, matured enough to savour the power from the water crawling in abundance on her woman body. The brilliance grew in power. And the red colour appeared to detach itself from the arch. The shred revealed itself, as a broken heart, a narrow incision describing her own story. —Love hurts, she observed. The weight of her thought collapsed deep in her core. She didn't have time to write a cerebral essay, as a golden light transpired in the sky. She felt a soft breeze infiltrating her body, and her arms unfolding, like the flapping wings of an angel. Preparing herself to fly, she witnessed a deep blue colour, covering the sky. It looked like a satin carpet, protecting planet earth. Strange energy glowed from that blue colour. A force was communicated with her, through a language sounding familiar to her soul. Completely absorbed by that luminous effect, she allowed herself to blend in the middle of indigo decor.

— Indigo blue plant, of course! she let out. This plant is recognised as the most famous and widespread dye plant in the world. There and then Issata recited loudly: '*Ice is made of water, but colder it is than water. The blue dye comes from indigo, but when something is repeatedly dyed in it, the colour is better than that of the indigo plant. The Lotus Sutra remains the same, but if you repeatedly strengthen your resolve, your colour will be better than that of others, and you will receive more blessings than*

116

they do.' A passage from the Gosho, *The Supremacy of the Law,* written by Nichiren. The word Gosho signified, the writings of a respected person and represents letters of encouragement, from Nichiren to his disciples, a form of written instruction, in which he offers his profound appreciation for their support and in which he pours his heart in instilling the importance of faith. Today those letters are published into two large volumes entitled: *'The writings of Nichiren Daishonin.' Similar as the process used by the indigo plant, this passage denounced the importance of faith in order to obtain more vitality and good fortune.*

A torrent of gratitude crawled on her face. —The rainbow is regarded as a new departure, she expressed overwhelmed! Carrying on with her meditation, she contemplated images galloping in her mind. The sign of a station caught her focus, then a room filled with people. — Possibly travellers, she observed as they carried luggage and bags. She met this woman again. This time, she noticed the red jacket on her, similar to what she was wearing. She touched the hem and realised: —It's me! her cry guided her that crucial moment:

—Dan, she exclaimed, —You stood me up!

At that same moment, a nurse entered the room.

'Where am I?' she panicked

'You are talking?' The nurse approached her, moved to hear her voice.

'I am Anna, you are in hospital.'

'In the hospital?'

'Everything will be explained to you! Your sister will be so happy!'

'Sophia?'

'Good morning, Miss Sherif,'

She looked up towards the voice, calling her name. She saw a man, whose blackness made her feel safe, and a woman, she wanted to believe came from India. She stared at them, and felt millions of emotions, filling her heart. Those same sensations, weighed down on her, beneath the emptiness of the moment. After Anna's visit, she had time to drink a coffee, ate a toast with butter and strawberry jam, discover the date, 23rd March, to urinate, without the help of anyone. She was able to observe that she was alive, most importantly, she adjusted the luxury to remember. She conversed with people. Everyone, she met, rejoice at the sight of finding a woman, animated by a powerful vitality. 'You are very brave!' 'Everything will be fine!' 'What a great joy, to hear you speak!' For seven days, she plunged into a mutism. She woke up and those formulas of kindness, welcomed her back to life.

'I am Dr. Reynolds and this is my assistance, Dr. Morgane.' the voice added.

'Good morning,' said Dr. Morgane.

She acknowledged by a nod.

'I hear, you are talking?' checked Reynolds.

'Yes,' she sighed.

'And how do you feel?'

She narrowed her gaze. —If only, I knew, she didn't dare express. A feeble glow twinkled in the middle of her pupils, a clear reflection of her own despair. The question drew on her own interrogations, as to what has happened to her? Her revendications, on how long she has been there? And the major demand, as to why?

'How do I feel?' she repeated and broke down in tears.

Dr. Reynolds brought a chair located in a corner of the room, near the bed, and invited his comrade to sit, while he sat on the bed.

'Do you know why you are here?'

She sniffed and made the 'no' movement moving her head.

'Your colleague told us about sarcoïdosis.'

She stretched her eyes, wanting to know who.

'Michael, he called the ambulance.' Reynolds understood, the message, behind her pulling face.

The face of a black guy, hair plaited on his scalp, smiled at her.

'Michael?' she called. Her memory led her to see him, holding her in his arms.

'Do you know Jimmy?'

'Jimmy?' she cut in. 'He was there, he knows everything!' Her tears flowed again.

'Issata,' tried Dr Morgane.

'I want to see him,' she sobbed.

'Jimmy explained about the date and the suitor didn't turn up.'

'No, no, no! I don't want to hear this!' She threw her hands in the air. She gave the impression that she was searching to wipe away, the souvenir from the night of 16th March.

Unfortunately, she didn't succeed to let go of it. The unfolding exploded in her mind. The scene looked like a firework, amplified by pain, rejection and humiliation.

'He is a bastard!' Her wail, stimulated more tears, tears which invited more shivering, and sniffing.

Morgane grabbed her arms.

'Issata calm down! You are a remarkable woman!' she tried to control her movement gently.

—To calm down? spurred in her brain, before she riposted angrily: 'So why? Tell me why?' A colossal force took over. She could see herself breaking everything.

'Issata!' Morgane held her wrists tightly, forcing her to confront her.

Surprised, her instinct responded to the intentional demand from a woman doctor.

'Deception hurts deeply. It hurts because it often sends us back to something else,' she spoked softly.

Issata kept her eyes on Morgane. The sentiment that she was talking to that thing inside her, intrigued her.

'What is it then?' escaped from her mouth.

'I don't have any answers to your question?' she let out.

'That seven days of silence, denounced a trauma!'

Reynolds intervened. 'You are coming out of it. You have just expressed your pain through your tears. Try to add your own words to it, now.'

Tears crawled on her cheeks.

'What words? I just wanted to believe!' burst from her lips.

'You have just found the words!' empathised Morgane.

'No one is stopping to believe!'

Like a click, an avalanche of words jumped out of her heart. Those same words vibrating under the melancholic sound which summarised her life. The sound of solitude, the sound of pain, the sound of a broken woman. She looked like a wounded sheep, counting her final days. 'Look where I am now, in a hospital bed.' was the only correct sentence, she managed to say.

Morgane clapped her hands, softly. 'Now, you have to work on what is stopping you to believe,' she empathised.

'What was the catalyst?' Dr Reynolds wanted to know

'The rain! I recognised the sound of the rain!'

'I knew it! A beautiful woman like you couldn't have fallen in the abyss of madness!' He felt proud of his anticipated intuition. Proud, because he was a black man, a black doctor who refused to give up on a young black sister, a human being.

There were no words to express how Jimmy and Sophia felt when they found their Issata. Hearing her speak, to feel her alive, represented the best present the universe could offer them. Tears flooded the face of three people who loves each other dearly. Sophia called Mum. Relieved and faithful to herself, she cried and spoke about herself. Agnes and Michael joined them.

She returned home, a week later. Our two doctors were adamant about the diagnostic. 'I highly recommend that you take time off from work and I advise you to start a therapy urgently.' were the words of wisdom from a black doctor.

Jimmy by her side, she passed the threshold of her door, and shook from shame. The black dress, her underwear, her *LKB* shoes were laying on the floor, the way she had left them. A reminder of that rendezvous. The odour of the nicotine emanated around her. She didn't think, she wouldn't return home. Her astray was full of buds.
'You will be fine darling!' Jimmy embraced her.
'I need to move out of this place.'
'With time!'
At that instant, they heard a knock. Curious, they stared at each other.
'Who is this?' she asked.

'It's me Rajeev,'

'No,' she sighed.

'Who is he?' Jimmy's eyes questioned.

'Hello,' she answered, opening the door.

'Oh, you have someone with you?'

'Do you need anything?'

'No, I noticed your blinds were shut for a week and I was worried,' he mumbled.

She watched her friend with that look which claimed: What's the F...? —Will he be approaching me if I was a man? 'I was in the hospital, but you didn't have to come over for this!'

'Sorry to hear this. Nothing serious I hope?'

'I am fine as you can see. And I have company.'

'Right, if you need anything don't hesitate to contact me. I am like a brother for you.'

'Good.' She closed the door. 'It was my landlord.'

'I have guessed so. There is something vicious about him.'

'You are right! It is his sweet talk which disgusts me. And can you believe this, he said he was worried about me.'

'I know, but don't let this affect you. You have other worries.' 'Yes,' she sighed.

'Why don't you rest? I'll come back later. I am sure you will want to meditate.'

'Thank you,' she hugged him.

She picked up her clothes from the floor and dumped them in a plastic bag. As well as her shoes. —They hurt my toes anyway, she commented, and threw everything in the large black bin, stationed outside. She cleared up her home and lit up a cigarette, after ten days away from the nicotine. —Marlboro, I have missed you! She inhaled her favourite poison, an orgasmic pleasure inscribed on her face. *'Issata belonged to this type of smoker, who associated smoking with pleasure. As a consequence, the hospital not being regarded as a place for comfort, entertaining an egoist need, was not a required luxury.*

She opened her fridge. A bottle of Prosecco half full was sleeping quietly. —Not for long, she smiled. She poured herself a glass and let that refined sirup, slid in her throat. The bubbles fizzled on her papilla sharp and cold. —How could I ever live without you?
She swallowed another sip, her eyes lingering towards her sanctuary. —I am coming! she gulped the drink and poured another one. —So what? We all need inspiration! Especially, since I need to find some answers about my life! she giggled. —Alcoholic? I knew it already! And chuckled. While smoking, the spontaneous laugh faded away quickly. In the middle of her room, she watched the smoke infiltrating the heaviness of the atmosphere. Through that suffocating weight, she felt a deep hole, digging inside her being. She had to face her reality.

—The reality, is that I am ill! Tears filled her eyes and vibrated in her voice. She inhaled her fag quickly, cleaned up her butsudan and knelt in front of Gohonzon. —I need to know; she contemplated and began.

Her voice resonated in her room, on the same frequency of the desire to discover the truth. The truth behind Dan, she had thought to be the perfect man, sarcoidosis an incurable illness, her job whose only purpose existed to serve the elites of the world. That urge to find answers, enticed her to revisit a guidance from Daisaku Ikeda.

'Illness is not just an inconvenience to be suffered. It is a signal for growth in one's spiritual life. From the perspective of the eternity of life, it is an indication of a great change, an opportunity to deal with. From illness arises the mind that seeks the way. When the karma of illness appears, we have the opportunity to change it once and for all. This karma has been deeply embedded, perhaps for many lifetimes, causing us to suffer. When it appears in such a concrete form, we can be assured that we have already come to grips with it. We have already changed it enough for it to surface in a physical form so that we can recognise and deal with it. From the approach of faith, it is a cause for delight.'

—Karma, she repeated. Five letters, expressing sounds and thoughts, translated through our actions as a consequence.

—So, I have to change my karma, Sensei? Is that so?

—You also had yours to change, she murmured.

At a very young age, Daisaku Ikeda suffered from a very fragile physical constitution, aggravated by tuberculosis. According to the doctors, he was doomed to never reach thirty. Those predictions must have clearly helped him establish a vision for his life, a way which had defined his personality. He was not to waste time. And guess what? In 2012, he was breathing through his eighty-four years of age, with the vitality of a young man in his twenties.

But who really is this man? A Japanese Buddhist philosopher, educator, author, and advocate activist, for world peace. It was through Josei Toda, at the age of nineteen that he converted to Nichiren's Buddhism. His meeting with Toda had set the course of his life. From the start, he had Fallen under his charm, his righteousness, his passion for justice which Ikeda himself had searched to establish, after losing his brother during the war. As we have discovered pages before, Toda carried an impassioned love for youth. They bonded at a Buddhist meeting and he found in Toda, a spiritual mentor for eternity.

After his passing, it became the mission of Daisaku Ikeda to serve as the third president of SGI. He had chosen to devout his life in spreading Nichiren's philosophy worldwide, through the concept of *Human Revolution*. As the word implies, a revolution is defined as a fundamental and sudden change in political power, which occurs when the people are revolted.

In terms of Buddhism or any spiritual paths, the change takes place inside the human being. The central idea lays on observing the self; starting by developing immense compassion, in regard to our own emotions, learning to understand them, and working on our impulses. In other words, the human revolution consists in transforming one's life on the deepest level, and to give it a sense of purpose. That sense of purpose illustrates the template of Kosen Rufu, the main goal of SGI.

This sentence found in the Japanese translation of the Lotus Sutra is translated as world peace through the happiness of the individual. In a more detailed explanation, *Kosen* can be understood as: widely declared, spread, promulgate; *ru*: flowing like a mighty river, and *fu* means 'to spread out like a roll of cloth. In other words, Kosen Kufu represents a vision largely declared which flows freely to reach all.

The mentor of disciple relationship was intriguing to her. She worked at it! —It is common sense, she told me! In any sphere of life, exists someone with the skills, the qualities to guide and teach. —Sensei, as she calls him, represented the only religious leader, she trusted. To her, he demonstrated how to apply the mystic law in everyday life. From that perspective, she believed that if many people were to engage in polishing their lives and inspiring others do the same via the pathway of Buddhism, society will without a doubt bloom into a gigantesque flower, the lotus flower of mankind.

She was even more determined to deepen that bond, when she discovered that SGI had acquired *The Chateau de Roches* in Bièvres and decided to call it, *the house of Victor Hugo,* with the aim to open it to the members of the public. That propriety belonged to a certain Louis François Bertin. He was the director of *Journal des Débats* around the time, between 1789-99. Then it was in 1804, that he bought, this famous castle and began to organise a literary salon. He invited many artists, hence Victor Hugo. Since 1989, Soka Gakkai France is the owner of that building. Mr. Ikeda himself declared: '*This house will be the bridge between two civilisations, French and Japanese and I would like it to become the point of reference for the literacy world.*'

—Sensei has done it! Me too I can do it! At that moment, she made the determination to sincerely chant to understand her mentor's heart and to use her illness as a life-changing experience.

Jimmy returned, transporting two large bags full of goodies…and champagne. 'To your great health my darling!' they raised their glasses.

Where to start? Issata was alive, but something was missing inside her. She felt like a part of her story in this world had died, a part of her. But what? Do I really need it? she would question.

Jimmy travelled to Amsterdam, for work. 'I am with you Issata!' he made sure to tell her.

Dr. Vanessa from her surgery, summoned her after she took possession of the medical notes from Dr. Reynolds. She signed her off sick for six months and mentioned the therapy as he suggested. Issata refused. She didn't insist. But she organised two stays in the hospital.
—Brompton hospital, where she had to undergo a biopsy, concerning the lymph nodes. It went well. However, they had to cut one of her vocal muscles, because it was not really important. Sarcoidosis was building its own empire inside her chest, was observed. This explained her difficulties in breathing when chanting, and when doing the slightest physical exercise. —At the Royal Free hospital in the rheumatology department, due to muscle pain. Fatigue and irritability animated her everyday life. She spent her precious energy engaging in inflamed conversations with the nurses who were only doing the very best to assist her. The doctor in charge accused the

illness and was seriously concerned. He suggested that she took antidepressants to relax her nerves. What did she answer for: —No! Why? —Because if the sarcoidosis is produced by my own body, then my body can cure it, she concluded when she went back home two weeks later.

Amsterdam had kidnapped Jimmy. She reintroduced the millions of vitamins in her diet. It cost her a fortune and she decided to base everything on faith. At least, her belief was free. Jeanne had always encouraged her to chant abundant daimokus. —Daimokus cultivate the life state of the buddha, she used to tell her. She ventured herself to practice three hours every day with the determination:
—*Fuck you Antigen! She could be so profound as we will discover.* Japanese members of SGI qualify this activity as toso. It implies engaging in a spiritual campaign of chanting a quantity of daimokus, invoking the great life force of the buddha. There is no rule as to how much people should chant. Nichiren himself declared: —To chant to your heart's content. Buddhism is reason.

—This illness manifested in my life when I was looking for Mr. Right, she realised and studied the letter, *Earthly Desire are Enlightenment* from Nichiren. The title explains very clearly, the importance of desire and its function. Nichiren confirmed categorically that no separation existed between earthy desire and illumination. Because both facts of life surged from the same source: —Happiness. —So where is the illumination? —Dan what a bastard you are, she wept! —And you are married, the scandal it could have led to! There and then, weeks of silence infected by virulent emotions exploded in her, drawing litres of tears, she tempted desperately to use, to wipe away the idiot she observed in herself. The sentiment of shame and humiliation was slaughtering her heart. —Why didn't you come? And where are you? According to Michael, he hadn't travelled since.

Weeks went by, she received the same message in the letter box of her heart, stained by tears and sealed by the stamp of her own pain. She tried desperately to pierce through her agony, looking for the way to its source. She happened to even personify this suffering. She imagined it as a woman terribly hurt. Issata only wanted to help her. She embraced her with positive energies through her prayers. —You can trust me, she would whistle. —I just want to hold you in my arms, and together we will find a solution.

On one occasion, concentrating in front of her Gohonzon, her iPhone rang. —Oh no, I don't have time for you, was her reaction, when she watched Agnes' name flashing. The vocal notification printed on the screen, intensified her resentment even more so. Agnes was only calling to check on her, as she had been doing since her friend had fallen ill. Issata just didn't want to talk to her. Her heart screamed repetitively inside her chest to an obsessive sound. She felt chased by an enemy determined to suck her blood. The energy crawled through her being like a galloping horse. Then her anger exploded. As if she had just named the wild beast, emerging from the ruins of her existence, she let out: —Sarcoidosis is a condition where the immune system attacks the body! Heat possessing her sense, sweat dripping under her armpits, she repeated the realisation aloud and asked: —Is this illness linked to anger? —And Agnes in all this? Let's remember she has a big weakness! She is very careless! Tears inflamed her eyes, leading to a tsunami of emotions possibly locked for millions of years, in a secret part of her life, ready to explode, like a volcano. It is explained that volcanoes form when the magma, molten hot rocks found beneath the Earth's crust, move towards the surface. They then turn, into lava which allows the volcano to erupt. Following this example, Issata's disease would be the physical manifestation of the volcano, lava, perhaps anger. And what would magna represent in her life? She cried and cried and wept with her wrath as a guardian of her own peace of mind.

—It's official, I'm angry, she confessed! According to Google, it is a healthy and natural emotion. —I have hope then, she reassured herself. However, it could take on disproportionate measures. —Damn too good to be true. To her surprise, she discovered that three types of anger existed. — Passive anger, aggressive anger, and assertive anger. —It's all very well, but how do I deal with this fire inside me, now? —Detect the signs of anger, the therapists would advise. Issata to analyse: —If someone is not able to read on the face of an African woman, who chips between her teeth with the violence which could shake the bones of their ancestors in their graves, who rolls her pupils following you in your worst nightmares, the nostrils wide open to suck you alive, ready to hummm, followed by the *wallahi* (I swear to Allah, in Arabic) before uttering the sentence, then that would lead to a serious problem. She clearly knew her roots. —Take the time to process triggers! —What triggers? These are Toubab's ideas! The word Toubab or *Toubabou* most commonly used in Central and

West Africa was used in colonial times to describe white men, mainly associated with wealthy travelers. Issata could also be labelled as a Toubab by an African person because of her European lifestyle. —Finding control techniques, such as deep and slow breathing to regulate the heart rate, mindfulness, is also viewed a good meditative way, to direct the mind away from anger. —I am a Buddhist, so I already have a vigilant approach to consciousness.

— I write, as well! —I read a lot! She took a deep breath, realising that these techniques were already implied in her life. Her eyes briefly lost towards her windows; she spotted the serenity in the blue sky. —And I love walking.

'Sayon,' she placed her arms around her trunk and proceeded to her ritual. She breathed through her bark and placed her beating heart, against her tree. Her tears rolled in her eyes and she felt, Sayon's invisible arms resting on her shoulders. 'He did not come,' she murmured. 'I need you so much!' She embraced her tree, looking to open what every New Age believer would call the chakra. Even though this energy had existed for many years. And what is it? Quite simply, the point of gravity where the energy is concentrated. Chakra is a Sanskrit word. It means a wheel, a disc, and derives from the word *Cakra*. In the past, it represented the rotating wheel or energy disk, which helped to generate the flow of light, from the body. It was explained that when a chakra did not function or appeared blocked, this obstruction would lead directly to the disease. 'Sayon, I am so lost!' her heart bled. Gripped to her tree, she heard like a whispering: 'Sometimes the answers are lodged at the beginning of our lives!'

131

'Mum 'called Issata, waving at her, when she arrived at Montargis' station, her hometown. Her mother was leaning at the front of her red Fiat Uno. The two women hadn't met since Christmas. Her heart trembled with anxiety.

'My daughter, are you okay?' She hugged her against her chest.

'Yes, Mum, thank you.'

'Are you sure? Your face is swollen, darling.'

The side effects of steroids, came to light, hence this round face forming her new image. —That's all you can say, criticise me, she ignited inside?

'It's the cortisone and I'm just very exhausted.'

'Well, let's hope you can rest with me a little bit.'

—Hopefully, she responded silently. They jumped into the car, heading to Corquilleroy where Mum lived with Antoine. He came out to greet them, when he saw the car entering the courtyard. True to himself, he wore jeans and a white shirt, which highlighted his Mediterranean complexion.

'Issata, nice to see you' he hugged her.

'Hello Antoine, equally.'

'And how are we keeping?

'I keep going.'

'Make yourself at ease and use the time to rest.'

'Thank you.'

Lunch was ready. Mum had prepared a quiche with salmon, served with lettuce salad, and the famous French vinaigrette sauce.

'So how is life in London? And the queen?' Antoine inquired. English politics was one of his favourite subjects, and Issata always explained the same news. The English still drove on the left and Queen Elizabeth had still not invited her to the Royal Palace. This was as far as their conversations led to. Antoine also loved to talk about retirement. Her mother remained silent on the subject. After their meal, she accompanied Mum for her walk, clinging to her arm. How to start a conversation?

—I could investigate my childhood? —No, Mum didn't belong to that generation where we discuss childhood psychology. —We are taught to study, to graduate, get married, and to make babies, she smiled, internally.

—I guess I should just enjoy my moment with her. And that was what she did. She listened to her stories while she smoked. Her life as a receptionist, her routine with Antoine, her neighbours, the latest promotions from Leclerc supermarket, her high blood pressure problem, the life of a woman in her mid-sixties who didn't know any better.

—Sarcoidosis is a bitch! Dan screwed me up! —No, he didn't fuck me! — I don't want to see Agnes! —I'm angry! She contemplated facing, her *omamori* Gohonzon. What is it? — a narrow version, of the one kept at home. To give you an idea, it is about the size of those little matchboxes found in any tobacconist. But the power remains the same. Only members from advanced experiences in their faith could receive it. —What about my mum in all of this?

—I just want the truth, nothing but the truth!

But she did not swear. The truth about the world surrounding mankind, that enigma had seduced thousands of men and women, to find answers, and draw on their own theories. Some rely on dogmatic truth. The truth becomes the object of belief, an opinion that is a matter of faith. Others, work in accordance with mathematical truths, obtained by logic and mathematical proof. Exists also, scientific truth, only accessible by scientific methods where evidence is analysed with the utmost attention. So, what is the difference between Maths and Science one might wonder?

According to Galileo, philosophy would be inscribed in this immense book entitled, the universe. His fascination towards the mystery of this infinite kingdom spurred him to dedicate his existence, to deciphering the universal codes which requires mathematical language. We can all recognise that Italian man, his eyes always behind an astronomical telescope, a tool he perfected, and exploited as his everyday glasses. So, rather than looking for a difference, we can deduce that science needs math and philosophy to describe the world as it presents itself. And we must learn to interpret all experiences in rhythm with the time. Science is knowledge, so is the truth for that matter! And Issata had to decode her own scientific truth, based on the mystical law. Something was emerging from her heart, a spontaneous invitation that her voice was suggesting to accept. A slideshow of different moments of her life scrolled into her mind timidly. There was no chronological order, but all images contained one thing in common. Issata was present on each one of them. She was a little girl. Petrified, her heartbeat accelerated. She sensed something inscribed in her childish stare. She hesitated to confront the upsetting glare but recognised the old wooden oak cabinet, bought at a flea market. It was then that she saw Mum's shadow rushing into the living room. Standing near a chocolate-coloured leather sofa, she stared at her mother's face. It was dripping with sweat. Behind the frame of her oval golden glasses, she witnessed her garish, cold, rigid-looking eyes. Issata shuddered and, paused from chanting to catch her breath. —But at what point did I witness her dark gaze? She remembered the sclera turning black and the iris brick red. She knew what was coming. The hardness in the fixation would last a few seconds, but enough for her to remain motionless. Paralysed with fear, she would cry: 'I'm sorry Mummy!' before her mother exploded like a tornado.

'Issata, are you okay?' a voice interrupted that memory. She startled with dread and replied: 'Yes, I'm okay, I'm finishing my chanting and I'll see you later. »

'Okay pray for me!'

'Of course!' she sighed. —Why was she screaming at me? —Why did I ask for forgiveness? —I must have done something bad, as she used to tell me: —I'm sick of you, she recalled. Issata was only six years old. —Maybe she didn't want me! — Maybe I was an accident, maybe… maybe… maybe…

A week with Mum and no answer to observe, except for that growing knot in her heart, every time she tried to talk to her. To tell her what? Issata didn't even know why so much bitterness filled her soul. She stopped in Paris for two days to visit Sophia. Her nephews were growing up so fast. Touched by their life force, she promised to heal in order to see them develop into good, respectable, authentic people

135

In July, began the Olympic games. Each athlete, gave their whole body and soul, to support their own nation. Issata engaged in her own marathon. She immersed herself in her faith, meditating and studying Nichiren's writings and Sensei's guidances. Nevertheless, the anger was killing her inside, to the point that one day, so engrossed in it, she vomited that poison on a young employee who had just presented to her where the queue was. —Poor little girl, Issata confided to me. —Alas, she took away her right to be angry, to say shit and fuck you. —So what? I was wrong, I want to pay now, was her argument. She knew that the fault rested on her, but it proved impossible for her to admit it. Her anger was right. That's the way it was! The store manager had to intervene to unravel the situation. She left the store, her ego hurt for allowing such embarrassment publicly. She walked home, consumed by shame. —I am not the Buddha who removes suffering to offer joy. —I inflicted distress on this poor girl, who could have been Sophia, my younger sister! —I am a monster, she accused herself and slammed her door.

'I want to see Dr. Vanessa!'
She yelled, tears covering her face, she stormed into the surgery. Shocked, the two receptionists looked at each other. One was wearing a chador, the other looked Indian. 'Do you have an appointment,' the Muslim woman

136

checked. 'Are you listening to what I have just said?' She banged her fist on the table and walked off towards the stairs.

'Miss, please wait!' the Indian lady let out, and followed her.

Too late, she had already pushed the door of her doctor's cabinet.

'Help me,' she wailed.

'I got this,' Dr. Vanessa rushed to her patient.

'Issata take a seat and tell me what's going on?' She offered a Kleenex. Issata was clinging to the chair, searching to prevent a fall from her violent tremors. Shaking through every sob she managed to let out:

'I am angry all the time! I am a bad person!' She explained the incident with the girl at the cashier.

'Issata, you are a very brave woman. It's very serious what you are dealing with and you're going through it all on your own. Do you get support from your Buddhist group?'

'No! I don't want anything to do with them! They disgust me!' she yelled.

The violence in her statement shook them both. Dr. Vanessa stared at her, analysing millions of scenarios which could force her patient to make such a statement. — Maybe she is involved in a sect, and doesn't know how to come out, she even considered?

'But I thought Buddhism…'

'Buddhism is about people! People's lives! My life!' Her rage escaped from her mouth! The words vibrated around her. Those words she chose spoke for themselves.

'Issata, if you are in danger, you have to report it! There is a lot of new age movement who seduced vulnerable people…'

'I don't have to justify myself!' she cut in, embarrassed to hear such comments. —It's just that I do not know anymore why I chose Buddhism. Plus no one needs to chant to achieve goals in life, she argued inside.

'Ok, I think you should seriously consider therapy.'

'I am not mad, you too, you are like them.'

She broke down in tears.

'I am just trying to help you, at least you can try.'

'Trying what? I want to kill this rage and I wish to never wake up,' she screamed.

'Issata, don't talk about yourself like that. I feel so responsible and I'll never let you down.' let out Dr. Vanessa, trying to show a brave face. How heartbroken a doctor must feel, when hearing their patient, not wanting to live anymore.

She continued to sob like, that ugly duckling rejected by all and sniffed the sadness congesting her chest.

'You are a fighter!'

'I am fed up to fight. I ached all over. All I do is swallow pills all day long.

'What are you taking?'

'Codeine,'

'Let's have a look! I see, my fellow doctor only prescribed the codeine,' she checked on her screen. 'I will change to Co-codamol, a combination of codeine and paracetamol.'

'I want to sleep.'

'It will help and let' s try to establish an objective together.'

'What is the point? Look what has become of me!' she rose her voice. 'Maybe to consider a part-time return before the end of the year?' 'I said, I want to sleep, and you are talking to me about work,' she yelled. 'I am trying to help you focus your mind.' 'I exhausted!' she wailed.

'Let's start with antidepressants and I really want you to consider a therapy.'

'Whatever!' she let out.

'I see you soon.' She handed over the prescription.

She definitely noticed a difference in her mood. She found herself more relaxed and less angry. But she could feel a lurking sensation of exposure, like a fraud. She increased the dose, because she didn't want to think. She didn't want to face the stress, of engaging with herself. Before she knew it, an emotional confrontation animated her mind. She began to hallucinate and spent her time in bed, hiding beneath her duvet.

—Is this normal that I no longer feel myself? she managed to reach Vanessa. But didn't mention to her, increasing the pills. The prescription was altered. It got worse. She woke up nauseous, with headaches, and more tired than the definition of the word itself. She studied the side effects of her treatment and what she discovered frightened her. —That stimulator only controls the mood. That's how many people became addicted to it. Everything ended in the bin. What is left for me then? she sighed.

—Shijo Kingo was an angry man, the monster of rage, one day she acknowledged! And revisited a passage from the Gosho, The Three Kind of Treasures: '*Your face bears definite signs of a hot temper. But you should know that the heavenly gods will not protect a short-tempered person, however important they may think he or she is. If you should be killed, even though you might attain Buddhahood, your enemies would be delighted, but we would feel only grief. This would indeed be regrettable.*'

Shijo Kingo, represented one of Nichiren's loyal disciples. He excelled in his role as a renowned samurai and physician, but he was known for his fiery temperament and penchant for sake. This often got him in trouble. Shijo suffered the persecutions of his lord, a certain Lord Ema who did not adhere to his religious beliefs and who confiscated his lands. Nichiren, knowing all too well the weakness of his disciple, felt the need to warn him about his tendency in life, hence this stern letter, an expression of his deep compassion. A message clearly explaining: If Shijo Kingo should die, it would be sad, but if he succumbed because of his own negligence, the negative functions of life would rejoice, even if he was to reach the state of the Buddha. Later, the story tells that his lord had fallen seriously ill and Shijo Kingo, being a skilled physician was invited to cure him. He healed his lord and to thank him, three times more than what he had lost, was offered to him. —He also possessed his own weakness, she analysed! —And that did not prevent him from receiving the blessings of the universe and putting his knowledge at the service of his boss!

— The Ten Worlds, Issata realised that she had neglected these key principles of her practice. These worlds are not destinations where men and women and children would travel every day to come back exhausted. Mind you, some are very tiring, especially, when we don't know where we are going. —But let me explain! These worlds express the nature of our states of life! They demonstrate the fundamental orientation of our state of being, at a given time which determines everything.

—What we feel, how we think, our attitude, and how we interact with others. Everything stems from our state of life, which paints the picture of our existence. They are called:

—Hell, which resonates with the world of deep suffering, but experiencing such misfortunes can help us strive to improve our circumstances and better understand the suffering of others.

—Greed, belongs to the world of insatiable desire, but we also can crave to see others happy and fight for a better world.

—Animality, the world of instinct, represents the fear of the strong and bullying the weak, but it can also give rise to protective instincts such as self-preservation and the protection of others.

—Anger, Issata's best friend, and her worst enemy, is dominated by ego, a state characterised by arrogance, the spirit of comparison, rivalry, and domination of others. Anger can also rouse us to stand up for justice.

—Rapture, a state of momentary pleasures as expressed by the word itself. However, it can often be motivated by external factors.

—Tranquility, or Humanity is a state marked by the ability to reason, and make calm judgments. However, this state can also represent a fragile balance that yields to one of the lower states when confronted with negative conditions.

—Learning, is defined by the desire to learn about ourselves with the help of others and through existing knowledge, but can also lead to egocentricity.

—Realisation, a state where one awakens to the truth through one's own intuition and observation. It can also lead to self-absorption and a tendency to prefer using reason rather than wisdom to solve problems.

—Bodhisattva is intended to exercise compassion and kindness, but without paying attention to one's own needs, one's life can easily move towards the lower life.

—The Buddha state, finally, which reveals itself in perfect harmony with its environment, based on courage, compassion, and vision. *'What we need to remember is that we have all these life trends. They manifest positively or negatively. Apart from the state of Buddha! It demonstrates no negative aspect and exists in every state of life. The purpose of Nichiren's practice is therefore a way to awaken this Buddha state on a daily basis. When 'the buddha' wakes up, depending on 'his' mood, 'he' makes good use of his skills, in illuminating all others. Thus, everyone can express their personality while remaining true to who they are.'* —I'm not arrogant? —I'm not trying to compete with the others, am I? —I just don't tolerate people who lie and cowards!

'I get you the door!'

August had arrived! She was meeting Jimmy at his home in Brixton. She didn't have to press the intercom. He saw her from his kitchen window. She waved at him and listened to the buzz. She pushed the door, ran up the stairs and they hugged tenderly.

'I missed you so much!' she exclaimed.

'Me too Issata!'

She followed him in his large apartment which he had inherited from a lover, fifteen years ago. Glen was his name, older than him and rich. He died from leukaemia.

They walked through the corridor painted in bright and warm colours, or rather, the walls had been decorated with black and white photos of naked men, and arrived in an

American kitchen. Two large windows overlooked an immense balcony. This jewel arrived equipped with two bedrooms and a large bathroom with a bathtub, baroque style. A bottle of Veuve Clicquot was waiting for them on the terrace of his balcony.

'Get comfortable, I'll get the appetisers!'

'Thank you. I love your flat so much! If only I could have a place like yours.' She sat and saw him arriving, with a platter of charcuteries, olives, cheese, and a basket filled with rolls bread, from Paul, the French patisserie.

'It will happen. You just need to follow the course of your life.' 'Right, I don't' see how.' she muttered.

'In due course!'

He opened the champagne and filled their flutes.

'To you, my friend!'

'To us!' They toasted and swallowed the elixir of their friendship.

So have you thought of commencing a therapy?' Jimmy grabbed a slice of salami.

'To be honest, I don't know where to start! It is mainly, this anger in me!' she lit a fag and took a deep drag. He copied her.

'Professional counsellors exist out there, trained to help you free yourself.'

'Everything is so confusing for me. You know my girlfriend, Agnes; I can't stand her anymore.'

'How comes? It's true that she is a little too much, but she was present for you.'

'I am not comfortable with her anymore. I feel like our friendship has been wrong from the beginning.'

'Have you seen her lately?'

'No! She did call me when you left a few times. And I think, they are away now, possibly back in September, for the return to school.'

'Trust how you feel.'

'Just hearing her voice, makes me sick! Everything is about her. And she just goes on and on and on. Then after an hour, she finishes by saying, it was nice hearing your voice. Sometimes, I wonder how Abdul can live with her?'

'Let's be honest, she is beautiful!'

'Absolutely true, but so vain!'

'I guess, after the diva's life, having to raise children must be hard!' 'She made a choice!' Issata rose her voice.

'You are truly upset with her!' Jimmy fixed his friend.

'She is so over confident! You should listen to what she says about her husband. —Me, if Abdul cheats on me, it is over! It wouldn't occur to her that if he feels the need to visit a different territory, it is possible that hers, might not be to his liking anymore?'

'They are a lot of people out there who feel invincible. Often, they are expressing their own insecurity. Do they share goods in common?'

'All I know, the house has been in Abdul family for more than one hundred years.'

'One hundred years, impressive!'

'I wouldn't be surprised, to hear that he is fucking around. That would be the biggest slap to her ego!'

'What makes you think this?'

'We all know the expression, 'Beware of the sleeping water'? Abdul is a very reserved man, too elegantly quiet.' Jimmy smiled.

'Obviously, there is definitely something profound, emerging from you. And tell me, do you receive support from your Buddhist community? Because what is happening to you, is very serious.'

'My GP had asked me the same. There was Agnes, but right now, I can't care less.'

'But you used to be so active. I remember you were always so excited to report about your Buddhist meetings.'

Sadness invaded her gaze. She recalled the time of every meeting, she attended. Chanting with members, she enjoyed. She grew within the organisation. She took on the leadership role. Then something changed. —Stories, she heard; —Long-lasting members, left that so-called movement for peace; —People committed suicide! How to explain that those people, so strong, so courageous, filled with compassion, had reached that point of profound loneliness? —They might have suffered so much to end their lives? She recalled observing! What is the responsibility of such a movement? An organisation which places people at the heart of its activities? —For sure, there are a lot of people, not related to any kind of group, who end their lives, she couldn't ignore. But doubt has found a seat in her heart. —Well, look at me, I am suffering from an incurable illness, and where is SGI? Me too, I feel lonely. Those words surfaced in her mind, before, she could answer.

'It's true! I was so active! Right now, I do not feel inspired! I need to keep away from all of it!'

'I understand, it is important to take time to reflect! That kind of movement can lead to fanatism! It can be very dangerous!'

'Exactly!' said Issata.

'On this note, santé then!' Jimmy rose his glass.

'Santé!' she joined him.

'Let's eat! You haven't touched anything yet!'

'Oulala! Yes!' She grabbed some salami and olive, that she shoved in her mouth. Jimmy got his hands on the cheese. Chewing happily, he looked at his friend, deeply moved.

'You know, maybe you could think to return to work part-time?'

'To the lounge?' she panicked.

He understood from the sound of her voice. 'Have they seen him?'

'No, he hasn't travelled since! When I think that I so wanted to believe.' 'You can still believe, but not with him!' 'Jimmy, I am so scared!' she cried.

'I have read somewhere that anger is linked to fear.'

'How is this possible?'

'Anger is like a shield to protect us.'

'From what?'

'That is why you need to start a therapy!'

'I don't know!'

'I know that Madame Clicquot is calling us.

—I have to start somewhere at some point, became her daily motto! October 1st, she met Ray the head of human resources and his assistant Catherine. They discussed the possibilities to help her return to work. She confessed how disappointed she felt toward Pascal. 'Eight months, since I had fallen ill, and not once he contacted me.' They assured her to look into it and agreed that she could try part-time the following week. —Is this the right thing to do? In the tube, her heart beating fast, she heard herself questioning. Of course, the real motivations behind her doubts, were more hidden beneath: —Where are you? Why did you disappear? She panicked. —I can't, she sighed! Words attacked her brain. She felt like a tight bandage, crushing her skull. White spots dazzled around her, similar lights to those, she experienced when it all started. —They don't care about you, her mind continued. — Pascal, do you think he would have come? —Leave me alone, she mumbled. Aware of the people around her, she lowered her head in her hands. Arriving at her destination, she ran home, tears crawling over her face. —I'm not ready! I don't want to go back! A frightening sentiment assailed her. She saw those eyes everywhere, laughing at her. — Fuck you, she yelled! Passers-by looked at her, not sure how to respond. She kept running, shaken by dizziness. She was about to open the entrance. But someone else did it from inside. 'Is everything okay?' a man, with dirty blond-looking hair asked. 'No,' she muttered and collapsed.

'You are awaked!'
Issata had just opened her eyes and watched a woman, dressed in a blue uniform, approaching her. She noticed a thin tube attached to her right arm.
'What am I doing here?'
'I am Michelle, you are in hospital. How do you feel?'
She widened her eyes.
'You collapsed in front of your house. Your flatmate called the ambulance.'
She tightened her face, searching for who. Her memory took her back to the man with his dirty-looking blond hair.
'Fortunately, you had your passport with you. We found you in the system. Are you able to confirm your name and date of birth?' Mechanically she confirmed her identity.

147

'Perfect, I am going to do your observation and call the doctor.' As she placed the cuff monitor on her arm, to check the blood pressure, Issata's eyes began to move rapidly, leading her pupils to roll beneath her eyelids.

'Issata?' she exclaimed.

Shaken by uncontrollable movements, both arms, and legs, assaulted her, forcing her tongue to unfold from her mouth. Watching the saliva dripping alongside her lips, the nurse immediately called for help. She then turned her on the side, to release the tension. Issata fainted.

When she regained consciousness, she perceived a masculine umbra floating in front of her tired eyes. Effectively, a tall man, presented beneath a silhouette neatly conserved, his peppery hair kept short and slightly parted on the right side of his head, was standing not far from her. A long white blouse covered him, not to mention the stethoscope, the fetish necklace that every doctor carries around their neck. He was reading some notes. Sensing a movement, he lifted his head and she met some brown eyes elegantly worn, and as smooth as a *Michoco*, French candy chocolate, delicious for its unique mixture of soft caramel, coated with dark chocolate. She was seduced by the gentle confidence which emanated from him.

—Gary Grant? she wished.

'Miss Sherif, I am Dr. Clark,' he approached her.

—No, he was not Gary Grant. *No need to explain to you that at certain point of the novel, I will refer to him as Clark or Gary Grant.*

'I am a neurologist consultant.'

'What?' she let out.

'I checked your file. You were hospitalised this summer for sarcoidosis. Tell me how you feel.'

'Why neurology?'

'I specialise in maladies which affect the nervous system, and spinal cord anything which coincides with troubles related to consciousness, sleep, and reasoning. And I treat 'neurosarcoidosis,' he replied quickly, not wanting to worry her.

'I'm angry all the time, and I feel like someone else is inside me,' she sobbed. In that moment, a sentiment of embarrassment invaded her being. Having to admit her weakness seemed as painful as Jesus carrying his heavy cross on his back and not the least glorious.

'When exactly did it start?'

'A few months ago, before I collapse at work.'

'We need to have an MRI scan on the brain.'

'The brain?'

'Miss Sherif, it is common in sarcoidosis sufferers, for the disease to affect the brain. This could explain your mood change and seizures.'

'I knew something was wrong,' she cried even more.

'We will take care of you.'

'I want the voice to stop!'

'What voice?'

'In my brain, I hear it all the time.'

'Do you hear it now?'

'No!'

'I will prescribe you some treatment for your epileptic seizures and immunosuppressants to rebuild your immune system.'

'What kind of treatment is that?'

'I'll evaluate after your MRI'

'But why? What did I do?' She sulked.

'You're safe here.' he said confidently.

As suspected by Gary Grant, Sarcoidosis found refuge in her brain. This explained clearly her confusion, the voices, her mood swings. Those existential vertigos denounced clearly her fight for survival. In this most disturbing form, Issata was shouting: —Help! She began the treatment of methotrexate used orally to treat certain types of cancer, a kind of oral chemotherapy. Why chemotherapy? Let us remember that no one knows the cause of sarcoidosis and there is no cure for it! Just like cancer. Methotrexate is a cytostatic agent deriving from a group of chemical containing drugs. Because of their toxicity to cells, these products could therefore prevent replication or unhealthy cell growth. In the case of our patient, it would help slow the growth of her immune cells. And therefore, reduce the sensitivity and responsiveness of the immune system. Issata was clearly in no position to go back to work.

It was dark. Her heart beat slowly at an infinite rate.

She couldn't see her membranes. Her body blended into the immensity of the darkness, but she felt in harmony with a cosmic serenity. She heard the profound silence of the emptiness filling her existence at that precise moment, like a calculation of the past, present, and future. — A future which wouldn't exist, if the present did not contain a past, a past that needs the present to manifest, and a present which can only decide the future. It was then that she perceived a flickering glow above her. It began to shine, traversing the galaxy. The light intensified like a shooting star, illuminating the vastness of the night. She noticed a woman lying peacefully on a bed and the warmth of that light enveloped her like a caress. The woman's eyes were opened. They stared directly at the light. She recognised herself in her. Except for the fact that her skin tone, resembled that of an expired dark chocolate bar. Issata walked up to her, still unable to see her body, nor the shadow of her own figure. As she was about to touch the woman's face, she became aware of the long thin scar on the right cheek. —There is only one person whose cheek is tattooed like that! Shocked, she exclaimed: —I can hear my voice? Without understanding what was happening to her, she infiltrated the body placed flat on the bed and felt an exhilarating sensation. She had the power to travel back in time. The brilliance of the light illuminated the path of a tunnel which grabbed her, like a mystical force. The pleasure she felt, in throwing herself into this flow of energy, reminded her of her first orgasmic experience.

At the age of fifteen, she discovered Emmanuelle, the erotic character played by Sylvia Kristel

The boys at her school talked about her and what they saw her do in her films. But for Issata, she represented, an image of women, that only existed in people's fantasy.

Her mouth, with her lips, rolled up, like juicy tangerine quarters, was just waiting to be invited, to the pleasures of life, and everything such possession could deliver. Her round, firm breasts inspired coconuts, which any connoisseur could delicately crush on the floor before sucking, crunching, and chewing the soft and sweet juice from the fruits. Her legs, whose toes were dressed in red, exuded the elegance of the Siamese cats. As for her private part, her pubic hair kept the surface largely covered, because at the time, the Brazilian, had not entered the fashion trend, but the trim made it possible to imagine her swollen lips, which contained her secret bud. Issata too wanted to discover her own bud. In the middle of puberty, she felt it growing inside her panties. —What can I do? the question tormented her.

—Who to ask? Mother? Certainly not! We're not talking about sex! —Sleeping with a boy? —No, because I don't even know how to kiss! Her hormones drove her crazy, especially when she saw Arthur, the new school boy who came from Canada. He was training to become a champion tennis player. Apparently, her best friend Carine had slept with him and he had made her cum. All she had left was Mrs. Claude's expertise. She was her professor of Natural Sciences, a woman in her sixties, tall and skinny, single and childless, always dressed in black, and who honoured Mireille Mathieu's hairstyle.

The school entrusted her to the sex education of her class. — I am sure you are still a virgin, Issata told herself, when her teacher attempted to explain the difference between the female and masculine organ. Even though it was obvious!

On her way home, she would always pass by *Emmaus*, an international solidarity movement founded in Paris in 1949 by Father Pierre. And there she saw in the window, the cover of a book: an apple fashioned into a woman's buttocks. The skin revealed a snake's tail. Panting, she stared at the book. Her eyes beamed with pleasure, imagining the lovemaking of this woman hidden in the manuscript. She hesitated before entering and saw a mature lady sitting behind the counter, dressed in a pink and green sari, the traditional Hindu outfit. Timidly, she murmured: 'How much?'

The shopkeeper observed Issata for a second and greeted: 'Hello, how can I help?'

'How much does it cost?' she muttered.

She left her seat and advanced towards her.

'Want to read Emmanuelle?'

Embarrassed, Issata rushed to the door.

'Wait!' The woman took the book from the window.

'It's for you!' She handed it over to her.

Perplexed, she let out: 'Free?'

'I was young too! And my grandmother taught me the Kama Sutra.' Issata widened her eyes.

'I also attended classes to learn all kinds of techniques to discover my own body and I learned to please men. The most important thing is to find your pleasure.'

—Find my pleasure, she repeated to herself. 'Take it and learn. Once you know your body, you can reveal your own sensuality!'

Issata grabbed the book from the woman's hands. It must have contained a hundred and eighty pages maximum, but it weighed so heavily on her imagination.

'Thank you' she said, hiding her new Bible in her bag.

She reached her house and did the usual; supporting her sister Sophia with her homework, helping Mum with housework, and discussing her future with Dad. Her father had already decided that she would be a lawyer or a doctor. Then her moment came.

'Good night, everybody!' And she escaped to her room. Fortunately, she could lock her door. —I'm in bed with Emmanuelle, she sighed and started reading. Her eyes shining with excitement, Emmanuelle revealed herself exactly as she had imagined. She discovered her adventures, her heart trembling with sexual urges. Then she heard a noise and panicked!

— Maybe Sophia needs me? False alarm, just Dad emptying his bladder! How did she know it? —By the violence of his water. So, she went back to her reading. Slowly, the fingers of her right hand, because she was right-handed, began to follow the rim of her panties. She struck her intimate part over the nylon fabric. Instantly, a lukewarm heat penetrated her senses. She placed her book on her nightstand and I let you use your imagination.

A new sensation vibrated within her. Pure madness and she loved it. She gave in, inviting a small stream to emerge from her flesh. The pleasure grew faster inside the hollow of her ribs. She couldn't describe that feeling. For the first time, her female side wept with joy and she was in control of her tears. She would have loved to hold on to that pleasure which had seduced her body and senses for longer, but she was only an amateur and could no longer resist. She cried silently, for a long time. Her hand, locked between the warm place she listened to her heart regain its human rhythm.

—My first orgasm, she sighed! It's so good! This was what these exhilarating sensations sent her back to. A choice, a conscious decision to make and honour. Her choice was not limited to a pill like Neal in the Matrix. She could create her own matrix. She had all the codes, just as she had chosen to discover her own pleasure. Then everything went fast. The glow changed its trajectory and headed towards the bed. The lustre on the face lit up a new way. Through a lost glare, she felt her body lying on the bed, tightened, and the energy pushing her towards a mysterious gulf. She was not afraid. But it was not normal! It was so not normal for her to be able to hear her voice while watching her body prisoner on a hospital bed. That is why, she let out: —No, not now! An electric shock travelled through her. She felt a brutal punch hammering her chest. She jumped, then nothing.
The next thing she knew, her eyes moved slightly. It was daylight. She looked around and saw the light in the hallway of the hospital. The spectacle looked as similar as the tunnel and its luminous strength.

—Have I dreamed? She touched her face and felt relieved to see her body. A nurse entered the room to do her observations. Everything was in control. —Something happened to me, she wanted to tell her! —But who would believe me? In this moment of transition, because that was how she had perceived this experience, she realised that there was no separation between her body and her inner state. She had the choice of following the light and leaving this world or to stay and finish what she had begun. She chose to stay. That morning, through her prayers, she imagined the characters of the Mystical Law: *Myo* being her head, *Ho* her throat, *Ren* her chest, *Ge* her stomach, and *Kyo* her legs, deeply rooted in her daily life.

—Nam is the action which kept me alive, she observed in front of her Gohonzon, when she returned home, two days later.

Part 2

KHRYSTIAN

-Turning Poison into Medicine-

3

Sitting at her bistro table, she smoked her Marlboro in front of her black coffee.

—I witnessed the eternity of my own life. I defied all laws of physics. Surely, I must have something important to accomplish, she thought, or else…A sound came from her phone. —A message from Catherine? she checked.

She couldn't believe what she read. Catherine, the HR assistant, was informing her about health insurance, she had taken out when she started her employment with Voyage Europe. Since she had planned to return to work part-time, she would be entitled to income protection. Because from November, her company's sick pay would go down to fifty percent. Grateful, she expressed: —Is that what we call protection? In Buddhism, protection is a blessing in disguise, and Issata estimated that her relapse with her health before her return to work was the Buddha's compassion manifesting through her own body. —What a great victory for someone who had just escaped death, she smiled and busied herself sorting out her flat.

She began with the piles of letters, from the council. There were notices stipulating that she owed £4000 pounds of council taxes. Since she had signed her tenancy agreement, bills had never been part of her contract. Shocked and panicked, she contacted Rajeev. 'My Dear, I will look into it! I can never do this to my tenants.' —I wait to see that! she sighed when she closed the call. She continued with her cleaning and put on 'Les Amazones de Guinée' famous band formed by women. Those women were part of the army. They decided to lay down their guns and replaced those weapons with instrumental music. Issata was brought up with their sounds. She didn't understand the lyrics, but their voices of warriors spoke to her heart. Submerged by emotions, she lost herself in her thoughts. So much had happened. And still no answers. She readied herself and left her flat. As she was locking her door, a voice with a strong accent arose:

'Hello,'

'Hello,' she answered politely.

'I see you are feeling better,' the voice continued, coming down the stairs.

She watched carefully and saw descending, a man strongly built, wearing white trainers. The kind of cheap trainers bought from the corner shops, which keep your feet smelling for life. As the umbra was revealing itself, a blue jean and a leather coat made their appearance before she could see a face. She met a pale and unshaven visage, blond and bushy eyebrows, straight blond hair, square cut. Simply said, she was facing the bad boy, looking like those musicians from the seventies.

'Did you call the ambulance for me?'

'Yes, I did.'

'Thank you, I am Issata!'

'I know, Rajeev told me! I am Khrystian!' She stood in front of him, fixing his eyes. 'Do you need something? I am rushing to the shop.'

'Me too,' she muttered.

'Let's go then!' he moved away to open the main door.

Rapidly she discovered, he was Polish, unemployed and lived in London for twenty-seven years. He had moved to

162

Valley Park in March. 'You are Buddhist,' he said. 'I heard you recite Nam-myoho-renge-kyo. Issata was gobsmacked. He told her that a friend took him to the centre in Varsovia. They reached the supermarket. Khrystian carried her basket and followed her like a puppet. —The mystic law will have to explain this to me, she observed! To thank him for his kindness, she invited him for dinner.

At eight o'clock, he knocked on her door.

'You are beautiful,' he let out, when she welcomed him. Indeed, Issata had changed into a black woollen dress, with a huge turtle neck, and was wearing a pair of prune tights which she slid into her golden ballerina flat shoes. They sat at the table, straight away. A large bowl of couscous mixed with peppers, eggplant, red onions, olives, and feta cheese, aromatised by mint leaves, waited for them.

'Wow, it looks delicious!'

She served the wine. 'Cheers!' they drank. Then she watched him grab his fork. He controlled it as if he was holding a shovel and pushed it in the pile of grains like a farmer would manoeuvre a rake to work in his land. He shoved three large bites in a row, and chewed loudly in front of an Issata, disgusted by the noise his tongue was making. His face was almost touching his place.

'So, you are looking for work?' She began, hoping to move her attention from his way of eating.

'I am trying,' he let out. She witnessed the food sliding in his throat. He burped loudly. 'I am forty-nine, at my age, it is not easy.'

—What a pig! He didn't excuse himself! She took a deep breath:

'You know, it is difficult for everyone. Anyway, how did you end up here?'

'I spotted an advert on a shop window.'

'Like me!'

'He thinks he is still an officer!'

'He told you, his story?' She was not surprised. She remembered clearly, the first time, he told her his time in the army.

'Yes, and you should see the look on his face!'

'I think something has happened to him over there.'

'You are right because he likes to feel important!'

Issata shivered. The word important in that context inspired her the criteria of a narcissist. This is when she recalled the character of Commodus, in the movie *Gladiator,* who killed his own father, Marcus Aurelius, for choosing his loyal General Maximus as the next Emperor after his death. Driven by jealousy and an excessive need for attention and admiration, Commodus tried to kill Maximus and plunged Rome into a deep carnage.

'He is a narcissist, someone with an inflated sense of their own importance. Rajeev expects us to recognise him as superior,' she added.

'That is exactly that! He sounds so nice but there is something off about him!'

'Just like his house, it looks so clean!'

'Too clean!'

'Do you see the other tenants?' she inquired

'I know John, the black guy who lives opposite to me. He works in IT.'

'Yes, I see who you mean.'

'Anyway, tell me about Buddhism!'

'What would you like to know?'

'I like the philosophy and I would like to try.'

'I am amazed, why not!' she exclaimed.

'Do you think, you can save me?' he asked, a naughty smile printed on his face.

'Because you need to be rescued?' she giggled. 'The only thing, I can share with you is my belief. That practice helps me take responsibility for my life. At the moment, my health is my priority.

'I have nothing to lose,' he smiled.

'Ok.' She kept her eyes on this Polish man, who could hardly speak English. The contrary of Mr. Smith and definitely not the kind of person, she would associate with, not even as a friend. This guy was having dinner at her home, the day after she left the hospital. That same man was seeking enlightenment.

'Ready?' she met him the next day. —You are seeking happiness? We might as well start somewhere! What about tomorrow at eleven? Issata had suggested before they parted.

'Try me,' he laughed.

She presented the Gohonzon to him and explained the ritual. He preferred to sit on a chair, whereas she knelt as usual.

'What do I need to think about?' he asked curious.

'Very good question. First concentrate on reciting the syllables correctly. When you feel confident with the rhythm of your voice, naturally, everything concerning you will arise. Maybe you could chant to find work?'

'Do I have to say, I need to find work?'

'Just determine to find work between now and next week.'

'Next week,' he laughed, not convinced.

'You never know. But it is not magical. You must take action!'

'Ok.'

'Repeat after me, Nam-myo-ho-renge-kyo'

'It is not easy, to say' he giggled, trying.

'You will get used to it.' She led the prayers and listened to him dragging his voice behind her for two minutes, then rang the bell.

'How do you manage?' he let out, when she faced him.

'Now, you can try at home.'

He stared at her mysteriously. 'You are beautiful, you know.'

'Well, thank you,' a perplex voice responded.

'That was all I could think about! So, if I can't find work, it will be your fault,' he defended.

'You are cheeky!' she giggled.

'What about diner at mine, tonight?' He leaned towards her.

—Am I dreaming? Her eyes jumped out of her face.

—First, he saved my life and now, he wants to invite me to his place?

'I would you like to make you taste some Polish recipe.'

'Khrystian, I don't know what to say.'

'Say yes!' His gaze begged her. 'Only diner and nothing else,' he winked.

—Because, you actually think that something could happen? 'Ok, you have won!' she sighed.

'Hooorrrray!!!' his eyes beamed proudly. 'Come at seven.' He stood up and wore his jacket.

'You can start by looking for work then,' she smiled.

He left without commenting. She had no words. But her hormones were screaming to be heard.

'Are you the same woman, I left this morning,' Khrystian asked, amazed by her transformation when she presented herself at his door. A black jean was dressing her legs which we now know make a lot of men dream to caress. A beige jumper fitted to her torso, black lace decorating the round collar, was covering her girly chest and her prune mini boots highlighted the fact she was not as innocent as the description depicted.

'I am afraid yes!' she smiled, and her nostrils were greeted by a strong smell of stew.

'You are gorgeous, come in!' An effort was also observed on his part. He cleared his face from his beard and wore a black shirt which accentuated his wild and fragile side. His studio looked like hers, with one difference, he possessed a balcony. The table already set up, he suggested in his enigmatic smile, confident she would say yes: 'Some wine?' He was right. He served their glasses and 'Cheers,' they both let out. 'Please take a seat.'

Her eyes lingered towards the large pot placed on the electric cooker. The smell of the food made her sick.

'So, what's for dinner?' she wished to know while she executed herself.

'Bigos!'

'Bigos?'

'My country's specialty, made with pork, cabbage, onions, and red wine. It was in the freezer. It needs to be served extra hot, so it must boil for some time.'

'Oh?' she sighed. —Oh what? You didn't cook? —Oh, because you think it is normal to travel with food already cooked in a plane. —Oh, and how long did the food have to be cooked before it reached London? —Oh, and oh and oh!

167

'You will love it!' He walked towards the cooker and stirred slowly the cooking of his mother, with the wooden spoon already in the pan.

'I look forward to try it!' she lied.

'And what did you do when I left you? Khrystian continued, still busy in front of the stove.

'Nothing particular, I make some order in my flat and here I am.' —I was not going to tell him that I am horny since this morning? We don't know each, but I feel so itchy in the middle of my legs that I am afraid to not remember! It has been such a long time!

'I see,' he interrupted her thoughts.

—Surely, what am I thinking? Embarrassed that he could have heard her, she trembled.

'Tell me, how many people practice your Buddhism in the UK?' he pursued.

'Well, I don't know. Ten thousand, I think.'

'That is enormous!'

'Italy is the country with the highest membership in Europe.'

'It must be in their blood! Italian people are passionate. I had an Italian girlfriend, years ago.'

—He had an Italian girlfriend! Why is he telling me this? A bitter feeling squeezed her heart as if he had touched in her what she was finding intriguing in his person. She watched him bring the spoon to his mouth. He blew softly, before tasting the *bigos* of his mother. Sucking slowly, the end of the spatula, an exciting glow appeared in his eyes.

'It is ready!' he claimed victory and met her at the table carrying the huge pan. A brown and thick liquid landed on their plates. Issata fixed that maroon texture, in front of her, which resembled everything, except for an inviting meal.

'*Dobry Apetyt*' said Krystian in Polish.

'Good Appetite too,' she faked a smile. Then drank a slurp of wine before trying her first bite. She chewed the food like a connoisseur looking for specific's spices, subtleties between all aromas, which could help her express a fair critical verdict. She didn't like it. The food had been boiled for hours, and perhaps stewed for days before travelling from Poland to Luton airport, from the airport to the national express coach, from the national express coach to Kilburn, from the local buses to his home.

'So?'

'It is an interesting taste!' she concluded. The word interesting represents the most popular English expression. Everything is interesting in the mind of an English person. When someone behaves in a rude manner, a polite English person wouldn't say, what a cunt, not at all. They would express themselves in the most eloquent manner and would denounce: He or she has demonstrated a rather very interesting mood today, don't you think so, my dear? And when they differ in opinion, they wouldn't dare labelling you as an ignorant person. But they would admit that your participation has attired a lot of attention. At least, Issata knew how to juggle with the subtlety of the language.

'I am pleased that you love it! I will make you discover more dishes.'

—I have never said that I loved it! A fake smile still dressing her face; she washed the very interesting taste with more wine. 'And you? How was your day? You haven't said anything.

'I went to the Job centre. I have to sign on every week. Then I went to meet a friend.'

'A girlfriend?' She regretted her question, instantly.

169

—Surely, if he had a girlfriend, he wouldn't be spending the evening with me? —Maybe they had just split up? Maybe he is gay? —No, because he had an Italian girlfriend.

—Mind you these days, it is difficult to say. —Perhaps she had left him because of his mother's bigos. Within a fraction of seconds, Issata managed to write millions of theses in her head, in response to her single question. 'A girlfriend?'

'Would it matter?' A cheeky smile illuminated his face.

'Forget it, it was a stupid question.'

'No, I don't have any girlfriend! I want my freedom! What about you? Is there a man in your life?'

She could have told him that she was seeing somebody, but that he was too much in love with her and she dumped him because, like him, she wanted her freedom.

'No, I don't have anyone. Plus, I have my health problem' she hurried to conclude.

'I understand. But your bigos is probably cold now. Shall I warm it up!' —Again? I would be very lucky if I didn't have the turista tomorrow! 'That is fine!' She forced herself to finish that national Polish dish. She chewed ruthlessly, while he contemplated her as if admiring a oeuvre d'art. He caressed his lower lip, with his index finger, concentrating on the movement of her mouth, a childish pleasure animating his eyes.

'Thank you, it was really good,' she murmured.

'There is more, I can prepare some takeaway for you.'

'No, no, no, I am full! But I would like to smoke.'

'Of course, I should have suggested this to you. We don't have any more wine, though.' His look suggested an evident alternative.

Everything went fast. They got to her place. She prepared some drinks. Music was playing. They danced. He devoured her with a dangerous gaze. Her heart beat quickly. Before she could anticipate what was happening, Khrystian's mouth was sealing her lips. His big hands lost their way on her chest. She drove him to her bed. Their clothes flew everywhere in the room, to accommodate more daring touches. Both naked, Khrystian revealed a tool as huge and thick as an elephant horn, that he dressed with the appropriate accessory. Without warning, he plunged inside her, she gasped loudly, watching the fire in his eyes. His instrument grew to its capacity, while he visited her ferociously. She had to wrap her legs of warriors around his back, forcing him to go deeper in her fountain. They exchanged furious kisses and groaned noisy animalistic grunts until they couldn't hold anymore. One more deep push and they both exploded in a powerful climax. He laid on top of her, quivering, savouring the release of his milky stream. Slowly, he gained his breath. He pulled out from the warm place, the plastic jacket full of sperm. He rolled aside, holding the condom in one hand. Issata, overwhelmed by what had just happened, remained in her position. Tobacco smell, sex, sweat, alcohol embalmed the air. An enthralling silence reigned in the atmosphere. Who will break the silence? Khrystian volunteered by touching one of her feet. 'Did you like it?' his masculine voice investigated.

'Yes!' she let out, a confirmation that her orgasm was real! She turned to face him.
'Me too and where do I put this?' referring to the little bag, in his hand.
'In the bathroom, there is a bin,' she giggled.

171

He jumped out of bed. She heard him pee, then listened to the sound of the water coming from the tap.

—He washes his hands, it's a good sign! She thought, when she saw him, coming out of the bathroom.

'Do you want yours?'

She watched him, walking towards his pants and taking his cigarettes.

'Yes please.'

'Sex makes one thirsty.' He smiled and went back to the bed, their glasses still full of wine in his hands.

They smoked silently, inviting the nicotine to spread in their lungs. A strange malaise weighed in her. What was the reason for this? Her naked body, next to a masculine naked body, or the fact she just had sex with a stranger. The most frightening of all laid in the fact that a need to start again was eating at her. An eternity had passed by since a man could enjoy a glimpse of her expertise in the matter. The art to fornicate belonged to yesterday, those moments of her life. She attended many parties and made good use of the number of opportunities that presented themselves. She never brought back someone to her place. How did she survive? A panoply of gadgets waited quietly somewhere in a draw. One could discover a very interesting collection of toys:

—The Geishas balls, also called Venus balls; one day those naughty beads remained prisoners where you know. Panicked, she was doomed in her bed for ten minutes, because she didn't dare pull the string. Then a shiver crawled through her. She sneezed and the balls were free.

—Never again, she swore! She did it again because she liked the sensation. Her favourite is the silicone rampant rabbit, multi-speed, phenomenal, specialised on the 'G' spot! *Let's remember, she discovered the mystery of that precise location, thanks to Bach. The G spot, not the rabbit!*

'But tell me, is the mystic law, the same as the Kama Sutra?' Khrystian let out in the most natural manner, a man, in the truest sense of the term male, would want to know from a partisan, faithful to the mystic law. She burst into laughter. No one had even asked such a question.

'I don't know, I had never studied this disciple!'

'There are sixty-four positions. Maybe we can discover them together!' He embraced her in the neck and stroked the black point of her tit.

'Khrystian,' that was all she could let out.

'Issata, I love your energy! Do you know, I have never had sex with a black woman before you?' Falling from the clouds, she fixed him. —You have never had sex with a black woman; —What do you want me to say to this?

—I hope you are not one of those white men who fetishises black women. —Maybe there are no black people in Poland. Naturally, the colonial era, synonym to slavery period flicked through her mind. —Relating stories describing the white master, curious about this unknown beauty that every black woman carried; this unique beauty, which contains many names, such as: —different but intriguing, docile but fierce, wild but determined, black and proud, —she recalled the particular scene in *Roots*, where *Chicken Georges,* the grandson of *Kinta Kinte,* discovers that Tom More his owner had raped his mother and was his own father. —And the tale of *July,* a young slave, narrated as a memoir in the *Long Song* novel from *Andrea Levy, an English author.* The story is set in ninetieth century colonial Jamaica and the transition to freedom which took place thereafter. There was a white

173

master, Robert Goodwin, he was the son of an English Clergyman, revolutionary, pro-slavery abolition, who enjoyed an intimate relationship with *July,* his maid. Together they had a child. Then the Baptist war also known as *Christmas Rebellion* erupted, leading to the emancipation of the Jamaican slaves; therefore, the right of black people had to be honoured. Well, Goodwin forgot his liberal principles and hired white thugs to massacre their home and their livestock. That was what Khrystian's comments, '*I have never had sex with a black woman before you*' brought home to Issata. Why does everything have to be associated with skin colour?

'I have a vagina, like every woman,' she commented.

'Now I know that, and I would like to explore that African well, furthermore.'

'Suit yourself!'

'Only you can write such a story! Jimmy was so not surprised when she met him at his place, the next day. 'So, what is next?'

'He left this morning, and wants to meet tonight.'

'But do you like him?'

'Do you know what, he reminds me of someone! In his eyes, I read control, danger…'

'Daniel Smith,' Jimmy cut in.

'Exactly, I didn't dare thinking about it!'

'It sounds very mystic! After your successful man, you meet the jobseeker.'

'Surely Khrystian cannot be the response to my prayers?'

'Darling at least, you got laid!'

'I admit, last night, I felt so powerful! I was a completely different woman.'

174

'So, enjoy then!'
'I was meant to return to work, you know!'
'There is a message behind all this, no doubt!'
'Which one?'
'Nothing is stopping you to prepare your return to work.'
'It is just a weird situation!'
'Issata, enjoy what you have to live! And let's just say:
—Cinderella is not for you! So, let's observe how you get
on with Lady and the Tramp!' 'Jimmy!' » she exclaimed.
Together, they burst into laughter.

Khrystian's odour was still floating in her studio, when
she got home; an intense perfume of perspiration, sex, the
smell of a man, in which she wanted to bathe and fall
asleep. As she knelt in front of the Gohonzon, a knock was
heard.
'I told you I'd be back,' Khrystian defended, when she
opened her door.
'Yes, you told me so!'
She closed the door and he covered her with kisses.
'That's the only thing, I could think of!' he whispered.
Issata gave in and they performed what they experienced
the night before. They exploded in a violent cry.
Sounds of heavy and rhythmic respiration dominated the
atmosphere. Khrystian's lips rested on her neck. 'You are
my miracle,' he managed to blow to her ears. Issata had no
word. —First Mr. Smith, and he disappeared. And now I
am in bed with Khrystian, performing a new version of:
Lady and the Tramp.

A new chapter had begun! Issata and Khrystian. They met night and day for a specific purpose. Impossible to describe the carnal need unifying them. They fed it with an indescribable voracity. After all, he did suggest studying the Kama sutra.

Despite her acrobatic performances, with her lover, she welcomed her days, consumed with fatigue. Often, accompanied by violent urges to vomit. Nothing to do with premature pregnancy. Her symptoms were pronounced like the flu watching her. She felt worse and more disoriented. She began to question her new treatment. —Oral chemotherapy. 'I think my condition is getting worse,' she complained to Dr. Clark, but he insisted that she continued, assuring her that her body would adapt.

Jimmy met Khrystian at his friend's home. He offered to cook. And prepared some spaghetti Bolognese, Polish style. He added several slices of sausage. Jimmy discovered him, the same way Issata had painted that colossal guy, thug-like looking, the kind of geezer, a lot of women would try to rescue.

Here we are, 18th November!

That date represents the foundation of the Soka Gakkai, created in 1930 and the anniversary of the death of its first president, Tsunesaburo Makiguchi, in 1944. This movement spread thanks to its central pillar: Zadankai, a Japanese term regarded as a discussion meeting. These meetings serve in sharing the benefits of Nichiren Buddhism with others.

That morning, while sitting before her Gohonzon, Issata realised that she hadn't applied herself to her practice wisely, since the appearance of Khrystian in her life.

He spent more time in the middle of her legs and other parts of her body than her in front of her spiritual mirror.

Thoughts flew in her mind. Words were selected, as if she was trying to justify herself.

—That is the Sarcoidosis's fault! She chanted, but with no real conviction. She was searching for answers. Why my path crossed Khrystian? —How incredible that this man activates my sexual appetite! I want him all the time! Perhaps I suffer from nymphomania? —Surely not! Disgusted she felt! Dirty she felt!

Her eyes surveyed those black lines that she had studied at the beginning of her practise, because she was a good student. Thirty-four characters, she discovered. They all have profound meaning. The signs for the mystic law and Nichiren, if you had followed the story carefully, you already know where to observe them. But all the other signs, how to understand them? They simply represented all aspects of life, both positive and negative, as well as the ten worlds. There are also the natural elements that support us, such as the sun, the moon and even the stars. And Nichiren, the wise man, as we know him, used all these representations in the form of little figurines, borrowed from Buddhist iconography. Rather than just watching those lines, neatly drew on the Gohonzon, it offers a different perspective as to what we are looking at.

Issata was fascinated by four icons, beginning with Shakyamuni, the symbol of wisdom. He was the first recorded historical Buddha, known as: —Namu Shakamuni-butsu. 2500 years had passed by, since his birth. Heir of the Shakya, a small tribe whose kingdom was located alongside the Himalayas foothills, at a young age, his discovery in regard to the four sufferings of life, which he observed through being born in a troubled world, illness, old age and death, forced him to renounce his throne. Desperate to understand the fundamental cause of mankind suffering, he ventured himself through a spiritual quest, in order to find a solution. After years of studies and trying all kind of different religious schools, he decided to reject all of them, judging those ways, not suited for the answers, he was looking for. One day, sitting under a body tree, he meditated deeply and then reached enlightenment. Shakyamuni understood the true nature of life which spurred him to expound the Lotus Sūtra. In which he revealed his own illumination, according to people capacity to learn, to feel, to seek, to understand.

For fifty years, he travelled everywhere in India, sharing his comprehension of life with everyone on his path, and mainly explained how to access the immense potential, existing in each one of us. This is what we discover in his doctrine, exposed in the emblematic description of his interaction with a large assembly of buddhas. He points out the great benefits that could be gained in believing in it. After he had finished explaining the depth of his teaching, a gigantic "Treasure Tower" decorated with precious jewels, emerged from the earth, to the astonishment of his assembly and lifted all the participants into the air, disappearing far away into the sky. This event is described as: *The Ceremony in the Air*. Then a voice spoke from inside the tower, declaring that the Lotus Sutra expounded by Shakyamuni was the truth.

Shakyamuni confirmed to the assembly that the voice came from *Namu Taho Nyorai* also called *Taho*.

Taho Buddha is the second name she cared to remember. He is known as Many Treasures Thus Come One and recognised as the symbol of the law, that is to say the Teaching. According to the eleventh chapter of the Lotus Sutra, he lived in the world of The Purity of the Treasure, an eastern part of the universe. While he was still engaged in the practice of benevolence, he promised that even after he entered nirvana, he would appear, and attest to the validity of the Lotus Sutra wherever it would be taught. That moment came. Shakyamuni opened the tower, and, at the invitation of Many Treasures, sat beside him.

—Why Shakyamuni, himself opened the tower treasure? Issata had always wondered when she discovered his story.

Shakyamuni then, exhorted all people present, to support him in propagating the mystic law for the future time. And the propagation commenced.

She also met: —Kishimojin, known as the mother of Demonic Children, shown somewhere at the right-side bottom of the parchment. This mother, daughter of the demon Yaksha of Rajagriha, in India would have had 500 children. Some sources even say 1000 to 10,000.

—What a naughty woman, you were, Issata to joke! Apparently, she was also killing other people's babies to feed her children. —And psychopath on top of it! She had point out. The terrified and grieving population sought help from Shakyamuni. Master of wisdom, he hid Binkara, the youngest son of Kishimojin. Distraught, Kishimojin searched the world for seven days, but to no avail. In her despair, she finally approached the Buddha. Shakyamuni reprimanded her for her misbehaviour and had her pledge allegiance never to kill another child again. He returned his son and Kishimojin became venerated in India as the goddess who bestows the blessings of easy birth. Subsequently, her myth was introduced to Japan and in the twenty-sixth chapter of the Lotus Sutra, it is discovered that she and her ten daughters committed themselves before the Buddha to safeguard the practitioners of the Lotus Sutra.

And of course, —Dai Rokuten no Mao, recognised as the Demon King of the Sixth Heaven. He is the most formidable enemy of the Buddha who freely uses the fruits and efforts of human beings. His only pleasure rests on obstructing believers from their Buddhist practice. He enjoys seeing others suffer, seizing every opportunity to perpetuate bad causes.

She sat for hours praying from the emptiness of her life.

After all, it is the mystic law!

The law follows its course.

—You can do it! she reassured herself.

After nine months off work, she arrived at work by taxi. The last time she took the night bus, she didn't go back home. As she penetrated the terminal, she saw them all, in their uniform, impregnating the pride of Voyage Europe.

'Issata is back,' Kwame let out, when he saw her, heading in his direction and he welcomed her in his arms.

'Please sister, take care of yourself. I prayed hard for you!'

'Thank you very much brother!' He scanned her badge and she walked away, deeply touched. Michael, who saw her passing security, left the reception to meet her.

'Issata, I'm so happy to see you! We missed you so much.'

'I missed you too Michael,' she whispered. They hugged tenderly.

Stupor animated, the face of all, colleagues and travellers, when she stepped onto her floor. Their host was back. She was alive. They exchanged kind words and kisses.

To her surprise, she saw Pascal, coming out of the elevator, walking in her direction. She observed the costume in cheap material covering his skinny body. The kind of suit at the image of its owner, on which sweat remains well incrusted.

'Issata, it is a real pleasure to have you back!' he declared, when he reached her height. She fixed his light blue eyes, buried inside his eyelids. He was Asian from Hong Kong.

So, Pascal, the so-called manager of Issata, how can I describe him? A tall, skinny, very dry specimen, whose hair cut into a brush, made him looked like a hedgehog. His face beautified by red spots made his skin as hideous as his lack of capacity to care. His personality was as inexistant as his management skills. Do you see the picture?

—Right! Issata thought loudly. —Not once you contacted me, since I had fallen ill. Yet —*It is a real pleasure to see you,'* are your words to me. 'Thank you,' she answered politely.
'And if you need anything, we are here to help.'
She hesitated, then tried: 'Well, since you are asking, for now on I'm going to have to come by taxi to work. I was wondering if I could get some financial support with it?'
'Of course, leave it to me, I'll see what I can do!'
She watched him, walked off. — What a wanker, her pity wished to spit at him!

She pursued her shift, letting the compassionate comments of all, soothing her heart. 'Issata, is back!' 'Issata, we missed you!' 'Issata please keep well' rose around her.' Their kindness made her return special.

The time for her break arrived. She stepped out of the lounge, away from the terminal. Determined to regain her routine, she pulled on her cigarette thoughtfully. The smoke carried her, through the number of times, she had to quickly kill her Marlboro, afraid of missing his arrival. Then, a familiar scent emerged around her. This scent infiltrated her being. It belonged to her, for having breathed that aroma every Monday and having kept it safe in her fantasies.

—That's not possible! She glanced around her, watching the black taxis parked in front of Voyage Europe. Lighting up another cigarette she asked herself: —What if I was to see him today? She was frightened and excited at the same time. —I deserve an answer anyway!

Back to the lounge, she visited the ladies. While washing her hands, her iPhone rang. Her heart pumped madly.

—It is normally the time, he arrives.

'Yes,' her voice answered nervously.

'He is here,' Michael whispered.

'Who?' She already knew the answer.

'Mr. Smith! He's going through security.'

'I could feel felt it,' she mumbled.

'Now you know the truth, he can't play with you anymore,' Michael said very firmly.

She remained silent.

'He's coming.' He hung up.

Rushing out of the toilets, she looked towards her usual spot. —Yes, it is my job, but it is not stipulated anywhere in my contract, that I had to wait for him at the top of the stairs. Nor was it stipulated that I should get sick for a company whose staff's welfare was not at the heart of their business. A flame ignited her heart; not for the reason, we got to discover. The decor appeared the same, empty and noiseless, but the actress dressed a different role. Standing firm on her Amazonian legs, she positioned herself in the middle of the private area. —I need to know! Dan's feet stomped on the stairs and her vital engine trembled under the rhythm of that devilish melody, that air which stimulated her desire to believe. His odour grew in the atmosphere, and she recalled the first gaze they shared, his contagious smile and his enthralling voice. She shivered, desperate to run to the balustrade, to feel one more time, that breath of heat, crawling through her body, when he will lift his head. She didn't move an inch and perceived the reflection of his silhouette through the translucent divider. His shadow grew at the speed he was reaching the top of the stairs. She then froze when she met his eyes. Her nostrils quivered. Her heart dropped down her stomach. Dan's beauty was radiating through his manhood, his charm slid around the vastness of the room as if dropping spells of magic. And his intelligence controlled the destiny of his victims. —You seemed so perfect Dan! Those were the only words, covering the sphere of her brain at that crucial moment.

'Issata,' he called, marching towards her. His blue intense eyes fixed her. She felt so crucified. —You hurt me, Dan! she wished to scream. He reached her and kept her prisoner under his vicious stare. Searching for the courage to protect herself, a strong voice intervened inside: —I don't own the power to take away your eyes Dan, but I have the power to decide!

'I have waited for you,' her mouth said.

'I begged your pardon?' Dan arched his eyebrows.

Issata waited for a strangled breath to escape her throat and repeated: 'I have waited for you!'

Surprised, his eyes moved quickly. Then a ray of light illuminated his face.

'Didn't you get my message?' He plunged his hand into his jacket's pocket.

'What message?' She watched his finger scrolling on the screen of his iPhone.

'Here it is?'

She read: '*I am in the obligation to cancel our dinner tonight. I am rushing to New York. But I will make it up to you! I am missing you already! Yours, D.*'

She noticed the time; —12noon the text had been sent, but didn't go through. She smiled.

'I understand,' she pointed the warning sign on the screen.

'Oh no! I am so deeply sorry Issata! What can I do for you to forgive me?' He approached his hands towards her. She moved a step back while observing: —You are married, so get lost!

'It is best not Mr. Smith!'

'No more Dan?'

'No more Dan!'

'But Issata, is everything alright? I find you changed!'

—You find me changed? —I truly wanted to believe! Look where it led me! Nine months without any news from you! Possibly too occupied, to add more trophies to your hunting board. And now, you have no one to entertain your miserable existence. So, you are coming back to me! Little Issata, plus she is black! The black girl, who to the eyes of some white men, will always be the slave, ready to serve the master. —Yes, I have changed, she wailed inside!

'Mr. Smith, I am fine!' she let out. 'I just don't want to mix everything!' she added, raising her chest, and letting her arms fall, alongside her body.

'Please, give me a chance!' He copied her posture, his blue eyes sealed to her brown eyes, he caressed her fingers deliberately. A sexual chill ran through her body. Her heart ran quickly. It was tempting. She was anticipating the ride. His gaze became the master of her senses. She foresaw his lips, kissing her neck; crazy, she was going. She wanted him badly. A warm liquid escaped from her private lips and the boarding was announced. Rapidly, she removed her hand.

'Goodbye Mr. Smith,' came out from her mouth.

185

'Issata, I am coming back tonight. Why don't you meet me at the Ritz for dinner?'

—Don't you ever stop?

'Goodbye Mr. Smith,' she repeated again.

'After, I will remain in New York for several months. I have a big case to deal with.'

She kept her silence.

'Anyway, I still have your number. I will call you.'

He walked away, the same way he arrived.

She watched him going down the stairs and murmured:

'*Voilà comment ce lundi-là, il s'en allait.*' This song is a reference to Michel Delpech the French singer.

'My dear, I was waiting for you.'

Her eyes rolled when she saw Rajeev in front of the house.

'Hello,' she forced a smile.

'I see, you are back to work?'

'As a matter of fact, yes!'

'Do you feel better?'

'Fine, thank you. And what did you want?'

'I am actually looking after the problem with the council tax. You know how it is, with bureaucracy?'

'So?'

'Well, they want a testimony of all tenants residing in the propriety.'

'But can't use the contracts?' she verified surprised.

'I am just trying to speed up the process,' he defended.

'Ok, I will write my statement!'

'Many thanks my dear, truly appreciate it! Take care of yourself!'

'Goodbye!' she said and rushed inside her flat. Her back against the door, she burst into tears. —I have succeeded!

Now I must get rid of Khrystian! Our relationship is so not healthy! In fact, it is not even a relationship! We are both sex addicts.

'We are so happy to see you!'

'We missed you!'

'Issata is back!'

'My children did a drawing for you.'

'You are the soul of the lounge!'

Two weeks since her return, messages of welcome landed in the human resources office. They congratulated Voyage Europe, for having found a gem. Of course, Issata was more than touched. Did Voyage Europe really appreciate her talent?

13ᵗʰ December, she turned thirty-eight. Jimmy, Khrystian, Michael, and a few colleagues participated in the celebration.

Christmas, she went to Paris. Khrystian flew to Poland.

—*Honey, we are expecting you for New Year's Eve!* The invitation from Agnes, she was so dreading. —I so don't want to see her, she sighed when she read her email!

—And there is Khrystian! Somehow, something in her, enticed her to ask: 'Can I bring someone?' Sure, little sausage! was her reply. Her heart danced with excitement. —For once, someone will be my side!

Both very well-dressed, Issata and Khrystian made their way to Agnes by taxi. Her eyes dropped from her face when she saw him dressed in black, from head to toe, except for the woollen white scarf, cascading on both sides of his shoulders, because elegance didn't seem to fit with his lifestyle. Yet, that evening, a cap covering his head, added a special touch to his dirty blond hair. He had on a cashmere coat, over a fitted silky suit, which enhanced a shirt, slightly opened, on the muscled body, she cared fucking with. Armed with some Charleston shoes, he looked like the gangsters from the fifties.

'You told me they were leading a very expensive lifestyle, so I made an effort,' he answered to the surprise on her face.

'I see that.' She also rolled the dice and slid into a strapless black lacy dress, retro style, cut straight, embellished by a silver bow tie beneath her bust. To refine her look, she dressed her feet in her glittery Minnie's pumps. Twenty minutes of drive and: 'Look at this house!' Khrystian exclaimed when they got out of the taxi.

'Wait till you see inside!' Issata pressed the doorbell.

'Honey, I am so happy to see you! You look good!' a voice greeted them.

'Good evening, Agnes, thank you for having us, this is Khrystian.'

'I see...!'

Khrystian remained glued to this Scandinavian beauty.

The texture of her white pearly skin, similar to sweetened condensed milk, did not leave him indifferent. But it was her luscious lips painted in red, which accelerated his heart beat. It reminded him of: —*Egyptian women! That's right! Everything seems to lay on Greek mythology! The story tells, painting one's lips in red denounced one's sexual preferences. Even more so, that statement evoked a clear message! My mouth is consenting to practice oral sex. And for a woman to expose herself in such a way, she must feel confident in her skills. Cleopatra herself loved to paint her lips in red. Her dress code must have influenced Caesar to marry her or what she did for him! All this to confirm that the red lipstick was already fashionable in ancient Egyptian culture and these women were definitely experts in performing BJ, initial for blowjob, whereas in French, that special activity is contemplated as 'Tailler la pipe'.*

That is very clear, that these women loved sex in all its shapes, especially the shaping of the pipe. So why so much fascination with fellatio? Have you ever heard about the myth of Osiris and Isis? Osiris the god of the afterlife and death was killed at the hands of his own brother Set, the god of storms, violence, and chaos. He cut his body into pieces and scattered them all over the world. What a tragic death for the poor chap! Isis, in addition to being Osiris' wife, was also his own sister. Antiquity represented the time when many royal houses practiced incest to preserve the purity of their lineage! Thank God, thank Buddha, or thank someone, because today incest is a crime! A forbidden crime! Devastated, she ventured around the world, searching for the body parts of her precious love, with her mission to bring him back to life. And she found them! But, but, but, but, but, a small problem arises, I will even say a

big problem. His willy was missing. —Guess what she did?
She made him a willy in clay and blew life to it! —How?
I let you use your imagination. Thinking of it, this is where
the expression 'Tailler une pipe' comes from! An Egyptian
romance. Morality dear readers, all experiences matter.
Thanks to Isis's infinite compassion in blowing life into her
fetish tool, so many sex toys exist and Ann Summers is
recognised worldwide.

'Nice meeting you Khrystian,' Agnes opened her arms and
brushed herself against him, placing two huge kisses on his
rough cheeks. Her red lips touched the hollow of his ears
as if she was whispering a message to him. He held her in
his unique way, the left hand on her shoulder and the right,
sealing her waist. A kick of jealousy hit Issata. That was
how he held her.

'Nice meeting you too, Agnes,' he breathed, a gleam of
admiration shining in his eyes, which Issata, didn't fail to
notice.

'Let's get the party started!'

A jubilant pleasure emerged from Khrystian, when they
crossed this famous interminable corridor, leading them to
the dining room. Abdul and the other guests were happily
quenching their thirst already.

'Issata' Abdul called, advancing towards them. In line with
his Hindou Somalian beauty, always maintained by the
elegance of its tailored suits, he sported a traditional outfit,
in silk red and gold embroidery which consisted of a
sherwani, a long jacket falling over pants.

'Good evening, Abdul,' she hugged him.

'My dear, you are beautiful!' He stood away from her,
holding her hands. 'I heard what has happened to you. You

look like new! And I am so happy to see you, before moving away.'

'How come?' she asked surprised.

'You haven't told her darling?' Abdul looked towards his wife.

'I was going to announce it tonight. Yes, we are going back to Sweden temporarily. But you two will have to come and visit!' She smiled taking a stand by her husband, where the mistress of the house owes to be.

'Great news!' Issata didn't know if she should rejoice.

'Why don't you introduce Khrystian, to Abdul?' Agnes fidgeted around her husband, grabbing his hand.

—You have just done it, typical of you! You always have to be the centre of attention; she was about to let out but bit her tongue and said: 'Indeed, here is Khrystian!'

Both men fixed each other, as if inspecting their manhood.

'Good evening, Khrystian, I am Abdul. You do take care of our friend, I hope?'

'Good evening, Abdul, you should ask her,' he smiled and accepted his hand.

'I will!' he paused, checking him out. 'But give me your coats and darling Agnes look after our guests, will you?'

'Certainly Abdul,' she stole a kiss from him.

They removed their coats and mixed with the other guests. Agnes made the presentations. When her husband joined back, she offered a toast:

'My dear friends, Abdul and myself are very happy to celebrate that New Year's Eve with you. And like most of you know already, we are moving to Sweden at the end of the month of January. You are obviously, all invited!'

The guests clapped.

'I would also like to offer a special toast to my dear friend Issata, who has fallen very ill but is on the mend. And I am even more delighted to finally see her with a man by her side.'

Self-conscious with embarrassment, she felt a painful warmth rising through her cheeks and her anger burning her eyes. —You didn't? —Thank you for reminding me that I was always the one alone at all your parties. Dominated by her own humiliation, she didn't take notice of the comments around her. In that instance, she was begging to be buried alive. Khrystian, witnessing her uneasiness, smiled at her and raised his glass. 'Cheers!' he let out.

Issata felt obliged to follow the mood of the evening.

'Yes, thank you, and cheers to you all!'

They drank up their fizzy drink, then Abdul escorted the crowd to a luxurious dining room. A feast for ten people was prepared. And the children? They were all teenagers, so diner was served in a private room. As soon as all guests sat, Issata noticed that Khrystian's beaming eyes were constantly heading in Agnes direction. And she caught her sending smiles which she had found suggestive. Abdul on the other hand, seated next to his wife, didn't seem preoccupied. In fact, they all looked clearly joyful. So why was she feeling a strange vibration resonating in her? A feeling of not belonging, a chorus which she knew so well. Her African nostrils shuddered, each time she watched them exchange quick glances, followed by an uncomfortable squeeze stabbing her heart. —Surely, I am not jealous.

4

I want you,' these words pronounced by an enflamed voice, announced the beginning of *The Year of Victory for a youthful SGI'* for 2013. That same voice spurred a determined hand to palpate the little grains sticking out of Issata's chest, while the other one, made its way blindly towards a tight fissure difficult to access, especially when its borders are closed. Unable to express a word, she felt a huge lump rubbing, below her back, a mouth licking her neck, some teeth nibbling her right ear. This is when images from the party surged in her mind. She wrestled, looking to envisage the chronology of their night. Khrystian, desperate to take his breakfast in bed, tried to turn her around.

'No, I want to sleep,' she answered, with a dry mouth.

'I will be fast,' he insisted, pressing against her.

'I am telling you that I am sleepy!' she pushed him.

'Please, last night, you fell asleep. We couldn't do anything.' Excited, he grabbed her buttocks.

'Are you mad or what?' Her elbow landed violently in his stomach.

Shocked, he let go of his prey.

'What is wrong?' He fixed the black woman, discovering how strong she was.

'What's wrong with me? You were going to force yourself inside me?'

'We have shared so much together! Watching you lying naked, in a posture that is so you excited me.

'I excited you!' she threw, that is when Agnes face came into her mind. Her little smile, her eyes always directed at Khrystian and the way she kept touching him, like a female dog in a need of a good fuck.

'Listen Issata, if you don't want, it doesn't matter! We will do it later!' He pleaded, trying to hold her.

'Do you think, I didn't see you?' She abruptly pushed, his arm.

'What are you talking about?'

'Agnes here, Agnes there! What a wonderful host you are!'

'Are you jealous or what?'

'Why? Should I?'

'I think you are still drunk and I should let you rest.' Khrystian began to push the duvet. —What? Her mind lost track. —That's all you have to say? —I know you want her. That is why you are finding excuses to leave early. You have planned everything together, right? —You won't get away with this! Khrystian noticed the change in her body instantly and absorbed the odour that her hormones produced when she was excited. The spicy smell was so enthralling.

'Yes, it matters!' Issata pushed the blanket away and climbed on top of him. 'You still want me? I am going to show you!' Her mouth grabbed his lips and she kept Khrystian's tongue prisoner to hers. Both organs swirled, on the same tempo, like twin sisters. They stretched, stomped, and pressed, reciprocally. Which of which will swallow the other one? Well in control, Issata established the rules. As she was going up and down, on top of Khrystian, she could feel her own elixir, springing out from her source, scrawling alongside her thighs. It went rapidly.

194

The wild animal, vibrating inside her, grew each time she swayed. In a hard hit, escaped from her pelvis, an intense tremor. A seism, which inspired her, the sensation of the cold wind, during the winter season, similar to those slaps which keep your face frozen in your memory. A violent moan, forced her to contract her intimate muscles which lead to explode in an exciting feeling. She quivered so generously, that the sound of her pleasure stimulated Khrystian to cum too.

'I don't know what to say!' he sighed, catching his breath. 'I just made your wish come true, that's all!'
'Yes,' he mumbled, 'It's just that I didn't recognise you. You were like another woman!'

'And, you don't like it?' she provoked him.

« Not at all! » A fake smile, masked his voice. 'I think, I must go now, because I have to call my parents.'

—Your parents! 'Good Idea, because, I go back to work tomorrow.'

He got off the bed and disappeared to the bathroom to pee. She was smoking when he joined her. She watched him slid in his clothes silently. He came close to her.
'We catch up later,' he whispered to her ears and placed a peck on her lips. —Right, it's Agnes, that you would rather visit, she murmured after he closed her door.

The salon was overcrowded with passengers. The regulars turned up on time for the rendezvous of the year. She offered her wishes to all of them, neatly wrapped by the ribbons of her warm embrace. She met Pascal who informed her that Katia, one of her colleagues from the train, would cover Thursdays and Fridays, the days she didn't work. Katia was a loud little brunette, trapped in a Brazilian body. I leave you to guess her measurements. Issata did not find any inconvenience at the news but felt so let down when he told her that her taxi's allowances could only be granted if she started at half-past five. That was VoyE policy.

—Whatever! Just kill me, she could only think. That response not anticipated, destabilised her. The days which follow, she experienced heavy headaches and the muscular pain reiterated with violence, as if the flame always visiting the same part of her body, responded to a stimulus. She decided to keep a clear record regarding each setback. One morning, she lost count of who she was and where she was going. Panicked, she trembled with fear. Her eyes blinked on the tempo of her beating heart. Alone in the middle of the night, her voice resonated in her head. The seizure began to nag her and in the movement of her eyes, she managed to recognise a key element, which illustrates Voyage Europe's location: the big clock build on the building of the station. Tears of relief rolled down her cheeks. She mentioned that episode to Dr. Clark. 'Those neurological troubles belonged to the neurosarcoidosis symptoms. We need to keep a close eye on it,' he reassured her.

—Darling, I hope to see you this Sunday at the Zad. I have invited Khrystian, I think, it will be better for him to meet the men in the group. Ag.X.
Issata received that message, two weeks after the New Year Eve's celebration. She was one hundred metres away from the entrance of the terminal.

196

Let's remember that the *Zad* or *Zandankai* represents the monthly Buddhist meeting, members attend at the end of each month. In this instance, the January reunion was scheduled earlier. Reading the message, there was nothing offensive in it. After all, Agnes a fervent bodhisattva of the earth was only putting into practice the lotus sutra's theory: —To take action in encouraging others to reveal their potential. But in Issata's mind, in the heart of a woman, who has been racking her brain for years as to how to approach a sensitive subject such as their friendship, that message was not acceptable. Plus, —Why did Khrystian never mention anything? Standing against the wall of the station, she reassessed the words in her brain. —Who do you think you are? Her anger woke up, that was enough! —You love playing the diva! —Here is your scenario! She typed on her iPhone, like a secretary expert in shorthand typing, her tears running on her cheeks, throwing up her anger. She looked like those poor people, suffering from gastroenteritis. A deep cleaning had commenced and that negligence coming from Agnes's part denounced the result of a large wound that had been infected for many years. Now everything had to come out. She sailed throughout her souvenirs where one night, in particular, marked the birth of that fissure that expanded as time went by. They had met at their local pizzeria and Agnes spent the whole evening talking about herself. Not once, did she question her friend's feelings? —*A real movie!* —*Can you not shut up; she was dying to yell on many occasions?* —*No, keeping her mouth shut was not part of her education.* —*What about Issata? Couldn't she tell her to keep quiet? It looks like expressing herself was not her strength either. She mainly didn't want to hear, her famous argument: This*

197

is who I am! Because it was true, Issata couldn't change her. So, who was at fault? Agnes, with her big mouth? Or Issata for not being able to be assertive?

At that precise moment, it didn't matter anymore. She pressed the send touch and listened to the *swish* sound, proof that her message had been sent.

—I truly hope that you will reflect on yourself, now. Because precisely, this is who you are!

Feeling exposed by her behaviour, she walked towards the entrance. She was about to cross the doors when her eyes met the image of the black woman. —You? A cerebral hysteria took over her brain. —That's her fault! She forced me, she yelled. Her sight multiplied. Then nothing.

She ended up at A&E. The result showed that the sarcoidosis was progressing in her brain and lungs. But Dr. Clark's reservation laid in her mental state and insisted, she commenced a therapy. Jimmy joined her and met the consultant. 'Issata, he is right! Don't ruin your life!' he begged her.

A week later, she was discharged. Dr Clack advised her GP, Dr Vanessa to keep her off work for at least a month and that he referred her to a psychiatrist.

No news from Agnes, let alone Khrystian. He didn't answer her calls, nor reply to her texts.

'I had to leave for Poland! Good Luck KX' said the note she found with Jimmy slid through the door, when she reached her flat.

'We go to my place!' he decided.

'Why is everything happening at the same time? I can't even explain what is most hurtful? Agnes' betrayal or Khrystian's departure?' she sobbed, sprawled on Jimmy's sofa.

'You will find your answers.'

'The answer is to stop my Buddhist practice!'

'You are kidding?'

'Buddhism brought all those problems to me! My life would be better if I stop desiring. It hurts to dream! Dreams are not real! Jimmy, tell me that I am right, she wailed!'

'Do you know what, I find it very interesting that Khrystian disappears at the same time, you are having a conflict with Agnes?'

Surprised by the remark, she analysed the equation in her mind. 'But he doesn't know about my relationship with Agnes!'

'That is the mystic law responsibility, isn't it?' he smiled.

'The mystic law,' she sighed. 'He left without saying goodbye!' her voice trembled.

'Issata, now is the time for you to take care of yourself! Stay here as much as you need. But I want my friend back, the Issata, I know!'

'Issata Sherif?' A hoarse voice, with a distinctive Latin nuance, called her name.

She rose to her feet and faced a woman dressed in a prune suits trousers, shedding the light on her cream turtle neck jumper which enhanced her fair skin. Beneath her frizzy black boyish cut, she incarnated the image of a modern woman in her late fifties, whose life's experience was engraved on her face but whose eyes shone with a sincere desire to help others.

'Hello, I am Dr. Benedict,' she added… *And Lady Kondo to say, I will refer to her as Dr. B, because B. is shorter to write.*

'Hello,' Issata replied and followed her into a spacious office. The walls were painted in lilac. A black desk made of ebony wood, and two chairs in brown leather furnished the room. But it was the immense black and white photography suspended on the wall, which attracted her attention most. It was composed of several children from diverse nationalities, laughing and playing together. The photographer succeeded in capturing the soul of each kid, their enthusiasm and innocence; the candour of the little living beings destined to achieve huge dreams. She later discovered that the artist was none other than Dr. B.

'Please take a seat.'

Nervous, she took off her black woollen coat and sat in front of B. who did the same.

'Can I call you Issata?'

She nodded affirmatively.

'You were referred to me by Dr. Clark. So first, I would like to tell you about myself rapidly. I have been a therapist for twenty years and I am fifty-five. I chose that profession because I had to undergo therapy myself which saved my life. That is why I decided to help others.'

Her approach touched her heart. She could hear the words of an experienced woman, a human being who chose to use her life to help others. 'Not everyone benefits from therapy, however, it is important to try and I am pleased to see that you are willing to try.' She took a deep breath and added:

'You know my story so why don't you tell me about you?' Her voice accompanied by a tender stare watched out carefully.

'Like what?' escaped from her lips.

'Like what brings you here?'

—What brings me here, she repeated in her head?

During her time at jimmy, only her suffering mattered.

—That's all, I have, she would cry! Suffering represented her story. A story, she didn't want to read, nor write anymore; a story, she clearly didn't want to use as her handbook for life anymore. Yet Life, the greatest scriptwriter of the universe kept offering her the same scenario. Issata always accepted the role. Why couldn't she turn it down?

—Karma, I always go back to it, she observed! —If karma is something that occurs continuously, it is not by hiding at Jimmy's that I will change it! She decided to start therapy.

'I am angry!' she wailed. Her face entered into a stage of decomposition. The veins in her eyes were ready to explode and she burst into tears. She threw everything contained in her heart. —Work? They have let me down! The illness? I am a codeine addict. Agnes and Khrystian? I hate her! — He disgusts me! 'I'm just tired of being alone! All I wanted was to meet someone and live in a beautiful home. It is too much to ask?' Tears flooded her face.

B, wanted to know what happened when her rage emerged. 'I scream in my head! And I talked to myself!' 'How do you calm down?' 'I guess through writing, and I am a Buddhist. I like to go to the park too.' 'Your family?' She confessed that she was angry with Mum.

B looked at her deeply.

'Have you ever heard about a condition called bipolar?'

'I am not manic depressive!' she exclaimed

'So, you know?'

'That is an illness of the mind! I am not mad!'

'Bipolar can become an illness of the mind, if not discovered on time and treated. Having said that, it is mostly regarded as mood instability.'

'I know all this, and that is not me! I am not a hyperactive woman who falls into depression most weeks after a rush of adrenaline!' she defended, tears burning her eyes.

'We can be bipolar without suffering from hypomania.' She looked at B, perplexed.

'Issata, I am only trying to envisage all kinds of possibilities. That anger that dominates your life comes from a deep suffering. We are going to discover it together. I am going to prescribe you some lithium carbonate, to help you stabilise your mood, and I would like to practice with you what we call CBT.

'What is it?'

'It stands for cognitive behaviour therapy, a therapy goal orientated. This method lies in helping us change our perceptions and habits by placing the emphasis on thoughts, values, behaviours and beliefs. The concept is simple.

If our thoughts guide our vision of life and consequently our reactions, by changing how we view the problem, we can then transform our perception and obviously chose the appropriate action to tackle our struggles.'

'If you say so! I just want the anger to go!'

'I am determined to help you unlock all mechanisms behind your emotion.' She sighed. 'Shall we meet weekly for a month?' Issata nodded and the session ended.

Lithium pills played their trick. She felt the big difference from the first antidepressants, she had tried. B confirmed that it was a slow process. She found herself meeting the relaxed woman in her.

March 1st, on her return to the lounge, Pascal informed her that for the business need, VoyE had decided to keep Katia. —For the business's need, she repeated silently. Her hope to return to full-time had just vanished. She watched the one door, she had worked hard to keep open, shutting itself brutally. For Voyage Europe, she was only a number.

—Please, not him, her eyes screamed out of her face, when she saw Rajeev coming out of his car.

'Hi Issata,'

'Hi Rajeev,'

'Sorry to disturb you, but I think we have to renew the contract.'

'Yes indeed, next time let me know in advance, as I am just back from work.'

'Of course, my deepest apology. I have it with me.'

'Ok, follow me!'

'Thanks, and how is your health?' he asked when they entered her studio.

'Getting there,'

'I have noticed that you and Khrystian were quite close'

'Listen, are you here to sign a contract or to talk about my personal life?'

'I didn't want to interfere.'

'You just did!'

'I am very sorry! Regarding the contract, you have to pay the council tax now.'

'Why?'

'Because that is the law!'

'If that is the law,'

'But there is a little problem,'

'What again?' she snapped, losing patience.

'You have to pay for the arrears'

'How come? I thought you have dealt with it!'

'I have tried but you are responsible to pay because you live here and you wrote a statement.'

'What?' Her eyes grew big.

'You admitted it!'

She fixed him and identified the monstrosity inherent in his life. His eyes shone with evilness. Staring at him, she thought to herself: —From the moment, I met him, I knew, there was something twisted about you. Her intuition being confirmed, she let out: 'You have used me! I know I shouldn't have written that statement!' She felt so itchy on her fits, that she was ready to knock him off.

'My dear, I am just informing you about the situation, because I am an honest man!' he smiled.

Her anger rising to come out, she exclaimed strictly: 'Get out of my house!'

'And the contract,' his dilated eyes exclaimed? The veins in his pupils ready to explode turned red. He looked like a drug addict in need of his fix.

'Since you are an honest man, get advice about your rights and I shall check out mine as a tenant.'

'My dear, you are so not well that is why I forgive you,' he sneered. She slammed her door.

She was in a mess when Dr. B, welcomed her into her office. Ok, she couldn't gain her job full-time. But she had the option to move out. And according to Jimmy, everything happened for a reason. She registered with estates agents looking for the perfect flat. Because everything had to be perfect for Madame Sherif. Despite the amounts of actions she took, she was not finding anything within her budget. Or if so, there were pure slums.

Council tax had to be paid. And since she was still living in the property, she paid. She didn't receive any bills in arrears. —Maybe Rajeev was just trying to make money from me, she deducted with disgust in her heart. He didn't approach her either, since. But his car was parked in front of the house. The sight of the monster, stationed in the street, made her sick. She would hear his nasal voice and uneducated timbre. Trembling with anxiety, and fear knotted in her stomach, her heart would race at the thought of seeing him. She couldn't stand him! His whole being repulsed her. She became convinced that he deliberately kept his car parked at that specific spot to make a point. — You will never be important with such a desperate voice; she would scream in her heart. —That is your punishment! Your voice is your identity, you will always hear it.

Working for Voyage Europe could be inscribed in the annals of the saddest moment of her existence. Issata would just cry on her way to work. She described her experience as being a suspect under judiciary review who had to present herself at their headquarter Monday to Wednesday at half-past six in the morning. The only element missing was a bracelet tag. But she still had a badge to swipe. She was left alone in her battle to gain her health back. And solitude followed her home as an ever-present reminder that she had become ill doing her job. It had become her world, an immense continent, cold, empty, and ugly. It represented her only dependable friend. Loneliness dragged her around inside a grand and heavy coffin full of despair, hurt, memories, painkillers, pills, and anger. That was the life of Issata Sherif, who was looking for Mr. Right to dance through life with.

In October, a studio flat appeared on the market in her area, at the same price as her own flat and inclusive of bills. She contacted Rajeev straight away, to give him her notice, and asked him to present her with proof that her deposit had been put in a deposit scheme, as per the law. From the sound of his voice, she knew he hadn't followed the procedure. She packed everything ready to move out. Having given three hundred pounds to secure her new home, she had one week to obtain a reference from her landlord. The day of her moving, as she was finishing her shift, the agency called her to say that Rajeev refused to give her reference, therefore she couldn't move into their property. Devastated, she called to try to reason with him, but he insulted her, shouting the worst language a man of his age could possibly express. Shocked and scared for her life, her instinct drove her to the police station. An officer called Rajeev, reminding him of his legal obligations, and gave him a verbal warning.

—Why, she cried, back home, looking at all the boxes packed in the room? Everything seemed to be linked to her desires. —Mr. Right and the right flat, two simple and natural desires and yet impossible to achieve for Issata. Desires can draw the greatest suffering from one's life, such as a woman not being able to conceive, that gift unique to women, a man embarrassed to find himself always at the bottom of the ladder, for not being able to shine in the eyes of his family, his friends, his colleagues. However, desires can also become the source of a catalyst for growth, explains Nichiren's doctrine. —Guide me, her eyes begged her Gohonzon.

What about the deposit? She sought legal advice and was able to get her three hundred pounds back.

18ᵗʰ November, she met Dr. Clark who informed her that the ACE level had increased. 'It is time to consider, intravenous treatment,' he suggested. —Whatever Gary Grant, her mind replied when she left him. He was not as charming as in his role in the movie: '*To Catch a chief.*'

—Is that what it is? People have to die to receive the support from the universe? In front of her Gohonzon, her tears crawled on her face. —Nich, you said it yourself:

'I Nichiren inscribed my life in Sumi ink, believe in this Gohonzon with your whole life.' What is there to believe? I thought that chanting Nam-myoho-rengekyo connected to everything. —I am just a lost cause! My body is proof of it!

Her 39 candles, she blew them with Jimmy. He offered her to move in with him. His offer sounded perfect. It was so simple! — However, it wouldn't explain WHY, she realised. —Why have I fallen sick, when I felt ready to find a soul mate? —Why when I decided to buy a flat, I was not able to have my position back full-time.

—Why didn't Rajeev let me go?

5

Daisaku Ikeda declared 2014 as *'The Year of Opening a New Era of Worldwide Kosen Rufu'*.
A new era gives rise to change. Issata entered that new turn, still overwhelmed by her time in Paris. For once in her life, she needed her mother. She had wished to tell her how lonely she felt.

—How can I ever open a new era when I can't even leave this place? —How to draw faith, when I have never experienced it, she prayed with her heart and soul? Working was not bringing her joy anymore, even more so when she received a letter, informing her that the contract in the lounge will terminate at the end of May.
'We are looking forward to having you back on board the train in July as per your original contract, that was how the notice ended. I am not surprised, she concluded!
—But what future lays ahead of me? I am the prisoner of a chronic illness, eating me from the inside. An invisible illness that only my suffering makes it visible!

She pursued her sessions with B.
'Issata, would you be that desperate to move out if you didn't have those differences with your landlord?' B, asked her one day. Instinctively, she shouted: 'I hate him! That man is evil! B observed the pain expressed through her traumatised eyes. For the first time, after many months of

therapy, she could read in them, a pain, associated to an experience, which tainted her stare with sadness and loss.

'You despise him, that is a choice but by dedicating so much energy in hating him, it will be difficult for you to advance. 'You can't understand me! What if each time, I find a place he refuses to give me a reference?'

'I understand perfectly Issata! At the moment, you need to free yourself from this rage and I have faith in you. I sense that a terrible wound exists within you and is revealed through your light brown eyes. This pain is affecting your vision of the world. Don't let it destroy you. Your experience will help you to grow and you will touch many people.'

At that moment, a metaphor, her mentor had used on many occasions to illustrate the concept of karma, came to her mind. *'No matter how much we polish a mirror, if we don't polish our own life, the reflection will still be the same.'*

She knew that her therapist was right. From the mystic law point of view, the environment only responded to the profound cause deeply rooted in her life. —I don't know what are the causes yet, but I must focus on gaining her health back. She decided to stay. As she made that choice, she felt a real sense of freedom emanating from her life.

Maybe that is what it means to have faith, she contemplated? All her stuff returned to its original place.

The month of February manifested as fast as January ended. One afternoon, while she observed her nap, she heard loud knock on her door. She woke up suddenly. Her heart beat at a rapid speed. She checked the time on her iPhone.

—4pm, she read! The knock erupted again.

'Who is this?' she let out, trembling.

'It's me Rajeev!'

The sound of his nasal voice made her sick.

'What do you want?'

'Can you open the door for me please?'

—Why? she was so tempted to reply. She rose to her feet, reluctant to be standing next to him.

'Have you found a place?' he inquired when they faced each other.

'As you can see, I am still here!'

'Listen, I am deeply sorry for my behaviour. Sometimes, I get frustrated and I lose it. You are like a sister to me. I am not chasing you. Stay as much as you like.'

—Is he serious? All these months without news? She fixed him shocked. That man who vomited the worse insanities was saying, sorry.

'I have the new contract with me. Let's sign it and I leave you in peace.'

She fixed him. Torn, she knew she had nowhere to go. She swallowed her pride.

'Fine!' she sighed.

He pulled out from his pocket a piece of paper folded into four.

'One more thing, I increased the rent to twenty-five pounds more,' he said without looking at her.

'Ok!'

'Thank you so much for accepting my apology. I am indebted to you,' he expressed after they signed the agreement and left.

Minutes later, she hears him say: 'She is not leaving and I can't throw her out. She is paying the rent.'

—Who is he talking to?

—That is not possible, her mind screamed, when she saw him the next day, standing in the communal kitchen. He was facing the sink. Her heart drummed like the train will whistle three times. She inspected this giant guy, his torso covered with a stripe blue jumper. His blond dirty looking hair caressed his large and square shoulders. A jeans protected his military legs and, faithful to himself, he had his white trainers on. His presence sent her back to those months, where she wanted to believe it could work. His absence haunted her everyday life. It pounded under the sound of a bell, the sound of that desperate gong that attracted Khrystian in her life as a reflection of her own solitude. — No, she moaned in her heart, petrified that this man who transported her to places, she had never visited before, would doom her to go back. Breathing deeply, she kept her laundry basket against her belly and moved towards him. 'You are back?'

Khrystian turned around slowly. She stopped halfway. He undressed her with his gaze, like a hunter provoking his prey. His eyes slid all over her. She shivered and felt the hairs in her panties, bristling on her skin. His look reminded her, his skilful hands on her body. He was a proud man and he controlled her. Paralysed by her own desire, she was already anticipating his return in her African well.

'Yes,' he responded softly. 'Sorry, I am using the washing machine.'

'I will come back later.' She was about to walk away.

'Issata wait!' How many times, did he whisper her name to her ears.

'*Issata you excite me...Issata I am coming...*' He walked towards her.

'How are you?'

212

—How am I? You left without giving me any news and you wonder about my state of being. If she had a machine gun, instead of her eyes she would shoot him, until his body turned into a porridge of blood.

'I am fine!' she succeeded in replying.

'You do look well.' He lifted his right hand and stroked her face with one finger.

'What are you doing?' She pushed him away.

'Issata please?'

She marched towards the door but he caught her.

'Wait, I can explain to you.' His hand grabbed her shoulder.

'Leave me alone!' she wrestled, freeing herself from his embrace.

'I finish what I am doing and I come to see you.'

—It is only a bad dream, she tried to convince herself back to her place. —I will close my eyes and when I open them, he will be gone. —No, that is not a dream, she understood, when she heard the famous knock on her door.

—I don't have to open, she observed, perambulating.

—But I need to know why did he come back? —No, why did he leave without giving any news? The knock resonated again.

'What do you want?' she demanded when they faced again. She was afraid. She resembled a small girl, lost in a world far too big for her. A world where men are vicious and powerful, and where she didn't know who to trust anymore.

'Let me in please, I won't be long!' He passed her door and headed straight towards her bed, where their story began.

'My mother died,' she heard him let out when she closed her door. Tears vibrated in his voice.

213

'Oh?' Came out of her mouth, not sure if she should believe him. —But why would he lie? 'Sorry to hear,' she empathised.

'When I left, she was in a critical state. My parents had an accident with my father. He was driving and she died.

'What a sad story!'

'My dad felt so guilty. He needed me, that is why I didn't give any news.

'You could have told me about the accident'

'It is true, but I was devastated. Plus, you had your own worries.' —You left for a year, and you couldn't inform me?

'I thought about you a lot, you know,' he pursued.

—Right, Dan too thought about me a lot when he disappeared for ten months.

'When did you come back?' she counter-attacked.

'Last week. I wanted to surprise you.'

'Khrystian, you and I, that is the past! I need to focalise on my life and, so should you.'

'Rajeev told me he knew someone who could help me find work.'

'And you believe him?'

He rose to his feet and went close to her.

'He is not an angel, but I need him. And I can protect you.'

He caressed her face with his right hand.

'Stop this! I do not need protection!'

'Rajeev is a psychopath!'

'Are you mad or what?'

'I have never told you, but there are some strange activities going on in this house.'

'Why are you telling me this?'

'Do you remember John, my neighbour?'

'And?'

'He told me Rajeev is a pimp, he runs a brothel!'

'Khrystian that is enough!'

'Issata, don't be naive. John happened to see young women, in the company of older men, entering Rajeev's office at the top of the house. Do you know that they smoked cocaine? That is why John left.'

Horrified at what she was hearing, she remembered the number of times, she heard strange noises, creeping through the walls of the house. She couldn't say if there were cries or moans. Often, she could detect rancid smell too, traversing the hallway.

'Why did you come back then?'

'I admit, I was desperate. He told me you were leaving. Then, I thought we could chant together, and get him. You said it yourself; the man is creepy.' he smiled. She was confused. Why should she believe the Polish guy, who had left her a year ago, without giving a damn single news?

'Issata, I missed you so much,' he insisted and began licking one of her ears.

'Stop this, and you can chant by yourself.' she wrestled.

He grabbed her wrists fiercely and rubbed himself between her legs. 'I know you want me.' He sneered.

Khrystian was back! She didn't love him but couldn't find the strength to refuse that toxic invitation, which seemed to respond to a recurrent theme existing in her life. The only answer laid in a chemical attraction, which tied them. The connection was activated like a firework, leaving her most of the time, addicted to the sexual voyage he offered her. After the trip was over, she would feel ashamed, guilty! Why guilty?

I had to investigate and I came to a very enlightening realisation! It is the fault of Hippocrates, because according to his theory, the clitoris, that erectile organ was able to produce the semen and played a primordial role in the sexual reproduction. Just like 1+1=2, by adding the feminine semen to the masculine one, we could only observe the making of the embryo. But my lord, the proof that the ovule was produced during the menstruation cycle came to light. No need to say that The Church was offended in seeing the true nature of the clitoris. To their eyes, it looked like a device for masturbation, encouraging a form of contraception, and a fortiori the invigilator, destabilising the process of procreation. The clitoris became then, the enemy number one of the Church and was banished from school books because the woman's sex only served in receiving the sperm of the man. Hence the function of the vagina, for Mr. Spermatozoid to find refuge in the uterus for nine months in the company of Mrs. Ovule. Our poor clitoris was doomed to live in the shadow, for at least a good one hundred years, animating the cerebral fantasies of us women, as the world perceives us. History had to wait until the end of the nineties for Helen O'Connell, Australian urologist to shed a light on this mystery entitled: 'The clitoris our dearest unknown.' In it she explains, what is its function? What does it look like? She resurrected it, freed it from its religious cross, giving back to it, its real place in the feminine sexuality. As far as my own opinion, the clitoris has only one function: —The pleasure or 'Pour le plaisir,' Herbert Léonard would sing. I can clearly conclude that the myth between clitoridean orgasm versus vaginal is outdated. Because like everything in life, it is the journey, the voyage we undertake to arrive safely which marks our life. That is the same for the climax. Some women orgasm during the penetration, whereas some, mostly need a caress on their pink button. Speaking about the pink button, let's remember that, black women are part of this world too, so let's rectify the thoughts of our time, and let's baptise our dear friend Mr. Clitoris with a new name where black women can recognise themselves too. Not that they don't, but interestingly, even sex seemed to have been designed for white people. So, what about the black flower, or the black pearl? It definitely sounds better than the pink button? Because frankly speaking that analogy reminds me of the time of puberty when all spots on white skin come out completely pink. I am only observing, here! Anyway, all this to say, to all of us women of all ages, cultures, education let's explore our sex life and honour our dear friend, the clitoris, existing inside our legs to make us vibrate.'

Jimmy? what did he think? 'It looks like an unfinished business my darling, so just enjoy!' Dr. B? She was fascinated by her patient journey and felt useless sometimes. 'But I need you,' Issata couldn't cease to repeat.

Too busy, entertaining her legs in the air, if you see what I mean, I know the French always adopt a sexy way to life, she didn't see the month of April arriving, where the French would say: "*En April personne ne se découvre d'un fil*" and the English will argue that: '*April showers bring May flowers*. For Issata both expressions suited her perfectly. She kept her legs in the air and made sure her black flower got showered, well before May arrived. After all, as the saying would say, sex and money governed the world and Issata couldn't argue with that. Until the day would come, where she will be forced to remember that, as uniquely designed, African women's derrière look like, it wouldn't help her, pay her bills. The good news, Khrystian found work as a lorry driver. It involved long-distance travelling. Sometimes, he stayed away for two days. She didn't mind, plus he was almost living with her. Let's just say, he was spending more time in her bed than he would in his own. They would argue daily about little things and even about what to cook for dinner. They looked like an old couple. And since fulfilled relationship ought to be based on honesty, she dared ask:
'Did you have a story with Agnes?'
It was a sunny morning; they were drinking their coffee. She was smoking and found him absent. He had his phone in his hand, an Android brand, which kept beeping.
'What?' He looked at her puzzled.

'Tell me the truth!'

'Agnes who?' he mumbled.

'Don't pretend! Why didn't you tell me that she invited you to the discussion meeting?'

'Oh, her?'

She fixed him deeply, like a lie detector. It was proven that the body possessed its own language and that the eyes represented an indicator crucial to analyse someone's sincerity. A liar would look away when confronted with the truth. Would his eyes move around looking to prepare what to say next? Issata osculated him like a doctor, searching for the right diagnosis for his patient. He didn't look away. In fact, he seemed at ease.

'Listen, it was late. She mentioned it. I said, yes out of politeness. She insisted that I take her number. I took it and answered that I would probably come with you.' he explained.

'You had her number?'

'Issata, she is a married woman! What would she do with a guy like me?' he put down his mobile on the table and caressed her left hand.

—Precisely, because she is one of those wealthy married women, who spend their time in saunas and clubs for elites, all looking for an escapade to satiate their lack of fulfilment, I wouldn't be surprised, that she finds interest in someone like you, she was ready to yell.

'Answer me!'

'Yes, I had her phone number! No, I didn't contact her!'

'Why should I believe you?' Her eyes began to fill with tears.

Khrystian stood up and moved close to her. He squatted in front of her and placed his hands on her knees.

'She is your friend. How can you think this of me?'

219

'I don't know what to think!'

'I could have never done such a thing to you! Plus, anyway you have news from her, don't you?' A puppy look was printed on his face.

She hesitated to answer. She didn't want to lie but didn't want to tell the truth either. The truth was that she hated her. She hated what she represented. The kind of woman, who inspires, men not to respect women, to these days. She saw in her a faded sadness.

—*I cannot say that happy sadness exists, however, there is some sadness which can move us, sadness which leads to inspiration, sadness which touches people's heart, I want to believe.* Nonetheless, the mystic law put this woman on her path. Agnes converted to Buddhism because she wanted a bit of spirituality in her life. Chanting was more of a relaxing technique for her.

'Khrystian, you are right, Issata breathed deeply. 'I don't know what got to me. When you left, I felt lonely. And the mind has its own way to influence our perception of reality.

'Don't worry!' he embraced her hands. 'Come,' he rose to his feet, his eyes lingering towards the bed.

That was how their story continued.

Sometimes, they would bump into Rajeev. 'Issata, you look better,' he would address her. 'Thank you,' she would reply politely. 'You two form a beautiful couple, Khrystian you are lucky,' he would observe at other times.

Issata didn't know how to respond to his new visage, even though, he was no different to the man she didn't trust from the beginning. That new face sounded exactly how Khrystian described him. —Perhaps that is my mission to reveal the true face of Rajeev. Perhaps Khrystian is only here to help me realise it. Mr. Right or not! And at the end of the day, how to know we have found the one?

That fascinating question still remains a big debate in today's society. Even Adam and Eve had to face their relationship problems. Who's bad, Michael Jackson would say! —Eve! She encouraged Adam to eat the apple. This poor Adam, no male figure to inspire him, had no other choice than to bite it. However, he couldn't swallow it and found himself doomed to live with a piece of that fruit stuck in his throat. An image that stayed with him, hence Adam's apple. And at that time, couple therapy didn't exist, so they had to seek guidance from the holy spirit. This could explain why so many men prefer bananas these days. It is a softer fruit, which slid easily in the mouth. —Morality gentlemen, choose your apple carefully because some women detain the art of transforming, the apple into a compote and the taste can seriously turn bitter.

Issata had devoured millions of books on the subject:

—*How to attract the right one?* Numerous writers invested their time and knowledge in sharing the key formula which would illuminate the mystery behind 'Why' men and women shine in differences and that through their differences they can find a common ground.

Let's look at *The Book of Rules,* by Ellen Fein and Sherrie Schneider, is placed in the first category of book on the topic, she studied. As suggested by the title, according to these two women, ladies had to follow some rules to attract their husbands. Issata notorious for debate, took note of it, for the only purpose to defy those rules. The hidden message behind those rules is to encourage women not to chase men, but to let them do the chasing. It was said that a woman who follows *The Rules* is called a *Rule Girl*. Issata smiled at the end of her lecture. —Not my flute of champagne!

'*Men are from Mars and Women from Venus*' revealed by John Gray, the American writer, and relationship Counsellor, joined the rank of the second book, she read. By using Mars, the god of the war, and Venus the goddess of love as actors to establish the differences, through his work, he explains very clearly that men and women don't speak the same language, and from this fact, those two opposite sexes, differ from their way of expressing their feelings and their actions, hence, the misunderstanding, the frustrations, and the hurt. Thanks to his personal experience, he succeeded in using it as a source of inspiration. The book remains the best seller of the time. Why? Simply because, the content helps men and women to better learn from each other, express themselves, and better respect each other.

The author sheds the light on a very crucial fact.
In comparison to women, when a man is anxious, he keeps himself in his private space, a cave states Gray; an inner place to think, and to prove to himself, he is able to fix his problem.
At the end of her lecture, she exclaimed:
—Alleluia, the answer is in the cave! Everything is linked to the cave. —I took note Mr. Right, I will refrain from entering your cave, only if you invite me!

Next, —*Why Men love bitches* a New York Times Bestselling self-help book by Sherry Argov; she was not impressed. —How sad that women had to be seen in such a degrading way to demand respect, was her conclusion! She didn't doubt that the intention of the writer was for women to stand up, but why choose such a title? What about:

—Why do Men love strong or confident women? —Mind you a strong woman can scare men! I am going to stop here. We can all observe that she studied a lot. Now, let's read and see, if she understood something.

June 28th 2014 is a date Issata will remember, like those dates we commemorate to mark the history of mankind on the planet. The Hundred Years War, —in fact it was one hundred and sixteen years, but there was also some peaceful gap, —anyway, commencing in 1337 till 1453 plunged England and France into a bloody fight all this for a sad disagreement over the throne! No, a sex story! But thanks to the great mercy coming from the holy spirit, Joan of Arc, the universal heroin, made her appearance and led France to victory. But at which cost?
No one can speak about France without evoking The French Revolution which began in May 1789 till 1799, giving birth to the Declaration of Human rights signed on August 26th in 1789.

The twentieth century emerged too with its own story, the calamity of the two world wars, which revealed the atrocity of a single man, Adolf Hitler; a nobody who used his desire for recognition to make the world pay for the way he perceived himself. Well, the world does recognise him for the monster he was, and as an example of what evilness looks like. *Now, we could question, in terms of Buddhism, where does this man fit, because the lotus states very clearly that everyone is the buddha? Yes, he was a buddha, but he must pay for his crimes toward mankind. Interestingly humanity didn't have to kill him. He killed himself. That was for the little story, because it goes for every single one of us, we are buddha, but each one of us must take responsibility for our actions.'*

Back to Issata, obviously, she was not going to war, however, that was how she perceived her last day in the lounge. What about going back on board the trains then? The last MRI showed some worrying changes in her brain and Dr. Clark didn't permit a return on the train. She could consider a new role? No new position was offered to her.

—Occupational health therapy? —Nope, but Ray made sure to inform her, that if her health didn't improve, she would be dismissed on capability ground. The word capability hurt her alter ego. —It is not my fault that you did not take care of me, she pleaded! Since she didn't possess any juridical weapons to fight those giants of the capitalist world, that little black woman had only one choice, to say goodbye to her travellers.

Deeply sad, they all promised to contact the big boss of Voyage Europe to tell him that the salon without their favourite hostess would just be a room full of people. She was touched. An hour before her departure, she sat one more time in the private section, her eyes directed towards the lift. She observed the young woman, dressed in a red uniform with elegance, black hair short to the skin, her sexy legs cat walking on the Vienna marble floor. Excitation shinning in her eyes, she inspired youthfulness, she inspired life. All eyes were turned towards her. 'Hello Issata!', 'Issata how you?' 'Issata thank you!' 'Issata is back!' 'Issata, we missed you!' 'Issata please take care of yourself!' Three years later, where was that person who dreamt of making a difference? Tears flowed on her cheeks, she heard her mind singing on the tune *Capri c'est fini,* French song from d'Hervé Villard: —VoyE, it's finish, when I think that you were the name of my first job,

—VoyE it's finished! Never will I forget that I have fallen ill because of you.

Curtain! And it fell down like a guillotine cutting the head of an innocent woman. To one difference, she managed to save her head when she left the salon. She hugged Michael who wished her the best of luck and she disappeared into the terminal. Sitting on the train, she burst into tears, not bothering about people looking at her. She was hurt and didn't want to hide. That was all she had! Few commuters approached her to offer their support. 'They sacked me!' she replied crying loudly. 'They don't know your real worth! That is their loss!' some voices reassured her. And Issata, did she know her true worth?

No more waking up at five-thirty. No more red uniform, reflecting the image of a company that didn't care. How much money do they earn at the expense of their employee's well-being? —And me what do I get?
Jimmy left for a new project in Paris. She had Khrystian.

It was Summer. Her sunny days were animated by deep anxiety, named: her future! Let's remember that she used her time at university to study the pleasures of love. —Yet, I still don't know how to apply it in my life!

Throughout the hot season, she perceived her Polish man differently. When together, he spent most of his time on the phone. A lot of whispering, she could capture and sensed he was hiding something. It affected their intimacy. He dedicated less time to their favourite activities. He would take his pleasure and would fall asleep. Sometimes, he would escape to his flat, using the argument that he had to call his father. When she confronted him, —I am worried, he would defend! 'You could understand me?' 'Work is hard!' Yes, she understood. —Why now? she tried to make sense. —Now that I am out of work! Then, would follow, enflamed words, blaming her for being selfish. She would dwell in deep culpability and suffer out fear of seeing him disappearing again.

14ᵗʰ of August, Issata remembered clearly, as the date marks the Assumption Day, often mistaken by Ascension Day. To understand, the difference, let's look at their etymology. In Latin, —Assumption represents *assumere,* which means 'to take off. That assumption is related to the Virgin Mary. When speaking about the assumption, it is explained that God would have had pulled her to the sky, in order to keep her by his side. —Ascension, on the contrary, celebrated in May, forty days after Easter is, *ascendere* in Latin, which signifies, to climb. Jesus meets for the last time, his disciples, forty days after His Resurrection. Being the son of God, he rose to the sky, through his own strengths. That was for the little story, a little story which made the following of the story, big.

Sunday, precisely, in the middle of the night, she felt someone slipping out of bed. A little breeze passed through the sheets, a sign that the whole bed belonged to her. She heard the sound of a door closing. Khrystian was leaving her flat. Work was picking up. He was absent for five days. Issata actually thought that it would actually do them good. She didn't wake up, because the smell of his perfume remained still impregnated on the duvet, keeping her warm and safe. Wrapped in her blanket, she resembled a little girl attached to her father's shirt, holding onto a virtual presence.

A vibration sound caught her ears. She opened her eyes and checked her phone. —9 AM, she managed to read, but no message. —So, what is it? She recalled Khrystian's departure. She jumped out of bed to lock her door. The noise manifested again. —Maybe it is my vibrator? She searched in her handbag. Her device friend was there but switch off. She emptied all the contents. The sound was still resonating in her room. Then, nothing.

—Surely, I am not mad! Her eyes travelled in the studio. Her bladder then called her attention. —I need to pee, that is a normal and natural observation! Sitting on her throne, she let her yellow water splash in the toilet sink and heard the rumbling again like an explosion. She trembled with fear, listening to where it was coming from. Her senses were guided to her laundry basket. She rose to her feet without wiping herself. Leaning over it, she saw a phone ringing.

—Whose phone is that? She picked it up and read the name of the caller. Her eyes widened. —It cannot be! She recalled Khrystian's behaviours, his evasive replies, 'Not important,' 'Just a mistake', 'you don't know.' And now a person named Agnes was calling a phone, forgotten in her laundry basket. She shivered, watching the name written on the screen. She didn't want to believe that the name belonged to a woman, she once respected. The vibration stopped. She wanted to identify the caller, but the phone was locked. Tears flowed in her eyes.

—This Agnes, she cannot be... The mobile rang again.

'Hello,' she hurried to answer.

A faint, sound came from the receiver.

'Hello?' she insisted.

Then a respiration rhythmic came as a reply.

'Agnes is that you?'

The caller gasped and hung up. Issata walked back to the main room, her eyes fixing the phone. —He told me you never spoke! She met in her memory, a Khrystian completely obnubilated by Agnes theatrical beauty on that famous New Year's Eve. He behaved like a virgin boy, desperate to have his penis sucked by a mouth as vulgar as those of her friend. —How could they? —This explains why he left, she sobbed! —But why come back to me?

Her mobile on her bedside table rang. Khrystian was the caller. Tears crawled on her cheeks. She let it ring till the fanfare stopped. 'I can explain,' a text message followed.

—What is there to explain she ruminated, deeply hurt?

—That she manipulated you? —And you, as lousy as you are, you had no other choice? Her mobile rang again. The cruel and modern sound, proper to iPhone, activated her murderous rage. She felt it, sliding beneath her veins, looking restless like a dirty bitch. It stimulated in her, the ramping snake, the watching snake, the dancing snake Baudelaire would describe. Her eyes screaming for revenge, she abandoned herself to the vertiginous sensations, provided by her priestess. Fulgurant thoughts weighed down her mind. Her heart craved to honour her fiercely. Seized by an astounding power, she felt spur to flirt with a deep need to scream, to punch, to destroy everything in her way. Pearls of transpiration scrawled on her body. The mistress was to arrive any minutes. What to wear to welcome her? A mask to preserve a damaged look? A cape to dissimulate a dagger hidden in the corner of her soul? Some gloves to wipe any prints leading back to her? The world around her multiplied in several parallels. Her adrenalin rushed inside her at a speed she couldn't control. Determined to establish her own justice, she declared: —A man and a woman betrayed me, and they have to pay for that hurt. Owning her decision, she watched the name of jimmy flashing on her mobile.

'Jimmy, he is fucking Agnes!' she answered heartbroken.

'Darling, I don't get it! What is wrong?' 'Khrystian and Agnes! I hate them!' Jimmy gasped.

'Try to calm down and tell me exactly what's the situation!'

She mumbled fractions of her own interpretations, crying. Feeling sorry for his friend, he hardened his tone of voice out of compassion.

'Issata, I understand that it is shocking for you, but it was bound to happen. He left without giving any news. At least it is clear now.'

She knew he was right. It was the humiliation that she could not accept.

'I want to kill them!' she wailed.

'It is normal, because you are hurt and angry.'

'I will do it!'

'No, you won't! If you do so, I will have failed you as a friend!'

'Why Jimmy?'

'Have you had breakfast yet?

'No, I haven't even smoked.'

'Swallow a coffee and smoke as many fags you want and go for a walk.'

'I am scared to be alone.'

'Do you still see B?'

'Yes,' she sniffled.

'Contact her and ask to see her.'

'I want to see you.'

'Soon my darling, I must go now, only checking on you.'

'Don't leave me please!'

'Promise-me to call B,' he ordered.

'Ok,' she muttered through her tears.

'You will be fine.'

—If you say so, she sighed, after he hung up.

'Please come in, I am so pleased that you called me.'

B welcomed in her clinic, a young woman looking like a lost teenager, dressed in black, to the exception of her white converse. She had no socks on. Her face, hidden behind her dark Prada shades, she was wearing, a large round neck t-shirt beneath her linen jacket and her jeans. How did she land there?

Shortly after Jimmy's call, she remembered her cold coffee, the entire pack of Marlboro she smoked, without finishing any of them, the fifty missed calls from Khrystian and the text messages begging her to give him a chance to explain.

'I can't cope anymore' there and then, the fountain erupted from behind her mask.

'I am listening when you are ready.' B, placed the box of tissues near her reach.

'I cannot cope anymore' she repeated. 'Life is absurd! Life has no sense,' she wept like a sheep in distress and shared her news of the day.

B fixed this woman, who like many women including herself and men as well, arrived at this point that awareness where the decision to be alive didn't bring any sense anymore.

—What is the purpose of life? That is the question?
If there was no sense to live, how to explain the main goal of human beings on this earth? To continue to live and deny the absurdity about one's own existence, like Sisyphus and his rock? The myth of Sisyphus described the life of a young man punished to have defied the gods and escaped death. So, he was doomed to roll a huge stone to the top of a mountain, knowing too well that the stone will constantly go back down. The gods thought to have found the perfect form of torture for Sisyphus who would attempt everything for the stone to remain at the top of the mountain.

The name Albert Camus belongs to the French Philosophy era of the twentieth century, the time of existentialism, that philosophical and literary trend in which we find numerous big names, such as Jean-Paul Sartre, Simone de Beauvoir. That movement of thinking places at the heart of its reflection, the individual existence determined by subjectivity, liberty, and individual choices. In other words, an existentialist claimed to be the master of his own destiny.

Having said this, that way of living embraced the intransigent atheism of Friedrich Nietzsche, German philosopher, based on his theory: The will to power. His theory underlines that the purpose of pulsion is to realise exactly this: —The will to power! He used his concept, as a key instrument to observe the world, to interpret human phenomena, and revaluate a future existence.

He was not the only one looking for answers. His philosophical approach before anything, was inspired by French philosopher Blaise Pascal, and his religious thoughts. He defended that Man, because of his arrogance and his insatiable concupiscence can never find internal peace and absolute happiness outside God. According to him, it is the divorce between Man and its Creator which produces the dissatisfaction experienced by Man and makes him doubt the true purpose of his life.

Soren Kierkegaard too, a young Danish philosopher added his personal spiritual touch on the concept of existentialism, through his book: Either/Or. In it, he explores in a humorous manner, the choice each one of us makes to lead the life we aspire to. So how to lead this life the way we wish to, when no instructions have been brought to us and no one is around to provide answers.

Where to draw the will to power, when that will, the big theory of Nietzsche deserted us without taking into account our personal pulsion's? Or perhaps the suffering, the expression of the human condition shared by men and women doesn't match the real pulsion which would spur the will to power? And God in this? Pascal said, we have to believe in God!

This is what Camus attempted to explore through the theme of Absurdity. By analysing, the myth of Sisyphus, it would seem almost simple to lend him the need to die, because that was the result the gods were aiming to generate, an undeniable frustration, based on Sisyphus unrealistic hope that would plunge him in the cruel absurdity of life, that incomprehension leading to the decisive act. But Albert Camus couldn't let such a thing happen! He too challenged the Gods, by changing the destiny of Sisyphus with this declaration: "There is but one serious philosophical problem, and that is suicide," and approached the daily burden of this young man from a different angle. For Camus, even if life didn't look like a significant adventure, it was still worth living it. The right to was what defined the true purpose of our existence, to find and create it. So, he decided to make Sisyphus live the absurdity and honoured him as the hero of his own life. A human being who had no other choice than to live. Albert Camus will always remain one of my favourite philosophers of the twentieth century, for his commitment to analyse the human condition, and for his audacity to denounce that the essence of being human exists through: —The Revolt, the positive revolt, that he developed in an essay untitled: — The Rebel.

'Issata, you are right, life can seem unfair and take us to doubt the purpose of our existence, but precisely, the fact that it doesn't make sense gives all the sense to the absurdity. Like Sisyphus, the lack of sense gave him a sense of his misery. '

Issata exploded in tears. She felt her strength crumbling under the weight of her enormous stone. A stone, seeking to crush her, till she disappeared in the ground. The thought revolted her.

'I don't want to end up like Sisyphus, he was the victim of the absurdity of life.' she exclaimed.

'That is your own perception Issata, Camus made him choose: —Either to free himself from the illusion that one day the stone will remain on the top of the mountain or accept that the function of such a big rock, mathematically speaking is to continue to roll down to the ground. You can also choose what to do during these present circumstances, in that absurd moment of your life.'

'I just want to understand.'

'Bravo Issata!'

'Bravo for what? There is nothing glorious about my life!'

'Yes, there is! You are revolted. And you are going to give a sense to your revolt!'

A series of sounds coming from her iPhone resonated in the room. She fixed B.

'Check while you are with me.

She tugged her mobile from her handbag and saw a number of emails on the screen with different subject: 'Thank you Issata', 'Give us back Issata', 'I am so disappointed', 'That is absurd,'. This time tears of gratitude emerged from her eyes. One traveller thought her dismissal was absurd.

'You see your life has a meaning Issata,' B exclaimed when she showed her the email. 'Maybe not for Voyage Europe, not Agnes, nor Khrystian, but for all these people you have touched with your humanity. That is the purpose of your life. To touch people, you must have experiences to share. You have a profound meaning to me.' Tears filled B, eyes. 'Your life will unveil in a meaningful sense if you give sense to it.' 'I don't know,' she mumbled.

'But you have Buddhism, and if I may ask, don't you have someone in your group who could guide you?'

'Everyone keeps asking me, this question. There was Agnes' she sniffled,' 'But our relationship was mainly built around champagne as opposed to spiritual connection.'

'Surely, she is not the only one?'

'No, she is not the only one! But to be honest, right now, there is no one who inspires me to pick up my phone and talk to them.'

'That is deeply sad. I visited their website and from what I understand, SGI is that movement that proclaims to not leave a single person in obscurity. I thought the focus was on the welfare of their members, especially with everything which you are going through?'

'Dr. B, don't get me wrong, I chose Buddhism because it made sense to me, so I thought...' she sighed. 'And the person who introduced me to it, explained clearly to follow the law, not the people. And there is Sensei, somewhere in Japan.'

'There is Sensei,' B repeated, 'and you have me!'

Sitting in that massive office, animated by the magic emanating from the white and black photo of the children, who could have been theirs, they stared at each other, complicity reigning in their eyes. These two women who borrowed different paths were sharing the same story. A hormonal story, the one which implies the disfunction of the menstrual cycle and determines the mood swings. A gene story, making them unique in millions of ways and similar at the same time. A story, rich in cultural values and experiences. Very simply, the story of being a woman.

'So, what do I have to do then?' she begged.

'I am not here to tell you what to do because you have to decide. But today, I am changing the rules. Khrystian, Agnès, VoyE are part of your past now. Don't give them your present now!'

'How?'

'You need to rebuild yourself.'

'I feel that I have never been built'

'We are going to do it together. Perhaps you could go to visit your mother and she could surely help you. Family reflects our perception of society.'

'I am not ready for this!'

'Did you inform her that you lost your job?'

'No,' she cut short. B. smiled.

'It won't be easy Issata, but you will find the way!'

'Right now, I just want to stop thinking.'

'I can prescribe you some sleeping pills with Lithium, for one week only, to help you?'

'Make it two please.'

'Ok.' She gazed at her, compassionately.

A violent flare-up erupted, right after the betrayal.

It vibrated under her physical and emotional pain.

Dr. Clark brought up again, the intravenous treatment when he assessed her. She couldn't commit to the change of treatment. In the meantime, Sarcoidosis was delighted. She broke out, scrawling beneath her skin. She stabbed her joints, she messed up her mind, she was flirting with her emotions. She was vicious. Issata, being so generous had plenty of food to give her. She was angry, she felt humiliated, she was hurt.

Jimmy called every day, encouraging her to trust. 'I love you, my friend,' he always ended by saying.

Sometimes, she spoke with her family, mainly via texts messages. Of course, she refrained, to tell them that she didn't represent the image of VoyE anymore.

She increased the doses of lithium and kept asking B for more, complaining she couldn't sleep. Of course, B hesitated, but she would rather prescribe them, than pushing her patient to help herself on the black market.

The word absurd painted her new reality. Sadness rendered her daily life sublime and accommodated her emotional emptiness. That hole in her, contained a dominant energy, like a shadow, the umbra of a woman, whose mission laid in harassing her mind. Heavy thoughts weighed in her head. She couldn't encode them as the words have deserted her, like traitors. She often found herself sitting in front of a white page for hours, paralysed with fear.

—Why am I being the object of such a sanction, she would sob? Even writing, that universe where I feel in total peace with myself, armed with that liberty to assemble letters together, letters forming words, words evoking sounds, sounds expressing feelings, feelings rising to memories, memories being shared, giving birth to experiences, experiences which make great sense to life, writing that exquisite pleasure has abandoned me. The only criminal is me. I am responsible, as my life has no sense anymore. Night-time revealed itself as the worse transition period of her existence. And this is when Madame Anger, that woman of nocturnal pleasures, the goddess of every broken soul, would make her entrance on stage with vigour. She had a friend, Sarcoidosis. Craving for strong sensations, a deep need to resonate and shine in most lost souls, she commenced her demoniac tirades. Issata formed her only audience, and she received that privilege to listen to her perverse thoughts. Terrified by the noisy fanfare drumming in her brain, she bled with agony. Her existential anguish was piercing through her nerves like poisonous arrows. She was dying to scream, and smash everything around her, but her will to defend herself had abandoned her long ago, at the view of the bloody scenery passing through her mind. It resembled a battlefield, smelling like a butcher shop, where every piece of her body laid on the screen of her mind.

And Buddhism? The sight of her butsudan was breaking her heart. The thought of her Gohonzon, disgusted her and felt alienated by the sound of daimokus.

She felt constantly attacked by this mantra. A melody was emerging and she didn't want to hear it. —Leave me alone! she would shout. —You are evil! —You manipulated my mind, the mind of people to control us!

—No, you can't control me!

She knocked her head against the iron bars of her bed, but the voice kept persisting.

One day, she grabbed a big knife. She wanted to slice the throat in her head. She wanted to choke it for eternity.

Ready to act, her eyes crossed her image in the mirror. The violence observed in the scenery, forced her to drop the bladed weapon. Frightened by her own rational behaviour, because it existed a rational logic to search to put an end to the voice which was making her suffer, she hid her head beneath a pillow and pressed her skull, with all her physical strength, till her brain stop functioning.

—Maybe it is best to neglect my sanctuary, she deducted with time. She had hoped that the sight of a cemetery would kill the voice inside.

She assisted to her own funeral. She let her fruits to rot, the greenery to dry up. She noticed spider webs slowly growing around what had become the reflection of her life condition. —Good appetite, sometimes she would joke.

She didn't want nothing to do with the mystic law. But the voice was still alive. So, she entertained a dangerous desire to grab her object of worship and tear it. No to burn it. '*I Nichiren inscribed my life in Sumi ink, believe in this Gohonzon with your whole life,*' she would recite.

—Well, go to hell, she will then answer! I don't believe in all this bullshit! In fact, I have never believed in it!

—What did you really prove? You are not the only one who has been persecuted! —Jesus too was persecuted and he also realised miracles. —He turned water into wine. He gave a blind man his sight. So Nich, admit that your philosophy is not valid. Twenty years that I am waiting for Mr. Right and see where I am now. —It is over! I don't want this life anymore! —I don't want to carry that stone anymore like Sisyphus. —Sisyphus didn't even have a choice. Camus made it for him.

'*C'est fini, c'est fini la comédie…*' famous song from
Dalida *translated as* 'The comedy is over.' It was one of
those mornings where she had spent the whole night trying
to understand why. Issata had to admit to herself, she
didn't possess the strength to live anymore. She drew her
inspiration from one verse of the song: ' *Le décor n'a pas
changé et moi je n'ai plus rien à jouer…*'

    *translated in English as: The scene remains the same
and I have nothing to play.* —I want the perfect death, a
romantic ceremony, to be remembered.

    —Soon, I wouldn't have to put up with the sight of that
hideous image, she commented once outside. She was
referring to Rajeev's engine. She walked to *Nicolas* the
wine shop and ordered six bottles of what you know, to be
delivered home. —In a few hours, my suffering will cease,
vibrated in her heart. She strolled and strolled and strolled,
borrowing streets she knew so well, pathways which soon,
would belong to the story of her passage on this earth.
Determined to keep her secret safe, her senses captured a
red light in the sky, denouncing the arrival of Autumn. In
her stupor, she realised that she had reached the entrance of
the park. Her heart pounded with shame. She felt huge
tears, burning her eyes. 'Sayon, forgive me, I have tried,'
she whispered and rushed back to Valley Park.

She found her delivery in front of her door. The champagne in the fridge, she pulled down the blinds and ordered her favourite food. She waited patiently, sitting on her bed. An irreversible lucidity propelled her. The kind of beaming clarity highlighting her solemn choice. It dawned on her that every act of suicide is most often explained in a letter. What to say? —I don't have to justify myself! This is my life! I do as I wish! Look what she did to me, the bitch! This is payback time! —Jimmy, she asked? I can't take it anymore. — Mum? I have always been a big weight for her anyway! Sophia she is living her life with her children, her husband. And me, I have nothing. I refuse to reach forty with nothing. So, she wrote on a white paper: *The life of Issata Sherif has no sense anymore, therefore I am leaving. I.S.*

Her eyes read the words neatly written by her own hand, thought carefully and dictated by her heart without any remorse. The food arrived.
'Good appetite,' the delivery man wished her. 'Thank you.'
—You are the last person, I am interacting with, she sighed when she closed the door. She lit up thirty-nine candles, all organised in a circle on the floor. She fetched the tube of her pills and spread some on the table. She opened a bottle and poured herself a glass. —You wanted my death; I will perform it for you! she let out.

Bach opened the ball and she absorbed the drugs with the champagne. She had planned to swallow as much as her liver could tolerate. She drank, ate, mixed her pills to what looked like homemade porridge in her stomach. And smoked. The fume added a mystic experience to her performance. She opened her second bottle. Rising her hands in the air, she swayed on *Air in G string*, feeling intense sensations penetrating her body. Radiant, standing on her legs, her flesh yearning for sensations, she implored the African sorceress, to answer her only wish, Mr Right who will make her dance through life. Desperate, Issata wanted to believe. Her breasts swelled and she felt her tits rise. —I am here, I am waiting for you! She moved her head from left to right. —Come and dance with me! Her arms opened, in front of her, she invited her invisible lover to join her. Her heart drummed like percussions, responding to the chorus of her desire.

—Can you hear my body? He is an artist. My body isn't the most beautiful one, because he has suffered, suffered a lot. But within the suffering, he has to learn to exist, to use all the scars to write me poems. Through my tears, beautiful melodies were composed, often sad, but the notes my body chose, accompanied my life perfectly. —That body, I want to share it with you. Come and dance with me, that is all I wish for, before my departure. Issata brought her arms around herself.

She held tightly; the way she would want to be embraced. Her hands moved slowly towards her breasts. She groaned and felt a presence. Submerged, she trusted what she was feeling and pulled out her tee-shirt. The points of her tits turned into the mouthpiece of a saxophone. Hard and intense, those black glass bead expressed a very high pitch. Mesmerised, Issata offered to this mysterious mouth, the pleasure to vibrate. Her female body trembled. An electric shock crossed through her being. —I knew, that you would come! Excited, she removed her old leggings. She didn't have any knickers.

—After all, I don't need clothes anymore. —So, what is the purpose of all this material? To hide? —I don't want to hide anymore. She looked around her for that energy, that was spying on her silently. —I am ready! Look at that body, he is waiting for you! Imagine my skin like a canvas, a shagreen. You will be able to paint whatever you like, with the colours that inspire you. —Come! Issata presented her hand, in the room lightened by candles. Impatient, she anticipated caresses made by each brush, drops of oil, he would throw all over her, those splashes of the final touch, that will immortalise the painting of her existence. While she waited, the music changed to Serge Gainsbourg single, *Je suis venu te dire que je m'en vais.* In her horror, she saw her shadow and the reflection of her own fingers, dancing on the wall. Looking like a worm in her nudity, her body eaten away by her existential anguish, she stood in the middle of her stage, the projectors directed towards her, magnifying her silhouette through the penumbra of the night. —No, escaped from her mouth. Issata realised, that the ancestors had failed to answer her call. No one was going to accompany her, on stage, that immense galaxy called, life. Broken with deception,

—Me too, I am going, anyway she added. —There is nothing for me to do here, but not like that! She waddled towards the fridge as if her life was depending on it. The third bottle in her hand, she released the cork. It flew in the room. She opened her mouth and poured the golden liquid over her body. With the help of her left hand, she caressed her breasts, her belly. Her fingers fiddled through her pubis hairs, then massaged the mount Venus covering the stone of her prune. —I am leaving, her mouth uttered. —Finally, I am leaving and I am not coming back, she giggled savagely. She emptied the third bottle, staggering happily. She was anticipating, the moment her skull would explode, the sensations to feel her brain vessels turning into a bloody purée, and the extinction of her mind, which would mark, the official termination of her thoughts. Her eyelids became heavy. She couldn't stand on her legs. Ready to give in, Dalida's song, *Mourir sur scène,* rose in the room. The time had come. —I decide! All my life, I have obeyed orders. Today, I chose when and how I leave. Her tired eyes, stretched by dolour, she felt into the fridge and grabbed the fifth bottle. A silly smile, printed on her face, she gathered the little strength, she could manage and succeeded in opening the sparkling wine. Her perilous achievement, led her to lose her equilibrium. She fell down on the ground, champagne splashing everywhere. The candles lights caught her attention. She crawled towards the glowing scintilla; her hand glued to the bottle. Something burnt her skin. It was fast. She took her place in the middle of the stage.

Flat on the floor, —Really? That question passed through her mind, as if she was hesitating. — You don't want to go anymore, do you? —Yes, a panicked voice, defended! That sense of justice, stimulated the awareness, as to why, her life didn't make sense anymore. She felt like a deep warmth, invading her being, and a sense of harmony with her choice of departing. —First of all, I want to talk to her! She moved with great difficulty and was able to kneel. —Mistress of the darkness, I am calling on you, because you are the only one, I have left. Her eyes shone with hope; the luminescence of freedom. Her breasts pointed with pride on her chest. She resembled a statue in stone, ebony shade, shaped, from her creation, in the deepest sufferings. Thirty-nine years, brutally shaped up, sanded with unfair treatments, which nurtured, her childish illusions. Thirty-nine years, without a break, thirty-nine years, during the length of time, she wanted to believe. This African soul, didn't want to have anything to do with Life anymore. She was dragging her to court; the court, based on the laws, she has established, human rights declaration.

—It is the second time that I am meeting you. The first time, *Life* your greatest rival beat you to your own game and snatched me from you. And what for? Look what she had made of my existence! —First, she made me ill, she planted the seed of wrath in my heart. This poison is killing me! The more my mind suffers, the more it affects my body. —For months, you followed me! —I have felt your presence! In my greatest despair, I waited! —Tonight, I am ready! Her hand reached the tube with the remaining pills. She threw everything in her mouth, brought the champagne to her lips, slid in the middle of the lights; she had searched all her life, that light to exist, that light to be loved.

A man was sitting in a room, his face gnawed by anguish. His heart wanted to believe that the spectacle, the unreal dream he was witnessing for some days, would end soon. That the woman, lying in the bed, whose dark marron skin which in the past inspired the robust flavour of coffee beans would open her eyes and savour the joy of living, the joy she always delivers. That man, you already know him and that woman too. Oxygen tube inserted in her nostrils, perfusion attached to her right hand, lights from monitoring machines flashing around her, she was between life and death again. Did she know? Her heartbeat was stable.

B. who was expecting Issata, called her the next day, several times, to no avail. Two days went, Jimmy, who was in touch with her daily, didn't hear from her, despite the messages he left. Suspicious and worried, that something was wrong, he asked his manager to return to London. He travelled on 12th September to be precise. As he reached her home, he noticed that her blinds were closed. Since he had her keys, he opened the door. His nose was welcomed by a rotten and smoky smell. 'What is that?' escaped from his mouth. He entered the room and spotted the sushi tray filled with white worms. The kind of little living beings who happen to visit the bins during heated summer. Horrified, he covered his nose and saw her naked and crumbled on the floor in the middle of the candles. Ashes and empty bottles laid by her side with pills spread around her mouth.

'No, you didn't do that,' he cried out and called 999.

'Yes, what is the emergency?' A female voice asked.

He explained the facts. 'Help is on the way,' the person on the line assured Jimmy. He hung up devastated; his heart aching with rage and guilt. —I should have anticipated this! He watched her fragile body, afraid to touch it, by fear it would turn into dust. Tortured with remorse, he rushed to the bathroom and returned with her dressing gown. While he covered her body, his eyes caught her letter by her Buddhist altar. At the same time, the ambulance got there. He hid the letter in his pocket. One of the paramedics searched for a pulse on her neck. 'She is alive,' he confirmed.

'Is she going to be, ok?' Jimmy begged.

'We will do everything to support her.'

Rapidly she was placed on a stretcher, an oxygen mask covering her face. Once outside, Jimmy recognised Rajeev.

'What's happening?' Rajeev asked, sincerely worried.

Jimmy hesitated in answering, recalling the differences them two shared. 'Only a malaise, he managed to say and rushed to the ambulance. 'She is lucky to have you! I will pray for her.' Rajeev watched the vehicle drive away.

Sitting next to his friend, he couldn't believe that she had lost hope. —Why didn't you talk to me, he asked silently? She ended up in the board theatre where her stomach was cleaned. Twenty pills, she managed to swallow on the night of the suicide. The rest slept on the floor. A small hematoma was located in her brain but it was not too alarming. This is when Jimmy met Garrison. 'Why did your friend try to kill herself?' he asked. Jimmy explained that she was suffering from a chronic illness, lost her job, going through depression and betrayed by a friend. He mentioned the name of B and Dr. Clark. 'Your friend is very lucky! Thanks to you she is alive. Let's hope she grabs it when she opens her eyes.'

'Can she really make it?'

'We have to trust.'

He left the hospital devastated. —And her family? How to announce to them such news? He read the words of his friend several times when he got home. He impregnated himself through this universal suffering that attacks the human soul, the pain emerging when the light of hope has faded away. —Hope, he whispered, losing hope is the worse suffering someone can experience. —Issata you must have suffered so much, to reach that point, he sobbed, overwhelmed. —*Now let's ask ourselves how to reconquer that flame, that scintilla which spurs us to believe. To activate a fire, one would add logs or inflammable materials. In relation to the matter of the heart, how to revitalise that vital organ?*

Jimmy cried in the dark, praying hard that she woke up. He didn't practice any religion but remained open to the idea that a spiritual force governed the universe. So, standing on his balcony, his eyes looking toward the sky, he called on them: —God, Allah, Sky, Star, stone, Somebody, please, help her to wake up! She is a winner! She must live!

He decided to protect her family and kept her friend's secret to himself. He took an enormous risk and was prepared to assume the responsibilities. But for how long?

Issata still remained at the crossroad of her existence seven days later. Jimmy spent his days with her and even brought, her *omamori* Gohonzon as well as her Buddhist items. —So that when you wake up, you can pray, he wanted to believe. Garrison encouraged him to talk to her. It is said that the voice activates our sensorial memory. So, he did! He spoke about the first time, they met. It was love at first time. He hadn't felt this way even with his boyfriends. He evoked their trip to Barcelona, where he had fallen in love every night for one week with a different Spanish God. The crazy nights, showered with champagne and illegal stuff where they swore never again and came the weekend, they both returned to hell. Despite all those clear souvenirs, his friend didn't open her eyes. He played French music: —*l'hymne à l'amour*, from Edith Piaf, *L'aigle Noir* from Barbara, *La Montagne est belle,* from Ferrat and even *La Marseillaise.* No improvement coming from her, he began to wonder if he should contact his family. —After all, the voice of a mother is such a powerful sound. It is the bridge between the internal and external world. —Is that what you want Issata? he touched her fingers. They didn't move. —Where are you? —If you hear me, please come back. Only you can make this decision now! Issata, I am waiting for you. Tears filled his eyes, he surveyed her face and imagined the moment, her eyelids would move, her nostrils would open and her suave glare would lay on him. Nothing! —Think about all the champagne we have to drink! In fact, you have two bottles sleeping in your fridge, he reminded her. —And what about bringing them here?

—Do you know what I think, they should insert that golden liquid in her veins, he smiled tenderly. At that moment between his thought and the smile, a strange energy travelled through the room. It moved slowly. Jimmy fixed her and almost believed that her fingers had moved.

—Am I dreaming? he murmured, feeling a tingling sensation crawling along his right arm.

'Issata,' he called softly. Her eyelids trembled and he anticipated her eyes rolling inside them. 'Do you hear me?'

She blinked her eyelashes and slowly opened her eyes. The face watching above her, looked familiar.

'Issata, you are alive!' he exclaimed, both hands, touching one of her hands. They stared into each other's eyes. She watched the visage, as if like she was searching to remember. The shape of the eyebrows, the clear and generous gaze, where did she see those details, so impregnated in her memory?

'Jimmy?' she called, naturally.

'Issata!' he burst into tears and rang the bell.

'Where am I?'

'In hospital,' he held his hands tightly, in case she was to disappear again.

'Hospital?'

'Darling, you will be fine! You took an overdose; everything will be ok, now!'

She widened her eyes, saw some pills white and blue. She was naked; The light was shining, then nothing.

'I'm sorry!' her voice rose, trembling, as if she was realising her act.

'I am so happy!'

'What's wrong?' A nurse rushed inside the room.

'She is alive!' Jimmy cried even more loudly. Another person was witness to her friend's emergence to life.

'Incredible! I am contacting the doctor!'

'It is a miracle,' Garrison declared, when he met them. He introduced himself and asked if she knew her name.
'Issata Sherif.'
'Madame Sherif, how do you feel?'
'I don't know.'
'Do you know why you are here?'
'I told her,' Jimmy intervened.
'Are you measuring your act?'
She watched him not saying a word.
'Nothing to be alarmed, we are going to keep you with us for some time'
'How long have I been here?'
'A week,' said Garrison.
'What date is today?'
'Monday 19 September,' Jimmy replied.
'Does it mean I am here since 12th September?'
'Yes,' Garrison confirmed.

For me to have mention it, I must now explain the significance of 12th September. It marks an important moment in the life of Nichiren. In 1271, on that date, he demonstrated the validity of his teaching. It was certainly clear, during Nichiren's time, his big theories of promoting compassion, wellbeing, equality for all, and a fortiori for women, that every human being is worthy of respect, didn't sit well with the government. From their point of view, he was an agitator who came to sabotage all their plans. So, he had to go. On that famous 12th September 1271, his execution was programmed. And guess what? As the executor was about to slash his head, a meteor crossed the sky, frightening the poor chap. The guy had no other choice than to run away. That planned persecution validated Nichiren's teaching in regard to the mystic law. His life vibrating in rhythm with the universe, he was able to draw the support he needed at the crucial moment. His experience is named in one of his letters: "The Tatsunokuchi Persecution". In another writing: "The Opening of the eyes", he expressed with his own words: "On the twelfth day of the ninth month of last year, between the hours of the rat and the ox (11:00 p.m. to 3:00 a.m.), this person named Nichiren was beheaded. It is his soul that has come to this island of Sado."

—It's true, no one could kill Nichiren, she contemplated, and I am still alive. That's what the date, 12th September 1271, refers to. On that same date, 743 years later, Issata destiny took a different turn.

'I am going to observe you quickly and more tests will be organised for the days to come.'

She shook her head and let him do.

'Nothing to declare, you are alive,' Garrison said.

—I am alive, she told herself!

'Will see you later. I am going to inform Dr. Benedict, and Dr. Clark that you are awake. They will be so pleased.'

'B, Dr. Clark,' she pronounced. Their names sent her back to the reality she had tried to free herself from. Her medical appointments, the millions of pills part of her daily diet, without forgetting the oral chemo, and the physical and emotional pain. —I can't go through that again!

Garrison left. Alone in the room, Jimmy came close to her.

'Issata, I missed you so much!'

'Who found me?' she, knew the answer, already.'

'It is me!'

'I know,' a guilty sound came from her mouth.

'You can't imagine how I felt when I saw you curled up on your floor. The world stopped at that moment. —Why? I kept asking myself. I felt so responsible and so powerless!'

—Why? Me too I have asked myself this question on many occasions and I still don't have the answer, she whispered in her heart. 'I don't know,' she spoke out.

Jimmy's eyes became wet. He had waited for this moment. He had summoned all gods of the universe to listen to his prayers. Today, his prayers were answered. Hearing her voice, represented the best gift the universe could offer him.

'I don't know what has got to me,' she continued. 'I just had to do it, to experience this pain, that suffering. I needed to impregnate my body with those contagious emotions. It was a vital necessity for me to feel the significance of losing hope. Jimmy, it hurts so badly and the body bleeds with ache, she sobbed.

'I know, it hurts. Me too, I had lost hope. For the second time, I was afraid to lose my friend. Issata, I prayed! I prayed like never before and here you are.'

—To pray, maybe that is the answer to find hope again! The fact that we can pray, open our hearts, express clearly our desires, denounces that an ounce of hope still exists inside. And that is the scintilla of prayer which revitalise those ambers of fire in our heart. Prayer gives birth to hope.

'But tell me what made you open your eyes?'

'I heard your voice.'

'Seriously?'

She nodded yes.

'What else?'

'Just your voice. I heard it all the time. I didn't know if I was dreaming. Then your voice painted an image, your face.'

'So, you heard me talking about the champagne?'

'Yes.'

'This is when you opened your eyes.'

Issata managed to smile. 'I was drawn by the sound of your voice. I was searching where it came from.'

Moved by the bond they shared, he watched for a second and said: 'I didn't tell your family.'

'Mum, Sophia,' she let out, 'Jimmy it would have killed Mum,' she cried.

'I know! You see, you have made it Issata. You can't give up. Think about all these women, just like you who suffer from loneliness. Think how you can inspire them.'

'Jimmy, I feel naked,' she doubled her tears.

'I have already seen you naked Issata, so nothing to fear. Now you have to choose the right clothes to dress up your life.'

She remained silent. He pulled out from the chest draw in the room, her Buddhist bag, and placed it close to her.

'I can pray with you if you want.'

'I don't want to dance through life alone anymore.'

'Your fairy tale will come true. There are always villains in every fairy tale story.'

'It is true! Villains always have a function. I must go now; I will come back tomorrow with clean clothes.' He kissed her tenderly.

Alone in the room, she couldn't avoid her Buddhist bag. She could feel, a violent resistance vibrating under the rhythm of her own anxiety. The idea of articulating those words which betrayed her, sounded impossible. In one movement, she could break her mini Gohonzon. She wouldn't have to hear about the mystic law, nor SGI anymore. But she couldn't ignore 12th September. A mystical reality! With a trembling heart, she pulled the little white and flat box, from her bag. She looked at this thing, which contained the immensity of the universe, according to Nichiren and opened the box. At the sight of the characters, she was shaken by an electric shock. Her lips moved spontaneously. A force emerged from her and that melody she had refused to hear, rumbled via the timber of her mantra. Guided by the harmony through her voice, she let her tears flow.

'I am alive,' her heart was screaming.

'New departure Issata!'

'New departure Jimmy!'

They raised their glasses, ten days later, at the terrace of Harvey Nichols.

Jimmy collected her from hospital and took her to Covent Garden where a beauty session waited for her.

She revealed a new woman. The African mama whose hair hadn't been combed for a very long time, found her Deedee Bridgewater look.

She didn't recognise her place when she stepped into her studio. Jimmy had scrapped all the dirt, changed her bedsheets, even did her laundry. She knelt in front her Gohonzon. —Mystic law, it is between you and me now!

She offered *sansho*. On finishing, a vibration surged from her phone. *I heard you had a malaise; hope you are feeling better. Kind regards, Rajeev.'* She read. —I hope he didn't see me. Her blood pumped through her heart quickly. 'All is good thank you.' No, it is not good! —What do you want from me?

Step by step, she was able to get a grip over her life. And found her joy of writing again. The word hope spoke to her differently. She would scribble the word in capital letters on many pages of her notes book, and imagined an injection of the word's definition, in her veins. Her heart had to reverberate on the sound of hope.

—Hope is the spiritual medicine of mankind.

—Hope should be the motto; we human beings must transmit to mankind.

—Not everything, is about revolt Sir Camus! Or perhaps, the revolt is a crucial ingredient to nurture hope? she was to analyse. This is when, the death of this philosopher intrigued her observation. —Even the death of Albert Camus is quite a mystery, she came to analyse. He died following a very tragic car accident. It is quite incredible, that this great man, who won the Nobel price, pondered so deeply on the theme of suicide, chose to travel with the son of his publisher, renowned for being a demon on the road? One could almost think that by flirting with death, he was looking to die himself. The more she thought about this man, he clearly demonstrated by his recklessness, the absurdity of his own life through his death.

Issata was back. She could feel that her own desire to find answers behind her illness, saved her from hell. Her desire to understand, shone deeper than the desire to die.

The word, hope, made her acknowledge how lonely, she felt. It existed, a separation between her entity and the world surrounding her. Most of her connections had their family lives and belonged to the working environment, which had let her down.

'I have only Jimmy,' she confessed to B.

'Why not join a group for sarcoidosis sufferers? This could help you meet new people who share your struggle.'

'Why not,' she sighed. Two years that the sarcoidosis invited herself in her life. The idea had never crossed her mind.

'This could be your next mission.'

'I would love to meet people!'

'Anyway, you are making big progress. What about your anger?

'My anger?' she repeated, 'It's still part of me.'

'You will confront it, when you are ready. Now I think it is high time to reduce the lithium in conjunction with a smaller dose of antidepressant.'

'I trust you B.'

Gary Grant? He didn't give her the choice, when he welcomed her in his clinic. 'Miss Sherif, your case is difficult, I sincerely encourage you to begin the intravenous treatment, especially considering what you have been through.' His soft and delicate gaze, begged her. She heard the compassionate voice of a man devoted in helping his patient. —If you say so, Gary she mumbled to herself before acknowledging a: 'Ok.'

—In October 1994, I encountered Buddhism, she wrote in her personal diary. 2014, twenty years later, I receive the last correspondence from VoyE, confirming that I am no longer part of their big family. —This is what 20 years of practice represents for my life: —*Je suis malade, complètement malade,* would say Serge Lama. I tried to kill myself. I am alone, unemployed and trapped in that sordid place. —All the pillars of my life have now collapsed. —Where is the enlightenment? —And these men, Mr. Smith, Khrystian, what were their purpose? Why did I attract this in my life? —That is right, I have invited them into my life? She was gobsmacked at her observation. For the simple fact, that she was ready to accept a part of her own responsibility, in regard to her suffering. Sincerely, she prayed. —Dan illustrated *Power,* he made me dream and I wanted to believe, she analysed.

—Khrystian, furnished the emptiness of my life. —Ok, sex was great, so mea culpa! And I had a story. —But this doesn't explain why I crossed their path. She chanted for hours every day, as she used to, but no answers emerged, no signs to help her understand. —Maybe there is nothing to understand because in both scenarios, I have suffered, one day, she concluded. In that second of acknowledgment, the word suffering revealed itself in the most concrete form of its significance. —That is exactly how it was unveiled!

With Dan, the prestigious lawyer, who represented my ideal, I suffered a great deal and my health worsened.

—Same with Khrystian the loser, who made me cum, I plunged into suicidal depression.

—So, nothing to do with them. They continued to live their lives, whereas I lost myself. —I am the weakest link! I have to change! Issata realised that both these two men performed a role completely different, however, the nature of her own attraction, guided her to the same suffering:

—Rejection! If they both manifested with prestige or as losers, she wouldn't have identified her part of responsibility. —That is the reason I had a relapse in my life when I thought I was ready to go back to work! she saw it crystal clear. —To meet Khrystian and put the light on my own insecurity. Tears shone in her eyes. —Only I, must respect my life! —Mr. Right exist, I must define him.

—4o, a little voice whispered to her ears, Issata opened her eyes, on the 13th of December, overwhelmed with gratitude. She had closed the thirtieth chapter of her life, proud to have experienced the *Grand Mal,* that many men and women, unfortunately, had not managed to emerge from. Messages were waiting for her. A lot came from her ex-colleagues. And she heard: *Ladies and Gentlemen, welcome to Paris; the onboard team and myself would like to thank you for travelling with us and we look forward to welcoming you onboard very soon.*

She smiled. —No, you are not going to see me again. I have landed, with great difficulty. But I am safe! I don't know where I am going, but I won't take that train anymore.

Naturally, a rebellious sentiment rose in her, underlying Camus's message in *The Rebel*. This essay denounced a metaphysical rebellion. From his point of view, a revolt against something is necessary to give sense to human existence. We just have to contemplate the origins of every revolution. How it began? People were angry. They had to express why they were angry. All those revolutionaries used their revolt as a catalyst to raise the life condition of mankind. —It does make sense! —Nichiren too used his revolt to bring a sense to his own mission.

—Why were Buddhist teachings failing to guide people to happiness? There was an urgent need to understand 'why'. And from that need, rose his profound desire to bring a personal answer to mankind. He left the Gohonzon.

—It was necessary for this depression to manifest, overwhelmed, she admitted. — That existential anguish had helped me express the woman in me, I had long suppressed. —I am a revolted woman! she declared, crying with joy.

There was only one place, she wanted to be to explore the new Issata. A clear sky, guided her to the park. She was excited. Even more so, she carried a bottle with her. 'Sayon!' She approached her tree, embraced her trunk.

'I am forty today! I am alive! Let's celebrate!'
She took a step aside and opened the champagne.
'Thank you, Sayon!' she said and brought Madame Clicquot to her lips. Enjoying the effervescence of the liquid on her being, she set to dance around her tree, one hand caressing her barks. 'Drink with me!' she offered, and poured some drops on the ground, targeting her roots. Pursuing her hysteria, she sensed the earth rumbling beneath her feet. Her eyes riveted to the ground and saw nature moving. Her ears perceived the sound of little bells

ringing in the air. Her gaze travelled around and the sound climbed in crescendo. The music persisted on a very distinctive polyrhythm, the rhythm of African music. —It sounds familiar, she spoke. Spontaneously, that curious melody emerged from inside her. Slid, from her lips:— Nam-myoho-renge-kyo,dadadadouidada,dada,Nam-myoho-renge-kyo,dadadadouidada,dada,Nam-myoho-renge-kyo, dadadadouidada, dadouidada…Amazed, she watched Sayon and continued to sing her mantra. She heard drums, tambourines, saxophone. It sounded like the opening of a ceremonial march. The fanfare intensified into the infinite space of the park. She let go of her friend and captured the movement of nature. The leaves had turned brown, prune, orange, yellow, that romantic season, described by Autumn. Winter was preparing its entrance. She could smell its icy and necessary perfume. Captivated by this show, she wondered: —Am I dreaming? A cold breeze slapped her face. She was not dreaming. The wind blew strongly, taking the role of the Chef d'orchestre. That natural gas, spurred her to chant, confidently. She expressed her mantra in a suave and authentic tone, mixing her timber in perfect harmony with the imaginary instruments. Her voice rose towards the sky, crossing the cosmos. Blasting away, her hands waved in the air. She felt a force lifting her. Her eyes looked up. The sun pierced through a huge cloud. In a split second, a blue blanket covered the sky. A stream crawled in the little path between her pupils and her lower eyelids. Overwhelmed, she grabbed her iPhone to immortalise that instant, with her melody, in the background.

—I will never be a singer, she cried, but I can manifest my revolt as a WOMAN! And I will live for that revolt in me!

—Is that what it means, '*Turning poison into medicine?*' came into her mind. —*To change poison into medicine is to transform even the greatest evil into the greatest good. One does not return to zero as it were, but one actually gains from the experience that once seemed so poisonous,*' Daisaku Ikeda explained.

'Happy fortieth!' exclaimed Jimmy, in the evening. They met at Zuma, a very hype Japanese restaurant in Knightsbridge.
'It could help you reveal the princess in you!' he expressed when he gave her the whole Disney collection.
'My Jimmy, why can't you be my prince?' she hugged him.
'It is against the Gay law!' They both laughed.

In Paris for Christmas, she announced her dismissal. The news shocked them all. Mum and Antoine announced their retirement for March 2015. Mum also added, that she didn't wish to spend the festive seasons with the family anymore. 'It makes me tired to come to Paris all the time!' she defended. Her remark vexed her daughter. —What about me? I am always alone. I wanted to finish with life and that is all you have to say? You, my mother? She didn't express her mind. In fact, no one reacted to it! It was Mum.

Part 3

EDWARD JONES

-Honnin- myō – From this moment-

6

The *Year of Dynamic Development, in the New Era of Worldwide Kosen Rufu'*, Daisaku Ikéda decided. And: —*The year of the rebellious woman,* Issata to add! —I now belonged to the world of unemployed women. —I could almost launch a group for 40+ she surprised herself to joke and become an influencer! Her surprise grew even more so when her health insurance became effective, in relation to her income protection. Moreover, she was receiving support from the council for her rent.

—Sarcoidosis, this is where I am at now! Every single day is a fight to get out of bed. Every day, I am having to face an unbearable pain stabbing my body; my brain gets confused and tired, forcing me to control any seizure activity, by more pills. There is not a day, I do not cry, because of you. So, please tell me, why did you choose my body? she addressed in her prayers!

—New tenants, she began to notice throughout January! Mainly young women, a bit too young to her logic, coming in and out of the house. All nationalities were represented, in a very ordinary way, however, their dress code and make-up were hiding a worrying vulgarity. They remained polite. A 'Hello' there and then, followed by 'Have a nice day,' summed up her encounter with these girls.

—Where do those girls come from? Sometimes, she happened to meet some of them conversing with Rajeev. He addressed her in a particularly kind manner.

She commenced her intravenous treatment, with *Remicade*, the name of brand which composed infliximab. What is there to know? First of all, this drug is used to treat a series of autoimmune illnesses, such as the Crohn disease, Rheumatoid arthritis, Psoriasis. It is a chimeric monoclonal antibody which neutralises the TNF alpha (Tumour necrosis factors) and induced the T lymphocytes apoptosis activation. Do you understand a thing? Neither do I! Issata explained that she understood it as a temporally biological therapy.

In theory, the time of treatment should have lasted three hours. It took her the whole day as the blood test and urine had to be checked, the medicine had to be released by the pharmacy and she needed to be monitored. She didn't complain, because Gary Grant passed by to say hello.

She discovered a different man. This time, no white robe covered his lengthy body. But a metallic blue pair of glasses dressed the shape of his generous gaze. The rectangular frame accentuated his cultivated face and the colour blended perfectly with his light blue shirt. —Are you casting for a new role Gary? she surprised herself to think. —Can he be an ideal man? followed through her mind, while she lost herself in his smooth look. She couldn't tell whether he was married, he never wore a ring. —Maybe he removes it when he is about to see me!

—After *The Lady and the Tramp*, why not *The Shrink and his Patient,* she had time to observe while he checked her neurones. —I am exhausted, she sighed when she reached home. —Will see in four weeks' time.

In the meantime, the book title, written by Iyanla Vanzant became her daily mantra. The Author helps us free ourselves by explaining that, relationship is an ongoing process of discovery and growth, starting with the *Self.* So, in the meantime... She was thrilled to have found a group for sarcoidosis sufferers in Central London. She met Julia, the tall, blond Australian woman, equipped with soft blue eyes. Like Issata she was the PR for an advertising company when the illness manifested in her life. She also connected with Gary, an ex-banker, originated from Ireland. Sarcoidosis flared up during the stressful time of his career. 'So do I, the illness infiltrated my body, while I was working under very difficult conditions.' Issata introduced herself and told her story. She didn't share her desire to die, but expressed: 'I am truly grateful for being alive.' Everyone was moved by her spirit. She met them every month.

In the meantime, ...She pursued her therapy with B. She was satisfied with her progress. Issata managed well the new dose of antidepressants.

In the meantime, ...February arrived and so was the time for her second injection.

In the meantime, ...Time flew as fast as a shooting star. In March, she received her third injection, in April the

269

fourth…No side effects from the treatment, such as runny nose, numbness, or feeling sick, but a bloating sensation, like a strong need to urinate were presenting itself as a concern. Dr. Clark was notified. 'It will get better,' he reassured her.

In the meantime, … As time went by, the rebellious woman was finding her place in this world which didn't seem absurd anymore, as she gave it a sense through looking for answers, about the purpose of her own existence. She read a lot, wrote her realisations.

3rd of May, Issata was making her way home by train, as usual when leaving the hospital. This time, her treatment terminated at four o'clock. Spring was smiling at her and she was hoping to sit at a bar terrasse before the sun disappeared. *—For me to mention that date, it must surely represent a key moment! —Touché! The 3rd of May is again considered as a symbolic date for SGI. Josei Toda was appointed the second president of the organisation on that same date in 1951 and Daisaku Ikeda the third in 1960. A date that represents a new departure and the commemoration of Mother's Day within SGI. The message behind 3rd of May is about advancing and never giving up.* Dressed in her jeans blue robe, with long sleeves, reaching her knees, a large woollen scarf, protecting her neck, her red Ralph Lauren handbag strapped to her right arm, she was reading: *Le bouddha dans votre miroir,* in French, a book explaining in a simple way how to realise the life state of the buddha in our modern time. Captivated by her lecture, she was not paying attention to the people climbing on the train. When out of the blue, she heard a

270

'Hey'. Not knowing who it was addressed to, she didn't try to find out. But the voice carried on, revealing a masculine tonality.

'Miss, excuse me.' She lifted her head. Sitting in front of her, a man dressed in black in a suit designed with elegance, looked at her with interest. Some locks of wavy greying hair, generously padded out, were slightly falling over his shoulder and a goatee beard, nicely shaped on his square face, revealed the maturity of a man carefully preserved. Fixed on each other, she could only admire, the light brown shade, on the skin of his face. It enhanced a natural complexion, and revealed an authentic portrait, painted for a modern time. A mixture of Asian and African blood, emanated from his aura, she aimed to analyse. He wore some white converses, labelling him as the rebellious artist. He made a sign of the book he was holding in his hand. To her surprise, he was reading the same novel in English: *'The Buddha in your mirror'*.

'Wow!' she expressed.

A childish smile escaped from the mouth of this man so charming.

'You are Buddhist?' he asked in the most natural manner.

'Yes,' she threw.

'Nichiren Daishonin?'

'Yes,'

'Me too' he giggled.

At that same moment, the train stopped at Kilburn Park station.

'I am getting off here,' she mumbled.

'Me too.'

Grabbing their stuff, they got off the train. Straight away, she absorbed a wild odour, emanating from being, sweet and woody, like black musk. Observing his silhouette, she took note of his tall and slender body. —He looks like a professor, she thought.

'I am Edward,' he presented his hand, once outside.

'Issata, nice to meet you.' she smiled and shook it.

'Beautiful name. Would you like to go for a drink? It is incredible to meet this way,' he went on.

—A drink? The only drinks I take are with Jimmy or alone. 'Ok' she accepted.

'There is a pub not too far,' he suggested.

'That is right, the Black Lion.'

'Are you coming back from work?' he asked on their way to the pub.

'No, I was in hospital.'

'Oh, everything ok?'

'Just a treatment, I have just started. And you have an accent?

'I am Italian and a Jazz musician.'

'I thought I had recognised the Italian passion in your voice.'

'And you are French?'

'Yes,' she managed to answer as they reached the pub. They found a cosy space on the garden terrace and he asked while she sat:

'What would you like to drink?'

'A desperado.'

'Oh, what is that?'

'A beer with Tequila.'

'Sounds good, I am going to try,' and walked away to fetch the drinks.

She lit up a cigarette, wondering if she was dreaming. Smoke evaporating around her, she concluded: —Maybe, life after death does exist after all! I have purged my sentences, I have been acquitted and I am at the Black

272

Lion, in company with a perfect stranger. —No, an Italian man, whose English is impeccable.

'Desperado for Madame! You smoke?'

'Yes, one of my favourite vices.'

He placed the drinks on the table.'

'Me too!' He lit up a Philip Morris.

'Thank you and cheers.' Issata raised her bottle.

'Salute,' he nodded.

'Oh, that is very strong, but it is good. Do you want to make me drunk?' he teased her.

'It is up to you!' she teased him. She felt the flamboyant woman, once she knew, emerging from inside her.

'So, you are a Buddhist?' she asked.

'Last year marked 40 years of practising.' This is when she discovered, —His name was Edwards Jones. He came from South Africa, bassist, divorced, father of two girls, Alexandra aged twenty and Valeria thirteen. 'They are beautiful and they mean everything to me!' he insisted on this fact. Issata observed the scintilla shine in his eyes when he ended his sentence, the pride of a father. He explained that he lived in Sicily with his adoptive parents Roberto and Rosalina. They transmitted to him, their passion for music, especially African music. Rosalina died five years ago. Roberto, aged eighty, lived alone in their big family's house because he was their only child. —Why did he divorce, she wished to know, impressed by his résumé?

'What about you?'

'Me?' she smiled, 'Last year, I turned 40 and marked my 20 years of practising.' She added, what we already know but didn't talk about wanting to kill herself.

'I celebrated my 60th birthday, last year too. We need to celebrate!'

—Twenty years gap, she had time to recognise, and read the sincerity shining in the eyes of that stranger.

'Absolutely, we have one number in common.

'Twenty!' he raised his glass.

'That' right twenty!'

They gulped their drink and she pursued:

'Do you live around?'

"On Kilburn Lane.'

'So do I, I can't believe it!'

'Actually, I am looking for a Buddhist local group.'

—Local group, she told herself. The light on her face faded away. Buddhist meetings, she had stopped attending them. Since she had fallen ill, she looked at SGI from a different eye. A woman's eye, deeply hurt and who kept going. From the outside, what a great initiative, peace in the world, because we are all buddhas, we are human beings with immense potential, but as an insider, that movement well-observed and recognised throughout the world didn't inspire her anymore. She breathed deeply:

'To be honest, I am not going to meetings anymore,' she sighed. He stared at her and sincerely assured her:

'I understand you. I went through this phase too, where, I didn't feel inspired to do activities. I lost faith in all those national leaders.'

Touched by his sincerity, finally, someone understood her, she let out: 'That is exactly how I feel. I lost faith in those leaders at the top. I understand why people leave SGI after many years of practice!' Tears shone in her eyes.

'Maybe you could seek guidance with your woman leader'

'Would you believe me if I told you, I had contacted her on many occasions, and she dismissed me?'

'I see, but regardless of her behaviour, she is still a human being.'

'For sure she is a human being,' Issata acknowledged, politely.

'I have learnt throughout my years of practice, the importance of not judging. As Gandhi would clearly say:
—Be the change, you wish to see, so, let's be that change we wish to see!' Edward continued.

—I clearly do not aspire to resemble that woman! And find myself at the age of seventy, prisoner of an unfulfilled desire, she talked to herself. 'You are right, I must focus on becoming the change I would like to observe around me, she answered. 'Having said that, for the moment, I refuse to give them my energy. After all, Buddhism manifests itself in daily life.'

'Well said! You are clear! The most important thing is to never give up. I made myself a promise to never stop practicing and to never leave SGI. We do not practice for an organisation, but we are ambassadors of Sensei. And it is up to you and me to continue what he had started.'

'Do you know what, — I feel free, that is the irony of it! Free not to have to attend those Buddhist meetings and to listen to all those leaders, who are only seeking to grow the membership of the organisation.'

'I am here now and we can chant daimokus together.'

'I would love this,' she smiled.

Their eyes remained locked to each other, the time to write a new scenario. That joyous moment led to another desperado. Issata was inviting. The evening followed its course under the sounds of laughers. —To laugh, this verb had deserted her vocabulary since the dawn of time. It reappeared instilling inside her, that sublime sensation that the word itself describes. She felt good.

—If someone had told me, one year ago, that after spending my days flirting with suicidal thoughts, gnawed by the lack of hope, that one year later, I will be sitting at the garden terrace of the Black Lion, with a stranger, I have the feeling to have had known long ago, drinking a desperado, I would have never believed them.

Around eight o'clock, the sun was getting ready to sleep and the wind was getting excited.

'I must go now; I have a gig in Brighton this weekend.' Edward let out.

'I understand, it is getting a bit cold, as well.' She threw back her woollen scarf on her shoulders.

—And what is next, passed through her mind?

They readied themselves and left the pub. Outside on the pavement, he approached her. His lips caressed her cheeks and he whispered to her ears: 'I would like to see you again.'

He pushed his head back slowly, waiting for her answers. Speechless, she got carried away by the gentle stroke of this man who wanted to see her again. The artist, uttered these words as if he was denouncing the title of a song, presenting a chorus to which, she had no other choice than to add her own poetry.

'So am I,' her lips trembled.

They exchanged numbers.

Indeed, the story continued. He was sitting at the *Dolce Vita*, an Italian restaurant located on Kilburn High Road, and watched her, walking towards him.

On his return from Brighton, he phoned her.

Issata trembled with excitement when she saw his name flashing on her iPhone's screen. —Shall I answer, her ego questioned? —I don't want him to think I am desperate. —Who cares what he thinks, what matters is you, whether you want to meet this man again? —Yes, I do! —So, answer now, an honest voice ordered to pick up. 'Hello,' she answered softly. 'Issata, it's Edward.'

All this to state, that he didn't send a text confirming the time and the place, for a rendezvous. But his warm Latin voice, took the courtesy to call her. A musical voice, imbued by the romantic tonality beneath which, we recognise an Italian man.

He was draped in a velvet dark blue suit, highlighted by a soft white shirt. A silky violet foulard around his neck, fell on his shoulders. Issata chose a blue petrol robe for the occasion; the famous boubou design, honoured with pride, by men and women. A large butterfly was embroidered in black, at the front of the dress, where each wing felt on both side of the garment v neck. While he listened to the sound of her black wooden high heels sandal, opened toes, lapping on the ground, like a horse trotting in a meadow, he didn't fail to notice the red vibrant polish, on her toe's nails. He rose to his feet and greeted her, by kissing her hand.

'Bonasera Issata.'

His perfume hypnotised her. It smelt deeper than the first time. And she could recognise a deeper note completing the primitive fragrance.

'Good evening, Edward,' she giggled surprised.

'I am old school.'

'I love it!'

'And you are sublime.'

'Thank you so are you. What is your parfum?'

'Terre d'Hermes and yours is Chanel 19.'

'That's right!'

'How incredible that we chose blue tonight,' she pursued taking her seat.

'Well spotted, to a blue evening then, after *La vie en rose.*'

They burst into laughter and a waiter came to assist them.

They ordered a bottle of Prosecco, olives and focaccia for aperitif. He shared about the gig at the Verdict in Brighton.

'The room was full! The audience loved it!' he threw. He explained that he will be on tour in Europe for three weeks. In awe, she listened to the glamourous life of this man, she had the good fortune to meet, thanks to the treatment to cure her sarcoidosis.

A woody smell, with a hint of a dusty patchouli dominance, floated in the air. A soft snoring sound, could be heard rising around her. She opened her eyes, to the murderous light coming through the blind. A warm presence caught her attention. She turned her head on her right and saw him, peacefully asleep, an exquisite smile, printed on his lips. What has happened? She remembered the joy; she experienced in his company. She chose, linguine *al cartoccio* for her meal. 'I already know what I want, I love their *spaghetti al salmone !*' The waiter opened a bottle of chianti, selected by Edward. The master tried it and liked it.

She didn't want it to stop.

'What do we do?' he asked when the dinner was over. 'A last glass at mine?' she suggested without any hesitation. His smile contained the answer, she was hoping for. A taxi drove them to her place. 'Wow, you have a lot of stuff,' he commented when they passed the door. 'I know, the story of my life! Ready for that last glass?' 'Deal!' She served two glasses of Bordeaux and: 'Santé!' They clinked. Enjoying the robust aroma sliding inside her throat, she wanted him so much and felt her tits reaching an erection. As if he had heard her call, he murmured slowly in a courteous manner: 'Do you want?' 'Yes, I want to!'

They put down their glasses on the table.

Edward's hands moulded the shape of her face, as if he was trying to impregnate his fingers with it. Then, he placed his lips on hers. This quartet of luscious flesh engaged into a tango of kisses. Issata allowed the desire to grow through her. Carefully, she listened to the concise musical sounds, his mouth performed with grace. He kissed her, like no man had ever kissed her before. She savoured a nectar, mixed with multiple tastes. The coulis flowed in her mouth and slid, in the same way, a stream would determine to return to its source. Her breasts began to swell. She trembled, she quivered. Her theory was being confirmed. A man who knew how to kiss a woman, knew how to make love. Those same hands landed on her narrow hips. She pulled him to the bed. They enlaced and continued their passionate kisses. The mouth of his lover, changed it trajectory and reached her neck. With his tongue, he zigzagged alongside that elastic trunk, which separated her head, from the rest of her body. Issata shuddering, caught one of his hands, and placed it on her chest. He got the message and played around the dunes. As soon as he touched her, she felt a familiar flame, reviving her whole being. Lost sensations, were returning. The pleasure kept growing, inside her.

Then Edward decided to try something different.

With his fingers, he brushed those two black spots, like a pianist would press a keyboard. Both nipples looking extremely similar, sounded completely different on this African melody. Their breathing intensified. He lifted his eyes towards her. Their gaze sharing the same complicity, he raised up, to take off his clothes. She admired his slender, fit and beautiful body. His sex attracted her, most. It looked like a piece of art; the kind of precious item conserved in luxurious galleries. That famous night, she was the owner of it. He took out of his pocket a pack of two condoms and placed it on a side table. Smiling, he pulled down her coral blue panties. She shivered when he brought his face near the entrance neatly shaved.

A special piece of art emerged within her dark hairs, and appeared by the same occasion to Mr. Jones's eyes, a rare treasure, only a fine connoisseur could afford. In order to attest to its own uniqueness, he smelt it. Rapidly, his nose quickly detected the particularity, emanating from the exotic scent. It was not Gauguin's signature. It was not Modigliani's special brush stroke. He was discovering, a sculpture authentic. No one could reproduce such a jewel. He freed her from her dress.

Both naked, he laid on top of her. With his talented hands, he caressed her, as if he was practising his own instrument, strolling back and forth on her flank. She could feel him rubbing against the entrance of her fountain.

As she was about to guide him to the secret passage, Edward stopped her. 'Let me do it!' he whispered.

His lips travelled down to her ebony forest. Issata's body was shaken by an immense pleasure, which no man who ever visited that hidden territory, could offer her. The caresses, she received, described a new beginning. It was soft, the way it should be. Even more so, that delicate touch, was an indication, that finally, the cloud of good fortune had found refuge above her destiny. Edward lifted her slightly and indulged himself with the rich liquor escaping from her crevasse. She moaned deeply. He continued to massage her and followed the path towards her black and pink bud. She spread her legs and swayed like a black panther, ready to leap on its prey. She felt the concentrated pleasure in the middle of her hips, burning the lower part of her body. The orgasm climbed through her.

While she caught up her breath, she furrowed her fingers, in his sliver hair and pressed his head inside her legs.

A scream of ecstasy escaped from her mouth. The sound came from far and resonated on the same tempo of her warm body. Her body continued to jerk. She was submerged by joy. Then Edward lifted his head, his face covered with sweat. She pulled him to her and kissed him.

'Thank you!' she murmured.
'It's not over!' he let out.
He rose to his feet and she watched him dress the private part of his body, with one of the plastic socks, he had brought. When he returned to her, she helped him slid inside her legs. A wave of heat, crawled through her again. Edward began to paddle. On the way, he greeted the little man on the boat, with utmost respect and dove into her vagina's waters. Was he writing a new version of *'The old man and the sea?' — Little reference to Ernest Hemingway, here. Santiago, the protagonist was a skilled fisherman... The moment arrived when he had to confront oldness. Eighty-four days passed by and he was not able to catch any fish. He kept going, and ventured to the Gulf Stream...Eventually, he captured a marlin. One can only envisage the joy beaming out of the life of this man, the joy of perseverance.*
So, Edward pursued his path at his own rhythm, looking inside her eyes. Moved, he was, to be sharing that journey with her. Issata let new sensations emerging from her flesh. She was called for a new adventure, towards a dynamic dimension, a sexual and spiritual path. She was seduced, and just wanted to eradicate, any traces of Khrystian in her life; to rinse the taste of his kisses, by moulding her lips to Edward. She used each drop of her

new lover's perspiration, to wipe out any sexual footprint from that gigolo. Each vibration represented new notes. She was composing a new melody under the magical caresses of that Italian man. Together, they were performing their own comedy musical. They were working on elaborating, a new symphony, based on sensational and overwhelming sounds, like those, revealed in love stories.
—The story of a man, twenty years her eldest, author and composer; and the experience of a woman, happy to have reached forty and who had dared to believe. They swam freely in the intimate ocean of their sentiments, when naturally, they succumbed to the delicious and spasmodic waves of pleasure. The Franco-African woman and the Italian man from South Africa exploded in a harmonious orgasm. 'Buongiorno,' she heard.

As if she was waking up from a dream, 'Buongiorno,' her voice murmured.

'Did Madam sleep well?' He moved close to her and his hand crawled on her belly. It didn't go further, but enticing enough to pull a laughter from madam.

'Yes, and mister?' she giggled.

'Mister too! And he is feeling famish!' His hand went back hunting, so did the rest of his body, inviting Issata's body to join him. She could not believe it!

The morning passed by like a dream. Before they parted, they took breakfast together, or rather a coffee, and managed to do Gongyo. On hearing herself praying with Edward, she realised how much she had missed chanting with members.

'So, Edward?' Jimmy began.

'He is wonderful!'

They were sitting on his balcony having lunch. She shared in detail the magical moments spent with that Italian man.

'Love at first sight, then!'

'When he kisses me, I feel dizzy, it is unreal, it is beautiful!'

'He is sixty, right?'

'Well considering his age, it is working perfectly fine.'

'When is he back?'

'Two weeks!'

'To your fairy tale!' Jimmy rose his glass.

'I am so scared!'

'Trust sweetheart! So happy for you. I feel the transformation in you!

What about your treatment?'

'So far, I am ok, I just feel swollen and find it hard to pass my water. Dr. Clark says it will pass.'

'Watch out then! And the Sarcoidosis Society?

'Everyone is lovely! My therapy, I have reduced on the antidepressants. And I have to admit that I am managing quite well.'

Jimmy watched her deeply moved.

'Yes, B knows and she is happy for me.'

'Issata, you are glowing.'

'So are you,' she said. She looked at him as if he was hiding something.

He offered her a cheeky smile.

'What?'

'Well, I met that guy.' His secret out, he blushed.

'And it is now that you are telling me?'

Jimmy explained how it started. He had just finished his cardio exercise at the gym. Heading towards the changing room, he noticed a man, tall and fit as a gladiator, caramel-looking skin, dark curled hair, watching him. He remained bewitched by his green eyes. The guy smiled, approaching him. 'I am Xavier,' he introduced himself.

'Jimmy,' our dear friend mumbled.

'I have been observing you for a while,' he expressed confidently, 'I am going to do twenty minutes of treadmill, do you have time for a coffee after?'

Blushing, Jimmy melted down.

'Why not?' he managed to answer.

'Super!' Xavier headed towards the sport room, and Jimmy disappeared to have his shower.

Excited, he had a hard-on at the thought of meeting this man who has been observing him for some time.

—And how come I haven't noticed him, he wondered. He waited in the cafeteria of the club.

The guy with green eyes, arrived dressed in jeans, black bombers coat, red Nike trainers, and was holding a motorbike helmet under his right arm.

He is French of Spanish origin, fifty years old, freelance photographer, father of two boys, Ethan twelve and Raphaël eight. Children? His ex-Vero had always known that Xavier liked men. She waited patiently for his coming out. At the birth of his second boy, he couldn't lie to himself any longer. He couldn't lie to them. They lived together till Raphael's fifth birthday. Because they wanted to install in them the awareness and understanding that life is meant to be lived and shared. And that to our present age, some men love men and some women love women.

Did they paint Van Gogh? Yes, ten days later.

After two rendezvous for drinks, passionate kisses, Xavier invited him to the New Grill, a restaurant modern cuisine, located on Liverpool Street. He wore a Bordeaux costume, highlighting a pink salmon shirt, slightly opened on the neck which revealed a gold chain with a black stone, diamond-like. Under that romantic accoutrement, he impregnated more the businessman looking for comfort after weeks of negotiations, rather than the athlete in his sporty outfits. He watched Jimmy conversing with a waitress. She pointed in his direction and escorted him through the warmth of this sophisticated venue, made from brick red looking, a mosaic of vibrant colours. Xavier rose to his feet when they reached the table.

'Good evening, Jimmy,' he kissed him tenderly on his lips. A deep emotion penetrated his heart. He lived his homosexuality with pride.

'Good evening, Xavier,' he let out and removed his three-quarter beige coat. Always very elegant, he had opted for a black suit and a pink shirt, exactly the same colour as his lover's shirt.

'It is a sign,' Xavier observed.

'I love signs!' They sat, and the same waitress returned, with the aperitif. Champagne of course and appetisers, Xavier had organised.

'Wow, I am starting to get used to that luxury life!'

'I hope so,' Xavier smiled.

The champagne opened, the waitress served their glasses, and placed the delicacies on the table. —puffed salmon pastries, olives, salami, and so much more.

'Santé!' they exclaimed when she left. They swallowed the liquid as if making love with their eyes. They haven't checked the menu yet, but their hormones were already thinking to savour the desert. —Well, this would have to wait, their accomplices' minds answered.

They attacked the nibbles, while they shared their daily activities, that is to say, work, Ethan and Raphael, and they realised that they didn't have much to share. Because they texted almost every day, since their first coffee. How did they resist?

They laughed a lot. Then Jimmy told him that he had just finished reading: *The power of now*, written by Eckhart Tolle. The book reveals the story of our ego, in our everyday life. Ego is the impostor, the identity thief. Xavier pulled out from his bag, a blue book. They smiled in osmose through that power of the moment, that power to share, to speak, to simply be.

The waitress approached them for the main course.

With that same complicity, they chose a côte de boeuf, served with its bordelaise sauce, accompanied by baby potatoes and green beans. For the wine, Châteauneuf-du-Pape. Then and there, they indulged themselves with their feast. An alimentary orgy was taking place publicly.

They devoured their meal with passion. Each time, they inserted those juicy pieces of food in their mouth, a smile was printed on their visage, followed by an erotic sigh during mastication. Came the degustation of the wine.

As good citizens of France, they swallowed the blood of the almighty, toasting to Eve's happiness. If she hadn't tricked Adam into eating the apple, they wouldn't have met. The most spectacular moment presented itself when they finished their meat. They had undressed the beast from its flesh, however, the sauce still remained in their mouth, tickling their palate. Their eyes fixed on the bone in the plate, a telepathic idea illuminated their imagination.

'Make me,' Xavier defied, laughing. Slowly, he inserted the bone measuring about twenty-five centimetres' long, in his mouth.

'No!' Jimmy let out, red from exposure.

'Someone is timid?'

'Is that so? Do you want to play? Watch me!' And Jimmy to take on the challenge.

After such a dinner, dessert could no longer wait.

A taxi escorted them to Hampstead, where Xavier lived. Burning with desire, they kissed savagely. They wanted each other, so badly, anticipating what they would do on arrival. Finally, they arrived, free from all eyes, any kind of boundaries. Naked, they found themselves in Xavier's bedroom, determined to honour, their right to love. Lying on the bed, they explored each part of their body through caresses, kisses more adventurous.

'Jimmy, I am so happy for you,' she smiled.

'Darling, it is the first time that I feel in complete harmony with someone. Xavier is the crystallisation of what I aspire to.'

'To our fairy tale!' they raised their glasses.

She arrived before a big Victorian house, the kind characterised by pointed roofs, painted bricks.

Those properties were named after, painted women. Why such an appellation? The architectural style of that time was inspired by the aesthetic movement, which celebrated the cult of beauty, observed through picturesque paintings. That era placed its focus on the image of women. A woman was regarded as an object of desire. Artists searched to define the ideal woman, the fatal woman.

The sun was still shining. She rang the bell, her heart trembling. —What if it was just an illusion, the mirage of my own fantasies? But the kisses, the orgasms, I didn't invent them?

'Good evening, Issata,' Edward opened the door and welcomed her, in a hallway bigger than her studio flat. Above her head, a big chandelier brightened the white ceiling and the green upholstered walls, very light green.

His voice sounded real. The brown gaze, she carried with her, in her sleep, was shining in front of her. The man who left her, one morning, three weeks ago, clearly existed.

A pair of black spectacles, designed by Christian Lacroix, accentuated the softness in his gaze. He had a linen cream trousers and a lilac shirt on, very simple.

'Good evening, Edward,' she smiled nervously.

'You are beautiful,' he placed a kiss on her lips.

A prune pleated dress covered her silhouette. She looked like a Coco Chanel model, daring to boast her feminine elegance. A golden black shawl protected her shoulders, and highlighted a cream tote handbag and her beige braided high heels opened toes.

'Thank you,' she whispered. 'Do you wear glasses?'

'Yes, mainly in the evening.'

'Oh?'

'The other night, I forgot them!' He understood her inquisitive look.

'It is magnificent here!'

'Wait till you see inside!'

He took her hand and escorted her inside his manor.

She was lost for words when they accessed the main room, painted in cream, equipped with vintage furniture from the time of Louis XIV. Her emotion amplified when her ears captured the music from her favourite movie, *Cinema Paradiso,* resonating in its grandeur. The film carried her throughout her twenties, a story about friendship, complicity, the greatest love story of our time. She had spent hours listening to the soundtrack, for many days, months, years, and up till today. She had dreamt of a story like Salvatore and Elena, and promised herself, to one day write her own version of *Cinema Paradiso*. He placed his arm, around her waist and let her enjoy, the sensorial pleasure vibrating in the room. She shivered. He felt her tension and searched for her fingers as if to protect her. She played the game, and immersed herself into his creative life, the baroque time, that she could feel breathing in the house. Every corner had its function. There was a place for his music, the first thing she had noticed. His contrabass, made from an oak tree, a mixture of cherry and chocolate colour, laid on the floor, looking like a woman after a passionate night. Issata felt her aura. A strong force was protecting the sanctuary of the master. —You are alive, she heard herself say. — And, thank you for welcoming me in your master's propriety. Plunging herself into an emotional trance, she also caught the black grand piano, *Fazioli,* the Italian brand, of course, an electric bass, drums, timbales, a real concert stage. Not far from the orchestral scene, she saw his black butsudan placed on a white cabinet. Standing majestically, it emerged as the reflection of his own personality, a sincere man. Issata couldn't believe what she was witnessing. He guided her towards a large red baroque sofa, the wooden legs painted in gold. Everything was set up on a tea table, champagne flutes, candles, and little white serviettes.

'It is my friend's flat. He left for New York and needed a tenant.'

'How lucky!' she exclaimed.

'I am!'

'And where do you sleep?'

'I will show you later if you want?' he winked at her.

'I should hope so!'

'Have a seat, I go and get the aperitif.'

'Oh, I almost forgot,' she gave him a bottle of Prosecco.

'Thank you, I will keep it in the fridge.'

She sat on that luxurious sofa, and watched him slipping off the room. Overwhelmed, her eyes stopped at the windows opened, dressed with cardinal red curtains. She travelled to a different century. —I would so much like to live here, she let out. Her eyes wandered in the living room and stopped at a round table covered by a white knitted cloth. Long red candles, firmly maintained within the candle holders, were waiting to be lit. Against the wall, an immense cabinet stood in the corner. Through the glass doors, she saw white porcelain dishes, little blue flowers printed on them. A whole set was exposed in it, telling a story. A story of inheritance, generations, richness, a story amongst millions of stories made to be shared. Such beauty burnt her eyes.

Edward came back, carrying a large tray with champagne and mini bruschetta for appetisers. Some with tomatoes, mixed with parsley and thin onions and some with avocado mousse, and prawns. He placed the goodies on the table and served their glasses.

'Señora,' he handed over, her flute.

'Edward, it looks amazing!'

'Do you know what?' he made her observe, when he sat near her.

'Tell me, Mr. Jones!'

'We met on 3rd of May!'

She widened her eyes and exclaimed:

'That's right! The day, Sensei became president!'

'It's a sign!'

'Absolutely! To 3rd of May!' she raised her glass.

'To 3rd of May, Issata Sherif!'

They gulped their drink. Joy brightening their faces, she asked: 'So how was the tour?'

'Super, thank you for asking!' He shared, how fulfilled he felt, when playing, his moments with the musicians and mainly Lelo. 'He is my best friend, an excellent drummer, so clumsy but so funny.'

'Friendship, is so important,' she echoed to his comments and introduced him to Jimmy, through her own words, how they met, and the bond uniting them.

'I look forward to meet him!'

'For sure! And the family?'

'Before we forget, let's eat!' he pointed towards the little sandwiches.

'Thank you.' She picked up the crackers with prawns. He chose the tomato's one.

'It's delicious!' she chewed politely.

'Please yourself!'

'Family?' he raised back, 'My father is fine. I often wonder how he manages without my mother. He inspires me so much. His daily routine carries him, through life. He is strong.' A note of emotion, resonated in his voice. 'But I am mainly worried for Alex.'

'Alexandra?'

'Yes, she wants to come to London.'

'Really?' she coughed.

'Everything ok?' He pated on her back, gently.

She received like a punch in her stomach, so that the food missed its turn. Her encounter with Edward had just commenced. However, she needed to acknowledge a big element. —The children! —No, the girls! A girl is more complicated to raise, than a boy.

'No worries, a crumb got stuck in my throat!'

'Drink up then!' He refilled their glasses.

'So, when is she coming?' she tried to investigate.

'Not decided yet!'

'To be continued then!' she smirked and swallowed more wine.

'I know, she needs me,' he defended, and sounded guilty.

What to answer to that? She fixed his eyes. They just revealed the love of a father, looking to protect his daughter.

'Can we smoke?' was the best, she could come up with.

'Of course!'

He went to get an astray.

'Very original!' she let out, when he joined her back. He had in hand, a copper recipient, made in the shape of a shell.

'Alex, offered it to me!'

'I see, very touching,' she sighed.

They lit up their fags. Edward's mobile rang.

'Sorry, but I must answer,' He walked away.

Pulling into her ciggy, she felt a hot flush, climbing up to her throat, with the same intensity, Edward's voice rose from a different room, the kitchen she discovered. She was not sweating, but the sensation didn't feel agreeable. She could sense a shadow, a sign, like a cyclical element. That pattern occurred each time, she wanted to believe.

'It was Alex,' he explained, reappearing.

'Everything ok?'

'A problem with her mother.'

'I see, Mother and daughter, the story of women,' she sighed. Her own sound, sent her back to her own relationship with her mother.'

'Anyway, let's focus on our evening,' he caught her hands.

'What about your treatment?'

'It follows its course,' she could only say.

'In that case, I wish you a speedy recovery, because we have so much to discover together.'

'Like what?'

He brought his lips near hers and kissed her.

'Like this!'

'I hope to match up to it!' she giggled.

'First, let's have diner!' His hand encouraged her to stand up. Of course, she followed him. 'Have a seat!' he readied her chair, like in the restaurants and lit up the candles.

Minutes later, a feast was laid in front of her. He served

pumpkin tortellini's, accompanied by a beef ragout. *Amarone*, Italian's grand cru, honoured their meal. 'That bottle comes from my friend's vineyard in Italy,' he let out proudly. He freed the wine, from the bottle and poured the smooth scarlet in a decanter.

'Bon *Appetito* Issata!'

'Bon *Appetito* Edward!'

A subdued light dictated the theme for the night. They ate, alongside the music soothing their senses. The food slid deliciously in her mouth. The wine's bouquet revealed the greatness of the perfect gentleman, and the special guest added her unique touch.

When? How? She lost track. She remembered the distinctive sound of trumpets, the HiHat thundering in the room. All instruments rose in a languorous sound, supported by the spell of piano notes. Then the contrabass brought the whole orchestra, together. By then, the dinner was finished. They had reached the dessert part. A fruit salad, served in a sauce made with rum, ginger, lemon, and honey, also belonged to the chef's talent.
'It is me playing,' he said.
Moved to tears, she only realised, he was inviting her to dance, when he reached her and murmured: 'Our Love is here to Stay...' She followed the rhythm of his steps, methodical and slow. And listened to the sound of each instrument traversing the room. Each note danced with her and guided her, to her sole and unique mission, — to be happy. On the way, they did a stopover on the sofa.
At the boarding, no cloth was detected on their body.
The tempo was set for the course of the voyage and they were both ready to take off. Edward was a man of experience —Nothing to do with age! He loved women

and knew how to love them. He knew his discipline with preciseness. A woman represented his musical source. He understood that every woman was unique and each woman possessed that the key to our own pleasure. He had learnt to vibrate with women; small shapes, slim, tall, corpulent bodies. He loves fusing with a feminine body and together exploring any forbidden games. A woman's geographical anatomy was no secret to Mr. Jones. Half African, half Asian, Edward's Jones made love like a professor, and remained an eternal student in the art of learning the pleasure of love. The story wanted that him and Issata shared that common ground.

Ready for landing, two hearts beat in one note. The pressure from their orgasm, intensified and a myriad of sensations burst through their wet bodies. Submerged, by a deep joy, Issata felt her body floating in the air. A mystical energy continued to overflow. They remained silent, enjoying the nocturnal peacefulness reigning in the warm air.

Marching down her street, her stomach began to ache. Shaken by a recurrent anguish, she was trembling.

— How to return to Valley Park after such a romantic moment with her Prince? Reality forced some huge tears to roll down her cheeks when she passed her door. She so wanted to believe! —Because in all fairy tales, the Prince Charming always rescues the princess. —Edward lives close by in a big house. —And together, we will live happily ever after and without children…That is the new script!

She spent more time at her lover's house than at her home. Her belly grew bigger. And Dr Clark had to admit that something was not right and accepted to send her for a scanner. The result came sooner than expected. There was a cyst on her kidney which needed to be drained. —So, I was not mad, she sighed, relieved!

'You are the famous Edward?' An excited Jimmy welcomed Issata and her lover at his home.

'And you are Jimmy?'

'Yes, her husband in her next life!'

Edward looked at his girlfriend, smiling.
'She forgot to mention that detail, but I will keep the place warm for you.' The all laughed heartily and hugged.

They went to join Xavier or Xaxa, would say Jimmy, smoking on the balcony. He was as handsome as her friend described him. Issata was surrounded by three men, tall, charming, and sincere. Two men who loved each other, and one that she loved.
The champagne was served. They shared their stories. Xavier talked about his life as a father, and being gay, and how grateful, he was towards his ex, Vero. 'I would have never been free. All my life, I would have been dependent on the way society looks upon me, just like we can be dependent on our husband or wife. A lot of us hope for someone else to rescue us. Vero did rescue me, only when I was ready to come out. This is what I want to teach to my boys.' Words filled with wisdom, from a man in love with another man. Jimmy faithful to himself, held his hand

297

tightly within his fingers. Issata explained, that she was waiting for a date to pierce her cyst.

The evening was flowing nicely, when the Italian man, the master of Jazz, the man in control of his freedom, announced that Alex was arriving in London 20th November.

'Are you serious?' They all heard, the black woman's scream. Edward as a father, was only echoing to another father's sentiments, in regards to his boys.

'I understand you,' he had to say. 'I am a father too, with two daughters, 20, and 13 years old of age. They are my life! For instance, at the moment my ex and I are facing a challenge with our eldest.' Then he dropped the bomb.

Both Jimmy and Xavier witnessed the decomposition on her face. Her nostrils began to smoke. They felt for her and spotted tears in her eyes.

'I only found out this morning and didn't have time to tell you.' Edward placed one arm, around one shoulder.

'How long for?'

'I can't say, she wants to try. It will give me the opportunity to spend time with her.'

An explosion of emotions burst inside her. Alex had just broken her dream. She watched her desire to settle with Edward, disappearing in the ruins of her imagination. And of course, her doubts invited her anger. Her demon didn't have time to explode, because the doorbell came first.

'Our dinner has arrived, go for a fag, if you want.'

'Great idea!' Xavier rose to his feet.

'Issata wait for me in the kitchen,' Jimmy suggested, walking to the door.

Xavier understood and dragged Edward to the balcony.

'Darling, everything will be fine!' He found her, smoking by the window. 'I feel so stupid! He should have told me!'

'He admitted it, she took him by surprise!' he lit up a fag too. 'Plus, you will be able to decide on what you want!'
'Jimmy, I feel I am losing it! I hate where I live!'
'Issata, did you hear what Xaxa said earlier? You have to free yourself! That is not Edward's responsibility! You were already in that situation before you meet him!'
'And my fairy tale then?' she breathed deeply not to shed tears.
'That is your job to write your own fairy tale.' Jimmy whispered. She sniffed loudly. They finished theirs fags quickly and joined the other men.

Issata had to force herself to remain polite, even in front her favourite dish. She found her comfort in the wine, the champagne, and cognac. They went back to Edward in the middle of the night. They managed to make love,

—The least he could do, considering his child is coming to ruin my life, she said those words.

Early morning, she left him, dressed with the costume of the revolted woman. Approaching the white and black house, she saw Rajeev entering his car. —What is he up to? her heart drummed loudly. It was about 8 am. Their gaze met. —That is all your fault, she wished to spit at his face! His vicious look was laughing at her, under that same diabolical sound, a sorcerer would make when everything falls according to plan. —Hihihi, I am the master! Torn by disgust, she passed him, pretending, she didn't see him.

Kneeling in front of Gohonzon, she cursed Alex, loudly crying. —Me at your age Alex, I arrived in London by myself. —I was twenty by the way.
—I found a job —And Basta!

—Miss Sherif, this is Dr. Clark, a bed is waiting for you to pierce your cyst. She received that message, on the morning of November 18th, just after she had finished her prayers.

Since the gathering with the men, Xaxa's words followed her. Finding a palace that would sustain her happiness, represented that one desire on her dream list, before she met Edward. That secret wish to be rescued like a princess, haunted her mind, since her encounter with Edward.

They kept their distance. She decided so, and took up the search again at her own rhythm, with that key date as her motivation. The hunt was hard and painful. No landlord wanted a tenant on DSS. Defeated, angry, she found herself lashing out: —Do you think that it amuses me, not to be able to work? —Do you know how it feels to wake up every day, eaten away by pain, addicted to codeine? Because one company was mostly focused on keeping their place on the market competition rather than looking after the well-being of their employee? No, they didn't care, because it was her battle! —What again Gary Grant? she told herself when she heard his voice, whispering like a mature bird.

Is it a joke? No, there was no joke in the mystical way of life! —How long for? She prepared a little bag.

Upon arrival, a nurse escorted her to a private room, bigger and brighter than her flat. —I was looking to be settled in my new home today and I am back in the hospital, the story of my life, she smiled.

Dr. Wagner, a black man from Kenya, in his sixties assisted her. His thin moustache made him look like Martin Luther King. He discovered a woman who looked ready to give birth to triplet. However, Issata was not pregnant. He sent her to the science department to unlock the scientific mystery. She received local anaesthesia, before inserting a tube linked to a bag. It was attached to the left side of her stomach, to empty the right kidney. Within seconds, a yellow liquid flowed into the plastic pocket. The lab team effectuated an analyse. It was confirmed to be urine. A scanner had to be observed, they all concluded. —Now, I understand why I had so much difficulty peeing! She returned to her room exhausted, with a nephrectomy tied to her stomach.

Edward, Jimmy, and Xavier, came to visit her in the evening. She was happy to see him until he reminded her of the arrival of Alex.

'Your case is unique!' Wagner declared, when he got possession of the result of her scan. False alert! It was not a cyst! Instead, they detected a large brown bag, growing around her kidney. It was filling itself with urine, preventing her organ to function. She had to undergo a small procedure on her urethral. A small stent was inserted between her kidney and her bladder, in order to temporarily relieved the urine. What a verdict! She informed Sophia, but not Mum. Worried for her elder sister, she wanted to come and assist her. Issata told her about Edward. 'I am happy for you sister, and I am also here if you need me.

—M*yoho,* the mystic law, she observed, during her stay in hospital. —Myo, means mystic, opening, and perfectly endowed. —Ho, phenomena as manifested. So, if the kidney is an actual fact of the struggle with my health, what could be the mystic aspect linking the essence of my life to the blockage, she had to investigate?

A week later, an ambulance dropped her at Valley Park. 'Let's see how you get on with the stent. We will organise a scan in January,' Wagner suggested. Dr. Clark adjourned her treatment out of precaution.

'Do you know them?' the paramedic man asked, when they approached her house.

A group of three young women, dressed in a frivolous manner, were slipping out of the house. Standing on stilettos heels, they staggered on the pavement, with their glittery mini-skirts. She managed to see their faces. Painted like prostitutes, the blurry look on their faces, saddened her.

Scandalised, and mainly not wanting to believe that Rajeev was running a brothel, she let out carelessly:

'No, they probably had too much to drink! Young people these days!'

'It is sad!' the man said.

Issata regretted her comments. —If that's the case, I should support them! 'You are right, it is deeply sad. Thank you!' She got off the car.

302

Upon opening the main door, a foul odour slapped her nose. The same rotten smell, which can only be associated to illegal substances. She couldn't miss the light coming from the top of the stairs. She heard the walls whispering, the stairs, whistling, Arabic sounds. She believed to perceive, Rajeev's voice, coming from each floor. —What a sad soul! I could just call the police! But what to say?

—Plus, I have enough of my own problem!

'Alex and I are deeply thinking of you, have a good rest! XXX' she got the message as she was about to chant.
—Right so deeply that you didn't come to collect me! Her ego was hurt. —*Thank you, I look forward to meeting her XXX.* —Such a great liar, she murmured!

—I love my new handbag! I can remove it during the day and use it at night. Someone had to learn how to live with the gadgets of science. Especially when meeting with Edward. They had to adapt themselves to the new device because sometimes the tube opened and happened what had to arrive. This didn't prevent them to make love as they enjoyed exploring it.

'This is Alex, my daughter,' said Edward, after he kissed Issata who had joined them, at the Black Lion. He turned his gaze towards a tall, slim silhouette. She was wearing a hoodie pink sweatshirt, generously opened at the front. Issata couldn't keep her eyes away from those boobs purposely put in evidence. —Right! crossed her mind.

303

A white slim jean elongating her legs, her black Puma for shoes, she incarnated the typical look of the Millennium generation. The more she watched her, the more she saw Edward. Same facial features, same eyes colour, thin lips, except for the freckles splashed on her cheeks and the top of her kitten nose. Her long chestnut curled hair was falling on her shoulders elegantly. Her skin was as flawless as coconut oil, she was the female version of her father.

'Hello Alex, I am so happy to meet you,' Issata, ready to hug her. Alex looked at her with her killer eyes. She presented her hand and let out with insolence: 'Hi!' The tone of her voice was clearly accentuating: —He is my dad!

If, she could, she would have called Issata 'Bitch!' And Issata would have slapped her, with her African hand and in the African way. But she didn't. —Ok, she thought, before accepting her hand. She studied the arrogance of her youth, screaming in her eyes, and decided to play the game.

'Well, you are beautiful!' 'Drinks?' Dad suggested.
'Desperado for me,'
'And you, my darling?'
'Lemonade.'
'Sure? You can have a beer you know?'
'I said lemonade,' a cold voice insisted.
He nodded and went to get the drinks. —What do I do? Issata alone with her wondered. Talking to her? About what? Even if I wanted, she is glued to her phone! Every second she could hear her phone ringing.
—Young people today, she sighed.
'Salute.' Edward returned with a tray.

304

'Thank you,' Issata took her beer.

Alex too busy with her phone didn't notice her father.

'Alex?'

'Yes, thank you,' she threw her nose on her screen.

'Please leave that phone alone!' Edward insisted, raising his voice.

Reluctantly, the girl slid her mobile in her pocket and grabbed her glass.

They slurped their drink and Issata began:

'So, what are your plans?'

'I want to be a model to travel the world.'

'Why not, you could register with agencies.'

'I did it already. I have a portfolio, everything that I need!'

'So don't worry!'

'Darling I sincerely think, you should find a job, make friends and see for yourself.'

'Look, dad, I know what I want. I am 20, I don't have to justify myself with you!'

Issata watched her boyfriend, feeling for him.

'I would love to watch your photos, me!' she commented.

'At least you understand me. I need to grow in this industry!'

'Alex, your dad understands you. He just wants to encourage you to grow as an individual.' Her hand caressed his.

'He should encourage me to believe in my dreams.' she riposted, taking her phone again.

They looked at the face of that teenage girl in a woman's body. A fresh sensuality reigned in her eyes, a sensuality when guided correctly could emerge into a powerful force.

'My darling, you are right, I should support you more in believing in your dreams' the wisdom of a father replied.

—You have a lot of work to do with your girls, Edward Jones, empathised Issata in her heart.

She finished typing something and stood up. 'I am going to smoke.'

They stared at each other and followed her. Out, she was more friendly. She posed and they played the photographers; useful tips to get closer to the new generation.

The photo's session, continued inside. She wanted to try the desperado, and ordered burgers. They posed with the food, then biting in the burger, then swallowing the chips. Overall, their first evening was a victory. Edward went his way with his daughter and she walked back home alone.

—My man's daughter is in town!

13th December she turned 41. Would you believe that Edward was also born on that same day, but twenty years later? Coincidence or mystic? They landed at Sky Garden, the greatest public garden of London. It was meant to be Jimmy's present to his friend. But a change of plan occurred. There was Edward, Xavier, and Alex. Sitting at the Darwin restaurant, they enjoyed a spectacular view. Champagne was flowing. They had ordered a seafood platter for starter, chicken Forestier and dauphine potatoes with spinach sautéed, for the main course, cheese, red wine, and black forest for dessert. And of course, Alex had to complain throughout the meal. —She needs a slap this girl, Issata cursed. Her anger visited her, each time she had to face the child of her boyfriend. As a gift, they received a Thai massage voucher valid indefinitely.

'Edward, you are clearly a man to marry!'

Issata spent Christmas with her boyfriend and...Alex.

He cooked roast lamb with vegetables. Issata bought a French Christmas log from Paul. He had just served the dinner, and well educated as she was, she ought to compliment the chef. Oh Lord, how dared she?

'Me, I don't believe in marriage! Look what has happened to you and mum!' the pest had to spit. —What a pain you are! Get yourself a job, instead of complaining! she bit her tongue.

'Darling, your mum and I had our story and you are part of it. Getting married is a choice and we have made the choice to divorce, that is all!' Alex rose her shoulders and deserted the table.

Issata pursued her with her eyes, till she crashed on the sofa. —She is holding a deep grudge towards her dad, just like me with Mum! —Maybe that is the reason, she irritates me. —No, nothing to do with me! —And my darling in this, how is he handling this? —Maybe he is feeling guilty?

—That is the scenario which always makes relationship dangerous, the culpability.

Heaviness floated in the atmosphere. They gave her an envelope with cash. She didn't even say thank you. —I am unemployed, you know! Give me back my twenty pounds! That's the price of two-pack of Marlboro!

New Year's Eve led her to Edward quartet's concert, at Pizza Express in Soho. Jimmy and Xavier met her there.

To her surprise, she saw Alex working. The restaurant was looking for extras. Alex was available, the manager hired her. —Let's hope she changes her attitude, she had to think. Dressed in a black smoking, white shirt, no tie, Edward was shining on stage. That was the first time, she saw him perform. She travelled with him to New Orleans, the place where the first forms of jazz emerged.

He incarnated the jazz era. Concentrated on his instrument, he closed his eyes, and she slid virtually in his arms, imagining him, striking the chords of her bra, the cords of her panties, the cords of her womanhood. They spoke briefly, they kissed, and... she returned home at three o'clock, alone and drunk.

7

Hello 2016, *The year of Expansion in the New Era of Worldwide Kosen Rufu.*
—Another theme from Sensei, she meditated sitting on the throne! —I only need to open the canal which links my kidney to my bladder. If you have some tips, let me know! At the end of the day, you are the master! Enlighten me! She had her scan in January! —I hope there will be a change! The year started well for Edward. Gigs emerged and he was meeting new musicians. She managed to attend all his performances, often with Jimmy and Xavier. He was beaming with joy. 'I am so happy with him, he confessed to his friend!' And just like his friend, he struggled with Ethan, the eldest son of Xavier.

Alex was still working at Pizza Express but continued to invade their lives. Edward was her papa and she made sure to remind his girlfriend of it.

One night, while at her place, living her romance with her man, the girl called in tears. Apparently, she had lost the house's keys. It was dark and cold and she was scared. Edward had to rush to rescue his child. —Bitch, Issata screamed in her heart. On another steamy occasion, this time at his home, she disembarked at the house completely crumbled and drunk. Our two lovers were entwined naked, on the sofa when a deep wail gave them a fright. 'Dad,' she sobbed, 'It's Kevin, he dumped me!' —A guy, since when? Furious because she was about to orgasm, Issata who was riding him, took the blanket to cover herself. Edward put on his boxer and walked to his daughter. 'Darling, tell me everything,' he held her in his arms. 'Dad, I feel so lonely, no one loves me!' she cried 'You have your girlfriend! You never have time for me!' 'What a comedian,' Issata observed them, burning to scream.

'Alex, I love you, I will always be there for you.' He then pursued in Italian and ushered her toward her bedroom.

Hurt, and feeling left out, Issata got dressed. —Who does she think she is! A violent desire to smash his instruments was itching her. —And you and your spoiled child will be free from me! She could foresee, the pieces of the body of his wooden mistress scattered on the ground, with her cords as slashed as her broken heart. The piano keys, exploded on the ground, ringing out of tune, on a disharmony, she knew so well. She didn't feel wanted, the soundtrack of her life.

'Where are you going?' Edward questioned when he returned. Shaken by her own thoughts, she jumped.

'It is best that I go home!' she answered grabbing her handbag.

'But it is late!' He came close to her. 'We will continue what we have started,' he teased, trying to reach her hands.

'Because you think this is funny?'

'Issata, she is my daughter, I can't leave her alone!'

'And me, who am I for you?' she burst into tears. 'It is all about her! Can you not see that she is trying to separate us?' 'Please understand me!'

'And who understand me?'

'Stay for the night and we can talk with her tomorrow' Edward insisted. He was sincere but she needed to make a point.

'Sort out your child! I have enough of my own problems!' She pushed him away. Edward listened to the slamming door detonating behind her.

Alone in her place, she texted Jimmy.

'Darling,' he called back.

'She is a bummer! You should see how she plays with him. She hates me! I think I don't want this relationship! It is too much for me!'

Jimmy listened with a lot of patience.

'Issata listen, Edward is a wonderful man! This is for you to see, what is waiting for you! Are you ready for it?'

'What about me? Can he not see that I need him?'

'Don't expect anything from him! What matters is what you feel inside! And it is up to you both to establish a balanced relationship.'

'Without Alex!'

'Not possible! And for what I remember, there is another child.'

'Why is that so complicated?' she wailed.

'Look at it from a different perspective; don't forget that you pee in a plastic bag. It doesn't stop him to make love to you.' A silence weighed heavily from her side, as if he was right. 'Sweetheart,' he called softly.

'Jimmy, that is so not fair!' she wept.

'Listen, it is 2am, go to sleep, we speak later, ok?'

'Ok,' she sighed.

'I love you, darling!'

'I love you too, my Jimmy!'

B, recognised the sadness in her eyes, when she entered her office. An ocean of tears ravaged her face while she tried to explain: 'He...he...he is nice, but his daughter, I have enough,' Issata howled.

She listened, observed and analysed.

'All those destructive elements from your life are emerging through your relationship with Edward.'

'I don't understand!'

'Life is testing you now!'

'Again?'

'Anger and rejection represent deep suffering in your life. Today those demons are attacking your love life. It is up to you to decide what you want to realise with Edward.'

'I want him to understand me!'

'Then tell him!'

'He knows already!'

'He needs to hear it from your voice.'

'How?'

'Like you are doing with me.'

'I don't know,' she whispered.

B looked at her deeply. 'Is the anger you carry for your mother the same for Alex?'

Issata remained speechless. The question exposed a fact, an image, a sentiment, a reality. And how to explain that reality? 'Each emotion hides an experience, translated by a sentiment, a happening, illustrating the depression of our own existence. You are almost there, Issata!' B, concluded.

Those same words escorted her to Valley Park.

She rose to her feet and followed the voice calling her name. 'Hello Dr. Wagner,'

'Please come in.'

'We looked at your scan,' he began, when he closed the door. 'Your kidney still contains a lot of fluid. Unfortunately, it is pushing the other organs inside.'

'What does it mean?'

'We thought we could fix it but it would be too dangerous for you, due to the location of your kidney. Right now, the only option is to remove it!'

'Oh no! You said it was healthy!'

'Effectively, but at this stage, we will need a miracle!'

'A miracle,' she threw softly.

'I understand your deception. I am going to discuss your case at our regional meeting and organise a date for the operation.

'I don't know what to think,' her voice trembled.

'Do you pray?'

'Yes,' she uttered, followed by: 'I am Buddhist.'

'Ask your Buddhist god to help you.'

'It is true they have left me down a bit.'

'Madame Sherif, you are very strong. We want the best for you,' he smiled.

'If you say so!' Tears shone in her eyes.

'Shall we meet…' he checked his calendar quickly, '16th March, so we can discuss the operation?'

16th March, four years ago, she had a date with Mr. Smith and ended up in hospital. Where would life lead her, 16th March 2016?

'Ok,' she agreed and left.

—A miracle, she reflected on her way home.

1 4th February *2016*, Issata had a date! No, she didn't update her Facebook status.

Alex? The story got sorted. Days after her crisis, her and Kevin got back together. And Alex apologised.

It was the first time a man had requested her company for this occasion, she confessed to me. In the past, she hated the fuss around that date, that day which dictated her happiness, which reminded her that nobody wanted her. She hated all the publicity around 14th February, on TV, in the shops, even in her workplace. She felt persecuted. Society wanted her to believe that she needed a man to be happy.

On arrival, in front of his house, she found a note.

—*Come in, it is opened.* Excited, she pushed the door and followed the tea candles, leading her to the salon. His legs slightly spread, holding his double bass, he watched her entering the room. His eyes encouraged her to meet him. She was mesmerised by what she saw. He had set up a bistro table, with her glass of champagne, a bowl of olives and peanuts, for aperitif. She also noticed an envelope with her name written on it. She opened it and found a card covered with red roses. —*Issata, I am your Valentin tonight, EdXXX.*

'Edward,' she expressed moved. Staring at her, he rose his glass and said: 'Salute!'

'Salute' she joined him. Slowly, they swallowed their drink.

'Take a seat and enjoy Issata.'

His left hand holding the neck of his instrument, his right hand controlling the bow, he caressed the four cords and rose in the room: —*Our Love is Here to Stay*...Her eyes filled with tears. They made love with this melody. She let the music strike her senses. She could feel a sonorous sensuality vibrating under Edward's fingers. The grinding of the arco, stimulated the memories of their intimate moments. Each time they made love, it led her to a new experience. Each time she climaxed; she came for the first time.

Her first private performance, Issata envied the posture of the contrabass. That voluminous machine, thick, solid and fragile, resembled a woman, a musical muse, completing the life of Edward Jones. She watched her dancing in her lover's arms and perceived the shape of a feminine energy, an aura. There was no colour, but she captured a smell, an earthy odour, a pure territory, well studied and well-maintained. The perfume emerging from the mud of life gave birth to millions of entities. Those living beings represent the protagonists of mankind's history. Her perfume governed fiercely, proud of her spiritual beauty. Issata could sense how the liberty to love, and the liberty to forgive formed her essence.

Bewitched, she analysed that shape, exhibiting itself, between her master's legs. In a need to express a legitimate desire, the points of her tits hardened. Issata wanted to be in her place and imagined the arco sliding under her dress. Panting, pearls of sweat crawled all over her body, while her black flower meowed silently. She rubbed her ten fingers together as if praying, and like a response to her call, Edward placed his bow on the ground to pursued his pizzicato. Issata rising to her feet, walked towards this man, who was ready to enter nirvana. She twirled around him. She implored him to take her on his journey. She admired the story of his life unveiling on his face. Edward Jones was a man who travelled the world through music. She tipped toed around him. She followed the movement of his fingers. She danced freely, moved by so much tenderness and respect.

— On the 3rd of May, I listened to my heart, my desire to dare to believe, she screamed inside.

Edward slowed down and squeezed the last note. Speechless, she clapped her hands. He put his bass on the floor. 'Happy St Valentin Issata,' he let out tenderly, and bowed to her. She enlaced his neck and kissed him…

—A miracle, those two words animated her mind every day. —Dr. Wagner advised me to pray, she ruminated over and over. That is why, one morning, while she was praying, she heard a profound call: —To realise the impossible,

I must do something impossible in terms of my practice, because faith is translated through prayers. She recalled on members' experiences, who dedicated their times in chanting abundant Daimokus for hours while battling their financial situation, marital struggles, or health. And they won. She mostly remembered the joy and pride in sharing their immense gratitude towards Nichiren's teaching. So, she dared to meditate for ten hours for ten days. She managed three hours, why not ten?

Her motivation impressed Edward. 'I can join you, if you wish,' he suggested. —I want to chant alone, she replied.

Day 1, the first day of March, at six o'clock in the morning, she observed deeply the mountain standing in front of her. Imperturbable, the mystical stone disappearing in the sky, was requesting her company. On her knees, she faced the Gohonzon. Her ten fingers sealed together, the expression of the ten states of life, that rainbow emotional innate in mankind, she ventured to meet her. Honoured by such invitation, she prayed with her whole heart. She climbed carefully with the sound of her voice as her guide. She called forth her prayers in penetrating each particle of her body.

—The heart has its reasons that reason ignores, would say the proverb. —Have reason on my prayers, her voice declared. And she visualised the geographical map of her body, through her mental screen. Hours went by. At noon, she took a break. She had just managed to chant six hours. How was she feeling? Hungry and dying for nicotine. She grabbed a bite, swallowed her favourite lemonade.

One o'clock, she continued her spiritual marathon, determined to win. At least, she wanted to try. She bathed her being, with the same prayers, under the same tonality, the same drive. Came five o'clock, she ended up tired. Her voice was broken.

Day 2, on time at the rendezvous, she begged her chi, the essence of her life in fulfilling her function, that is to be

317

alive. Life is an energy that needs training. When dead, the energy remains latent, when alive it becomes manifest. This explains the two phases of life, a rhythm that all living being goes through. Life travels through the universe and mixes through other material forms until it finds the right body.

—Come on push the walls of the canal, linking my right kidney to my bladder. —That is all you have to do!

—After all, that is your role! —You, Life, revive my body. Her voice resonated for hours in the sphere of her studio, strengthening her vocal cords.

Day 3, Day 4, Day 5, doubt came flirting with her spirit. —What if it didn't work. The thought saddened her, even more so, because she had never realised her goal through Nichiren Daishonin's teaching. Why did she keep at it? Her life took a turn, she would have never thought about. She borrowed some paths which offered her, a different vision of her destiny and spurred her in welcoming new ways to her existence on earth. Why couldn't she adopt the same strategy regardless of the result? —Because I want to be convinced that the mystic law is the religious path to follow for the rest of my life was her reasoning.

Day 6, she was sulking and gnawed by fatigue. Four more days to climb and she wanted to give up. She observed the mountain shining in its splendour nagging her. Issata felt mainly lonely in her challenge. But it was a battle she had to overcome alone. —What would Sensei do? she wondered during her break. —I am losing my voice! —I am exhausted! —Where did you find the

318

strength to continue? —You must have felt so lonely too when Toda died! Later, she received a text from Edward: 'I am with you Issata. You are the most courageous woman I have ever encountered.' The word courage, slapped her being, like a breeze of oxygen. Daisaku Ikeda always mentions it in his guidance. Nichiren himself explains: *'Spur yourself to muster the power of faith. Regard your survival as wondrous. Employ the strategy of the Lotus Sutra before any other. "All others who bear you enmity or malice will likewise be wiped out." These golden words will never prove false. The heart of strategy and swordsmanship derives from the Mystic Law. Have profound faith. A coward cannot have any of his prayers answered.* 'The Strategy of the Lotus Lotus'. According to the dictionary, *the word* signifies the ability to execute something which frightens us. The synonyms rhyme with bravery, audacity, heroism, and the list is long when taking the time to search. But let's observe its origin. It derives from old French, borrowed from the word *Coeur* which means heart in English. Then the rage was added demonstrating the fire burning inside us. Literally speaking, courage can be understood by drawing the flame blazing in our hearts. To be courageous lies in drawing that force colossal anchored within the heart. Often one has to dig it. Tears shone in her eyes. —But how am I going to succeed in drawing out that courage? I have almost lost my voice and four hours to do. On the verge of defeat, she caught the photo of Nelson Mandela with Daisaku Ikeda, she kept on her butsudan. Those two men were shaking hands. That moment was immortalised in Tokyo in 1990 after Nelson Mandela's release from prison. —Madiba, she sighed. It was the name of his tribal clan, the name of his ancestors belonging to the Xhosa ethnic. The name represents a sign of respect. Mr. Mandela himself preferred to be addressed by this name. So why Nelson then? Just a custom, chosen by African people during that time. His teacher named *Miss Mdingane* according to some source gave him the name. Issata remembered vividly the day of his release, 11th February 1990. She was sixteen, not realising the importance of his freedom. She didn't measure the suffering he has undergone for the cause of black people.

She was just happy to see him free. Nelson Mandela declared: '*I have learnt that courage was not the absence of fear, but the triumph over it. The brave man is not he, who does not feel afraid, but who conquers that fear.*' Who could have thought that after 27 years in prison, he would serve as the President of South Africa?

—Courage, she murmured, and how can I translate this in my life then? Because I don't want heroic courage, the world has changed, she pronounced, staring her object of worship. —Why have I started this campaign? —After all those hours of prayers surely, I must have shifted something? She asked herself.

—Ok, I am still alive, her consciousness analysed.

That awareness resonated to a different degree, inside her.

—I am still alive! she let out loudly. In that moment, she felt a warm feeling permeating her heart. —To be courageous means, developing the spirit of gratitude. Because without life no one can experience courage. Her heart filling with joy, she bowed to each character inscribed on the Gohonzon, who had promised to support her. Suddenly, she watched them floating before her eyes symbolically, as a response to her own reverence. The calligraphy began to sway, like thousands of volatile souls, revealing feminine forms, free to dance, free to sing, free to laugh, free to cry their right to exist. Free to be, simply! A mystical and natural force lifted her in a timeless dimension, inviting her to participate in this dance, staged by the true nature of her sincerity. She allowed herself to be guided and joined the dance with all those women who cheered and waited for her on an eternal journey. Then she heard: '*I Nichiren, inscribed my life in sum ink, believe in this Gohonzon with your own life.*' A passage coming from a letter called: —Reply to Kyo. A divine sensation exploded inside her being. Tears rolled on her cheeks. Issata had found the essence of her own courage, spiritual courage, the kind of courage guided by moral values. She was back in the race and finished her session confident that the right answer would unfold.

Day 10, she reached the top of the mountain.

—I have done it! Glorious, she watched her life from the view of her studio flat. —Ok, I still live in Valley Park, she giggled, but I didn't give up.

She was leaving her flat to meet her lover, and saw a young woman, with dark hair, descending the stairs. She discovered a visage painted under the brush of a traumatic red, for a very white skin. The colour looked like, sad eyes drowned by tears and bruised patches deriving from heavy punches. Speechless, she watched that fragile body, covered by a long blue, fake leather coat, reached the end of the stairs. She had on her feet, high heels sandals, without socks. The veins on her legs accentuated the colour of her coat. She carried a roll-up between two fingers damaged by nicotine. Issata saw straight away, that she bit her nails and read in her gaze, light grey eyes, the story of a lost and broken soul, who was no more than eighteen.

'Are you ok?' she rushed to ask.

'Yeah, I work for Rajeev!' A nasty sound mixed with an Eastern European accent escaped from the bruised lips of this young woman.

'But you are bleeding?'

'It happened all the time!'

'What is happening all the time?'

'Listen, I am tired, I worked all night!' She moved away.

'I am Issata, I live here. If you need some help...'

'Eva!' she let out, opened the door, and went.

Straight away, Issata heard the start-up of an engine.

—After such an intense campaign, this is what the universe is presenting to me? And why now? Her eyes looked up the stairs. She was tempted to go and check. —Forget it, she scolded herself, and rushed to Edward. She shared her suspicions with him. 'What do I need to do?'

'That is very serious! But you need proof!'

'I know, that is frightening and I live there!'

'Issata, you have your own worries! Why don't we focus on: 'In the search for the lost time,' he whispered to her ears.

'And to appreciate the time to create. You are right!' she giggled.

16th of March, the verdict remained the same. She kind of knew it and was ready to say goodbye to her right kidney. Dr. Wagner confirmed that he had secured the 3rd of May for the intervention. Does it ring the bell?

—I will have to inform Mum now, she worried on her way home.

For a long time, I have asked myself, does fate exist? Even more so, is it possible to change the course of one's life?

Karma, it is high time that I explain, because Issata must face it!

The word karma means, action and is created by three ways, thoughts, words and the act itself. We are all familiar with the expression: "Actions speak louder than words."

However, since these three expressions originate from a root cause, the motive of the action, the fundamental attitude behind the act itself is therefore very crucial.

Most of our problems and sufferings, stem from the actions and the decisions that we have made in the past. Following the process of causality, those events reflect the seeds planted in our lives. Seen this way, when difficult situations emerge with no apparent reasons, one would claim, we all have been asking ourselves: Why am I being the object of so much sufferings? What have I done?

—Same for Issata ! —Why sarcoïdosis? —Why is she not able to find her dream flat? —And her kidney? —Is this her destiny? —Can she change it?

Karma has two sides: positive and negative. And we mainly focus on the negative aspect, because it represents the source that makes us suffer in our everyday life. The Good news,

karma can be transformed, Nichiren assured through his
teaching. How? Before, I answer allow me to make one
point.

Buddhism establishes a very clear difference between
mutable karma and immutable karma. Mutable karma
represents causes that manifest, as we create them,
whereas immutable karma in the tradition was considered
invariable and destined to reappear lifetime after lifetime,
determining the course of our existence.
So how? By eradicating the root cause of the negative
karma.

—Maybe is it the karma with Mum that I need to
unlock? Issata observed, one morning during her prayers.
If karma is action, what actions do I take in my
everyday life? —Right, I am angry, nothing new!
—A fortiori with you Mum, so tell me why? Through
her voice, she searched Mum, the definition of those five
letters added together, embracing all the women in the
world. She heard screams from children, lost or frightened
in the supermarket or the parks: —Mummy, mummy
crying for their female heroes. She witnessed babies'
laughter, their hands clapping, joy in their eyes. Their eyes
shone with innocence; they were free. But Mum was
nowhere. She recognised Sophia's cries. When she came
into the world, she beamed with joy, she had a little sister
and felt responsible. Five years her eldest, she used to tell
her not to cry. Sometimes, she would give her, a bottle
under Mum's supervision. Overwhelmed, she surprised
herself thinking, I am searching for the core of my anger
and I am being taken to Sophia? —She cannot be the root
of my suffering? —No, I love Sophia, I will protect her
with all my might! She wrote those souvenirs in her

324

notebook. —I must find the root cause of my anger! In her quest, her mind invited her to revisit an experience which took place at the primary school. Shocked, she paused. She was about six, Madame Benoit a petite blond as small as a bird, with big blue eyes had written on the blackboard:

—Subtractions! That morning, the numbers were running everywhere on the board. —I can't concentrate, she wanted to cry. The next day, she received the worse mark in the classroom.

'Issata Sherif, 3/20' Madame Benoit threw, giving out her copy.

'The numbers were running Madame Benoit; I couldn't catch them.'

'Numbers don't have legs' someone laughed at her. The whole classroom burst into laughter. Issata cried, tears galloping on her cheeks. Madame Benoit watched her pupil. She had an idea as to why the numbers were running on the chalkboard, to the eyes of Issata. But she didn't stop the children from laughing at the little girl nor did she give her an explanation. She informed Mum when she collected her at the end of class. 'You have the weekend to look into it, Madame Shérif!'

—To look into what, Issata wanted to know?

On Monday she returned to school, her eyes fixing the ground. 'Look Issata is wearing glasses' someone pointed out. 'Serpent à lunettes' another pupil attacked, translated as snake wearing glasses. That is a vicious way of mocking kids with spectacles. She lifted her head and revealed some protruding eyes, covered by golden rounds frames. She incarnated the twin brother of Gary Coleman starring in Arnold and Willy. To one difference, Issata measured at least thirty centimetres more than him, in his adult age.

Trembling with anger, she refrained herself from crying. They were making fun of her and her only wish was to run away. Unfortunately, the bell rang. Everyone had to stand in line.

'Silence please!' Madame Benoit commented.

She didn't say —Good morning!

'Issata is wearing glasses,' the same boy ridiculed her.

'I said silence!' she rose her voice. Once again, she didn't protect Issata. She didn't scold the young man who harassed her either. —I was so little! I couldn't defend myself, she cried. —And what this has got to do with Mum? Instinctively, she felt as if she was falling into a gulf, no walls, no ground in sight, only a deep crevasse sucking her and no one to hold on to. Her tears rained on abundance on her face, she was afraid. That sentiment choked her, while she listened to her heart banging violently against her chest.

—What do I need to understand, she breathed deeply?

—Afraid of what? —All I want is answers, she panted, trying hard to regulate her breezing. Then she remembered a comment from Jimmy. —Anger is a response to a threat! When we feel attacked, we often search to defend ourselves. In that reflection followed the souvenir from Mum's eyes screaming on that little girl. She grabbed her notebook and described everything she remembered, as they arrived in her mind. Long cornrows braids on her skull, decorated by wooden pearls, hanging at the end of her plaits, she was wearing her pink dungaree, embroiled with two large white buttons at the front. She was trembling like a frightened animal. Her face was fixing the floor. She was crying for Mum's irascible voice to stop. Her hands were in her back; she was hiding something.

'Look at me, when I am talking to you!' the voice ordered.

The girl lifted her head and revealed a gaze broken and lost.

'What did I say? Show me your hand?'

That kid remained paralysed. Mum approached her and took from her hands what she was holding.

'I just wanted to try Mum!'

'It is called stealing Issata! That is how it starts!'

Mum presented to her, the chocolate Mika bar. That sweet, they bought it together at Leclerc, just after their rendezvous from the optician. 'Mum, can I have a bit?' 'No, that is for your snack after school' Mum said. After the humiliation she suffered, she needed comfort. So, she slid into the kitchen while Mum was looking after Sophia. She climbed onto a stool, opened the cupboard, and took what she regarded as her treat for being laughed at. Hidden behind the sofa, she was biting the forbidden fruit, ecstasy printed on her face.

'Issata, where are you?' Her adult eyes confronted that image which she knew so well, the reflection of her own, filled with an extreme fragility. She could read in them the deep fear of a little girl, whose only argument at the age of six was to say: —I just wanted to taste Mum! Although that was not the real reason! —They laughed at me and I was sad, she wished to explain but Mum never knew. At that moment, she had to admit to herself: —It is fear which governs my anger! An exposed gaze, upon her own weakness, she felt an enormous ball, climbing up through her throat. Her gullet enlarged, looking like a nightingale preparing its concert. Issata didn't sing but sobbed. Her sobs broke out on her cheeks; she could guess the sound of broken glasses. Dolorous and precious tears flared up from her heart. Like a sponge, the deeper she cried, her heart absorbed all her tears in order to squeeze them out. Slowly, the suffocating weight lost its heaviness. A breath of fresh air, infiltrated her being, leading her mind to contemplate:

—Fear is the principal emotion that feeds anger. —Anger leads to hatredness and hatredness brings the greatest suffering. Those three emotions vibrated in her. She went through each one of them. Simultaneously, she experimented the damages those words can cause just by their definitions. She observed floating in front of her very own eyes, the magna, the incarnation of fear, bestial energy arousing anger, the lava to explode, leading to the eruption of the volcan. —Here is the explanation beneath the eruption of the sarcoidosis in my life! That conclusion reminded her that at the age of forty-one, she was still that little girl who had never communicated with Mum. —All these years, I was angry with her! She did her best, Issata tried to raison with herself, submerged by emotions!

25th April, she boarded Voyage Europe, envisaging the true Issata. As exemplified by the lotus flower which blooms in the muddy pond, behind her rage, existed a woman, ready to emerge from the mud of her childhood. Her ex-colleagues were happy to see her. 'We all miss you,' 'You have given so much, it is not fair what they have done to you,' she heard throughout the trip. 'I know,' she could only reply.

'No mum today?' she asked Antoine, when he collected her from Montargis' station.
'No, today it is me!' He hugged her and grabbed her luggage.

'Get in, it is opened.' They sat in the car and he drove away.

'Is everything ok with her?'

'Yes, she is impatient to see you.'

'So do I,' she murmured, feeling a breath of terror rising inside.

'You must be tired!'

'A bit, I left at 5 am.'

'I see, and how is your health?'

'I keep going!' She was clearly not going to tell him about the operation. —That will be betraying Mum.

'Let's hope you can rest here.

'Thank you.'

They entertained polite conversations and before she knew it, they arrived in the courtyard. She spotted her mum, cutting the roses. Straight away, she noticed how much weight. She jumped out of the car.

'Mum,' she called overwhelmed, walking to meet her.

'My daughter' she embraced her. 'How are you?'

'I am fine, thank you and you?'

'I am ok.'

'Have you lost weight?' She saw the lines on her face looking more worn out than before.

'My blood pressure is high.'

'Maybe you have to change your pills?'

'Don't worry, I see Dr. Leroux soon.'

'Is he not retired yet?' Obviously, he was the family doctor.

'Let's get inside, lunch is ready!' Mum leads the way.

'Issata, I am keeping your luggage in your room upstairs' threw Antoine, catching up their steps.

'Thank you, I have forgotten'

'At your service my Lady.'

She smiled and followed Mum. Baked chicory with ham and crème Fraiche, served with a green salad was waiting to be served. Antoine joined them, with a bottle of Bordeaux. He opened the wine in front of them.

'Cheers!' they rose their glasses and followed: 'Good appetite!' Issata dug into her pie.

'Very good mum.'

Mum smiled without looking at her.

'Tell us the news!' began Antoine.

She froze. —How am I going to announce the news, passed through her mind. —What if I didn't say anything? —No, they have to know, especially Mum!

'I should be asking you that question. How is the life of retirement?'

'Tell me about it!' Mum snapped.

She watched her face and heard her kissing her teeth.

'I am enjoying it. I have the time to look after the garden and do some work in the house.

'That is great! You could be travelling somewhere?'

'I don't like flying!'

'Take the car or the train.'

'Anyway, he doesn't like anything this one!'

'Can you stop complaining?'

'Get lost!' Mum shouted.

—What is wrong with them? She witnessed the nastiness climbing in the atmosphere.

'Anyway, you don't have to travel together,' she intervened. 'Mum, you could go to Sophia. I am sure your grand-children would be happy to see you more often.

'Issata, enough!' Mum cut through, her fury gaze piercing through her. That same look, that authoritarian voice, sent her back to the girl in a woman's body. Tears began to sting her eyes and she felt the flame of her anger heating her

330

blood to boil. —You have no idea, what I have been through because of you! —You! you! you! Always you pounded in her head. —Without Jimmy, you would have lost me! She crossed Antoine's gaze. She understood that him too, couldn't stand her anymore. At that moment, she wanted to yell at her and make her pay for all those years of suffering, where she felt doomed to shut up. And that was what happened. She didn't answer back, only out of respect.

—I am on a mission, she reminded herself.

Lunch over, they went to the garden. Antoine retired into his office. Mum had transformed that corner, into a botanic paradise. Well, almost! A selection of flowers, Roses, tulips, orchids, all planted in a colourful harmony, embalmed the scenery. Issata often found herself assisting to a flower festival. 'The garden is always beautiful, you have the green hand,' she praised Mum.

'I do what I can, but let's go and sit under the charm tree.

They walked toward the tree also called charmille, or *Carnipus betulus* in Latin. It lived in the garden, well before Mum's arrival. They sat on the rattan garden chairs. Sitting, a fag sticking out of her lips, Issata enjoyed the movement of the foliage above her head. That specimen is often compared to the beech tree. But what differentiates them, lies in the grey bark which breaks through old age. Its elliptic leaves fall alongside the trunk so that one can almost imagine a green emerald evening dress, dressing the creature of nature. —How charming, Issata used to say!

From time to time, she would catch a glimpse of Mum. She saw the oldness crawling on her face at a lightning speed. Instead of reading, the story of a woman, proud to have explored the different phases of life, to have fought hard for having given a decent education to her daughters, she was discovering a woman whose wrinkles printed on her neck, her face, her hands, denounced an extreme loneliness, a woman who has stopped to fight, who was simply waiting for her time to come. She noticed her lips moving and heard her speak. 'Mum?' Her mother didn't move and continued to speak. She fixed straight ahead. She shook her head and pointed her finger as if she was addressing somebody. 'But mum, are you ok?' Her mother directed the finger at her, and attacked her with incomprehensible words. Issata rose to her feet and knelt in front of her. Both hands on her shoulders, she shook her gently.

'Mum, what is wrong with you? I don't recognise you!'

'He can never find someone like me!' Tears filled her eyes.

'What are you talking about?'

'I am telling you! I am not his slave!'

'Mum, look at me!' she rose her voice. 'And tell me what is the problem!'

'What were you saying? How is work?' her lips pronounced.

—What? She is really losing her mind! 'Mum, you know that I was dismissed from my work.'

Looking embarrassed, Mum lowered her head.

'I meant your health and my mouth said something else.'

—And she lies, she had time to think, but didn't allow her manipulation, to affect her. She fixed her mother and took a deep breath.

'In fact, I have to tell you something!'

'Can I join you?'

Issata saw Antoine approaching them.

'Of course, take my seat,' she stood up.

Mum remained silent.

'Ok,' she began, striking her hands together. 'I will have to undergo an operation.'

'Oh?' Antoine uttered.

'I need to have one kidney removed in May.'

'What?' Mum barked.

'I am sorry to hear this Issata, but nowadays we can live with one kidney.'

'Oh you, this is not your business, you have no children!' Mum attacked him.

'What a pest you are! You don't have to be nasty!'

'Please you two, that is not about you!'

'You are right, sorry about this!' he apologised.

'It is serious?' Mum asked.

She explained briefly the situation.

'And why you didn't tell me? Each time, I asked you, you say that everything is fine. I already have my own problems.'

'I wanted to speak to you face to face.'

'How are you going to manage? You are by yourself over there. At least, if you had someone by your side. I can come to stay with you?'

—I have to tell them now. 'No mum, I won't be alone! In fact, I have met someone!'

'That is very good news.' Antoine exclaimed.

Mum looked at her daughter. Her face went darker. Her lips trembling and dying from jealousy, she spitted out:

'Life is good for everyone! You don't need me!'

Tension rose inside Issata's heart. 'I just told you that I have met someone. You should be happy for me! Don't you want to know what is his name? Edward and he is a very nice man! She defended fiercely.

A deep silence reigned around them. The birds stopped singing, the flowers ceased parading, and the charmille faithful to *himself,* standing free, as the master of the garden, on that day, it served as witness to Issata. She dared talk back to her mother and saw herself taking place in the body of this little girl. She replaced her frightened stare with a fierce gaze, filled with compassion. There she was, the revolted woman, she had freed weeks before. Finally, she had her seat in the adult world. Her ego wounded; Mum ran away.

'Issata I am so happy for you. Everything will be fine.' said Antoine.

'What is wrong with her?'

'To be honest, I don't know. Even myself, I have enough. I am very worried.'

'When did it start?'

'Since we have retired. Mind you maybe before, but we were working and didn't see each other.'

'Let me go and see her.'

'And please don't worry, it is not your fault!'

She found Mum sitting in the kitchen, her head in her hands crying. 'Mum stop crying. There is more to life than losing a kidney. I am still alive, that is all that's matters!'

'Why didn't you tell me about Edward?' She doubled her tears.

—Oh, is that the real problem? Seeing me happy, reminds you how miserable you are, she contemplated, before answering.

'I was only waiting for the right moment.'

'I am here and no one tells me anything. When things get hot, you all come and get me!'

'Mum, stop always bringing back everything to you. I am the one who is going for an operation. Can you not try to encourage me for once?'

'I suggested to come to you and you told me you had someone already!'

'Effectively and it is your choice to decide how you want to encourage me!'

Sobbing like a child, Mum hid her face in her daughter's arms. 'I feel so lonely!'

'But you have Antoine!'

'You don't understand me!'

Her mother uttered a dolorous sound. Issata felt her pain and embraced Mum through the sound of despair.

She recognised it, for having experienced it, herself.

As a Bach lover, holding her mum in her arms, carried her to linger onto The St Matthew Passion, in her mind. That *oratio* was written for solo voices and two orchestras.

Some sources tell that the Passion was executed on 7th April, St Friday in 1727. That lyrical masterpiece came to life at the heart of the Lutheran movement, the protestant theology initiated by Martin Luther, his founder.

Why the Protestantism? Simply, the need to consider religion differently throughout everyday life. Salvation and death represented important questions in his spiritual quest. According to Luther, to obtain salvation from God, lies in a man's capacity to follow, and put into practice the voice of the Christ without the intercession of the church. The bible was the only legitimate source of authority for any Christian. He based his conviction, on *The Epistle to the Romans*, a long letter from Paul, issued from the New Testament.

That text, forms the doctrines for Christian churches, on the subject, of justification through faith, which is to say, serving God.

The first time Issata listened to that tour de force, she poured her tears all over her body. She was in love, but not loved back; only God by the grace of St Mathew's Passion. The religious orchestra climbed through her. Each musician, vocalist, flutist, expressed in their very own unique talent what was in fact, a universal message:
—Compassion. In order to reach a feeling of freedom, of spiritual joy, crossing hell was unavoidable. As Jung would say: *'One does not become enlightened by imagining figures of light, but by making the darkness conscious. The most terrifying thing is to accept oneself completely.'*

Years later, she discovered that the Japanese word for compassion is translated by *Jihi*. *'Ji'* means to offer joy to others. *'Hi'* to alleviate their pain.
She rocked her mother in her arms. She was suffering, she owed to alleviate her pain.

'Yes, I understand Mum, it is only another bridge to cross for me, but I will be fine,' she was able to say.
Mum breathed deeply but didn't comment.

Diner time, she immersed herself in their evening routine. They ate in the garden. No one dared mention the operation. Then they retired in the salon and watched *L'amour en Héritage*, an American series, the way America loves to write movies, broadcasted on France 3. From time to time, she watched them. —They so don't share a thing in common! —Not even retirement!

—28th April, that date made it all for her. When she woke up, she recalled the day before, with Mum. She helped her with some gardening, and witnessed the profound solitude inherent in her life. The solitude looked like a twin sister and copied all her gestures. She was reclaiming her existence in the world. She saw her encrusting herself, through every corner of that façade, Mum had built with Antoine. That image inspired her those Japanese weeds, which every gardener fears. In front of her very eyes, that trompe-oeil was dissolving itself.

Mum always strong and determined to protect her nest was falling down under the ruins of her own lies. Powerless at the sight of seeing her mum so vulnerable, she wished to yell: —How did you reach that point, mother? —Your desire has been realised and here you are unhappy.

Staring at Mum, she missed Edward. She lingered on how it all started, the connection and the struggle. This is when she realised: —Me too, I started my relationship with him, based on that same desire to be rescued! —That is so true! She ran towards her. Gratitude pulsating in her heart, she held her tightly. —I refuse to repeat my mother's karma, the revolted woman promised.

Lost, in her contemplation, she remembered that Nichiren had proclaimed Nam-myoho-renge-kyo, on 28th April 1253, for the first time and ventured himself in propagating his teaching. —Amazed, Issata let out: —Today, on Tuesday 28th 2016, I can confidently declare that I have changed my heart towards my mother. Everything is linked to my own lack of confidence. —That is what a negative karma is all about then? To transform the tendency to suffer, deeply rooted in a man's life!

'*It has become necessary to cancel your operation. We are sorry for this inconvenience.*' That letter was waiting for her when she reached home, on Wednesday 31st April.

—What again? How long do I have to keep that tube inserted in me? —I did my homework! The door should be opening!

'That is why I thought to celebrate our one-year anniversary tonight.' Issata's face turned pale.

On 1st of May, she met Edward at the *Dolce Vita*, their Italian cuisine and he announced to her, he was travelling to Italy on 3rd of May, because Alex was missing her friends.

—Alex, you again, she cursed in her heart!

'Because she cannot travel alone?'

'Issata, she is my daughter!' he caressed her hand.

—Thank you for the reminder, a comment, she refrained herself to say. She pouted, moving her head continually.

'Listen, I know you are upset about the operation, but I am sure there is a meaning to this. Let's just spend a good moment darling.' —What about me? I need you too! How can you do this to me, she wished to blow up. Her wrath climbed in her, polluting her mind, giving birth to her tears. Then, Mum's everyday tarnished mirror reminded her of her promise. Not to repeat Mother's karma! At that moment, she understood she had the choice, enjoy her time with her lover or suffer. I let you guess, what she chose.

'You do realise his daughter left just after you have made a change of heart towards your mother?' Jimmy told her when they met on 3ʳᵈ May.

'Typical of you my Jimmy, such a wise man! I haven't linked the two!' she smiled.

The hospital came to her. Via a phone call conversation, Dr. Marisa, gynaecologist, explained to her that Dr Wagner, needed her expertise. A fibroid was found beneath her lazy kidney. Plus, the cheeky bastard was laying at the front, on top of her pelvis. That extra flesh could explain the problem. 'I wanted to discuss with you if you would consider a hysterectomy?'

'Is this a joke? How couldn't you discover this earlier?' she asked shocked.
'I understand your frustration, we only want the best for you.'
'Well, thank you for your concern, but a hysterectomy at the age of forty-one is out of the question.'
'Fine, we keep the uterus, and I keep you in my calendar for 3rd July.'
—July 3rd, she repeated in her head. A date illustrating the mentor and disciple relationship. As I have already explained, the relationship between a mentor and a disciple expresses the quintessence of Nichiren's Buddhism.
It belongs to the disciple's responsibility to develop that seeking spirit, that spiritual aspiration to understand the mentor's heart.

Why that date? Simply because Josei Toda was released from prison in 1945 on that day. Daisaku Ikeda chose that date. After having spent most of his time close to his mentor, he became aware: '*I am the only one, who can truly let the world know about the true life of President Toda. That is what, he is expecting from me and it is my mission as his disciple.*'—Then, it must be my mission to free my kidney from this fibroid on 3rd July, she observed. 'Ok, I will have the operation.'

'The door is now opening.' B, reassured her after she flaunted her misadventures.

'At the moment, I feel everything is closing around me.'

'You have to believe that you are an exceptional woman. Exceptional scripts are performed by extraordinary people like you.'

'If you say so!'

'I feel we are reaching the end of your therapy. To be honest, the idea of not seeing you mostly saddened me.'

'How can you be that sure?'

'Because we all possess the key to our own happiness, let's open the door.'

'The key,' Issata smiled.

Her man was in Italy. She had to open the door.

The door, a word belonging to our everyday life's vocabulary. An important element, in the world around us. A personification of our life, a symbol of force, power, but also a mystery. What's hiding behind a door, we all happen to question? Sometimes we hear sounds, revealed by laughter, moans, tears. We can also hear a silence. A lapse of time, talking to us, touching our heart, seducing us.

Silence has its own music, a combination of notes, which penetrates us. We lose ourselves in that silence without taking notice of what's taking place around us. It was that silence, ignored by Issata, throughout her stay in Valley Park, that same silence occupying her thoughts, since her encounter with Eva, which began to beat loudly, behind the door, she had to open.

She saw her again. Issata was coming back from B and saw Eva walking towards a black Mercedes, parked opposite the house. Rajeev's car was still at its location.
Black shades covered the face of an Eva dressed in black. Issata noticed the redness, around her dark lenses, implying she had cried.
'Eva,' her instinct spurred her to call.
She didn't answer. Issata saw the passenger window, going down. She felt an intense gaze piercing through her, but couldn't see inside.
'Do you know her?' A masculine voice was heard, when Eva opened the door.
Issata didn't hear her response. After she got in, the same voice gave a warning:
'No one has to know, do you understand?'
The driver closed the window and she watched the car driving. —No one has to know what? She entered her studio, confused and worried.

'Why don't you come and stay with me, till your operation?' Edward suggested when he returned. She was thrilled. —No more Rajeev! —No more Eva! 'My dream is finally coming true!' she dared to believe.

341

She moved most of her personal stuffs at her boyfriend's house. Within a year, they knew a lot about each other, the kind of food that they both like, their favourite colour, what made them tick in bed. But living with him, sleeping with him every night, waking up close to him, every day, she couldn't hide any longer her daily suffering. —The pain!

One morning, he moved closer to her, rubbing himself against her nude bottom. Issata was in agony. She had just swallowed her pills. The heat emanating from his body, she couldn't bare it and broke down in tears. 'What's wrong?' he panicked. 'The story of my life, Edward!' Through her tears, she shared her relationship to pain. That there was not a day, she didn't cry.
'But why didn't you say anything?'
'I just anticipated the pain!'
'Issata, this is about your own happiness! You have to be free to express yourself! Cry as much as you need! I will be there to cry with you.' He moved away from her. Relieved, she pursued her routine freely, no more secret. And he listened to the sound of her wails, a melody rich and personal. Every day, they chanted together. His spiritual support, was more than needed. Edward encouraged her to have faith. One day, he highlighted: 'Do you know what, your voice is a real gift! There is so much strength in it!' 'Only the residues from the tobacco,' she joked. 'I am serious, when you chant, I have the feeling that I am listening to your life. I hear a story, your story.' —He hears my story! she spoke to herself. She hesitated and shared her melody, recorded on her iPhone. 'That is spectacular! Daimokus in music, even I, never thought about it! I loved it!'

'Issata, I am obliged to cancel your operation.' she received that call from Dr. Marisa at, the end of June, three days before the procedure.

'Why?' In shock, she was.

'We keep the date but you have to do a scan again.'

Tears crawled all over her face when she announced the news to Edward.

'Only the mystic law can explain this!' he comforted her.

July 3rd, she got the results on the day. The fibroid stuck between her kidney and her uterus measured thirty centimetres long. —That is enormous! She recalled the length of the plastic ruler, she used at school.

Precisely, the imposter had to go.

They gave her another date, 12th of September!

'Look,' she presented the letter to Edward. At first, he didn't get it.

'The date!'

'That is right!'

'Incredible to be that in rhythm with the mystic law!'

'I must admit, I am amazed,' he embraced her.

—What is more amazing, without Jimmy, we wouldn't have ever met.

September arrived and I let you guess.

No, I am telling you: —The operation was cancelled! They had some emergencies. —Because I am not an emergency? It was reported to October 12th, the date, Nichiren had inscribed the Gohonzon in 1279.

October came, a week before the D Day, same scenario.
—We don't have enough beds, was the story!
—I can bring mine, Issata suggested!
—We book you in, for November 18th.

November 18th was not the lucky number! It has never been, she thought! So, it had to be December 20th.

Happy birthday, Issata! On the 13th of December,

Dr. Marisa informed her that she couldn't take the risk alone about such an operation. 'We will meet you in January.' Issata had no words! —Why is it so difficult to open a door!

The end of 2016, she spent it at Xavier.
She met Ethan and Raphaël for the first time.

8

2017, The *Year of Developing the Youth Division in The New Era of Worldwide Kosen Rufu,* she opened her eyes in her lover's bed. Edward was on tour, that's the life musician!

—Aren't you tired Sensei? Development here, Development there. Your wife, poor woman, she must be so exhausted having to stretch so much. Soon she will cast as the new Elastic girl of SGI.

Slowly, she emerged and fixed herself an espresso.

A fag between her lips, she sat in the Louis XIV sofa.

—I must come out of that tunnel this year, ran through her mind. Everything seemed to be linked to my kidney!

According to Chinese medicine, kidneys are considered to be the most powerful organs, and regarded as the roots of life, thanks to their filtering power. Those two beans help to conserve and protect our vital essence. It is explained that the kidney meridian would commence under the foot plant. It would continue towards the foot arch, meet the leg, the thigh, and would climb the medial line of the abdomen, reaching the clavicles. Often, when speaking about Chinese medicine, we refer to the Yin and the Yang. The yin of the kidney stimulates birth, growth and reproduction, whereas Yang is the expression of the dynamic force innate in all physiological processes.

Therefore, a human being can only enjoy great health when those energies bond in unison. Her stupor grew, when she discovered that the emotion related to the kidney was fear. That anxiety, that emotional shock that paralyses us, and takes away our power. `

After three fags, and two coffees, she knelt in front of Edward's object of worship. While she recited daimokus, she saw a light emerging from a tunnel. She watched herself at the end of the tunnel. —This year marks my twentieth Gohonzon's anniversary, I am opening that door!

'Amore,' Issata welcomed Edward in his house after a month apart. 'My darling!' They kissed. He left his bags at the entrance. The sofa was waiting for them.

'Nice meeting you Miss Sherif, your case is so unique!'

At the end of January, Issata and Edward met Dr. Marisa and Dr. Wagner, who introduced them to Juliette Wilson a young urologist. She was going to take over her case, as he was retiring but would be overseeing her case. Wilson was an English woman, Asian looking. Tall, very slim, her black hair, cut into the square style, highlighted her light blue eyes.

— It must be a question of rhythm, thought Issata.

'Tell me about it!' she let out.

'Together with Dr. Marisa, we will do everything to help you fix this problem.'

'And the nephrostomy? It hasn't been changed since!'

'Oh indeed, we will take care of it. Now, what about 16th March?' An air of complicity was detected on the face of our two buddhas.

'Issata can you hear me?'

She moved her head slowly.

The voice called again.

'Yes,' she answered.

'Great, you are speaking! How are you feeling?'

'Where am I?'

'In the recovery room.'

'The operation?'

'Yes, you had it. They managed to remove the fibroid, but they had to take away one ovary.'

That is when she recalled her busy morning with Edward by her side.

'I see!'

'Are you in pain?'

'No,' she replied, still feeling groggy.

'The epidural worked. The pain will come later, and we will provide you with morphine.'

'And my boyfriend?'

'He has been informed and is waiting for you in your room. The nurse gathered her stuff and with the help of another colleague, escorted Issata to her ward.

'Edward,' she whispered when she saw him.

'Are you ok?'

'I don't know. Did you stay here all this time?'

'Yes, Dr. Marisa and Dr. Wilson explained everything to me.'

'They removed one of my ovaries, what do you think?'

'They wanted to protect you.'

'That is often what they say,' she sighed.

'Listen, you must be tired. Have a good rest and let's just hope that the operation has been successful, ok?'

She nodded. 'I need to go now; I will come back later. Do you want something?'

'Yes, champagne!'

'This will need to wait till we reach home.' He kissed her. Tears shone in her eyes. —He said home.

In the hours which followed, she was shaken by pain. She received some morphine drops. Jimmy and Xavier came to visit. They brought some chocolates, and a picture, Raphaël had painted. The drawing represented the festive seasons. He described Issata in dark brown skin, added a golden dress, some red shoes, and a black beret with a small veil as a visor. Deeply touched by so much sincerity, she knew that Jimmy had found his Prince Charming. As days passed by, she was encouraged to exercise little steps to support the healing process. At first, it felt impossible because each time, she tried to put her feet on the floor, a brutal pain reminded her that she had a cut, twenty centimetres length above her pubis. Then, she managed to control her agony. Dr. Wilson explained that it will take some time for her organs to position themselves.

Her face brightened when she got to Edward's house.
'I told you at home!' Edward smiled. Her favourite drink was effectively waiting for her.
'I could almost live here!' she let out. Either Edward didn't pay attention to her comments or he feigned to hear. The sparkling wine opened; he dressed the flutes with their unique golden colour. —Do I need to ask if he heard me? —Will this make a difference? —If he wanted to invite me to move in with him, he will have done it long ago.
'To your absolute happiness, darling!'
'To us Edward!'

She gained some strength. She attended her rendezvous therapeutic. She stopped by Valley Park, only to check the post. Nothing to declare! Always that same heavy and mysterious silence; the silence of nocturnal activities.

In May, they celebrated their two years anniversary. Issata couldn't believe it! At the age of 42 years old, Edward was her first real relationship.

'I am sorry,' the moment she heard Dr. Wilson, pronouncing those words, she knew it didn't work.
It was in July. Taking out the fibroid didn't help the problem. To make matters worse, the left kidney was losing its functions.
'No,' she screamed, 'I believed in this operation! Look at me now! And you stole one of my ovaries!' she burst into tears. 'I bet you sold it!' Tears crawled on her face. Edward embraced her in his arms and asked calmly:
'What are you suggesting then?'

'My honest opinion, I don't know!'

'You don't know??? What am I going to do?' She rolled up her tee-shirt and showed her the tube attached to her belly.

'Look at it! We are in 2017! It has been two years! I can't take it anymore! I can't!' Her despair exploded in the room, like an earthquake. Shocked and moved, Juliette Wilson felt responsible. Her tears? Her screams? Edward got used to it.

'Issata, I totally feel for you! I promise you; we will find a solution!'

'No, you don't know anything! I had a job! Earning money, all I wanted was to buy a flat! Look where I am at? I pissed in a plastic bag! This is science for you? I do not care about that fucking kidney! I just have to die, so that we will all be happy!'

'Darling, please don't speak like this!' Edward tried to calm her.

'I speak the way I want!' she wrestled.

'Dr. Wilson, it's best we go now. But she can't continue like this!' Edward the wild artist, a man of conviction, king at heart, had to protect his queen.

'I will do everything.' She rose to her feet and shook his hand. 'Issata, I promise you!'

Issata left without looking at her.

'I see,' Edward sighed. They just got back home. He was checking his letters.

'What is it?

'It's Ricardo, he wants his house back at the end of the year.'

'Are you serious? Did he say why?'

'He needs to sell it.'

'What are you going to do?'

'I don't have time to look for anything. I must prepare my tour for November.'

'But you didn't tell me this,' she raised her voice.

'Issata, I am a musician, I thought you understood this by now. And you must focus on your health.'

'You want to leave me?' she cried again.

'Of course not. But some things take time.'

She exploded in tears again. Her dream to move in with him had fallen apart. —How am I going to come out of this mess? My kidney, Valley Park? Et now you leaving?

'Darling, we are in August now, I have three months to organise myself, so you can stay here as much as you need. But remember, we all have our own karma to transform and our own mission to fulfil according to the mystic law.

'Perhaps we could find a place together?' she suggested innocently.

He embraced her with both arms, looking into her eyes.

'Issata, I never thought I could love again after my divorce.' Her tears stopped. Edward just expressed his love to her. 'You are an exceptional woman; I feel free with you. You have to be clear with yourself'

She could only lose herself in his gaze filled with immense wisdom and tenderness. It was the first time; a man spoke to her this way. What about her? Did she love Edward, or was it the idea of being rescued, that she had fallen in love with? She placed her head against his chest, smelt him, and let his embrace sing to her that love, he carries for her.

'Edward you are right, I can't escape my karma.'

The place remained the way she had left it when she got home, the next morning. She sat on her bed and looked towards her sanctuary. —So that's it, you are testing me? Edward has to move out. He is going away on a tour.

—And me where am I going? —Twenty years gap, two girls, one is a pest! —Our lifestyle is completely different! —Ok we share one thing in common, Buddhism, the spiritual magic which brought us together.

So, let's look at that fact! A spiritual magic, bound them. However, Issata felt lonely. Jimmy was busy with work. He was living his love story. Her too had her own love story. It was not over. But what was her story? Since her encounter with Edward, she was living through his soft and reassuring gaze, addicted to the taste of his passionate and spontaneous kisses, impatient to feel his respectful and enthralling caresses. She let herself live beneath the sound of their idyll, a melody, she had long searched and desired for. She existed through the life of a man, who chose to live his life, she was realising. Yes, Edward added a spicy touch to her everyday life. He described the fact that a man was part of her life. —What about me? Where do I fit in the middle of that romantic scenery? it dawned on her.

'Sayon,' she pronounced, hugging her tenderly. 'I left you aside for two years.' A wave of energy coming from her friend, invaded her being and she burst into tears. Drops of salted water crawled on her face, along her neck. Summer time was faithful to the rendezvous of the year. Birds were singing. Butterflies were dancing in the sky freely, in that vast space, known as Mother nature. Bees buzzed around. Life followed its course. Holding tightly to her idol, that strength which supported her, listened to her, well before the arrival of a masculine living, in her sacred territory, a thought borrowed from Antoine de St Exupéry, brushed her senses. *"Love does not consist of gazing at each other, but in looking outward together in the same direction."*

Shivering, she began to understand. Life was inviting her to live. Life was asking her not to let aside her hobbies, not to drown into a relationship. Life was ordering her simply, not to forget herself. —If Edward and I shared a common mission, the universe will guide our steps, her heart determined.

'You will come back, right?' she whispered.
Wrapped in her own nudity, Issata stood in front of her door, to say goodbye to her lover. It was November 9th in the middle of the night.
'I told you that I had a gig in London on 25th November.'
She grabbed his hand and guided it inside her legs. Tightly, she closed them: 'You promise me?' a weepy voice checked
'I promise you and I need to go!'
Water in her gaze, she spread her legs opened and freed his hand. They kissed and she let him go.

Here I go again, and my karma yet to remain,
Just have to deal with it, so, I can change my destiny, that is my only chance. Leaning against her door, she watched her bed undone and hummed on the tune, *Taking a chance on love.*

It was real, the Italian man was gone.

—*Nich, how did you escape from Sado Island, she prayed?*
The story tells: after he had reached illumination, Nichiren was sent to Sado Island, a sordid place for criminals doomed to die. The kind of place where no one ever comes back. During his time in exile, he composed one of his most important letters, titled Letter from Sado. It was addressed to Toki Jonin. He stresses to him, that the direct path to enlightenment was none other than dedicating one's life to Buddhism. Even in the direst situations, Nichiren continued to encourage his disciples. We can observe the extreme compassion which governed his heart. Nichiren also elaborates on the concept of karma, using his life as an example. He concluded that the persecutions he encountered were linked to the slander he had made against the Lotus sutra in the past. And the only way to change the course of his life was revealed in propagating the Lotus Sutra. The principal message of this letter demonstrates that any difficulties we face, are tailored made to transform our own karma. After he analysed his journey, he inscribed the Gohonzon. And guessed what, he was pardoned without any given reason. He was free.

—Well, it looked like Valley Park is my Sado Island!

—Me too I want to be pardoned!

—The moment Nichiren proclaimed Nam-myoho-renge-kyo, he was so convinced that his life will be protected, one morning, she realised. And a sentence from the letter *Happiness in this world,* came to her mind. —*There is no greater happiness than chanting Nam-myoho-renge-kyo.*

—Of course, everything lies in faith. Chanting Nam-myoho-renge-kyo, is the greatest joy a human being can experience, travelled through her mind. It was 16th November, late afternoon. —I followed your teaching Nich, she looked at the Gohonzon. —I even tried to kill myself! —It didn't work! And I am grateful to you by the way; that particular prayer has not been answered! Ok, I am not the virgin Mary, so Mea Culpa for not being a saint! —But 18th November must represent the beginning of the end of that nightmare. —I must move out! Surely, there must be the perfect flat for me?

Her iPhone made a sound. A no caller ID was flashing on the screen.

'Hello,'

'Issata, It's Dr. Wilson'

'Dr. Wilson?'

'I think, I have found a way to fix your kidney.'

'What?'

'Your kidney is healthy, and the only way to protect is to remove the blockage!'

—Has she heard right? —To physically remove the problem?

'Whatever, you suggest! Let's do it!'

'But it can be dangerous.'

'I don't care! I can't continue like that! At least, I want to try.'

'Great, we are waiting for you on November 29th at 7 am.'

She rushed back to the estate's agents, with that burning determination: —The mystic law, I am counting on you. I have two days to make the impossible possible.

—18th November, I will find my new home, somewhere safe and comfortable. —My kidney needs space to function, and my life needs to grow.

She walked all around Kilburn, Hampstead, West Hampstead checking adverts on windows shops.

17th November, Day -1, she ran everywhere. About five o'clock, she was in front of her shrine. —I have taken all necessary actions. —To all of you, protectives forces, I need your support, she prayed like never before. And used that particular quote from Nichiren in the letter, *On Prayer: 'Though one might point at the earth and miss it, though one might bind up the sky, though the tides might cease to ebb and flow and the sun rise in the west, it could never come about that the prayers of the practitioner of the Lotus Sutra would go unanswered.'*

The five characters of Myoho-renge-kyo slid freely on her lips. Her voice sounded new and singular. Issata was seeking to believe in the law of causality. The more her Daimokus emerged through her heart, the more she felt a presence vibrating in the air. A reassuring force was guiding her towards the end of the tunnel. For a long time, she regarded Valley Park as a contemporary donjon. She had crawled inside in total obscurity. Slowly, that wish to believe was turning into a certitude. She rose above with the help of an invisible army and that certitude transformed itself into a conviction: —I am an entity of the mystic law, I am a buddha! A buddha with female characteristics, French nationality, and coming from Guinea. —Simply said, I am a human being! At that moment, she felt free and in complete harmony with her identity. —It doesn't matter if I can't find a flat by tomorrow, I must continue reciting Nam-myoho-renge-kyo! Relieved and detached from all artificial sufferings, she heard the house praying with her, so she thought!

Then noises broke out in the corridor.

'I want to stop!' She heard coming from a feminine voice.

'No, you can't leave! I picked you up from the street! That's how you thank me?' Issata recognised the voice of Rajeev, followed by a sound which resembled a slap.

'I will give you back your money! I just can't continue!'

'Come here,' he yelled.

Some banging resonated on the stairs.

—What do I do? —Maybe it's Eva!

She called the police and reported what she suspected.

'We are sending you, somebody!' she was advised.

—I can't let this woman in danger! She rushed upstairs. The girl was begging Rajeev to stop. Her strident cries travelled through the walls, amplified by heavy moans, like those of a wild beast. The door was slightly ajar.

'You are a bitch! You deserve to be punished!'

Issata pushed the door and witnessed the horrific spectacle a human being could inflict to his kind. At first, she was

357

not sure it was Rajeev, as he was not wearing his turban. But the green uniform could not fail her perception. It was the first time she saw his hair or the little of what he had left glued on his scalp. He had pushed Eva against his desk and was forcing himself inside her behind violently. Shouting the worst, he was beating her up.

Eva had only her tears to keep her going.

'Let her go!' yelled Issata. She marched towards him and pushed him. Losing his control, Rajeev turned around, the purple piece of his flesh, looking like a deflated balloon, between his legs. His face was sweating like a pig. Issata was about to throw up when she saw blood on the tip of his ugly flesh and some around Eva's damaged body.
'Eva, I have called the police' she tried to reassure her.
'You have no right to be here! Leave my house!' he barked, embarrassed to have been caught this way. He pulled up his trousers.
'Not the police!' Her face smashed and bleeding, Eva collected what she could and ran out.
'Eva, you have to press charge.'
'You, mind your own business! I should have thrown you out!' He continued his prose, pointing the finger to her.
Her heart beast fast, standing in front of her landlord who had no scruples. His eyes screaming for blood, exposed the many years of cocaine's addiction.

Everything became clear! Rajeev was a pimp, using young women. —Eva is probably an immigrant to whom he promised some papers, if she was to work for him. Disgusted, she breathed deeply. 'What are you going to do, to me? The police are on the way!'
'I was a general! Everyone respected me!

'You are a disgrace, a less than a man! You have no right to abuse people! You were raping this woman! That is a crime and you have to pay for it!'

'I don't want to see you in my house!' he wailed, looking like someone whose throat was about to be cut. Issata remained calm and listened to the parodies of an individual, who had been seeking for glory all his life.

A living being, who had set in his mind that using the vulnerable would make a man of him. She read the misery, inscribed on the face of a septuagenarian, whose life has been nourished by the poison of his own ignorance.

He vomited his despair using the most refined vocabulary which portrayed the eloquence of a miserable man.

She heard the bashing on a door.

'It's the police!'

She went downstairs quickly.

'I am Constable Courtney' A female police officer, spoke showing her badge. 'And this is Constable Holmes. Did you call?'

'Yes, he is upstairs! You should arrest him! He raped this girl! I saw him!'

'Wait here for us.'

Issata sat on the stairs. —If only, I had a way to contact Eva. —For seven years, I lived in this brothel! —How couldn't I have seen this before? —Why did she cry only now? —And no one came to support her!

'We can't do anything without proof,' Courtney interrupted her thoughts.

'What did he say?'

'That she didn't pay her rent.'

'And you believed him? Didn't you see the look on his face?'

'We need the victim's deposition.'

'I want to give a witness statement, and perhaps you could check with the other tenants? I am the only one who heard her, that is not right!'

'How many flats?'

'Ten.'

'Holmes, you go and check!'

Very quickly, the police officer joined them back.

'No one is answering.'

'I am telling you, this man is a pimp,' Issata insisted.

'You should think of moving out of here,' Courtney advised. 'Here is my card.' she added.

'Thank you,' Issata said.

—Maybe, that was my mission to expose Rajeev, she contemplated, when the police left her. —And now?

A number she didn't know, called her phone.

'Hello?'

'Good evening, I am Jonas; you left a message for the apartment in West Hampstead. Are you still interested?'

Issata had left so many messages. But she remembered one in particular with a shared garden.

'Yes, remind me the rent again!' she answered.

He told her the price. —That's right, she acknowledged. She connected with the advert, but couldn't afford the rent alone. —I have to decide! 'Absolutely, when can I see it?'

'Tonight, at 7:30 as I have a couple interested.'

'Great can I have the address?'

'What's your name?'

'I am Issata, the flat is for me and my partner! He is a musician,' she observed the risk to respond.

'Yes!' said Edward with no hesitation.

360

She arrived on time, in front of a huge house. She met Jonas from Morocco, a senior dressed like a senior, wearing glasses like a senior, grey curled hair looking like a crown on his head and his curled beard made him looked like a nomad living in the city. She greeted the other couple by a nod but didn't care. —Exactly as I envisaged it, her heart pounded when she passed the entrance. Grand floor, living room, and kitchen combined together, luxurious cream paper dressing the walls with elegance. The bathroom's ceiling and the floor were made of wood, painted in red oak colour. It contained a bathtub which could welcome at least four people. The toilet was part of the scenery. The pick of her victory awaited in the bedroom whose French windows led to the garden. Edward rang using facetime. 'Take it darling!'

'So?' Jonas asked

'We liked it!' said the couple 'So do we!' Issata attacked.

'Can you pay a month in advance and a month deposit?'

'Absolutely!' She took control.

'We don't have the money; you have found your tenants!'

'When can you move in?'

'Tomorrow!' Issata declared.

'See you tomorrow at 11 am then!'

'We have the flat Edward,' she exclaimed, once outside, tears brightening in her eyes.

'Darling bravo! I am so proud of you! And honoured that you invite me into your life.'

'We are moving on 18th November; can you believe it?'

'That is right! Together, with Sensei!'

She was speechless, when she got to number 66.

Rajeev's car had disappeared. —Seven years that this monster was parked here! —It looks like the malediction has been lifted, she could only observe at the sight of the empty space! For how long? She entered her place and rang Jimmy.

'Sweetheart! You did it!'

'It would be real when I signed the contract. Now I must organise the moving.'

'I will ask Xaxa, he knows people. Last push darling, the universe is on your side!'

'Yes, the mystic law has answered my prayers.

The next day 18th November, Jonas explained to her that the previous tenant had lived in the flat for thirty years. 'She was alcoholic. It cost me ten years of legal costs to get rid of her. You are my saviours,' he expressed moved. 'Thirty years,' she could only repeat and felt even more convinced that a new era was beginning for her. 'Here are your keys!' Jonas let out, once everything went through and left. Issata went to the bedroom and opened the French windows to smoke her first cigarette in the garden.

Well, it looked more like a jungle in need of extreme care. Jonas did tell her that the neighbour was a gardener and was happy to take care of it. —I see, was her reply. Lost in her thoughts, she imagined her life with Edward. Then, the rain reminded her that she had some packing up to do. Back to Valley Park, she wrote her notice.

—I am curious to see the look on your miserable face upon receiving my declaration to you, Mr. Harijan! Xavier offered to pay for the removal. 'Prepare your boxes!' he said.

25th November, Edward came back to London. She took him to their new home. She had already moved a lot of stuff. They collected his belongings from the storage. 'We are going to be happy here,' he exclaimed, once all his instruments found their places. 'Yes, we will and here are your keys' she murmured. She attended his gig. They spent the last night at number 66.

—Goodbye Valley Park, she declared, on 28th November and left the keys at the door. She slept in her new home.

—My dear kidney, you've forced me to unlock the negative tendency which dominated my life all these years.

On the 29th November, at six o'clock precisely, on her way to the hospital. she addressed her organ: —I have opened the door! I need you to push wide open! On arrival, she was invited to change. Then a nurse guided her through the anaesthesia process. While the drug slid in her vein, an urgent desire to do sansho surged through her. 'Are you a Buddhist?' That same nurse asked. 'Yes,' she let out! 'Funny that you asked, I would like to recite my mantra.' 'Of course, do!'

In a peaceful voice, she expressed: 'Nam-myoho-renge-kyo,' three times. Issata felt at peace with herself. If she was to never wake up, her last words would have been dedicated to the mystic law. 'How beautiful' she managed to hear.

'You have won! The operation has been successful!'

A female's voice kept repeating three hours later. It was Dr. Wilson, holding her hands. By her side, she noticed Dr. Wagner proud to finish his career with such a victory.

'Did you remove the blockage?' Issata had the strength to pronounce.

'You and I have removed the blockage!' Wilson rectified.

8th December, the new chapter of her life had officially begun. —I could have taken VoyE to court, earned lots of money! But I have done better than that! I have given birth to my true self! Nothing and no one can take it away from me.

And still, I rise, I will always rise, she recited that verse from Maya Angelou, American black poet, the next day after her return from the hospital. Those thoughts denounced her own manifesto. She was standing in her bedroom, in front of the mirror, and watched the massive cut slicing her abdomen into two. She looked like a woman who had undergone a caesarean.

'Happy Birthday my darling! Now you can write your story.'

She celebrated her forty-three years with Jimmy and his new family. He organised the birthday cake which came served with a big present. Tears crawled on her cheeks when she saw what it contained. —A Macbook Pro.

'My Jimmy!' she embraced him.

'From Xaxa and the boys two!' he underlined.

'Is it true, you write books, we can buy like in the shop?' Raphael asked innocently. Moved by so much sincerity, she held him in her arms. 'I am going to try Raphael!'

24th December, she decorated her flat with a small Christmas tree. She dressed it with red and silver balls, added strings of light and stars. She cooked her first Christmas diner, moules marinières with fries. That choice of meal suited her perfectly. She sat on her sofa and ate in front of her television. She was alone and she was happy.

31st December, she walked to the park, slowly and with great struggle. It was snowing but she had to be there.

'Sayon,' she called. She couldn't embrace her as she would, but they both understood each other. She leaned on the trunk and felt the bark massaging her back. She was standing in the middle of a grey scenery. It was freezing, and Mother nature looked naked. Yet, the sun was burning in her heart. The universe appeared to her eyes, smaller than the palm of her hand. And life, on that last day of 2017 looked like a beautiful dance, she chose to dance. —I am Issata, *the one who struggle to become, a kind and willing person,* she declared.

Part.4

The Mystic Law the Dance of Life

'Shimei'-Using My Life

9

Sensei, it took the compassion of three men, for me to encounter such an extraordinary philosophy of life, one of them is You! For once, I am in rhythm with your theme for the year! Issata praised herself for beginning '*The Year of Brilliant Achievement in the New Era of Worldwide Kosen Rufu,*' victorious. —2018, I am ready!

Her soul was vibrating under a new energy, governed by the mystic law. —Tomorrow 2ⁿᵈ of January you will be 90, and I will always be indebted to you and SGI. You have dedicated your whole life in honouring Nichiren Daishonin's teaching as the new spiritual way for mankind. —Now it is my turn! How? I don't know but I shall try.

She was finishing her prayers and her iPhone rang. To her surprise, Sophia's name flashed on the screen.

'Allo,' she picked up, worried.

'My sister, I need to tell you something.'

Issata couldn't believe what she was hearing. Antoine had contacted them, completely devastated. He couldn't stand their mother anymore. She was threatening to kill herself. Sophia and her husband, collected her. They sought advice from Dr. Leroux. He told them that Mum had suffered from bipolar for years.

'When did this happen?'

'Since 29th November, she lives with us now.'

—29th November, she spoke silently. —The day of the operation.

'Why didn't you tell me?'

'We just didn't want to worry you. You had so much to deal with, the operation, moving out. And I felt it had to come from her. I pass her on to you,' Sophia suggested.

'Allo,' Mum said.

'Mum,' Issata let out, holding back her tears. Mum muttered debris of words, forming no sense.

—This explains her erratic behaviour. —B. is right, I must have inherited my emotional issues from her! she concluded when she hung up.

It is explained that the origin of manic depression is probably linked to an ensemble of genes which the influence remains unclear. At that moment, she understood the concept behind: —*Voluntarily assuming the appropriate karma.* That principle puts the light on the mission of the *Boddhisattva* emerging from the earth. It is explained that, if we believe we are buddhas, therefore we have made the pledge to choose the right conditions and the perfect difficulties, to demonstrate through our unique human revolution, how we became buddhas in the first place. Tears running along her cheeks, she whispered: Thanks to my human revolution, I have influenced my own mother to free herself from her unhealthy relationship. —I have truly won because Buddhism explains that when we transform our karma, that transformation affects seven generations from the past and the seven to come.

'Mum' she called.

A week after they spoke, her mother found an accommodation, not far from the station. Mum was waiting for her in the parking, as usual. —You are growing so old, she noticed, as she came close to her.

'Issata my daughter, I am so happy to see you,' her voice trembled. 'Me too Mum,' she embraced her. 'I can't wait to see your new home!' 'It's there!' She pointed with her finger.

Effectively in five minutes, they arrived in a complex, comprising ten houses in a dead end. They were built face to face. Mum lived on number seven. They got in.

She offered a guided tour of her new home. She also had a garden. It was less glamorous, compared to Antoine's mansion, but at least she could start to learn to live again.

A traditional dish from West Africa was served, the famous okra sauce. It contained oxtails and onions, infused with palm oil, which she used to call red oil, accompanied by Basmati rice. The smell and the taste sent her back to the time of her childhood. They were eating together, in the kitchen, sharing the food in a large wooden ball called a calabash. They ate the meal with their hand, where each portion was shaped into small balls, before being inserted in the mouth. Most of the time, she argued with Sophia to get the best part of the meat, the chicken's leg. One day,

Mum decided to cook legs for all, so that everyone could find their happiness. Each time, she inserted her spoon in her mouth, more memories emerged, like Mum plaiting her dark thick hair, adding colourful beads at the end of each tress. That was the only time, her white girlfriends at school wanted to be black. Came Ramadan, dressed in traditional clothes, she would meet the kids in her neighbourhood, comparing their outfits, eating with the grown-ups, and talking about God's blessings on them, or more or less their understanding of a super human being, watching over them. Through the taste of that African dish, she chased the souvenirs of her childhood.

'So, a brand-new beginning is in front of you Mum?' They both settled in the sofa, after lunch.

'My daughter, I am not mad!' Mum exclaimed.

'I have never said that! You must now take your own responsibilities.'

'You can't understand, when your father died, I felt alone. My parents abandoned me because your father didn't convert to Islam. I followed your dad because I didn't want to abandon you.' She rose her pitch. Tears vibrated in her words. 'And you, you went to London! And…And…And you abandoned me!' Mum exploded. Finally, that pain she had carried inside her, came out: ─Rejection, the profound cause of her fear to be alone, that she fed through her attachments to those she loved, by that need to be loved in return. Issata looked at her mother, respecting her suffering.

'Mother, wherever I am in this world, I will always be your daughter. But I cannot fix your problems. No one can do it for you. Not my father, not Antoine, only you!'

'But how? I am tired'

'We have to pray to find peace in our hearts.'

'Issata, it is over for me! I don't want to live anymore!'

Her mother's words vibrated on the leitmotiv of her own karma. She couldn't judge Mum. She completely understood her. To transform karma, demands so much courage, so much spiritual strength. When we suffer, when that force to hope desert us, giving up, dying, is the only answer. The mind is lost. The heart cannot cope anymore.

'Mum,' she took her hands and fixed her eyes.

'Me too, I had lost hope,' she confessed.

Tears rolled down her cheeks. Tears that were questioning, how after all the pills she had swallowed, she was still alive.

'Me too, I didn't want to live anymore,' a trembling timbre denounced. 'If I am still alive, it is for you.'

'For me?' Mum's face brightened with surprise.

'Yes mum, you gave me life. I am who I am, thanks to you.'

'Thanks to me?' She looked at her child as if she was meeting her for the first time. As if for the first time in her life, she mattered for someone.

'Yes, thanks to you, and if you believe in God, we all have our path to follow. He gave you a mission to fulfil, because he knows you can do it.'

'I did everything for Antoine. He never loved me.'

'He did it in his own way. He welcomed us. He considers Sophia's children like his grand-children. Now your story is over; you need to move on.'

'I miss your dad so much,' she cried.

'I miss him too. Dad is gone for a new mission. You still have us, Sophia, Malcolm, Nelson, and Rosa. And you have me, Issata Sherif, your eldest, and I am proud to have you as my mother.' She found refuge in the arms of this woman, who gave her life, forty-three years ago. Her arms, attached to her neck, she sobbed like a baby. Mum performed what a mother would do. She cradled her daughter. '*Ikana Kasi*' she whispered in Malinké, meaning: —Don't cry, in English.

'You have always wished for me to find a nice man. Mum, I have found him. Edward is a kind man; I have listened to your advice.'

'I did my best,' mum sighed.

'I know and I will do my best for you.' Two women tied by blood had found each other.

'You are probably right; I might be bipolar since it exists in the genes.' Issata met B, the next day after her return from France.

'If that is the case, you are at stage two, and I wouldn't worry about it. After everything you have been through, your life is equipped to unlock any truth.'

'Even bipolar?'

'Yes! And personally, your therapy is now over.'

Issata was not surprised. 'What am I going to do now?'

'You still have to deal with the sarcoidosis. How are you getting on with it?'

'The usual pain and tiredness, emotional instability and the seizure of course. I had to stop the infliximab treatment, because of my kidney. But Dr Clark confirmed that I can start again in March.'

'You see, there is still so much work to do for your health. You will have to learn to live with the sarcoidosis. Who knows, you might even become an ambassador for it!'

'First, I must understand the cause of it!'

'A Journey as exceptional as yours has to be shared. Each time you stepped into my office, you were reading to me your story and I was impatient to hear the next chapter.'

'Where to start?' a little girl asked.

'From the beginning.'

'The beginning' she repeated. 'But there is something I need to understand. How is it possible that I am still alive?'

B stared at her deeply and said: 'I have a confession to make.' Impatient, Issata fixed her.

'You kept asking for more pills, so I gave you empty pills, without chemical products. That is a technique used to fight addiction.'

'You did this?'

'You need to understand me!'

She rose to her feet and fell in her arms.

'Thank you, B! I didn't want to die!' she cried. 'I only wanted to stop the suffering! It was unbearable! I couldn't see a way out! It had to stop! Thank you, thank you, thank you!'

'I know,' said B, embracing her. Locked in each other's arms, they both shared the same mission, the mission of living the life of a great woman.

'Do you really think I am ready?' she asked, moving away from her slowly.

'Issata, an African proverb says: '*The fire that burns you, is the same fire that will keep you warm!*'

—E*arthly Desires lead to enlightenment,* Nichiren explained. '*Desire is the essence of man. That is to say, to which a man strives to persevere in his being,*' Spinoza concluded.

Sitting at the kitchen table, her coffee ready, a Marlboro inside her lips, her MacBook Pro on, thoughts wandered in her mind, observing a blank screen. A gigantesque mural fresco revealed itself in front of her very own eyes. It represented painted images, issued from her life experience and sealed by her own blood. The road appeared very long, guided by giant mountains, and just by looking in their direction seemed impossible to escalate. She could also observe palaces of wonders, as secret as Ali Baba's cavern, except for her treasures wouldn't come from stolen goods. Her richness will come through the treasure of the heart, the heart of faith, the treasure of hope. But her true richness can only derive from the story, that only she could write.

—Everything began with that desire to find Mr. Right, she analysed. A simple desire which forced me to open all necessary possibilities. In order to meet him, I had to welcome, Sarcoidosis, in my life. Sarcoidosis, you have helped me reveal the Mrs. Right in me. Because Mrs. Right, also has to make Mr. Right dance through life. Otherwise, it wouldn't be fair on men! Let's think about these young men, the pressure ahead of them, before they even step into this world. Plus, us women, we wanted emancipation! let's get on with it! Laughing, it dawned to her: —In all fairy tales, every princess had their own karma to transform. Poor Cinderella, she had the karma of living with an evil mother-in-law, and sisters-in-laws worse than the mother! Equally for Snow White, she had the intelligence to bite into the red apple, and her path crossed the seven dwarves…What did she do with them, we will never know the truth…And Sleeping Beauty, she spent her life sleeping. The list is long! —Morality, they all suffered! And more giggling from her part. —Enlightenment is all about experiences then!

That is what Shakyamuni must have understood, before he ventured to share his story. And thinking of it, it makes sense, that he opens the door of *The Treasure Tower*.

That door is the door of his own life. Then she typed:

—*Manifesto, From a Woman.*

As she typed the last letter, she heard a metallic sound, the noise of a key being inserted through the keyhole of a door. Her heart beating fast, she rose to her feet and fixed the door opening. She saw her Italian man dressed in a long cashmere cream coat, entering their flat. He resembled a businessman, returning home from a long trip. Leaving his luggage at the entrance, he walked towards her. She was paralysed with joy.

'Happy New Year my darling.' He held her in his arms and kissed her. Her tired woollen robe revealed her satin pink nighty. An intense sexual pleasure, crawled through her being. The little black button beneath the shiny clothe burgeoned. Two months without touching each other's, kissing, two months without making love.

'Happy New Year to you too,' she whispered, detaching her mouth from his lips.

'I have found a title for your melody,' he murmured.

'Really?'

'Since I have heard it, I couldn't help thinking about it.'

She opened her eyes, impatient.

'The Mystic Law, The dance of Life.' He took her hand and led her into a passionate dance.

'Oh! Yes, life is a beautiful dance and I want to dance it with you, Edward Jones!'

They danced in their living room on the tempo of the waltz: one, two, three... Following his lead, she also borrowed the path of her mind. —For someone looking for Mr. Right, who would make me dance through life, how incredible that I meet a musician! —Edward Jones, you didn't rescue me on your white horse, but you came with your sincerity, striking a contrabass. *'Everything begins with the courageous and noble dance of human revolution, in which each person strives to make its life shine to its brightest, in the place where there are right now.'* she remembered from her mentor in that instant. —B was right, I had the key in me all along, and Nam-myoho-renge-kyo, itself, hidden in the lotus sutra, guided me to find my own key hidden within my life; the key of courage, compassion and wisdom.

'Edward, we all have the key to our own happiness, let's open the door.'

'What about starting by opening the door of our bedroom?

Epilogue

The fact, that you had reached that page, reveals that you must have spent time with Issata Sherif. Perhaps for months, weeks, days, or you had just decided to read the last page. In any case, a desire, before anything, remains the expression of something missing inside our heart. Man, desires what he doesn't have.

 Hat about you?
What is your desire?

Thank You

Dear All,

L ife is a beautiful dance, which does not need to be danced alone.

So, I thank you all for sharing that dance with me.

Starting with my family, my mother, my sisters, my friends.

Deepest Thank you to the NHS:

Even more so, to _Dr. Maria_. She was the first Doctor who took care of me, when Sarcoidosis came knocking on my door. Then I met _Dr Arnold._ I am utterly grateful to these two women from the _Litchfield Grove Surgery_. Thank you to all the people part of the surgery.

Deepest Thank you, to the _Royal Free Hospital_:

Even more so, to _Dr Kidd_. This man is the Neurosarcoïdosis specialist for the UK. He dedicated his life in learning and finding solutions to this condition, which affects many people, everywhere in the world. He has established and run the Neurosarcoïdosis centre, in this hospital.

For 10 years, I have been under his care. Thank you, Dr. Kidd, and thank you to everyone who works with you.

Deepest Thank you, to the _PITU_ department (Planned Investigation, Treatment Unit), the reception team, the nurses, everyone.

Deepest Thank you, to the Urology team:

Even more so, to _Miss Maxine Tran_, Urologist Consultant. Miss Tran helped me save my right kidney through one sentence: _We remove the blockage_, she told me. That phrase changed it all for me. I still have both kidneys, and I have found the answer, I was looking for.

Deepest Thank you, to _Federico Parodi_ for designing the logo infinity sign. Federico is an animated film maker and a piano player.

Deepest Thank you, to _Astrid Brisson_ for designing the cover of the book and capturing the essence of the story. Astrid is an illustrator and graphic designer and a kind hearted, talented woman.

Deepest Thank you to SGI. (www.sgi.org)

Printed in Great Britain
by Amazon